SHANGHAI TANGO

SHANGHAI
TANGO

William Overgard

St. Martin's Press

New York

Grateful acknowledgment is made for permission to reprint
a selection from "There Goes a Man" from *Treasure of Proverbs
& Epigrams,* Ottenheimer Publishers, Inc., 1954.

Design by John Fontana

Library of Congress Cataloging in Publication Data

Overgard, William.
    Shanghai tango.

    I. Title.
PS3565.V427S5   1987   813'.54   87-4450
ISBN 0-312-00678-0

First Edition

10 9 8 7 6 5 4 3 2 1

There are several authors who I am indebted to for inspiration as well as information: Rear Admiral Kemp Tolley, Colonel John W. Thomason Jr., U.S.M.C., Jean Fontenoy, C. Martin Wilbur, Frederic L. Chapin, Harold Z. Schiffrin, R. deRohan Barondes, Lucien Bodard, and Emile Hahn.

I'll toss the cloak of dawn around my shoulders, my next to last whiskey will age in its glass, my death in love will arrive on a tango step, and I will die precisely at six o'clock.

—A. Piazzola—H. Ferrer,
Balada Para Mi Muerte

SHANGHAI TANGO

It was not remarkable. A ricksha stood untended, its delicate shafts dipped forward. It was parallel with the river and, backlit by the rising sun, at first appeared unoccupied. Then a suggestion of a head could be seen against the cushions, body sagging. As the first coolies on the job swung around it, terrible eyes just above the rim of the tall wheel watched them, whites colored pink by the sunrise.

By seven o'clock the wharves were crowded and noisy with the shouts of street porters and the clatter of ships discharging cargo. Still the circle around the ricksha remained uncrossed. At its perimeter a cluster of Chinese in padded robes stood spitting and talking in choppy sentences, discussing the occupant.

By nine o'clock the dock boss intervened. Annoyed, he pushed his way in and, dispersing the crowd, reached the ricksha. Looking down at the awful eyes, he turned quickly and ran to the phone in the shipping office of Butterfield & Swire. French Tonkinese police arrived an hour later and moved the crowd back, roping off the area. Other officials came and went in the next hours, each examining the occupant of the ricksha, but they all seemed to be waiting.

Just after one o'clock the Chief of Police of the French Concession arrived. He had been playing badminton at Le Cercle Sportif Français when he received the word, and came straight over after a light lunch. It wasn't the sort of thing his rank obliged him to do, but his interest was piqued. He got out

1

of the car, picking his teeth, hand held in front of his mouth in the Oriental way. Like other principals in the Concession police, he was Corsican—a hard man, known for his gallows humor and bad French. A correspondent followed, an Englishman from the *North China Daily News*.

They examined the figure in the ricksha, the police chief lifting the limbs and letting them flop back. As he did, the eyes followed him.

Walking back to the car, the Englishman was puzzled.

"It doesn't make any sense."

"No."

"What's been done to it exactly?"

"Hamstrung. The tendons have been cut."

"Really! But there's no blood."

"Very little, it was done by experts."

They got in the car, a Citroën, and it pressed forward, forcing its way through the groups of Chinese. The Englishman wasn't satisfied. "But why would they do that to an animal?"

The Police Chief took the toothpick out of his mouth and carefully put it in his breast pocket. "Well," he said, smiling, "it is the year of the monkey."

The car cleared the crowd and passed off the dock, picking up speed as it continued up the Bund toward the center of the city.

It was the 5th of February 1932, the first day of the Chinese New Year, 4531, the second new moon after the winter solstice, and the year of the monkey.

SHANGHAI, SUMMER 1931

SHANGHAI 1931
1 RAILWAY STATION
2 U.S. CONSULATE
3 JAPANESE CONSULATE
4 PUBLIC GARDENS
5 MASONIC CLUB
6 CATHAY HOTEL
7 GOTHIC CATHEDRAL
8 PALACE HOTEL
9 CUSTOMS HOUSE
10 HOSPITAL
11 CENTRAL POLICE STATION
12 SHANGHAI CLUB
13 RACE COURSE

NANTAO
Chinese City

ONE

RAMON'S EYEBROWS WENT up and he showed his teeth.
They were the wrong cigarettes.

"You gotta take what you can get, sport," Adrian said, warily holding out
the making. It was rolled as nice and tight as a machine-made, but Ramon
ignored it. Arms crossed, jaw set, he shifted his head toward the cloudy
mirror and plucked at the creases in his trousers.

Adrian was hurt. He prided himself on rolling one-handed: paper held just
so in the left hand, bag of Bull Durham tugged out of the breast pocket with
the right, drawstring opened with the teeth, tobacco (makings) shook along
the paper—then, after wetting the edge of the paper with the tongue, a deft
twirl sealed it and twisted up the end. You couldn't ask for a better job.
Ramon didn't think so. It was not his idea of a real cigarette.

The hell with it. Adrian sat on the Taylor trunk and, leaning back, lit up,
blowing the smoke toward him. The heat in the dressing room was blistering,
and he did his best not to move. He had bought an honest-to-God Palm
Beach suit in Frisco before coming out to China, but the damn thing had
shrunk. Pulled taut at the shoulders and arms, it was a mass of constricting
wrinkles.

He finally stretched his long legs out, carefully unlimbering the left—a
nasty bite above his knee was still healing. Settling in, Stetson shading his

eyes, hands in his pockets, he waited, smoking and listening to the queer squeak and squawk of the place. Then, connecting sounds: the slam of an outside door; scraping as something was dragged along; bumps as it came down steps—and finally a loud bang and the dressing room door flew open, flapped back, and was straight-armed into submission. A wide picture hat dipped in, and a pretty powdered face emerged from under it. "Do you know what the trouble with China is?"

"The Chinese?" Adrian said, the burn of the makings causing his eyes to squint.

"Besides that."

"You tell me."

"There's no place for a girl to pee—have you ever tried to find a ladies' north of Szechwan Road?"

"Not lately."

"Well, it's tough, cowboy—they don't call it the trenches for nothing." She began hauling a case of bottles in from the hall, sliding it along the floor. "And the damn Peking Five Star bottling plant is clear out by the Kieth Egg Factory—have you ever smelled that place? Every egg on the coast must show up there by slow freight—they make them into powder or something—in the meantime all those eggs are just sitting out there in the sun—got it?" She looked up. "What's wrong with Ramon?"

"Doesn't like his smokes rolled, I guess."

She straightened—"Oh for Christ's sake . . ."—burrowed in her straw bag, and came up with a crumpled pack. "How about that, Lucky Strike Greens!" Ramon's eyes cracked open a centimeter. She inserted the cigarette in his holder, smiling. "Do I get a kiss?" They kissed and she lit the Lucky. Ramon drew in deep and exhaled, blowing the smoke at Adrian.

"Why would you want to go clear out on Szechwan Road to get beer?" Adrian asked.

She fussed with Ramon's hair, straightened the part. "Would you look at that—I've got to do something, it's getting gray. . . ."

Adrian kept his eyes on her, but she wouldn't meet them.

There was the muffled wail of moon fiddles and hu-jings winding up. "God! How I hate Chinese music!" she said, squeezing a gob of Sta-Comb on Ramon's hair and working it down to crescent sideburns. "I'd give my left you-know-what for a real pit band with a wa-wa trumpet!" She moved her fingers along his slightly stubbled cheeks. "Do you need a shave?" Ramon expertly shifted the cigarette holder from side to side while she completed the inspection. "No, I guess not."

Getting up, she flipped the dress over her head and stepped out of the teddy. Naked, she wiped off existing makeup and began again in front of the wavy mirror. First, dusting her body with a huge puff, she sent up clouds of white powder that floated like a hazy scrim around her, circling the oil lamp and descending to settle on Adrian and Ramon, who sat and watched, cigarettes poised at their mouths.

"They like you white out here," she said, and having created a blank canvas, proceeded to draw in contemporary beauty: eyebrows as nicely arched as the swoop of a calligrapher's pen, heavy-lidded eyes kohled, and pouty lips coaxed into a bee's sting. A touch of rouge was blended at the cheeks, then circled boldly on the tip of each breast. Last, wetting an eyebrow pencil, she pointed up the outline of heart-shaped pubic hair.

"Damn!" Adrian said, unable to contain himself.

She didn't answer, hoping not to encourage him, but he got up and stood behind her, running his hands along the tight skin of her stomach, cupping her breasts. "C'mon, cowboy! You're getting fingerprints on me!" But he kept it up, hunching her. "You're going to upset Ramon!"

"To hell with Ramon."

But Ramon began to cough, and she instantly twisted away. "Ramon!"

"He'll be all right," Adrian said, annoyed. "Probably swallowed a hair."

The coughing increased—a terrible rasping sound, a sucking in, gasping for breath that bent him over almost double.

"It's an attack!" she said, her voice at an unnatural pitch.

"Easy." Adrian opened one of the bottles of Five Star Beer and shoved it under Ramon's nose. "Here, try this on your whistle." Lips pursed, Ramon was able to draw in some of the liquid. The coughing eventually subsided. "See?" Adrian said. "He just needed to grease the old chute."

She helped Ramon to a rump-sprung couch at one angle of the small room and arranged a pillow, stroking the damp forehead. "Don't scare me like that, lover—now try to rest."

She stood up, watching the irregularity of the chest rising and falling.

Adrian helped himself to a beer. "He looks long in the tooth—how old do they get?"

"I don't know," she whispered.

Adrian Reed had arrived in front of Frisky's a month earlier by accident. He had begun the evening (he thought) at a place called Gracie's, where the proprietress, a bulbous blonde in an electric-blue dress, had ordered up bubbly in a Southern accent. Arranged around a depressing Chinese Victorian parlor, pink-and-white beauties lounged against green satin, looking like a send-up of down home belles waiting to have their dance cards filled out. This was not the Oriental decadence he had in mind for himself.

He remembered later going on to other establishments on Kiangse Road, of sitting in the doorway of a brothel (on Broadway?) with a White Russian woman who swore she was a princess. When he got up to leave, she threw her dress over his head. Much later (or was it before?) another danced naked in a cabaret as sailors spun silver cartwheels across the floor. Bending low, she plucked them up with her nether regions while they shouted their only Russian, "Yellow blue vass! I love you!" and her cry coming back, "Yes-shaw! Yes-shaw! More! More!"

Everywhere he went the girls wanted his "cowboy" hat. It wasn't a cowboy hat; it was an "on-the-road" Stetson, and he would just as soon have given up his life. At the seamen's dives behind the Bund it got rougher and the booze got worse. He suspected they were serving dregs, but kept on.

Coming over on the *Gripsholm*, he'd heard tales of Shanghai's red light district—My God! they said. There were more whores in the city than the entire population of Toledo, Ohio! That was a fact! Adrian believed he had been propositioned by at least half of them, and he'd only been in town a week. If he learned anything, it was that they would rather drink than rut. In the end he didn't go with any . . . or didn't think he had. It wasn't the drink or high moral principles or even a concern about disease—he simply hadn't found a single erotic image that lived up to his heightened sexual expectations.

At dawn he made his way through the back alleys toward the Bund. This wasn't intuitive, rather a trail marked by the spore of countless seamen from the passenger jetties; sailors returning from an exhausting liberty to the warships tied up at the Man of War Buoys. There seemed to be one every block or so, standing up against a wall relieving himself, while a shipmate sat on the curb or sagged against a pole. This path was called the "Funnel" by them, and at the spout across from the giant cranes on the docks, Adrian had found himself opposite a theater. Even in his dim state he was arrested by English lettering spelling out the name in a hesitation of light bulbs across the marquee: FRISKY'S. Above, arced over a changing playbill, it announced: VAUDE-VILLE All Time Running. He crossed over, drawn by a very odd poster.

Frisky's was the one alert building in a waterfront of dead companions. Houses of sexual encounter were certainly not allowed facing incoming Dollar liners or Gray Funnel steamers navigating the Whangpoo River. But tucked into the far angle of the Bund was this small theater next to empty warehouses. It had been built in 1916 when vaudeville was at its zenith. The cast-iron facade, run up in Troy, New York, shipped out of San Pedro, was applied to a structure of local stone, its exuberant stamped decoration leavened with Oriental additions.

But it wasn't a success. Passengers on incoming liners for whom the bold marquee was intended thought it amusing, but had not come to China for fourth-rate vaudeville. For the *fanquei* on the Bund it was in a bad location, full of sailors and dock people. The sailors themselves streamed past it to the hook shops in the alleys behind. To survive, a policy of half-European and half-Chinese acts was begun; this along with a showing of the new talkies proved the right combination. The local Chinese merchants and those who could afford it enjoyed being entertained on the Bund (it was ordinarily off limits to loitering Chinese), and the sailors coming down from liberty could sleep off their wretched excesses just across from the sampan landing that ran a ferrying service out to the ships.

The performers who worked Frisky's considered it the worst. Playing there had become something of an in-joke with the vaudeville professionals of the Fuller or Tivoli circuits that were routed through the Far East. If you played Frisky's, that was the bottom; there was no place left to go. Still, it had a friendly connotation, was something to laugh over—except, of course, for the poor devils who ended up onstage.

Originally it had been named "The Palace of Illuminated Talkies and Frisky Acts," but that was too much for the marquee and it became simply: FRISKY'S.

What had stopped Adrian cold was a large poster announcing a dance team: LOLA & RAMON. It was done in old-style lithography and was extremely vivid. Pictured was a beautiful blonde in a slinky dress being held in the embrace of the tango by an *ape*. There was no doubt that it was an ape; however, his hair had been slicked back in the Rudolph Valentino style with crescent sideburns against shaved cheeks. He wore a full-dress suit of impeccable cut, key chain swagged to the pocket and white gloves with stitched darts.

It was the woman who got Adrian's attention. She was at once so sophisticated, so self-assured that he had to smile. The pose strained to conjure up images of terrible submission: beauty and the beast, dark unspoken primeval urges, degradation. Instead you felt sorry for the animal. This image produced in him more desire, more outright lust than the entire catalogue of the night's soiled doves had been able to do. Adrian paid and went in.

The house was a quarter full with a mixture of Chinese (in the back) and sailors. The Chinese called across to one another and talked animatedly throughout the performance. The sailors, almost to a man, slouched or slept. White uniforms were filthy with God-knows-what stains, hat and kerchiefs long since discarded or lost. No longer surly or combative, they were now sunk into the last hours of a wrenching forty-eight-hour liberty. Vendors went up and down the aisles selling tea and beer, and the floor was slippery with orange peels and suds. The smell of the place was like the unexpected waft of an open saloon door.

Adrian made his way to the front and, stepping over several sleeping sailors, settled in the second row. In the first, to his right, a large sailor with a cook's and baker's rating slept, leaning forward, his face on the apron of the stage. At each exhaled breath he sent up particles of dust.

Center stage, a Chinese singer in elaborate costume was singing in a voice pitched so high it caused pain. The placard announced: "Butterfly Wo." In the middle of a long aria she suddenly stopped and turned. An assistant ran out from the wings with a cup of tea, which she gargled and spit on the floor, then, turning back, continued. Adrian was appalled. Nothing he had seen in his night's carousing had seemed as vulgar. The crowd was unmoved, and when she finished there was scattered applause from the Chinese and a loud breaking of wind from one of the sailors, which everyone enjoyed.

The lights came up and another vendor passed up the aisle selling hot towels, which he tossed with practiced swings over the heads of others to the buyer. This seemed like a good idea to Adrian, and he was on the point of ordering one when he realized it was the same towel being passed.

The house lights dipped again, went out, and an amber spot circled the left side of the curtain. Then they were there, frozen in the attitude of the tango. It was apparent at once that the ape did not resemble in any way the tall, robust figure on the poster outside. He was a good two heads shorter than his partner, stooped, and in a dress suit that was shiny—a curious purple color—from age. The animal itself was in fact very old. From his seat down front, Adrian could see it in the lackluster hair and sag of red-veined eyes.

But the woman was something else. More exotic, if anything, than the dancer on the poster, and despite the heavy makeup, beautiful with the half smile and arched eyebrow that said, "There's nothing you can show me I haven't seen."

Then the discordant Chinese musicians took up the strains of the tango and the two began to dance. As they glided out, cheek to cheek, arms extended in the embrace of the tango, the flap of his feet audible, they seemed foolish: the white satin dress against the purple suit; pale face pressed against a flat black sideburn—she seemed nearly luminescent, he lifeless, the refraction of light from her rhinestone headband sending out a dazzle of brilliant pinpoints. When they reached center stage, the ape suddenly stopped, as if automated, and with perfect timing reversed the beat.

Obviously the animal had done this routine a thousand times with the dancer guiding him firmly. Still, despite the stiffness and bowlegged lope, it was possible to see an amusing parody of an old gigolo. The audience was unimpressed, the Chinese rattling on while the sailors slept. The bill had been running all summer and had lost its novelty. Their steps varied now, knees bent, their heads turned away from each other in kinetic snaps. It was her vivacity that gave the illusion of excitement. Adrian could see that the animal's eyes were flat, evasive—he was now tugged along by her signals just a fraction of a second behind the beat. At the end of a long run downstage, with the pound of a drum mounting, she spun herself out in a whirl of white satin, then wound in, the ruffles coiling and uncoiling up her body like the shimmer of quicksilver. They paused as she pressed against him, he arching his back in increments to create the caricature of a flamenco dancer. Doing this, he inadvertently stepped on the sleeping sailor's head.

The sailor let out a startled howl, and Adrian could see from his point of view that the patent leather shoe tops the ape wore had no soles; his wide toes were suddenly curled in a prehensile grip around the man's face. The ape pulled back instantly, but the sailor, furious, reached across the apron and grabbed hold of his pants leg. The animal shrieked and clung to his partner, but the man hung on. The crowd loved this departure, and sailors began to wake and offer encouragement. The ape continued its terrified screaming, drawing its lips back and showing yellowed, doglike canines, worn but still impressive. The woman tugged him back, smiling at the sailor, coaxing him to let go, but he would not.

Adrian reached over and tapped him smartly on the shoulder. "Why not let go, sport?"

The sailor swung backhanded with his free hand, the wind from the intended blow riffling Adrian's hair. "Get stuffed, Jack!"

Still shrieking, the ape tried to shake loose its captured leg, but the sailor hung on, and egged on by his shipmates, regripped, leaning forward. As he did so, he braced his knee against the edge of the stage and his leg came up. Adrian reached down, grabbed the hairless ankle with both hands, gave the leg a terrific wrench and spun the sailor off the stage, sending him crashing into the front row of seats. Under his considerable weight, there was a buckle of mohair upholstery, followed by the shearing-off of padded armrests, then a final springy hump as several seats bottomed out on the teak floor. Amazingly, the man scrabbled up, shifting his bulk and cocking back an arm in a greasy sleeve that showed four hash marks above his cook's and baker's rating. Adrian discovered he was holding the man's shoe. Cocking his own arm back, he hit him with it as hard as he could. He was rewarded by seeing the heel's imprint transferred to the cook's forehead. The man fell back, *hors de combat*.

Turning to the onstage performers, Adrian bowed—luckily—for instead of being hit a solid blow, he was hit a glancing one on the shoulder by another sailor behind him. He swung around, and they grappled awkwardly, with his opponent getting a purchase on his knitted tie. Adrian brought both elbows up, slamming them together on the man's ears. As his tie was released, he scrambled up on the stage. When the other followed, lunging forward, Adrian used his foot to propel him backward with another explosion of substandard seating.

All this time the terrible racket of the Chinese tango continued. The musicians, confined to a narrow triangle at the far end of the pit, played on with verve, frightened eyes cutting toward the audience as the enemy.

The theater was coming to life. Sailors woke to find a last chance to make trouble before liberty was up. A rebel cry went up, then a rally of gunboat sailors, *"Villabobos! Panay! Monocacy! Palos!"* This had the curious effect of a Roman legion sounding off, and was followed by a full-out charge, a hopping of seats that resembled the onward rush of a dirty white wave.

Looking out at a rising tide of his own Pacific Fleet—*Americans*—surging forward en masse with the sole intent of doing *him* bodily harm, Adrian was appalled. The insane music continued to a galloping crescendo. He turned and tipped his Stetson to the dancer. "Excuse me, ma'am, but I think we'd better get out of here!"

"Who are you?" she said, cocking that eyebrow. "Tomfuckin' Mix?"

There was no time for further conversation, and Adrian reached for her arm, intending to make for the nearest wing. The minute he touched her, the nasty ape leaned over and bit him viciously on the upper leg.

TWO

ADRIAN MANAGED TO limp after the dancer through a confusing twist of dim passages to a tight, L-shaped dressing room. He was reluctant to enter the small space with the ape, but the animal instantly jumped up on a sagging couch and turned his back.

"Oh, boy!" she said. "How do I get messed up in these things! Ramon, damnit! How could you do that! Bad boy!" Ramon shook his head in an agitated uncoordinated way. She turned to Adrian. "You should have left that bonehead to me!" Then she smiled. "I did like the part when you hit him with the shoe."

"Thanks." He was not amused.

"She looked down at the tear in his pants. "How's the leg—does it hurt?"

"You're damned right!" He hopped to the one chair and let himself down easy, then had to laugh. "If you're going to be bitten by an ape, I suppose it's acceptable if he's in full dress."

She laughed with him. "You're a sport, cowboy—let's see how bad it is." There was nothing to do but let down his trousers and hope to God his shorts were respectable. The bite, two opposing rows of ragged punctures, marked the perfect outline of Ramon's teeth on his upper leg. An ugly purple bruise was beginning to color the wound. "Oh," she said, "that doesn't look too bad. We can fix it."

"Not too bad!" He thought it looked terrible.

"Think about that sailor you broke those seats with, he's going to be picking springs out of his ass for a week." This was as close as she ever came to thanking him for extracting the ape from the cook's clutches.

She fished under the skirt of the dressing table, took out a bottle of rubbing alcohol, and soaked a handkerchief with it. "The thing is to get it clean." She knelt beside him and gently pressed the handkerchief to the wound.

"Jeee-zuss!" He sucked his teeth.

"Yeah." From a worn first-aid kit, she produced a large bottle of Mercurochrome and carefully applied it. "Ramon is really gentle—but that bohunk scared him, and I guess he thought you were more of the same—honest, he wouldn't hurt a flea."

Adrian didn't believe it for a minute. He could tell by the way she handled the wound that she had done this before—and he was grateful. From his own experience with horses he knew how septic an animal bite could be.

"Look at him—he knows he did wrong. He's going to feel lousy about this when he cools down . . ."

"So am I!" Adrian said with some heat, but she rolled right over this.

". . . he really likes people, that's all he knows. Show him another ape and he'd turn up his nose. . . ." As she talked, head down, Adrian saw that where her hair grew out at the part, it was a lovely color of red. He wondered why in the world she would bleach it that awful platinum blond.

Finishing the bandaging, she patted his knee and looked up. "There you go." At that moment, unasked and without the slightest advance warning, his shorts rose and tented. He blushed vividly.

"I guess he just wanted to say hello," she said, smiling.

After that, Adrian came around to Frisky's nearly every night. He discovered right away that he and Lola had almost nothing in common except the powerful draw of sensuality. He had found in the first few minutes that she was independent, funny, with a husky voice, a raucous laugh, and a way of looking at you that suggested shared secrets. As he got to know her, he also discovered she was from a vaudeville family, was in the Far East on a "Farewell Tour" with Ramon, that they had gotten stuck in Shanghai and had taken this rotten turn at Frisky's only to get passage home. She was used to working Pan Time or the big presentation houses.

He believed about half of this and could think of only one thing—bedding her down. But despite her appearance, she was not easy and held back, making sure he did not confuse her with the professionals in the tough neighborhood. Never mind her show-business swank, she was a good Irish Catholic (a failed Catholic, she admitted) brought up properly. Despite this

naïve disclaimer, the romance heated up rapidly and galloped toward a foregone conclusion. The main block was the damn ape.

They took Ramon everywhere they went. Lola said if they didn't, he would
sit and howl or tear the place up. For the street, she dressed him in a loose
mandarin coat and a bellboy's cap with a chin strap and a button on top. The
Chinese found this amusing, following them for blocks. Under his coat and
circling his waist was a stout belt. When the crowd got too close, she
snapped a chain on through a slit in the coat and kept him on a tight rein.
Ramon didn't like this, but he accepted it from her. Adrian was very wary
around the animal and watched him closely. He knew Ramon watched him in
turn, but he couldn't catch him at it.

Because of Ramon there was no way in the world he could take Lola back
to the hotel. Shanghai might be full of bizarre people, but they did not come
into the lobby of the staid Palace Hotel with an ape in tow. Or, for that
matter, single ladies did not take the rococo elevator to a gentleman's room.
So the routine after the show was to eat in one of the local noodle shops that
would accept Ramon, then go back to her place.

This was close by, in what appeared to be a Chinese version of the theatrical boardinghouse, full of odd cooking smells and the occasional glimpse
of other professional animals. The boarders were Occidental with the exception of an Indian, who, she said, kept snakes. Lola had a large, irregular room
on the top floor under the eaves, dominated by a huge Herkert & Meisel
wardrobe trunk. The overflow of clothes hung on bamboo poles swagged
across ceiling beams. When a smart breeze sprang up from the river and
passed through the open window, the poles swayed and snapped, the bells on
Ramon's bolero jacket playing an accompaniment.

There was nothing to sit on other than the bed, and late one night toward
the end of the first week of sexual fencing, this is where they were. Both
edgy, smoking and trying to relax, listening to Al Bowley's soupy voice on
the new Vic (a gift from Adrian). After several beers Ramon had finally fallen
asleep in the small curtained alcove in the back of the room. This had taken
forever, it seemed to Adrian. It was like dealing with a kid—worse, a mean-
tempered old man. He was beginning to wonder if it was worth it.

Lola was wondering the same thing. She found Adrian puzzling. He had
ridden into her life like a knight on a white horse, the answer to a maiden's
prayer, complete with white cowboy hat. She had been taken at once by his
collar-ad looks and parlor manners, sure that he must be rich. But his face
contained puzzling contradictions. In profile it was handsome, almost elegant, but there were troubling scars: a curved crescent above the left eye, a
distinct break at the bridge of the nose, a nick in the chin, and—the most
disturbing—a piece missing from his right earlobe. This seemed to suggest

some kind of hard case—or barroom athlete—the last kind of hairpin she wanted to get mixed up with. Still—he was young, twenty-five or twenty-six, she thought, and there was a quality about the face, the way he talked, that she associated with the upper class—money.

When she finally asked him, he said the scars were from polo. *Polo?! You could get hurt like that playing polo?* He tapped his front teeth—caps—the originals had been knocked out at the Myopia Hunt Club in '29, he said, by a ball traveling at least sixty miles an hour. His teeth, still imbedded in the wooden ball, were on the mantel of his father's Pasadena home. He thought this was funny. Lola thought it was dumb. She found it hard to believe that if you were rich (and you had to be rich to play polo), you would go in for something that would hurt you.

She said so. "That is nuts! It doesn't make sense—why would a bunch of rich guys want to go riding around knocking each other's teeth out?"

He agreed. "Good question. It's certainly the only sport I know where it personally costs you a great deal of money to do yourself such damage."

"Is that what happened to your earlobe?" she asked, getting mad.

"Well—a horse bit it off."

"What!" She had to laugh. "Boy, you are some kind of guy for getting eaten on by animals."

"I taste good."

"I guess."

They lay on the bed watching their smoke drift toward the low ceiling. "Why do it?"

"What?"

"Play polo."

"Oh, I don't know." What he didn't say was, it was all he could do, really well—that if judged by the sport's own handicap of 10 (there were only four in the world), he was an 8 and must be good at it.

There was something else too. He had done it to please the old man.

Adrian did everything he could to be like him, and when the old man took up raising polo ponies in the twenties, Adrian spent his summers as a kid on Joe Short's Peachtree Ranch near Bandera, Texas, shoveling horseshit and trying to please the foul-mouthed, taciturn cowboys. He wasn't all that fond of horses, but he made it his job to learn and ride with the best of them, to please the old man and confound the cowboys.

After he had been thrown, bitten, stepped on, and had suffered his first broken bone, he "got the hang of it." At the end of the first summer even the cowboys had to admit "he had glue on his ass." It was the turning point in his young life. He had found a thing he was good at, and he would continue to pursue it from now on with a vengeance.

The next year he began to learn about polo. The government paid up to $175 for a cavalry horse, but Eastern clubs and private players would pay twice that for a polo pony. Each day, Adrian went with the cowboys while they culled the herd for saddle-broken horses. These they would cut out and take turns "swinging a mallet" on. Finally, splitting up into teams, they "stick-'n'-balled," testing themselves and the animals for speed and the ability to close in a flurry of flying mallets. At the end of the training a half-broken horse was made into a polo pony and turned a nice profit.

When he was fourteen, Adrian began to travel the polo circuit as a groom and by the end of the first season was playing as a substitute. From the beginning he played best at the number-two position, "scrambler." This required fast ponies, fighting for the ball, and an aggressive drive. It also helped to be young and resilient. His injuries would eventually include (besides the facial damage), a broken leg, foot, four ribs, and several cracked collarbones. At the Onwentsia meet in Lake Forest, Illinois, he was knocked unconscious for twelve hours and ended up with a serious concussion. It was a dangerous sport, and an average of one man a year died from polo injuries.

At eighteen, mounted on his father's horses and playing against first-class competition, Adrian and his team won twenty-five straight games, including the American Gold Cup. As a reward, the old man took him to Alaska hunting, and together they shot a Kodiak bear. Adrian still had the bone that had been taken out of its penis and polished into a letter opener.

After graduating from Stanford, he traveled the next years with an international team and played "high goal" polo. Impressive fielding was necessary to support the four team members, fifty horses, six grooms, and all the tack and gear that went with them. The expense was considerable and as usual was picked up by his father. The team won the Copa de las Americas, then swung through Europe, capping a sensational season by capturing the Westchester Cup in Great Britain. By August 1930 they were back in New York to a heroes' welcome. Adrian now had an 8-goal rating and was called the California Cowboy in the sporting press.

A year later it was all over.

Lola plucked out her thin cotton dress where it had stuck to her skin. "Talk about humid, the place is like a sitz bath. When Ramon and I hit stateside, I'm jumping in the first snowbank I see."

"Oh, I don't know . . ." Adrian said, hand-rolled cigarette held between his teeth, eyes squinted in an expression that annoyed her. "Weather seems to fit a place—Shanghai seems right humid."

What the hell did that mean? She gave up. Enough. She knew what was on his mind. Holding him off had hurt his pride. He was pouting, like Ramon. God save her from the care of cowboys and babies. She was damned if she was

17

going to roll over for a Victrola and a couple of records. Who knew Al Bowley anyway? It was time for so long and it's been good to know you.

They had both reached the same conclusion at the same time, and leaning over at the same moment to put out cigarettes, cracked heads.

"Ohh! Jesus! You got a head like an Irishman!" she said, rubbing her head, then burst out laughing. "Are you out to get me?"

There was a second's pause. "Yes," and he nicely kissed her. It lingered—accelerated, set up electricity that jumped back and forth between them like sexual sparks.

"All right . . . all right . . . wait a minute." Sighing, she skinned her dress up. "I don't want to ruin this." Pulling it off over her head, she expertly flung it up, where it caught and draped over one of the bamboo poles. *"Ta ta!"*

Adrian frantically unbuttoned his shirt, sending the last buttons flying and, whipping it around like a bullfighter's cape, sent it up and over one of the poles. *"Ta ta!"*

Leaning forward and unhooking her bra, she circled her head with it once and easily made the pole. His pants followed, then shorts. Kicking her legs up, she shucked off her panties, snapped the elastic, and dropped them perfectly on top of his shorts. "Top that, cowboy!"

He plucked one sock off, measured the distance, and lobbed it up where it caught, hesitated, then stayed. She squealed, clapping. When the other sock caught and held, toes pointing together, she was his.

It was the first time they had been totally naked together. Closing, she whispered, "I hope you're wearing something. . . . I don't want Ramon to have any little brothers or sisters." He complied.

For Adrian it was the culmination of his ardent pursuit. But as he rose and fell above her, one thing spoiled the moment. "Did you hear something?" he whispered.

"Huh? Whaa . . . ?"

He twisted his neck, looking back at the curtained alcove. "Ramon?"

"No, no," she said.

But he couldn't get it out of his head. The thought of that ape creeping up on him and suddenly sinking those awful canines in his bare ass was unnerving.

THREE

ADRIAN WENT UP the side aisle of Frisky's before the evening performance began, dodging sailors and the come-and-go of hucksters. Outside it was hot, and the heat continued, lying on the city with a torridness that would not lift until autumn, when it would drop thirty degrees in a few hours. He was surprised to see a large old limo, a Hispano-Suiza, parked in front. As he watched, a man stepped out of it, the epitome of the Chinese gentleman, gold-rimmed glasses tweezed onto a minute nose, moon face, ruddy cheeks glowing. He wore beautifully cut Western evening clothes; the linen was bright white and looked to be starched the tensile strength of tungsten. Behind him were Shensi bodyguards, the distinctive broom-handle shape of at least one Mauser automatic visible under rumpled suits.

As the gentleman came by Adrian, their eyes met and he smiled sweetly. Surprised, Adrian smiled back. It was unusual to see anyone of the gentleman's class in Frisky's. He had noticed others on occasion, voyeurs possibly, titillated by the woman-animal aspect of Lola's act.

Their meeting was noted down by a man across the Bund parked in lee of the cranes. The car, a Ford roadster, had the top up and curtains snapped in despite the heat, and his face appeared distorted, curiously flat in the dull gloss of the isinglass. When Adrian stepped out from under the marquee and hopped a tram lurching by, there was a moment of hesitation, then the Ford started up and followed, its narrow tires slipping in and out of the trolley tracks.

Shanghai had come as a surprise to Adrian. Contemporary fiction, films, and his own romantic bent had prepared him for a murky, mysterious place full of the clichés of junk sails, pirates, and opium dens. The reality was of an enormous industrial complex sprawling farther and wider than Chicago, with a population of millions and a skyline along the Bund that boasted of some of the tallest buildings in the world.

The streets were an inventory of signboards: hard-edged letters projecting out on shaky framework, neon blurbs signaling "BUY" in Chinese and English; crude murals illustrating devils at work on enlarged stomachs, cutout illuminated mothers holding the miracle of electric fans to overheated porcine babies—and one sign he found particularly puzzling: SQUIRT VARNISH ON MOTOR COMPANY.

It was the language of the commercial West. The European city was divided into International Settlements, each with its own police, street names, and regional prejudice—all committed to the galloping pursuit of the dollar, or Mex, as the local currency was called.

The original Chinese city, Nantao, sat behind what had once been three and a half miles of walls. South of the French Concession it had been described as illustrating all the worst features of Oriental sprawl without antiquarian interest or one architectural redeeming feature.

Chinese sweat lubricated the gears of European Shanghai. Squeezed between the double-deck buses and automobiles that filled the boulevards, wretched coolies bent under yo-poles, rickshas, or two-wheeled carts competing for space. The place throbbed, bustled, broiled, and had been called, in a burst of overstatement, "The Paris of the Orient."

Adrian made his way up Nanking Road past the Astor and Palace hotels, Futterer's German Bakery, and block after block of crowded shops; then, turning on Route Cardinal Mercier near Siccawei Creek, he came to the velvety lawns of the Le Cercle Sportif Français. Unlike the stuffy American or Shanghai clubs, which banned Chinese even as guests, everyone was seen at Le Cercle.

The club got its name from several tennis courts and a swimming pool that was decked over in winter for badminton, but the real sport was in the bar and on the spring-loaded dance floor. As he crossed the canopied veranda, the cocktail hour was in full cry, and the crosscurrent of languages had the squawk and pitch of a pet shop; multilingual, loudmouthed Baghdadian business deals, the machine gun chatter of a table of *jeunes filles* summing up the day in kinetic gestures and antic shrugs; freshly starched Navy wives up from Manila on the Dollar boat, Georgia-drawling about a summer at Chefoo, and White Russian beauties with the faces of Tartar princesses and bass drum accents as thick as *hai-sin* gravy.

Adrian checked the drinkers out, made eye contact with the unescorted ladies, and went into the crowded oak-paneled bar. Over the rattle of dice boxes deciding who would pay, he spoke to the manager, an ex-Navy man he had cultivated, famous for inventing the gimlet.

"Good evening, Chief."

"Mr. Reed—martini straight up?"

"On the rocks, I think."

"Of course." He snapped his fingers at the Chinese barman as Adrian sat on a tall stool, wedged between drinkers.

"Have you seen anything of Captain Bodine?"

"No, sir, I've been on the lookout for him, but he hasn't come in."

"You talkin' about Red Bodine?" a florid man, squeezed next to Adrian, said.

"Warren Bodine."

"The same, only he ain't a captain." The man had a west Texas accent and talked around a wet cigar.

"No?"

"Not unless you call holdin' that rank in the Haitian Constabulary as somethin'."

"I see." Adrian started to turn away.

"It was officered by the Marine Corps, mostly noncommissioned types— that's how Bodine got to be a captain. He was a sergeant in the Marines."

"Interesting," Adrian said, polite as always.

"I know 'cause I came over here with him on the *Claumout* in '26. Remember that old bucket, Chief?"

"Oh, yes, sir."

"She was a Hog Island double-ender, bow looked like the stern, you couldn't tell if she was comin' or goin'—and at ten knots flat out, shoot, it didn't make much difference. They were bringin' the Fourth Marine over, an' Bodine was one of 'em, back to bein' sergeant."

"Gunnery sergeant, I think, sir," the Chief said.

"Whatever, anyway he was full of himself—he and another fella named Hanneken had killed Charlemagne—and after that, the Haitian rebellion was dead as last year's love. It was in all the papers at the time—they made a big thing out of it. He got a couple of medals and a bile-e-do from Harding." He neatly rolled the cigar to the other side of his mouth without missing a beat.

"Well, you would have thought he was God almighty—a sawed-off meanlookin' little bugger, redheaded and full of freckles, with one of those insultin' mustaches that looked like it was drawn on with a pencil. I tell you he acted like he was the cock of the walk."

Adrian smiled and tried to turn away again, but the Texan gripped his arm with one hand and put out his other. "My name's Leon Matthews. I'm the manager of the Standard Oil compound up at Woosung." His eyes were a hint too close together, but the fringe of a white mustache mitigated the effect, bestowing a kind of late-blooming authority on the face.

"Adrian Reed." They shook.

"Well, Ade, you know what happened to him, don't you?"

"Retired, I believe."

"Retired, shoot! He and a couple of other fellas were sent up to Chingchow to ransom a missionary's wife a couple of years back. Instead of paying out, they shot the place up and killed one of the bandits. It was only dumb luck that Bodine's bunch and the woman got back. It was real hairy, and she raised Cain about it."

"But—she must have been grateful?"

"Grateful? Shoot, she was a missionary! She said she didn't want to be rescued, that she was savin' souls and Bodine had murdered her convert in cold blood! Not only that, she claimed he had tried to molest her. Back in Nanking she filed charges through the Missionary Council. I heard later he had been booted out of the service before retirement. He was a cocky devil, but he didn't deserve that. Only goes to show what religion can get a person up to. . . ." He stopped and took the cigar out of his mouth. "Well, by God, speak of the devil! You're in luck!" Adrian turned and followed his eyes toward the entrance to the bar.

Bodine had just come in.

"Jee-zuss!" the Texan said. "He's got a blister on his arm!"

Lola was mad. She regretted caving in to Adrian, was convinced it was a mistake. The next day he had told her he had to spend some time on business and not to expect him back until late (for the first time); if not he would see her tomorrow. Sure. Once they got in your pants it was good-bye and goodie. She was no round heels but had been through this before and should know better. But she wasn't going to moon over it. What was done was done—in sex like show biz you better get a contract up front.

What worried her was *time*. There wasn't much left. Ramon was what? Forty? In human terms that would be . . . eighty maybe? Did anybody know? He was looking very frail, and she had to get him home before he died on her. She felt guilty. She never should have brought him out on this last tour. But what with talkies and Hoover's depression, bookings were few and far between. Why else would they be on this lousy tour, at Frisky's, for God's sake! They were riding a dead horse, and it was called vaudeville.

Lola Ryan came from vaudeville people. Her father, Billy Ryan, had been a popular Irish comedian before the turn of the century. He married her mother, Inez, a dancer, in 1904 in Chicago while they were appearing at the Cleveland Theater. (Will Rogers, making his first appearance there, was best man.) In the beginning they worked together as an "in one" act—in front of

22

the curtain—and were modestly popular. But in 1910 they got their big break.

Adolph Mendl, the animal trainer, had developed a young dancing chimp. The act was built around a popular craze at the time, the *milonga* or tango. The ape, Ramon, danced it with a life-size Spanish doll strapped to him. It was a hit on Pan Time around the country. Most people had never seen a real ape, let alone a dancing one.

The problems began when he matured. Male chimps were notorious for getting nasty when they got older and impossible to control. That's why "male" chimps you saw in acts were females dressed as males. After Ramon had bitten several stagehands and the booker at the B. F. Keith office, Mendl was forced to retire him. By luck, Billy and Inez had stopped by his Catskill farm on their way back from Niagara Falls, and Ramon had taken instantly to Inez; she was able to handle him. Billy saw a chance and bought him, spending the entire summer on a new act. As it originally went, Billy danced with Inez and was cut in by Ramon, then vice versa. It was a huge success.

They were booked on the big-time Orpheum Circuit and eventually played the top variety and presentation houses in Britain and Europe. These were the great days; the money rolled in almost faster than Billy could spend it. Ramon could still not be trusted and had to be kept on a chain offstage, but he was a star now and tolerated. Jealous and possessive of Inez, Billy had been tempted many times to sell him off to a zoo, but he was their meal ticket and Billy could put up with a lot to stay in the big time.

When Lola was born in 1912, it helped. She grew up with Ramon, played, ate, and slept near him. As with Inez, he accepted and depended on her. As she got older, they began to practice the routines together for the time when she could take over from her mother. It didn't happen that way.

The act had long since evolved into "Inez & Ramon." Billy had gotten fat and spent his time arguing with bookers. But the truth was, once you'd seen one dancing monkey you'd seen them all. They'd played the major cities a dozen times and now had moved to split weeks in the sticks. When Billy died in 1926, her mother took what little money was left and retired with Ramon to Sarasota, Florida.

Although Lola had been around three-a-day vaudeville as long as she could remember, she was pretty and found it easy to move over to working night-clubs and speaks. She was dancing at the International Casino in New York City in 1930 when she got a telegram saying her mother had passed away and Ramon had gone berserk.

He had thrown all the furniture out of the windows and terrified the neighbors in the court. The sheriff wanted to shoot him and strongly advised Lola to put him to sleep. She was shocked. Ramon was one of the family. She paid the damages and for a while tried keeping house in Sarasota and working locally. But Ramon wouldn't put up with being left alone and went on another rampage. This time they sent the dog catcher armed with a shotgun, and Lola had to sneak Ramon out of the court. They lived for a while on an alligator farm out on Route 30 until she couldn't stand it anymore. Finally she wrote to her parents' longtime agent at the William Morris office. The best he could do was a Far East tour on the Fuller circuit.

After a year of playing the outback in Australia, Lola let them be booked into Frisky's. It was all that was left. She found herself in the vaudeville performers' nightmare: trapped out of town. She could live cheap by Shanghai standards but couldn't save enough for a ticket home—one way on a decent boat was nearly a thousand dollars. Even the rotten job at Frisky's would be over at the end of summer. Then what?

There was a timid knock on the door, and the Indian manager pushed the door open a crack. "Gentleman come see by now."

"What? Huh?" She pulled her kimono around her, and Ramon, sensing strangers, jumped to the couch and turned his back.

The door opened and a rotund Chinese stood there. In perfect evening clothes. A silver key chain at just the right angle from vest to pocket. Carefully manicured nails, plump fingers holding white gloves. He bowed.

> *"Truly she charmed all beholders,*
> *'Tis she hath given us such jewels,*
> *The jade of our delight.*
> *But this bright jewel-jade that smolders,*
> *To our desire doth add more fuel,*
> *New charms tonight."*

Lola laughed out loud. "Shakespeare?"
"Confucious," he said, smiling sweetly.

FOUR

BODINE CAME IN with his odd swagger of a walk, a kind of cocky bounce on the balls of his feet. His red hair was cut short in the military style and announced a Spartan, but the tough bulldog face was softened by a mask of freckles and a pencil-thin mustache outlined by an up-yours smile. Wearing an open-necked shirt, sharkskin slacks, and black-and-white wing tips, he walked down the bar, looking into every face that turned his way, and it was obvious that he would welcome a hint of disapproval—a glove thrown down. But there was only cordiality, handshakes, and back slaps.

"Talk about balls," the Texan whispered, "bringin' a blister in here—he's gone straight to the woofs!"

The Chinese girl on Warren Bodine's arm certainly wore the grotesque makeup of a street prostitute: chalk-white skin sectioned off with brilliant patches of rouge. She was a tiny thing, thin with a *cheong-sam* dress cut up the side and the teetering steps of bound feet. Her eyes were languid or perhaps just somnolent; she seemed to hang on her escort as though to keep from falling. As they came in, their arrival was noted not by those who looked at them, but by those who didn't. Le Cercle was certainly one of the most tolerant watering places in the city; charming companions could be found there at any hour, but no one would ever consider bringing a street girl into the club. No one, it seemed, but Bodine.

As Bodine came by him, Adrian stepped out, smiling, and offered his hand. "Captain Bodine." Bodine shook it casually and started to move on. "Ansel O'Banion suggested I look you up."

Bodine stopped and looked at him sharply. "Is that right? C'mon, bunkie, I'll buy you a drink." They passed out of the bar and sat at a table at the back of the dining room, nearly empty now. "You're not in the military?"

"No."

"How do you know an old yellow-leg like O'Banion?"

"He was a friend of my father's—through Homer Lea."

"Homer Lea?" His eyebrows went up. "You from San Francisco?"

"Pasadena. Lea was living in Santa Monica then."

But Bodine wasn't listening. He kept searching the room out, then suddenly got up. "I'm suppose to meet a gink here—let me check out the Ping-Pong tables." And he was gone.

Adrian sat looking at the Chinese girl. Her thick black hair had been shingled and the bangs cut across her forehead like a curtain; below, the stage was empty. He smiled but it didn't register. The level of her eyes was fixed someplace over his left shoulder. He resisted the temptation to turn and look, knowing he would find nothing there. Adrian was not unfamiliar with drugs, but this girl made him nervous.

A boy came to the table and poured a measure of absinthe into a tiny tank mounted on a wire tower. As Adrian watched, it dripped, drop by drop, through a piece of sugar held in place to a glass until the glass was full. Adrian stuck to his martini.

Bodine returned. "The peckerhead didn't show." He sat down and looked at his watch.

"Forgive me," Adrian said, rolling a cigarette, "is this girl all right?"

"I didn't get your name."

"Reed, Adrian Reed."

"What can I do for you?"

"I thought you might be able to help me—I'm looking for a Marshal Yü here in Shanghai—and I've been unable to locate him."

"You got anything on for tonight?"

"What?"

"Tonight. This gink was gonna help me out, but anyone who's white and looks reasonably bright will do."

Adrian had to smile. "Are you sure I qualify?"

"I'll take that chance." Bodine smiled back. His teeth were small and even, with a gap between the front ones. "I have to deliver this girl, and I need a witness that I did."

"I don't understand. Deliver her where?"

"Tell you what, give me a hand and then we'll go over to my place and talk about finding Yü."

"Well . . ."

Bodine was out of his chair, tugging the Chinese girl up. "You comin'? I got a set of wheels outside, we'll be there before you know it." Adrian followed, and Bodine steered the girl toward the door. As they came by the Texan, he rolled his eyes.

A motorcycle was parked outside on the sidewalk, chained to one of the entrance columns. A big Harley twin attached to a sidecar, it had been painted a drab military color; white numbers and U.S.M.C. were crudely painted out. It was dark now, and as the lights of traffic flashed by, Adrian supported the girl while Bodine unlocked the machine. Several ricksha boys hunkered down, watching them.

"Climb in," Bodine said, slipping on a pair of goggles.

"What?" Adrian laughed. "There's not room in there for both of us."

Bodine took the girl from Adrian. "C'mon! You could fit a squad of hippos in this tub!"

"If you say so." Still carrying his martini, Adrian tucked his long legs into the tight space and pulled down his Stetson as Bodine lowered the girl onto his lap. She curled up with one arm around his neck, thin legs dangling over the side. Adrian gave her a peck on the cheek. "Hang on, princess."

Bodine straddled the machine and, leaning down, tickled the carburetor. Then, adjusting the spark, he squeezed the compression release and came down on the starting lever with a vengeance. The Harley sprung to life with a deafening roar, the exhaust blackening the column and scattering the ricksha boys.

The traffic was fierce at this hour, and Bodine seemed to be waiting for a break. He positioned the Harley on the sidewalk, engine throbbing, hand blipping the throttle, head turned toward the oncoming traffic. There was a gap, and just when it seemed he was going to move, he paused for one more car, then shot out directly in front of it.

Adrian's head snapped back like a catapult, sending the martini olive past his left ear. Bodine put the bars over, and the back wheels gripped and spun out inches from a taxi's front bumper. The driver stood on the brakes, and they pulled away from certain destruction by a hair, with Bodine laughing like a madman.

The taxi stalled out, blocking the Ford roadster from following the motorcycle. When the driver of the Ford laid on the horn, the Chinese taxi man got out and began to scream at him, furious at the motorcyclist, and turning it on him. The door of the Ford clicked open and the driver, dressed in a tidy suit and cap, walked straight up to the taxi man and slapped him hard. The taxi man staggered back, his voice cut off in midsentence. He looked closely at his assailant, then quickly got back in the taxi and drove off, missing the gear changes. The driver of the Ford stood for a moment looking at the flow of traffic; it was obvious now he would never catch up with the motorcycle, and he decided instead to wait at the Palace Hotel. As he got back in the car, the angles of his face were highlighted by the oncoming traffic, and it could be seen that he was Japanese.

The Chinese in the elegant evening suit bent over Lola's hand. "My dear lady, may I present myself—Charles Min. And may I be allowed to say that being in your presence is a most great thing. I found your performance extraordinary. Yes. Yes."

He said this in oddly constructed English with the overlay of a British accent. The beaming face with its polished apple cheeks and curl of a smile was without a line. It appeared seamless, the color of yellowed ivory, framed by glossy black hair and a part that might have been incised with a scalpel. She looked at the hand holding hers. There was a ruby on his finger the size of a gallstone.

"Well, thanks. It was nice of you to stop around."

"I've come around for the purpose expressly of inviting you to a late supper on my yacht."

"Yacht?" She smiled. "Is that right?"

"I insist."

"I don't think so."

"Oh, I think you must not miss it, oh, yes, you will want to accept."

Lola could see the bodyguards in the shadowy hall. Both seemed to have crossed eyes, like a Siamese cat she had once owned. "Thanks a lot, Mr.—"

"Min."

"Mr. Min, but I'm afraid I've got a date with my boyfriend. . . ."

"Of course, the Mr. Adrian Reed. We have just passed outside and had a smile. He will join us at your permission."

"What! He will . . ." She didn't know what to make of that.

"My car will be happy to arrive for you after midnight by perhaps one half hour."

"Well . . . we'd have to take Ramon."

The motorcycle and its riders went through the stack of traffic on Nanking Road with the projection of an erratic rocket. Bodine's hand never once let up on the gas, dodging and slithering around trucks and buses, snaking through impossible gaps that closed instantly behind them. The rush of air dragged Adrian back. Eyes tearing from wind and the burn of exhaust fumes, he watched the blur of large objects whip by. The girl on his lap seemed ephemeral, weightless. Her small head rested against his, the trusting limp arm looped his neck, the extension of its pale hand vibrating at his right cheek. The fluttering fringe of her bangs was the only animation.

Bodine turned off the main drag, and Adrian lost track of the streets and alleys he navigated, cutting corners and banking turns that lifted the sidecar's third wheel a foot off the ground. They left the International Settlement and passed through one of the seven gates into Nantao. The Chinese city was a tight tangle of cobbled streets giving way eventually to a ragged countryside with an occasional house hidden in dusty trees. As they passed, the nasty rapping of their engine cut through the night and blew back the leaves, disturbing the parched lime and plane trees.

At last Bodine backed off the hand throttle and the Harley slowed. Ahead, stone walls sloping in from the dirt road created a formidable illusion in perspective, a mass pierced only by a heavy wooden gate and latticed windows at the second-floor level. The road was empty and Bodine shut off the engine, coasting the last hundred yards. He threw his leg over, got off at a trot, and gestured to push. Adrian shifted the girl, hopped out, and helped move the motorcycle into a narrow alley between two sections of the building. Under the filtered light of a second-story window, they parked the Harley and extracted the girl, setting her on her feet. The odor of sewage was overwhelming, and it seemed to Adrian they were wading in a sea of excrement.

Before exiting the alley, Bodine leaned the girl against the wall, positioning her head with his left hand. "Got a handkerchief, kid?" Puzzled, Adrian passed his over. Bodine spit on it and began to scrub at the girl's face, removing the makeup. "Fourteen," he said.

"But—why is she dressed like that—what's wrong with her?" Adrian was shocked. He had adjusted to her being a whore.

"She's had a few buttons of opium to calm her down, that's all."

"What does she need calming down for?"

"For her own safety." Before he could ask the next question, Bodine got a grip on the girl, turned the corner, and walked the half block to the entrance of the building. At the massive gate he rang a bell, and a minute later a small priest door rattled open in one side. Pushing the girl's head down, Bodine propelled her through and stepped after her.

No one had to tell Adrian there was something very wrong here and that if he followed through that door he would be involved in it. It's now or never, he thought. I can turn around and walk away. It would be tough finding his way back, but he could do it. He stepped through with only the slightest hesitation.

Inside, the courtyard was built in the old Chinese way so that importunate demons could not find their way past. There were fake entrances and the odd shapes of walls jutting in. At a distance Adrian saw a lantern bobbing and heard the shuffle of slippers. A servant appeared, gestured, and led them through a maze of obstructions to the interior of the building. Bodine tugged the girl along, and Adrian brought up the rear, darkness folding in behind.

They went down bleak halls with rugs rolled up, unused furniture, cases of bottled water stacked against the walls. The heavy odor of unidentified cooking percolated from the dark slots of doorways, and beyond were shadowy glimpses of men watching them. Crossing an inner courtyard between huge copper tanks, Adrian heard the flop of fish hitting the sides and saw a piebald flash of an enormous carp. More turns, along a red lacquered hall, and at the end—a perfectly square room.

They entered, ducking the low archway, and Adrian's head skimmed brass-bound beams supporting a ceiling of silk panels. Incongruously, a bare bulb hung from it and produced an intense glare. The side walls were fitted with elaborate grillwork, and through it came more unpleasant smells. He had the feeling of being inside a Mah-Jongg box or, more disturbing, the confessional. After he had seated them on stools at a low table, the servant left.

Adrian spoke in a whisper. "What is this place?"

"A yamen . . . sort of a palace," Bodine said. "Whattaya whispering for?"

Adrian cleared his throat. "Maybe you better tell me what I'm supposed to be—what's my role?"

"Role?" Bodine laughed. "C'mon, just try to look official. What I need is a witness."

"Who lives here?"

"A bigshot—he owns all the noodle factories on this side of the river. We'll be dealing with his comprador."

A door slid back in the grillwork and a man entered, wearing a mandarin robe, the azure button on his pillbox hat announcing his importance in the household. They bowed together, and he seated himself across from Bodine. Adrian was not introduced. The conversation started with polite bobs of the head, then began to drone on in the choppy singsong of Cantonese.

Adrian lost interest and examined the room. Squinting against the shine of the bulb, he made out a flicker of movement behind the grilled wall. It was like the confessional—someone was listening! He looked at the girl sitting apart on a low stool, head nodding, and again felt a pang of sympathy. He wished her eyes would respond, that he could smile and reassure her. Poor kid, probably a runaway. Her face, innocent now, made him very uneasy.

Voices got louder, and he turned back to see the comprador get up and, shaking his finger, leave the table.

Adrian leaned forward. "What's the matter?"

Bodine leaned his arm on the table, masking his mouth with his hand. "Ah, I told these chop you were a big official with the government—who had to be bribed. Naturally they understand that but don't like it—that way I can drive the price up on the girl."

"What are you talking about?"

"What am I talking about? Her—we're here to sell the girl!"

"I hope you don't mean for the night!" Adrian was appalled.

Bodine also looked shocked. "What do you think I am? A pimp or somethin'? Hell, no! I'm sellin' her, period!"

Adrian couldn't comprehend this. "What! You can't do that!"

"Who can't do that? I bought and paid for her, by God! I can damn well do with her as I please!"

"Wait a minute!" Adrian said, starting to get up. "I don't want anything to do with this!"

Quick as a wink, Bodine grabbed him by the shirtfront and jerked him back down. "You don't understand a damn thing!" Adrian was aware of the bright flush of freckles and the cold yellow eyes. "This girl was sold as a concubine to the noodle jockey, paid for—but before they could take delivery the silly slit ran off with a Frenchman. Now, ordinarily they would take care of it in their own way—but they can't be muckin' around with a white man in the International Settlement, so they contracted me to get her back and bend the frog a bit. I also had to pay—buy a piece of her to get her out—all I'm doin' now is gettin' my own back plus a little per diem. Got it?"

"Get your damn hands off me!"

"Sure, sure." Adrian sat down and Bodine smoothed out his jacket. "Now come on, bunkie, don't go pussy on me."

"Why didn't you just tell me what you were going to do in the first place!"

"I didn't think you'd be interested."

Adrian almost laughed.

"Look, you worried about the tomato? That little girl is gonna have a good home here with her own people—trust me. I'd hate to tell somebody from Stanford what the frog had in mind for her."

"Don't oversell it, Bodine!"

At that moment the comprador returned, carrying a small chest. Behind him were two others, with expressions so theatrically sinister that Adrian thought they must be joking. The chest was centered on the table and opened. In it were trays of molded lumps of silver bullion, *sycee*, in the shape of small boats.

"Damn," Bodine said, smiling for the first time. "I haven't seen any 'shoes' in years. They must have taken this lot offa Marco Polo."

The comprador set up scales. He weighed each piece carefully, marking it, and placed them in a row. Bodine reached under his shirt and took off a leather money belt. It was divided into many small compartments. He examined each piece of silver and tucked it inside. The total looked to be worth several thousand to Adrian. This seemed odd; he had been told many times that Chinese girls were worthless, a burden on poor parents—that many were killed at birth.

When Bodine had secured the silver in the belt, the comprador leaned over and placed his hand on top of it. There were hissed words, and the belt was left lying flat on the table. Adrian could feel the tension in the room. Bodine eased back on his stool and, crossing his arms, stared at the comprador, who stared back.

After a minute Adrian leaned in. "What's wrong?"

"The peckerheads are gonna be cute." Bodine spoke out of the corner of his mouth loudly, still facing the comprador. "They say the girl was guaranteed to be a virgin on delivery. They want to check her out before they pay."

"What!"

"I'm not going to let 'em, of course. They know damn well she can't be, not after jerking around with a Frenchman—they just want to push the price down."

"What can you do?"

"Call their bluff. These damn people are all bluff. Now listen, I'm going to reach down and pick up the belt—when I do, you snort, act official. We'll get up and stomp outta here, all injured dignity."

"Do you think that's smart?"

"There ain't a Chinaman alive that can brace up to a righteous white man—don't sweat it." He shifted back on the stool. "Get ready." Bodine rose and deliberately reached for the belt.

As he did, a sword appeared miraculously as though conjured, swung in a large arc, and sliced down toward his wrist.

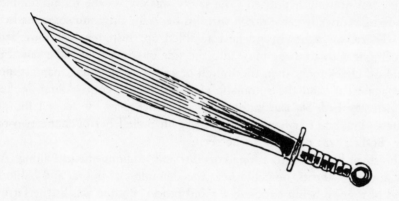

FIVE

WHEN ADRIAN SAW the sword's first flash, he kicked out, knocking the table forward with his foot. This movement threw the sword's stroke off by a hair, and instead of lopping Bodine's hand off, as intended, the blade neatly severed the last two compartments of the money belt, chipping the lacquer table. Before the man could shift his position, Bodine swung the heavy belt up and slammed him behind the ear. The man fell sideways, sliding on the polished surface of the table, collapsing one of its legs. As his head hit the stone floor, Bodine kicked him sharply in the left temple with the point of his right wing tip.

Adrian watched the other man's eyes, and when his hand moved, drop-kicked his groin, sending him flat against the grillwork, taking out a square yard. As he straightened too fast, Adrian's head hit the light bulb, and it broke with a loud pop. Lit from behind now, the grillwork went from positive to negative. In that instant Bodine was past him like a flash, straight-arming the door and disappearing through it.

Adrian pulled the girl to her feet and followed. In the hall outside, they immediately ran into a fat old man sitting on a stool, his face still pressed to the grill. He was knocked over on a young man wearing a black silk gown. Bodine jumped them, but Adrian, reluctant to step on the old man, lost his balance and fell. There were grunts, groans, then a small chrome-plated automatic was thrust up from the pile and pressed against his temple. Rotating his eyes, Adrian could actually see the finger try to squeeze the trigger, once, twice—but nothing happened. The safety was on. As the thumb fumbled for it, Adrian frantically came down with his heel, digging into someone beneath him. There was a howl, and he scrambled up, bringing his elbow around, whacking it with a terrific blow into the side of the first head he saw. He felt it skid off cheekbone, then the stretch of an ear. The young man clapped his hand against it, and the automatic clattered to the floor. Adrian looked for the girl. *My God! She was walking back toward the room!* He leaped the pile of Chinese, grabbed her hand, and once again pulled her over the two on the floor. Bodine was nowhere to be seen.

The small hall fed into a long corridor and, tugging the girl along, Adrian kept running. Ahead, he could hear the slamming of doors, and behind, the sound of a gong being struck in a rapid tattoo. Bodine was at the far end of the corridor, opening one door, then moving on to the next. Adrian caught up.

"What in hell are you doing!"

"We're on the north side of the house, right?"

"How would I know!"

Bodine ran to the next door. "It's got to be here! I can smell it!" There was a shuffle of slippers, shouts, then at the other end of the corridor Chinese burst into view. "Here it is!" Bodine ducked in the doorway, and Adrian followed him, dragging the girl in.

"Good God!" Adrian clamped his free hand over his nose. The smell in the room took his breath away.

The floor was covered with chamber pots: brass, clay, pewter—buckets, jars—dozens of them, all overflowing and few with lids. It was the night-soil collection, and from the looks of it a full month's worth.

"Any pot in a storm, bunkie!" Laughing like a madman, apparently enjoying himself hugely, Bodine bolted the heavy door. "They won't get through that in a while! C'mon, me hearties!" Stepping gingerly between the thicket of receptacles, they reached the window. Bodine shook the stout wooden grill, but there was no give. It was tightly fastened by a large brass lock. His mood plummeted. "Who in the holy hell would lock a window you throw shit out of?! Jee-zuss! A damn Chinaman! That's who!"

He began searching in the boxes and barrels against one wall. As he did so, the sound of chopping began on the door. Bodine worked a heavy bronze horse packed in excelsior out of one of the barrels. "This ought to do it!" Picking it up by the front legs, he carried it over and swung it toward the grill.

Adrian grabbed his arm. "Bodine! Look at it! That thing is a piece of art! It must be worth a fortune!" As he said this, the tip of an ax appeared in the door, splitting the center panel out.

"Yeah? How much is your ass worth, sport?" And he continued the swing. As he battered away at the grill, the teak gave, splintered, and when the last pieces fell away, the ancient bronze horse had been reduced to junk. Bodine dropped it and shoved Adrian through the opening. "You first! Then I'll let the tomato down!"

A hand now appeared through the shattered panel of the door and, leveling the chrome-plated automatic, began firing. As the low-caliber slugs splatted against the wall over their heads, Bodine shoved Adrian toward the window. "Don't worry, these guys can never hit anything! Go on!"

Giving him a heft up to the window ledge, Bodine leaned out, holding his hand until Adrian dropped the half story to the alley. Adrian hit hard, falling back in the filth of the open sewer. He got up in time to have Bodine lower and drop the girl into his arms. As Adrian caught her dead weight, they both went down this time, sliding in the slime.

In the night-soil room an arm and leg pushed through the smashed door as Bodine climbed over the window ledge and dropped to the cobbles. Clearing the sewage, he swung up on the motorcycle, while Adrian got himself untangled and, carrying the girl, slip-slided after him. Adrian climbed into the sidecar, struggling to get a grip on her slippery limbs, and just managed to pull her on top of him as Bodine went through the starting sequence. Straightening, Bodine came down on the crank with everything he had, hoping the big cylinders were top dead center. They gave a sooty cough—and refused to start.

In the room above, the young man with the bruised ear cleared the door and raced to the window, snapping a fresh clip in the little automatic. Below him, Bodine patiently repeated the starting drill. This time when he kicked the starting lever over, the engine ignited with a boom that bounced off the alley walls. As he let the clutch out and they skipped off, the young man at the window took careful aim and fired. The sharp crack of the small weapon was lost in the noise of the exhaust.

The Harley skidded in the trough, veering from one side to the other, the metal sidecar kissing off the stone building and sending back a trail of sparks. But Bodine held it, pivoted at the end of the alley, and shot out onto the street, twisting the hand throttle full up. At the corner he looked back and saw the lights of a powerful car pull out of the gate and start after them.

"Damn!"

Adrian twisted his head back and saw the same flare. "Can they catch us?!"

"Oh, hell, no!" There was a sharp detonation followed by an eerie whistle.

"Jesus!" Adrian yelled. "They're shooting at us!"

"Naw, it couldn't be!" The sound was repeated, twice in rapid succession. "Yeah? What's that?"

"Maybe you're right." Bodine whipped the bars over, and the motorcycle nearly stood on end, lifting the sidecar as though it were airborne. Adrian, convinced they were going over, leaned hard over the axel, but the right angle was negotiated and they cut down a dark alley, the thump of the exhaust bouncing between the overhang of buildings. A pause, then the flash of lights came up. Damn, Bodine thought, the car was still behind them, they knew the territory and had cut through a side street. Without the weight of his sidecar passengers, he could probably outrun them; with them, it was only a matter of time before they caught up. There was nowhere to stop, hide, get off, or make a run for it. This was the Chinese side; no helping hands would be out, and doors would remain shut. There was one possibility.

He leaned over, shouting in Adrian's ear. "When I get to the other end of this alley, I'll slow down and you drop off the tomato—maybe they'll stop for her."

"Oh, no!" Adrian shouted back. "Oh, no! You're not dropping off anybody!"

Bodine shrugged and twisted the throttle, but it was already full up. In the next minutes he exercised all his considerable skill, risking their lives, cutting corners, and using the sidewalks and alleys. But the car hung on, gradually gaining. He could see it now, a big German Horst, probably with a supercharger. At least they had stopped shooting, probably because they had approached the European section of the city.

Adrian hugged the girl's head close to his chest, trying to cushion it against the jarring bumps. Her arms and legs flopped erratically, and she'd lost a shoe. A few inches from his left ear the exhaust pounded, and the heat generated by the engine was nearly unbearable. Looking at Bodine crouched over the handlebars, shirt flapping back, the black-and-white wing tips on the pegs, Adrian had to believe he was in the clutches of a madman, but he also had to smile.

The chase ended at the outskirts of the International Settlement. Their lead narrowing, Bodine was forced into a configuration of streets that funneled into the river section. Ahead, through a break in the rooftops he could see the shine of Soochow Creek. There was still one chance. If he could catch a native ferry on the bank, they might—just might—be poled midstream before the car could close. Committing them, he whipped down a narrow road between warehouses. He was in luck! A wooden barge was moored to this side, and the poleman stood waiting.

As the motorcycle came roaring down at him, the coolie took one look, cast off, and dug in his pole. By the time Bodine locked up the brakes and slid up to the dock, the barge was already fifty feet out.

Bodine leaped off and shouted in Chinese, "Come back, you motherless son of an unclean dream!" But the coolie was poling for dear life.

Adrian looked back up the road. The car's lights flashed and turned in; the big Horst phaeton was coming straight for them. While Adrian struggled frantically to extract himself and the girl from the sidecar, Bodine calmly flipped open a toolbox behind the seat and unwrapped a regulation Army Colt .45 from an oilskin bag. There was a loop of cord attached to the ring in the butt, and after snapping the carriage back and taking the safety off, he looped the cord around his shoulder.

"Damn!" he said. "I sure didn't want to do this." Planting his feet firmly, he bent slightly forward, holding the gun with both hands, and pulled the cord taut to brace his aim.

The car came on. At exactly the right yardage Bodine squeezed off one round, the barrel lifting slightly as a dull report echoed up the street. The heavy slug hit the right front tire, blew it, and on the next revolution the tire came off, crossed up on the rim and set the car hopping sideways, shuddering against the rough paving stones. The car veered into the side of a stone warehouse with a shattering of glass and the horrendous sound of tearing metal. Scraping along the abrasive wall for nearly a hundred feet, it came to an abrupt stop against the projection of an abutment. The radiator was driven in, the hood pleated, and, in the front seat the driver went under the dashboard, taking out a half circle of wooden steering wheel with his jaw.

In the backseat a man was catapulted with a ripping sound through the top, hit the wall of the building, and ended in a sickening flop to the pavement. A third man rolled out of the rear door and landed on his hands and knees, apparently unhurt. He took one look at Bodine, jumped up, and ran down the street.

Bodine cleared the weapon and shook his head. "Damn, that looked like it hurt!" Then there was a shot, a ricochet wanging off the cobbles. A measured pace, then another, equally wild. The car's driver had somehow pushed himself up, and with the ruined jaw, eyes glazed, propped a Mauser on the windowsill of the car. He fired, keeping a slow, steady pace without aiming. Bodine walked toward him, his own weapon held at his side as the wild slugs clipped the stones near his feet. Reaching the car as the weapon emptied and the man continued clicking the trigger, Bodine gently shoved him down, saying in Chinese, "Take a rest, brother."

Behind him there was a sharp cry. He turned and saw Adrian holding the girl close to him, his shirtfront covered with blood. Bodine ran over. "Easy! It's probably just a scratch. Let's find the wound. . . ."

"It's not me, damn it! It's . . ."

Bodine reached out to steady him, then stopped. The girl's eyes were wide

37

open, opaque. "Oh, boy . . . oh, boy . . ." Cradling her head in his hands, Bodine parted the heavy bangs and there, almost dead center in her forehead, was a neat bloodless hole the size of a pea. The slug had entered from the back, bloodying Adrian's shirt. Bodine touched the hole and could feel the protruding nose of a small-caliber slug. Fired at low velocity, it had been stopped from exiting by the bone of her forehead.

"It was that peckerhead with the chrome-plated number . . ."

In the excitement of the chase Adrian hadn't felt or seen the blood. As he looked at her drained lips, it occurred to him that he had never heard her speak.

Bodine took the body from him. "What a rotten shame! Just when I almost had the kid fixed up. . . ."

"I can't believe this," Adrian said, anguished. "There must be something we can do for her!"

"No, bunkie, she's dead and you can't cure that. She's no good to herself or anybody else now. We sure can't take her body to the police . . . no." Bodine walked toward the ruined car, its radiator quietly sizzling, a postmortem of haze drifting up.

"Where are you taking her?" Adrian shouted, angry at the whole senseless episode.

Reaching into the back of the car, Bodine carefully placed her body on the seat, rearranging the bangs to cover the bullet hole. Then, straightening, he looked down at her.

"They paid for her, and after all is said and done, a deal's a deal."

SIX

A*T EXACTLY TWELVE-THIRTY* Lola came out of Frisky's, and the big limo was waiting. She was thrilled. It was tall, dark red, and shiny, just the way a limo should look. Wearing the same slinky satin of the evening performance, she had Ramon on a chain and hoped the Navy was getting an eyeful. One of the cross-eyed bodyguards stood holding the door open. In the backseat the smiling Chinese gentleman bowed.

"Most delighted that you might arrive! Yes, yes!"

"Where's Adrian?"

"He is to be picked up, of course, by us at his Palace Hotel down the Bund."

"All right." That made sense. She urged Ramon in. He was used to traveling in cars, but he didn't like this one. Finally with the right encouragement he jumped in, squeezing to one corner.

"Boy!" she said. "Look at this, Ramon!" The backseat looked as big as a Pullman drawing room, with inlaid wood and cut-glass vases at each side of the window frames holding wax roses. In front of brocade seats, an elaborate bar was folded out, displaying all the popular brands. Her host tilted toward it.

"Might I mix us a toast—perhaps you would have a gin sling cocktail?"

"Has Garbo got big feet?"

39

The car pulled away and continued down the Bund. Looking through the glass partition past the driver's head, she saw buildings slide by and realized it was the first time she'd been down the Bund in a private car. And what a car! He handed over the drink in a tinted glass, and they clinked.

"To a most beautiful arrangement, making friends."

She took a sip and wrinkled her nose at the gin taste. "This is swell. Ah, Mr. . . ."

"Min, Charles Min."

"Yeah—can I ask you how you happen to know Adrian?"

"I was the close friend to his father, Mr. Hugh H. Reed, the senior."

"Is that right?"

"Oh, yes, when he joined us here in 1911 at the successful making of our revolution—we were introduced by Dr. Sun Yat-sen in the person."

"Is that right?"

"You know of Dr. Sun?"

"Well—I haven't needed a doctor here yet."

"Dr. Sun is indeed a medical person, but we revere him as a patriot—he was our first president of the Southern Republic—a patriot—called by many the George Washington of China."

"Is that right?"

"Oh, yes."

The car stopped in front of the Palace Hotel and the bodyguard got out. A minute later he came back and, leaning down, talked to Mr. Min in rapid Chinese through a narrow gap of rolled-up window. Min took out a tiny silver pencil, quickly jotted a note on an equally tiny pad, and passed it through the window slot.

"Mr. Adrian Reed has not yet returned from business. I left a note instructing that my car would call at one half past one tonight."

Lola didn't like this, but she wasn't sure what to do. He knew Adrian—that was obvious—and Adrian had said he would be late. She looked closely at Mr. Min, but the lights from the street reflected off his pince-nez glasses and his eyes appeared opaque above a benign smile. She turned to Ramon to see how he was taking it, and saw that the wax rose was gone from its vase. He had eaten it.

Bodine's Harley came slowly down Kiangse Road, the hesitant pop of its exhaust the mechanical equivalent of a dog with its tail between its legs. Adrian slumped in the sidecar, dead tired, drained. His clothes were disgusting from the muck of the open sewer and from the Chinese girl's blood. The hot night was deadly, and the heat radiating from the motorcycle's engine baked the awful combination until its emanations made him sick. Worse, they were highly visible. At midnight the neighborhood teemed with noisy activity, and they passed the flicker of neon, windows lit and showing the sliding silhouettes of dancers, signs advertising "Deportment and Singing Taught," with lighted arrows that pointed upstairs to suggest more heavenly delights.

Gaily dressed strollers filled the sidewalk, surging into the street and tangling traffic. Even in his foul condition, hipless girls, in *cheong-sam* dresses split to the "upsides," propositioned Adrian curbside with two-finger gestures. No one had to tell him he was in the Nocturnal Quarter.

It was not the only one or the most notorious. Certainly no worse than the singsong houses of Foochow Road and a lot better than the Broadway area where they locked the girls in. Compared to "Blood Alley," the sailor's dives behind the Bund he had investigated, it was practically Sunday school. No, it was middle class, a family whorehouse neighborhood, where the apothecary shops displayed pickled sex organs in their windows, showing the ravages of V.D. as a warning to the young.

Bodine executed one of his sudden turns, putting the handlebars over and jerking Adrian's head back like the neck snap of a demented masseuse. It appeared that they were headed directly into the side of a building, but at the last minute an opening loomed up and they shot through the flap of canvas curtains into a ground-floor warehouse. The Harley skipped to a stop, and Bodine swing his leg over and shoved his goggles up. Unlimbering the chain, he locked the machine to an iron stanchion.

"Home sweet home, bunkie."

These were the first words since leaving the tangle of the car wreck and laying the girl away. No one had to tell Adrian that he could not go back to his white man's hotel looking as he did, and he had decided to go along with Bodine. It seemed almost too much of an effort to get out of the sidecar. Straightening, he unfolded one leg at a time and stepped out of his container.

Bodine gestured and Adrian followed, feeling every hard crease and unpleasant surprise in his clothes. Ducking through the low headroom of a door, they came into a scruffy backyard. Ahead, outside stairs led to the second story of a large, windowless building. Slowly climbing the steep steps, slippery with dirt, railings hung with damp linen, they squeezed around servants and neighbors who sat gossiping and drinking Jawbone Beer.

At the top landing, chauffeurs from cars double-parked on the street leaned against the open doorway smoking. Inside, a long hall painted vibrant green was covered with gilt grillwork constructed to look like bamboo. Brightly lit, the place seemed to throb with sensations. At least a dozen visible doors opened onto the hall, and out of each came giggles, the squawk of a Victrola, and from deeper regions, the wail of moon fiddles and *hu-jings* accompanied by another of those voices of such pitch that it caused the hair on the back of

Adrian's neck to stand on end. Clients and girls bustled in and out, exchanging advice; servants padded up the hall with chamber pots, small children and dogs tangling underfoot, and at the end of the long vista an immense naked man sat with his feet being washed by an old lady.

Adrian followed Bodine through beaded curtains into a parlor with blond art deco couches and dozens of canaries in cages. In the center of the room water jetted in a hammered metal fountain, bouncing light blue celluloid eggs about.

Here they were confronted by a furious Chinese woman. Of Bodine's height, she put her face against his and screamed, "Where you been, huh! No tell me you gonna leave! How come? You better not try same old excuse stuff!" Dressed in a skintight *cheong-sam* with the usual split to the thigh, she had a good figure, pillowy breasts balanced over a thin body, a handsome if hard face, and an elaborate hairdo.

Bodine walked on but she kept up a constant tirade, face inches from his. She pointed to Adrian, holding her nose. "What this? Some kind smelly fella? How come bring here? You want business to flop from big stink? Huh? Huh?"

Close, Adrian could see the faint tattoo of smallpox scars under rouge on high cheekbones. Her eyes were squeezed shut in fury, nostrils flared.

"Why you don't answer, chicken shit?"

Bodine stopped and cocked his fist. "If you don't shut your gob, I'm gonna knock those gold teeth I paid for down your sewer of a throat!"

She jumped back and in a flash whipped a wicked hatpin out of her hair. "You just try Mr. Big Boy, and I shove this up your buggery nose into pea brain!"

Bodine backed off, throwing his hands up, and went through another doorway to a bedroom. She didn't follow, and Adrian ducked after him.

"Who was that?"

"My wife," Bodine said, flopping on a white lacquered bed. "They call her the Dragon's Tail. She owns this place."

Adrian tried not to show his amazement, but it was difficult. Bodine sighed. "She's not always like that—you ought to see her when she gets mad." He thought this was funny, and Adrian did his best to laugh along. "She's right about one thing, bunkie, you smell like the rear end of a yak." He shouted in Chinese, and two girls came in. "One good thing about China, there sure ain't any shortage of laundrymen. Peel off your civvies, and Miss Golden Beetle here will give you a clean scrubdown fore and aft."

Adrian reluctantly removed his clothes, which were taken away at arm's length by one of the giggling girls. The other, Miss Golden Beetle, introduced a shallow pan of greasy water and, reaching up, began to dab at his chest with a damp rag. While she did this, others came in to watch—several

42

singsong girls and an old lady, who sat in a corner with a baby on her lap. Older children ran in and out, and the room sputtered with conversation.

Adrian had never adjusted to the Oriental lack of privacy, and he felt the social equivalent of a sideshow freak. He did his best to hang on to his shorts, but the girl tugged them down and, dusting off his privates, held them out for the others to inspect. A swell of "ohs" and "ahs" went up in polite admiration, and the conversation turned to comparisons. He blushed furiously, but there was no danger of sexual arousal; Miss Golden Beetle, like the other teenage girls, was painfully thin, no breasts or hips whatever, and wearing a dress that exposed rose-colored stockings with butterfly designs. As she bent over to do his feet, he could see a ring of grime between her carefully arranged hair and silk collar.

Mercifully, she finished, and he was given a skimpy robe. Clutching it around his large frame, he sat on a metal folding chair next to a shaky aperitif table. There was the scatter of watermelon seeds and pistachio nuts on its top, along with a bakelite fountain pen and a framed photograph of John Gilbert. When he looked up at Bodine on the bed, he was startled to see one of the girls behind him preparing an opium pipe. With the aid of a scraper and needlelike tools, she worked a dab of what looked like mud into a little pellet. She held it, already slightly cooked, over a small lamp to heat it.

"Care for a smoke, bunkie?"

"You're kidding?"

Bodine smiled lazily. "Listen, it's the best way in the world to relax your neck and ears after the cares of the day."

"No, thanks."

"You're in China, remember? Everybody smokes a little out here—from your white swells up in Frenchtown to the ricksha boys usin' their dross."

"Maybe, but I'll pass."

"Suit yourself, but don't get the rag on—you ain't peddlin' Bibles, are you?"

"No, and I don't care what you do! But I went along on your little business deal and damn near got my head handed to me. Now I'd like to talk about my business!"

"Bunkie, bunkie, I ain't goin' anywhere—I ain't a dope fiend smokin' to see heaven. I'm gonna lay back in the rack and relax while we chin-chin."

Adrian took a deep breath. "All right . . . like I said I got your name from Ansel O'Banion before I came out here. He knew my father through Homer Lea—"

"Homer Lea, the boy general, he was a real original. . . ." The girl handed him the pipe by the stem and he took a long drag, the pellet sputtering in the tiny bowl as air was drawn through it. His face was wreathed in clouds of

43

smoke, and the sweet and spicy fumes made Adrian pinch his nose in discomfort.

"Tell me about him. He said he was a secret courier carrying money to the Chinese revolutionaries, that he was Sun Yat-sen's military adviser—that he had fought at the battle of Po Lo, that he had been given a dragon sword—was any of that true?"

"Well . . . who knows? He was colorful, but one thing was for sure, he didn't look like a hero. He was a runt, came to about my shoulder. Couldn't have weighed more than ninety pounds on a full meal. From a distance he looked like a question mark . . ."

"He was a hunchback."

"That's right, but that face—Jesus! Big and wide with these heavy eyebrows marchin' across—and the eyes—it was the eyes that stopped you, they had command. I've seen some hard cases in my time, bunkie, roughhewed white men, and they all had those kind of eyes. It didn't matter if he was a shrimp, he didn't act it. You knew if he came at you, he'd keep coming. . . ."

There was a pause as the smoke rolled up, and for a minute Adrian thought he'd drifted off. Then he roused himself.

"I met Lea in Frisco . . . my ship had just made port . . . when was that. . . ?

It must have been 1903 or '04 when the Oregon was laid up at Mare Island before going on Asiatic station. He was ship's company with a platoon of Marines, in the Corps just a year. Lying about his age, he'd signed on for a "kiddie cruise" at the old Advanced Base Force at League Island Yard. Still a wild-assed kid with his first set of number-one liberty blues and turned loose in the greatest, God-damned, mean, dirty, no-holds-barred liberty port known to mankind. . . .

Frisco! Pacific Street, the main drag up from the waterfront, with every kind of good time, booze, woman, and vice ever invented. Gamblers, thieves, harlots, drunken sailors, homos, degenerates. The gutters full of broken bottle splinters, half-stewed bodies. Sidewalks bucklin' with pimps, con men, come-ons—steerers strong-armin' the suckers into black-holed dives, deadfalls, and dance halls. Every clip joint fulla loudmouthed hookers yelling out their wares. "Jiggi-jiggi-sixty-nine, Jack? Shag, Johnny? Plompay the cooler?"

Knockin' back milk whiskey and pisco with Chileno whores while they tried to fumble you off under the table. Then rollin' up Pacific, past Soloman Levi's trap shop, blankets and overcoats padlocked to huge staples driven into the walls, outfits hung on long poles over the street called Jew Flags . . . Painless Parker, the street dentist . . . and the book shops! The "Lively Flea," with its sign of a flea lying back in a field of clover surrounded by cupids . . . the Nymphia crib with a hundred over-the-hill hookers partitioned off in three-by-six spaces working bare-ass around the clock . . . Iodoform Kate and her Redheaded Jewesses on Battle Row over on the east side of Kearney. . . .

That year one thousand British seamen alone jumped ship in Frisco. They were working as streetcar conductors, bootblacks, clam diggers, anything to stay in the promised land—

heaven on earth! Then, in 1906 the quake shook and burned it down. . . . After that it was never the same. . . .

Of course the old salts on board the Oregon—the yarn spinners around the fo'c'sle bogey—most of them wind sailors who still griped about steam—said it wasn't what it used to be even then. Not the real Barbary Coast of the seventies and eighties, full of crimps shanghaiin' perks right out of their traps, dopin' them and givin' them a fast twenty-four-hour turn-around, then back to sea on a blood ship. It was a real gauntlet then, artists with the cosh, slungshot, blackjack, and knuckle-duster. The cops went in twos and threes, armed to the teeth with a pistol, nightstick, and foot-long knife. Now that was tough! And the girls! Hell, they were up to anything, lewd and lascivious women in black fishnet stockings, paps hanging out and no underwear! Feel 'em up for fifty cents! At Bull Run Ned Allen forced his girls to drink all evening, not cold tea like the rest of the slot-shops, but real booze dosed with Spanish fly! And hear this—during business hours they weren't even allowed to leave the floor for a piss-call—they all wore diapers! Diapers, for God's sake! Talk about your last stages of Sodom and Gomorrah!

And every other blind-pig had exhibitions, shows, tableaux vivants, *you name it! Girls with girls, dwarfs, giants . . . and animals, ponies, bears and . . . monkeys . . .*

". . . monkeys . . ."

"What?"

The singsong girl gently took the pipe out of Bodine's hand, cleaning it with her tools, and refitted another cooked pellet. She seemed unreal in the light fractured by the residue of smoke, her nubile face unmarked by the slightest sign of line or character. The glow of the lamp casting shadows above her eyebrows made the rest of her head vanish; she was a figure without substance, a container for services.

Adrian looked away uneasily. The room was nearly empty now; the audience had departed; it was not of the slightest interest for Chinese to watch someone smoking opium, and the voyeurs had drifted off. His own head felt blocked, thick—was it possible that he was breathing it in as well? He rubbed his forehead, pulling away a line of sweat.

"You were talking about Homer Lea."

Bodine accepted the pipe again, sucking in, rattling the pellet and projecting the smoke out in calculated puffs.

"I had run into Ansel O'Banion at some deadfall or parlor house near Chinatown, west of the waterfront . . . Dupont or Sacramento . . . all the Chinese whores back then were called Ah Toy or Selina. They sat at the doors of their cribs in black silk pajamas, chantin', 'Two bittee looksee, fo' bittee feeley, six bittee doey . . .'" He chuckled, sending the smoke dancing.

"What about O'Banion?"

"Yeah . . . he told me he'd been a yellow-leg, a trooper with the Fourth U.S. Cavalry, then a scout . . . a captain of the Philippine Constabulary. Now he had this job as drill master, training laundry boys and chop suey shuckers to be officers for the Chinese Reform Movement. He laughed about it. The HQ was down in L.A. with 'General' Lea as C.O.—they called it the Western Military Academy and secretly it was supposed to be a branch of the Chinese Imperial Army—C.I.A. They had 'em all over the country in those days before Uncle Sam cracked down . . ."

"What about Homer Lea?"

"Ah . . . he was speakin' a couple of nights later, and O'Banion took me along to hear him in this big hall . . . up in . . . in . . ."

"It doesn't matter."

"It had gas lamps . . . I can see 'em now in my mind's eye, sputterin' rows runnin' down a long, tall room with a sag to the floor and walls the color of dirty skivvies . . . and by God, the place was full of Chinks!"

Jee-zuss! There must have been five thousand of the poor buggers, every hard-luck laun-dryman, gandy dancer, and swill scrubber from the coast. Immigrants, Hua-ch'iao—most of 'em, natives of Kwangtung or Fukien brought over to carry the white man's load, live wifeless and grind for double hitches in jobs the lowest colored or Mex wouldn't take—all of 'em savin' for the day they could go back home. There they were standin' packed, bony ass to bony ass, every yellow son of 'em in identical Chinese getup with button skull caps and cues hangin' down their backs like greasy snakes. The smell alone was enough to knock back a bull moose! Hair resin, opium whiffs, spicy sour, sickly sweet unidentifiable hints of God-knows-what, and enough plain old body odor to induce a graveyard to rise up and walk! You could have got a footin' on the heavy layers of smells in that place and strolled to the ceiling . . .

"Bodine . . ."

"Ah . . . I stood at the back of the shebang with a few other white men, reporters and the curious, strainin' to see what in hell they were all there for. There was the ongoin' hum of their own mumbled foolishness, and from the front of the hall I could just see the head of a speaker and get that he was talkin' at them. It appeared to be another Chinaman, but with a kind of . . . swank about him, a mustache that owed more to the man-about-town than the old country."

"Sun Yat-sen?"

"That's right. Whatever it was he was sayin' wasn't goin' over, and the crowd of Chinks began to jabber louder and sort of shift like the meetin' was over. Then this voice came up, boomin' like a bass drum, reachin' out to every corner, buzzin' in your ears like a wireless set. I mean you could *hear it!* It talked to *you!*

"And I'll say this, *you listened!* You knew something very important was being said.

"The hall full of slopes shut up and all of us stood on our toes, leanin' forward, afraid to miss a word. I still couldn't see who it was—then all of a sudden this figure loomed up—I say *loomed!* There he was, ten feet high in a queer uniform I'd never seen in my life, blond hair tossin', arms workin', and speakin' to you personally, by God!"

"Homer Lea?"

"Homer Lea."

"He had been boosted up on Ansel O'Banion's shoulders, this hunchback, this cripple, and piggyback, both of 'em blending together, he looked like a giant stridin' that stage! He wore a black uniform with rows of brass buttons, curious medals, and a great sweep of a cape swirlin' out. His voice comin' up from that barrel of a chest rolled over us, compellin' us to his cause, haranguin', thunderin', speakin' with a halo and fire I've never heard since. . . . 'What's all the hubbub about? What's he talkin' about?' I says to this bird next to me, scribblin' in a notebook. 'Tsu Hsi,' he says. 'The Manchu Dowager Empress.' She was the fierce old spider who sat on China's Dragon Throne then, weavin' murderous plots. She'd been a concubine who gave the emperor a male child, then when the old boy died she grabbed the throne, killin' her own son and his pregnant wife to stay in power. She was a piece, I'll tell you. She *was* China in those days, stirrin' up the Boxers and causin' all kinds of hell.

"General Lea was tellin' the coolies this—that the very cues they wore down their backs were a sign of servitude to her and the Manchus, that the Manchu bannermen who conquered them hundreds of years ago were now weak, rotten wasters with their feet on the necks of honest men, pissin' downwind on them and all their children to come. That these dirty dogs who ruled China *were by God not even Chinese!*

"All of a sudden this howl goes up, *CH'I-IIIIIII!!* An I see the flash of a blade. I looked for the door, but the next thing you know one of the coolies has cut off his own cue with a pocketknife! In the next minute it was happenin' all over the hall, they were *all* cuttin' off their cues, swingin' them over their heads like lariats . . . and the *noise!* They shouted out in a banshee wail like dacoits, buildin' and runnin' your blood cold! I looked around and saw a solid mass of yellow fury, a dam of pent-up destructive energy waitin' to let go. . . . I tell you, it was no place for a white man. . . ."

SEVEN

"BODINE! ARE YOU awake?" Adrian was pacing now, and each time he passed the white lacquered bed he gave the leg a kick and Bodine's head jumped. Finally Bodine scrubbed at his nose and, heaving himself up, swung his legs over the side of the bed.

"Damn! You're a hard man, bunkie." He reached under the bed and withdrew a red-necked bottle of brandy. He took a long pull and held it out, but Adrian shook his head. "What in hell had Homer Lea or Sun Yat-sen got to do with you anyway?" Bodine asked.

"This. In 1907 my father, along with some other California businessmen, agreed to try to raise five million for a military uprising in China. Sun had been touring the country and was desperate for funds. The revolution was floundering, and he went after the big moneymen, promising them everything when he came to power—mining and rail concessions, trade monopolies—you name it, he was selling off a big piece of China. They were so confident—greedy—that they raised the ante to nine million and in February 1909 took the proposal to J. P. Morgan and Company. He turned them down.

"All that year the syndicate tried to interest other backers without success. When Sun returned to the United States in January 1910, they had to admit they'd failed. When the others pulled out, my father took Sun around to the

Union League Club and over cigars made him an offer. He would personally put up one million five for an iron-clad lease for drilling rights on *all* oil found in China in the next fifteen years. Sun accepted."

Bodine took another swig of the brandy, pulling his teeth back and shuddering. "Are you tellin' me your old man dumped a million and a half down the rathole of Chinese politics on Sun's promises?"

"My father was no fool, Bodine. He was gambling that the revolution would be won and soon. He was right. That winter Sun Yat-sen came back to China from sixteen years of exile to ride in on the tide of the Wuhan uprising; by Christmas he was president of the Southern Republic."

"And the oil leases?"

"They weren't his to give away."

Bodine chuckled. "They say Sun was an honest man, and I believe it, but he would have taken the dimes off a dead man's eyes if he thought it was for the good of China."

"He didn't get that money."

"No?"

"No one did. My father had stipulated that it be put in joint receivership in the safety deposit vault of the Hong Kong-Shanghai Bank. It could be withdrawn only in person by himself and/or Sun—together—or persons authorized by them."

"What?"

"When he pressed Sun for the leases and it became obvious he couldn't deliver, he refused to release it. Likewise, Sun wouldn't sign, so it became a stalemate. When Sun died in 1925, it was still tied up. I found this out last year after my father died and I came across the 'Sun Account' buried in his personal papers."

"You mean that money is still in the bank, here in Shanghai?"

"That's right. It hasn't earned a dime's interest in twenty years."

Bodine looked at him, pale eyes finally focusing. "What do you do, Reed?"

"Do?"

"Back in the states."

"I play polo."

Bodine smiled. "Polo?"

"You know, with horses, mallets, and a ball."

"I know! I know! C'mon, I'm talking about work—what do you do?"

Adrian hesitated. The answer was obvious: he had been born the son of a very rich father. Among his friends the question was never asked. He knew Bodine wouldn't understand that. "Nothing," he said simply.

Bodine's eyebrow went up again. "Nothing?"

Adrian was reminded of the men who used to work for his father: roustabouts from derrick crews, hard-luck wildcatters, oil-field drifters—men who smelled of whiskey and plug cut, talking loud, bragging in slurring accents with lots of hat tugs and nose wipes, spitting in punctuation—shit kickers, losers; men with greasy clothes, matted with horse hair, who shaved once a week and whose idea of freedom was farting whenever they felt like it. His father said they were the salt of the earth, good, hard men. Adrian didn't think so. Repetitive and sly, with clichéd folksy sayings and narrow prejudices, what they admired most was a "slick deal," treating his father as a kind of king—the one among them who had beaten the game.

The old man's up-by-the-bootstraps success story appealed to these men, because it had a lot of "dumb luck" and "seized opportunities" in it, something they clung to, something that made it possible to get up in the morning.

Hugh Hatten Reed came from Albert Lea, Minnesota, in 1880, looking for the main chance in California. Working as a picker at ranches around Fallbrook, he filled in off seasons cutting wood. In November 1892 he rode up to Los Angeles with a flat carload of eucalyptus poles hoping to sell them to the newly expanding telephone company. When they pushed the price down he stubbornly refused to sell. In the end, rather than abandon the poles for freight charges, he traded them to a young man named Eddie Doheny for an eighth interest in a lot on Glendale Boulevard he'd never seen.

Doheny said he was an "oil miner" and got all hopped up talking about deposits of "tarry stuff"—brea he'd found near Westlake Park. This was old news; the Indians and Mexicans had used it for years as waterproofing, and nobody had ever gotten excited about it before, but he was convinced there was oil underground. They rode the streetcar out to the property, about eight miles from the La Brea tar pits, and he met Charley Canfield, Eddie's partner. In the end he decided to throw in with them "for the fun of it."

The three knew nothing at all about drilling for oil and began by digging a vertical mine shaft with picks and shovels, shoring it with the eucalyptus poles as they went. At 155 feet they had had enough of the slow and difficult work. Sharpening the end of the last uncut 60-foot pole, they made it into a crude drill and at 460 feet struck oil, bailing it out with a bucket. It was November 4, 1892.

Two years later there were eighty wells in that twenty-block section, and by the turn of the century Los Angeles had more than three thousand, pumping like metronomes, to an output of two million barrels a day.

When Adrian was born in 1906, his father was a millionaire many times over. His father was also sixty years old.

Adrian's memories of his father were of an old man, tall and stooped, a tough old bird with soulful eyes that looked like fried eggs behind his rimless glasses, and a yellowed mustache that cut across and hid a whimsical trap of a mouth. He was everybody's idea of a foxy grandpa, clean as a pin, wiry, up

50

to all kinds of jokes boys love, with a crackling laugh and quick, strong movements that gave lie to his age.

Adrian's mother married his father when she was twenty-two, nearly twenty-five years younger. A pretty, vibrant girl from Ontario, Canada, she had been a local sensation as a faith healer and Pentecostal evangelist. The old man had seen her preach at the Angelus Temple where she was second on the bill to Aimee Semple McPherson, and he proposed straight away. It was his first marriage, and he said later he "never got the hang of it." Adrian saw very little of her. When he was six his parents were divorced and she went off to the "Holy Land" with a Dr. Footer to take slides. She now lived in South Pasadena, where she was writing her version of the Bible. He got a card from her every Easter.

The old man raised him, spoiling him one year by trips around the country in his private railway car, the *Eucalyptus Explorer*, then parking him the next year in some Prussian-style military school. But Adrian loved him fiercely, loved the look of his oil man's Stetson, the heft of the watch and chain with its complicated Masonic fob, the unembarrassed way he would grab him and kiss him, tickling his nose with the stiff broom of a mustache. Adrian did everything he could to be like him—grew up believing he was above the exploitations of the millionaire manipulators that newspaper cartoonists drew as fat bloated moneybags, riding the backs of the poor.

In his senior year at Stanford, the Teapot Dome scandal broke. The Secretary of the Interior, Albert B. Fall, had secretly granted twenty-year oil leases on the U.S. Navy oil reserves to Harry Sinclair and Edward Doheny for $400,000 in "loans." After a sensational airing in the press, the case went to court in a long series of trials. His father had perjured himself, testifying to help his old friend Doheny, and only a platoon of expensive lawyers managed to extract him. Eventually he was acquitted along with Doheny and Sinclair. Only Fall went to jail, but the public believed them all guilty, saying their money bought off justice.

It broke the old man. Always the outspoken patriot, he had seen himself portrayed as a "greedy despoiler of America," a "robber baron who would take the naval oil reserves and leave Uncle Sam helpless before his enemies." This attack on his patriotism crushed him. After it, he seemed to have lost all enthusiasm and diminished in size.

When he died in the winter of 1930, Adrian found that not only was there no inheritance, but the estate had been mortgaged to the hilt. Cleaned out. The whole structure his father had built had been pulled down by the monstrous legal defense, last years of neglect, and the first waves of the depression (and, he thought guiltily, his polo expenses). Searching through the labyrinth of personal correspondence, scribbled notebooks and bits of paper, he'd come across the Sun Account listed in a secret deposit box. It was the only evidence of money left. If the creditors found out about it, anything recovered would vanish in litigation. So, selling his string of ponies and tack, he slipped out of San Francisco aboard the *Gripsholm* on June 11, 1931. There had been something else in that box, something that seemed to him an even more compelling reason for the trip. He debated now whether or not to tell Bodine.

"You look tired, kid," Bodine said, not unkindly. Adrian guessed he'd been staring off in space.

"Bodine . . . I believe there's a thing even more important locked away in that bank vault."

Bodine smiled. "I know, Kubla Khan's jockstrap."

Adrian took his passport case off of the shaky aperitif table and carefully withdrew a much-folded letter from an envelope. "This is a letter written by Sun Yat-sen to Homer Lea—it's why I asked you about Lea's veracity." He handed it over.

Bodine read the letter carefully, eyebrow cocked. It was on stationery of the S.S. *Korea* and dated at sea, March 24, 1910. In it, Dr. Sun revealed that he was in possession of "some very important documents of a certain military power"—more than thirty big books outlined the war plans of the General Staff of that power. Sun asked Lea to try and find out if the U.S. War Department would be interested in obtaining these secret documents, "as they would be the most valuable things a rival power could have." The letter was neatly typed but not signed.

Stapled to the other side was a long list of the content of the "thirty big books." A detailing of Japan's mobilization attack and defense plans, regarding the United States of America as the enemy. Below this was the notation, Depos. H-S Bank, 3/21/10.

Bodine looked up, still smiling. "What are you, kid? A spy and a polo player?"

"No, of course not! But see that notation? It's in my father's handwriting. I think those secret books are in the bank along with the money. My guess is, Sun gave them to my father as a kind of good faith offering to seal their pact." He began pacing again, the skimpy bathrobe flicking the watermelon seeds off the table. "Do you know what they mean?"

"That the Japanese are plannin' to jump our bones? That's nothin' new to old China hands."

"Then we've got to get these books to our people! We've got to try to—"

"Why?"

"Why? Why, because it's the patriotic thing to do."

Bodine laughed out loud. "Please don't instruct me in patriotism, kid. Jesus, that's for the bunch down at the VFW hall. Why do *you* want to do it?"

What Adrian couldn't tell him, of course, was that he wanted to present those books to the government in his father's name. He believed it would restore his image, that he would be remembered as a patriot—not an oil crook.

"Does it matter?"

"No." Bodine handed back the letter. "Well, whattaya doin' about gettin' in that vault?"

"I've been in Shanghai nearly two months now, trying to unwind the legal red tape. I found that after Sun's death the authorization to cosign the account had been passed on to a Marshal Yü."

"Yeah . . . he was Sun's northern connection."

"If he agreed to sign—then we could split the money—and I'd have the books."

"You can't find him?"

"No, could you?"

"Maybe—for say a thousand Mex up front."

"I haven't got that much cash now. I'll pay you once the money is recovered."

Bodine clicked his tongue. "Looks like doin' nothin' don't pay too well."

"You'll get your money when the account's settled!"

"Sure I will."

"You have my word, damnit!"

"Hasn't it hit you as a little fishy that this guy hasn't come forward? I mean, there's a million and a half waiting to be split up."

"Maybe he's dead or sick or . . ."

"Maybe. You want me to work on promises? Okay, one percent of the recovered goods then."

"What!"

"Say you split half with Yü, then my cut would be seventy-five hundred. Fair?"

"No! Ever since I've been in this damn country people have had their hands out! The bank agents, lawyers, officials who would straighten things out for a 'fee'! I've had it up to here!" He let out his breath, annoyed he'd lost his temper.

"Well, maybe he's not that easy to find. Shanghai is a funny place, bunkie, boxes within boxes as they say, nothin' is what it seems."

"Spare me the clichés, it's highway robbery."

"I don't have to tell you that there are more stickups with fountain pens than guns in this old world—they call it the squeeze here, and it's what the country runs on. You ain't in Pasadena now, kid—this is China."

Adrian rolled his eyes at this hyperbole, then raised his arms and let them flop to his sides. "All right . . . all right."

Bodine stretched and got off the bed. "Done is done! And don't worry, kid, I'm gonna make you rich and a hero." He laughed and slapped Adrian's shoulder. "C'mon, let's find your civvies and I'll take you home."

They pulled up at the heavy overhang of the Palace Hotel at a little after one. As he got out of the sidecar, Adrian was surprised to see Bodine swing off the motorcycle.

"Tell you what, kid, I'll let you buy me a drink to put the seal on our deal. Every once in a while I like to mingle with my betters."

He laughed and they went in the entrance together. Like it or not, Adrian had to admire him. Nearly twice his age, and yet he seemed fresh after the hellish night. Adrian found Bodine cocky and insensitive, with a maddening push of his own importance—still he trusted him, not with his pocketbook, surely, but with his life.

They stopped at the highly varnished portals leading to the bar. "I'm going to check the front desk for messages," Adrian said. "Order for me."

"A martini, right?"

Adrian smiled. "At this time of night?"

"I thought that was what the polo players drank, kid. You gotta have numb nuts to play that game."

Seconds later Adrian hurried into the bar, obviously agitated. He found Bodine settled in. "I don't understand this—it doesn't make sense." He handed over a small square of paper. On it was a handwritten message in a tiny neat script:

> Dear Mr. Reed, sir,
>   Would you like please to see again the Miss Lola? If so, present yourself alone on the sidewalk laying in front of this hotel. At 1:30 this evening transportation will surely arrive.

"What in hell does it mean?" Adrian said.

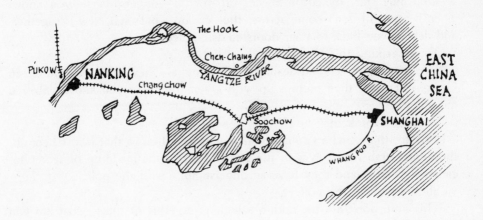

EIGHT

"WELL!? WELL?!"

Bodine looked at the note again. They sat in twisted rattan bar chairs of a highly complicated design, potted palms casting shadows on them from the overhead lights. Outside of the drinking area there was little come-and-go in the hotel lobby. Two tiny uniformed bellboys stood in a row behind the captain's station, and a sweeper pushed the same minute pile of dirt back and forth across the marble squares of floor.

"Doesn't say much, does it?"

"It's not *War and Peace*, if that's what you mean!" Adrian snapped. "It's the way it's written . . . 'would you like please to see again the Miss Lola?' And, 'present yourself alone'? For what? To go where? It sounds like a threat!"

"Who's Lola?"

"A dancer at Frisky's."

Bodine raised his eyebrows. "The one with the monkey?"

"Ape."

"Well, it is an odd piece of writing. Maybe she dictated it."

"What! Why would she do that—you're not saying she's been kidnapped?"

Bodine smiled. "You're a real romantic, bunkie. Still, you could be right. It's a regular industry around here."

"What happens if you can't pay?" It was the first thing Adrian thought of. He was nearly broke.

"Oh, they start by cuttin' pieces off of you—fingers, ears—you know. Then if you still don't come across, they cut up what's left, sew it together, and deliver you back to your doorstep assembled."

"You're making this up!"

"No, that bunch we had dealings with tonight—they belong to the Green Gang—they sew their victims up with green thread so you know who you messed with."

"You don't think they . . ."

"No, no, there isn't a Chinaman alive who could move that fast. Cheer up, they don't grab round eyes in the city. This place is made up of secret societies—Triads—and they have an understandin' with the police."

"Should we call the police?"

"This note don't ask for nothin'—it don't say this or that—what are you gonna tell 'em? That somebody took off with your girl and her monkey?" He saw the look on Adrian's face and held his hand up. "Okay, I'll tell you what I think. I think I just earned my finder's fee, that's what I think."

"What are you talking about?"

"Can she pay a ransom?"

"No!"

"Can you?"

"How could I unless . . ."

"Now you're getting it! Yeah! The million and a half in the bank! There's only one person that knows about it."

"Marshal Yü?"

"My guess is he's the bird who sent this note. He's tryin' to get your attention."

"But . . . that doesn't make any sense! All he has to do is get in touch with me! Why go through all this convoluted, complicated rigmarole?"

"Because he's Chinese!" Bodine said, as though instructing the retarded. "He's been watching you from the minute you checked into that bank, waited till you ran out of Mex and possibilities—you're broke, right? Then he takes the girl friend just to make sure the bargainin' goes his way. You were right about one thing. That note is a threat."

"What now?" Adrian said, sighing.

"There's only one thing I know of." He looked at his watch. "In ten minutes you be out front."

"But . . . what if they are kidnappers or worse! I'd be a damn fool if I put myself in their hands."

"Don't worry about a thing. I'll follow you on the bike."

"Do I pay extra for this?"

"You're gettin' cynical, kid. I like that. It shows your character is beginnin' to grow. When I signed on for the one percent, that meant that I was goin' to include in all expenses run up to get it. If I gotta rescue a lady and her monkey—well, that's my lookout."

"You've got a lot of heart, Bodine," Adrian said, smiling.

"I'd rather be told I had a lot of balls."

Adrian paced under the front canopy of the hotel, drenched with sweat, his shirt and jacket sticking to his back. Then the enormous old Hispano-Suiza eased up. For a minute it sat idling as he watched, listening to the tick of the type aero engine that had propelled Rickenbacker and Fonck in Spads above the western front in the Great War. Its burgundy paint had been rubbed until the bare spots gleamed and the polished wheel covers gave back his curbside image. In an open front compartment the chauffeur stared straight ahead like a cardboard cutout.

Adrian approached and leaned over the door. "Are you here for me— Adrian Reed?" The driver, a large Chinese with a face like a sulky moon, appeared to be mute. Finally Adrian got in the back of the car, and it moved off. When it was several hundred yards ahead in the stream of traffic, Bodine started his motorcycle and followed. Wrapped in an oily rag in the sidecar beside him was another relic of World War I; the doughboys called it a "trench-cleaner."

In the back of the Hispano-Suiza Adrian forced himself to relax against the brocade upholstery.

The inlaid woodwork displayed tortuous patterns of marquetry, and at each side of the window frames cut-glass vases held yellow roses, or rather one; the other was missing.

The smell of sandlewood, soy sauce, and French furniture polish permeated the car. Under the curve of the right armrest a padded cubbyhole appeared to be for top hats—an opera car. The glass partition revealed the back of the driver's shaved neck, bobbing in time with the car's suspension, as the three-ton behemoth absorbed bumps on Shanse Road. Adrian nervously watched the brightly lit buildings flip by and wondered for the hundredth time what his destination was. Bodine hadn't offered any clues and hadn't seemed particularly concerned. "We'll find out, won't we?" he had said. Adrian had to admit he had a pair of balls on him all right, real gall. Still, the only security he had was the thought that Bodine was back there somewhere, following.

Bodine was Adrian's first real experience with the career military man, and he guessed he represented an atypical example of the soldier that Kipling— somebody—called ". . . a bloody, ruddy, glory-bound hound of a paid hero, first to complain, first to charge into cannons' gape, first to fall carrying flags unfurled full, sword arm upright, bright . . ." Adrian agreed, Bodine was the kind of professional soldier in every nation that carried the burden of rash decisions made by politicians. He went where you pointed him—for a price, of course.

They turned right on Peking Road, moving toward the Whangpoo River. Adrian cranked the silver-plated handle, the window descended, and he could smell the heft of the river and the foul, somehow satisfying buffet of air from the sea beyond. They passed the imposing bulk of the Masonic Hall, and Adrian remembered how proud his father had been when he followed him "through the chairs." At the edge of the public gardens they turned right onto the Bund. On his left the second largest buildings in the world blocked out the moon. Along the passenger jetties steamships and passenger liners nudged up to berths. Beyond, anchored at the Man of War Buoys, were gunboats of half a dozen nations shouldering the White Man's Burden.

As they passed the Rue Colbert, on the boundary of the French Settlement, then the Boulevard des Deux Républiques next to the walled Chinese city of Nantao, Adrian's agitation increased. The Whangpoo docks were left behind. It got darker as lighting fell off, and the grading of ships seen dockside dropped to coastal steamers and coal barges. The car slowed and made a laborious turn between the scabrous sides of warehouses, godowns, built in the Chinese way with pitch of eaves turned up against evil spirits. Then at the end of the corridor of buildings a huge shape tied up to the quay became visible against the lighter sky.

Five masts rose above the curve of decks, the square lugsails folded now like Venetian blinds, each panel of matting secured to the mast by its own parrel. The car stopped, and Adrian got out, staring up at the massive junk with its thrust of bow, and the stern built up like stacks of irregular boxes. The only light appeared from a lantern hung above the enormous steering oar, sending pale yellow across the oily surface of the river. For Adrian it was an astounding sight, what he had originally believed China would be like— an ancient, unwieldy shape built so long ago nobody could remember its origins; an illogical container that carried all his childhood stories of sinister pirates and captured princesses. It suddenly occurred to him that was exactly why he was here.

Bodine saw the car turn in and, reluctant to follow it down the alley of warehouses, shut off the Harley's engine and coasted under an open corrugated shed. He chained the machine to a rusted-out donkey engine and made his way along the far side of the warehouse toward the tracery of masts. Reaching the point at which he would have to leave the concealment of the building, he paused and, listening, heard a familiar sound.

At the gangway two large Chinese searched Adrian. They seemed duplicated from the one in the car. They indicated Adrian should go ahead, and he walked between the two down the sloping deck toward the rise of the stern. As they went, Adrian felt a cold stream of sweat run down the trough of his spine, and he shivered despite the heat. It was very quiet, with only the shifting of planks somewhere, and the slap of tide against the hull. Ahead, the stack of superstructures rose in dark terraces of irregular shapes with odd corners and angles. Its silhouette against the sky suggested crenellated parapets, and he had the impression of a fortress rendered incorrectly in wood. Adrian had no way of knowing it, but this was called Castle in the West. Closer, he could see checkers of dim light piercing grilled ports. A low door opened, and they proceeded down a passageway, passing heavy, curved beams painted in vivid reds and blues.

They stopped before an imposing carved door, and one of the Chinese rapped. There was an answer and the door swung open. Bracing himself, Adrian stepped through.

He faced a long dining table, set not in the Chinese way, but with a white damask cloth, Rosenthal plates, and the shine of silver. A rotund Chinese with a cherubic face smiled up at him. Across from him sat Lola, and behind them on the long curve of a window bench Ramon crouched, chewing on a bone.

"Where you been, cowboy?" Lola said, smiling. "You missed din-din." They appeared to be on coffee and brandy.

"Dinner?" Adrian said dumbly, looking from one to the other.

"You must have got the note Charley left?"

"Yes, but . . ."

"We waited as long as we could, but I was starving. I wasn't sure you were going to show up at all." She smiled again, but he heard the hard edge to her voice.

They were both examining him, and he felt like the late dinner guest with a lame excuse. It was ludicrous, a bad joke. The Chinese wore a linen robe that gave him the look of a bishop. Bodine was wrong; there was no way this benign middle-aged Chinese was sinister, or Marshal Yü. A warlord? A playboy? He remembered now seeing him earlier in the evening under the marquee at Frisky's. The old boy was a stage-door admirer who had invited Lola to an intimate supper and had been forced to include him. How tacky. The problem had not been bad intentions but bad grammar.

"Sorry about being late—I'm afraid I didn't realize it was for dinner."

The Chinese stood and bowed. "It is my fault, of course! Please accept an apology. The invitation, I'm afraid, was badly worded."

Adrian smiled. "It did have me going." He reached his hand across. "We haven't met."

"So permit me, Charles A. Min."

"Charley knew your father," Lola said, sipping the brandy.

"What?" Adrian said, jerked back from his easy explanation. "How was that?"

Mr. Min shook his head in humility. "Nothing—I was one of a lot at Dr. Sun Yat-sen's taking of the presidency. I came to your father in company of Homer Lea in 1911."

Adrian allowed himself to be seated, alarms ringing. "You knew Homer Lea?"

"We all did at that time. But please—eat." Fingers were snapped and a plate was placed before him.

"It's not necessary . . . please."

"Of course, yes, yes."

A bowl of soup slid in. Adrian realized he was going to start from scratch. "What is it you do, Mr. Min, if I may ask?"

"Ah . . . travel when I may—Goodwood, St. Cloud—Saratoga even."

"You follow the races?"

"To my purse's discomfort—that being your pursuit, you would understand."

"Well, I played polo; I didn't ride."

"At your size, no."

The entrée arrived, and Adrian tentatively poked at it. It was rare pork and he had been taught to believe eating pink pork was akin to Russian roulette. "How was it you two met, Lola?"

"I wondered if you were going to remember little me," she said, propping her chin up with her hand, little finger waggling. Adrian had never seen her like this, and he wondered how drunk she was.

"Oh! Such a spirited dancer!" Mr. Min said, clapping his hands. "Such benevolent movement!"

"Vernon Castle said I put Irene in the shade." Lola winked.

"And he was, yes, right!" Mr. Min bent his bulk across the table and, finding her hand after several tries, patted it. "Such laughing toes! She delights our eyes with tiny steps of winged fairies!"

"I been a lot of things, Charley, but I've never been a fairy."

Mr. Min passed over this, indicating Ramon, who leaned against the transom glass, dozing, his bone a greasy streak on the silk windowseat. "Ah, I must also say, yes, I am including apes in my admiration. They have been considered ancestral in many cultures. Yes! Because they sit erect for long periods of time, the hamadryas baboon was thought to read and, oh, yes, write by the sometime Egyptians."

"Is that right?" Lola said, emptying her glass and having it instantly filled.

"In the North Africa there were ape cities. Diodorus, a Greek himself, describes such in 310 B.C., saying monkeys lived as commensals in the homes of men, dining and such."

"He knows all this kind of stuff," Lola said.

"The coastal people of Malay believed, yes, the crested ape to be their original ancestor."

Not mine, Adrian thought, plunging ahead with his chop, reconciled that trichinosis was the least of his problems.

"As you may know, part of the Buddhist dogma concerns the so tricky transmigration of the soul. It, yes, suggests the restless souls of the ever-dead repose in the bodies of monkeys. Yes! In our fourteenth century there was a Buddhist monastery in this Peking that housed both monks and monkeys." He giggled. "Amusing thought, I believe."

Adrian did his best to respond with a tired smile. Lola held her brandy glass out, sighting it against the reflection of the light.

"The introduction of Buddhism into this China was made to be paved by a mythical monkey, Sun Hou-tzu. He was the salty hero of *Hsi-yu-chi*, a drama book in which after eighty-one so terrible tribulations, the Monkey King embraces Buddhism and as, of course, a reward becomes the God of Victorious Strife and patron diety of official travelers."

"Is that right?" Lola said, yawning.

"India, of course, yes, is full of monkey cults. Why, the most regal Prince of Wales visited the monkey temple at Benares in '76."

She brightened. "Is that the swell-looking guy in the rotogravures?"

"His uncle."

"Adrian went to college, too."

"I'm sure."

"Tell him where, cowboy."

"Stanford."

"Yes, of course, a so-fine place. I spent much happy wasted time in California."

"He knows movie people."

"Please—Anna May Wong only."

"Your English is very colorful, Mr. Min. Did you attend a Western university?" Adrian had pushed his food around until it looked eaten.

"Oh, yes, I read Chinese classicism at Balliol, the many years ago."

"That's in Mississippi," Lola said.

"Well, it's part of Oxford too."

"In Britain, to be sure."

"Listen! There's an Oxford in Mississippi, damn it! I've played it!"

"You're right," Adrian said.

"Yes, oh, yes."

"I know a couple of things too, I can add a bunch of nines—I been to the fair—my folks traveled all over Europe with us! When I was three, I remember being in Egypt! I rode a camel! I've got a picture of it!"

"One hump or two?" Adrian said, smiling.

She focused on him. "Ha-ha. You guys think because you've been to some dumb schools you're wised up. . . ."

"No, no!" Mr. Min protested.

"Oh, yeah! While you boys were off playing boola-boola, I was on the road with Ramon, doing the three-a-day, learning the hard way! I sure didn't have any sugar titty to suck on!"

"No, no!" Mr. Min said.

Adrian was not smiling now. "Lola . . ."

"Who asked you, anyway, Mr. Rah-rah? Go hump a duck!" She stood up suddenly, rocking the table, unsteady on her feet. They both rose with her, and each reached out a hand to steady her, but she turned and took one step, flopping down next to Ramon on the windowseat. He instantly put his long arms around her, eyes wild, sensing something wrong. Lola put her head back against the glass with a *bonk* and shut her eyes. "Shit . . ."

Adrian and Mr. Min sat down in silence. Adrian was amazed. In the month or so he'd known Lola she'd never been drunk that he could remember. It was the late dinner and all that brandy—still, he was put off. She was not only a drunk—but a mean drunk.

Mr. Min lowered his voice. "Perhaps we should take the air onto the deck while our lady recovers?"

"Yes, of course."

They went down the passageway, followed by one of the Chinese body-guards, and stepped out on the deck. The heat continued, but a bit of pungent night air moved from the river and was not unpleasant. Mr. Min produced a cigar case.

"If you prefer the light smoke, you might so like the double claro."

Adrian selected one and they lit up, blowing the smoke toward the tall masts. "Thank you."

"It's a remarkable craft, Mr. Reed." Mr. Min indicated the stowed rigging. "With each narrow panel tied to the sheet line, it so allows the force of the wind to be taken in that it may be sailed into the wind. It was not till the nineteenth century that Western ships could match that, oh, no."

"What's it called?"

"The *Melodious Bird Song*."

"Ah." Adrian found Mr. Min an enigma. English manners and taste with their overlay of Oriental reticence were in odd conjunction. With his rosy cheeks and pince-nez glasses, Mr. Min presented the picture of the perfect gentleman in any culture. However, there was something about his affability, his eagerness to please, that was unsettling. Adrian decided to ask straight out.

"Mr. Min, might I ask if you are also Marshal Yü?"

"Oh, yes, that is my military title. But of course, you know that."

The sound Bodine heard was the familiar one of the clutch's return hitting floorboards. Searching the shapes on the cluttered dockside, he made out the half-moon silhouette of a wire wheel and part of a fender showing between two huge crates. Circling, he saw the car and that its left-hand door was open. Otherwise perfectly still, he moved his head in increments, checked out the area, section by section. On the third go-around, he caught movement. A man stood in the shadow of the sagging shed door. From the angle of his arms, he appeared to be looking through binoculars toward the junk.

Taking his time, Bodine worked his way behind him. He could see now from the man's line of sight that he was trained mid-deck, just forward of the tall cabin. While Bodine watched, there was a flare of light from an opening doorway and three figures came on deck.

It was Bodine's intention to grab the man in a sudden armlock and face him up against the door. But an instant before he could manage this, the man turned with such rapidity that Bodine was struck three times in succession by the flat of the man's hand before he reacted. Stunned, he stumbled back and went down, the trench-cleaner skidding off along the floor. Bodine put his legs up for protection and was instantly kicked twice in the calf. This caused such pain that he drew his body up to protect himself, expecting the next blow to his head. Instead he heard the sound of running feet.

Staggering up, he retrieved the trench-cleaner and limped across to where he would bisect the car. He heard it start, and when it crept by him, he stepped out from behind the crate and punched his fist through the side curtain at the face above the wheel. The isinglass gave with his blow, and he could feel his knuckles strike flesh. The man reeled across the seat, recovered, corrected the car's path, and stepped on the gas. Knocked sideways, Bodine raised the trench-cleaner as the car cleared the crates and picked up speed.

Before he could use it, someone grabbed him from behind, and he felt more pain.

NINE

ADRIAN HEARD A car start up on the dock, the sound of a scuffle, and seconds later one of the bodyguards ran out of the shadows and shouted up at the deck in Chinese. Mr. Min or Marshal Yü listened, gave a sharp reply—very unlike his lazy English—and turned to Adrian, smiling again. "Some small trouble—perhaps we should go below."

Adrian desperately hoped it had nothing to do with Bodine. He kept his voice level. "Would you prefer to be addressed as Marshal Yü or Mr. Min?"

"Whatever pleases you," he said sweetly. They crossed to the main transom and, with the guard, went down a staircase to the second deck. Marshal Yü laid his hand on the heavy bulkhead. "There are twelve of these partitions running both ways in the so wide hull. Watertight compartments, more, I must say, than on the *Titanic*."

Adrian was not interested in the guided tour at this point, but was surprised to hear the hum of a motor.

"The generators for our electricity. We are thought quite modern too. There are diesel engines to aid lazy wind." At the entrance to the sturdy door of another bulkhead, the Marshal paused, and his expression altered slightly. "I hope you will show no offense by what occurs further." And he opened the door.

Red Bodine hunkered down against the far wall of what must have been the crew's quarters. He looked badly used, breathing heavily and marked with several angry welts about the neck and head. A Chinese guard stood between him and a low table. On it rested a World War I pump shotgun—the trench-cleaner. Bodine smiled ruefully and gave the classic up-and-down gesture with his cupped fist.

"My God, Bodine! What happened?"

"He was found so armed near our warehouses. This, of course, cannot be permitted. I am, yes, embarrassed if he is an aquaintance or perhaps a most private guard—if we had but known it would have been avoided. Most distressing!"

"For Captain Bodine, certainly!" Adrian said angrily.

Chairs were brought and Marshal Yü gestured. "Please to sit. Captain Bodine, may we assist you?"

Bodine waved off the offer. "Leave me here for a minute . . . if you move me I'll break."

Adrian sat awkwardly across the table from Marshal Yü, still angry. The shotgun was positioned exactly at its center and had the shine of a well-used tool. "Marshal Yü, I would like an honest explanation, if that is possible!"

"So—where to begin—as I said, Mr. Reed, I knew your father, from Homer Lea and Dr. Sun. We were comrades together at the rising of our revolution and, alas, at its failing. Dr. Sun was the man for the formulation of ideas, carrying out of which he knew little—indeed he spent more time in Japan and America than he did in China. When he died in 1925, all factions of politicians scrambled to stake out their own constituencies—warlords, you colorfully call them. As surrogate appointed by Dr. Sun, I had much correspondence with your father over the years. Once we even met at the ocean house of Mr. Randolph Hearst in Santa Monica." Adrian looked startled. "Oh, yes, that's most correct. We discussed the using of his generous loan many times."

"I'll bet," Bodine said.

"I was a colonel in the old Tungpei Manchurian Army. When Sian was threatened by the Northern Army of Liu-chen-hau, I came to the aid of my friend Yang Hu-cheng, called the Tiger of the Cities, and we seized control of the city. Later, as warlord, I personally took down the five-barred flag of Manchuko and raised the sun flag of the Kuomintang. I was one of the few Northern officers who supported Dr. Sun's presidency. Oh, yes. He elevated my position to general, then marshal. At the end when the others turned against him and the scramble for power began, I alone in that place held out. Ahhh, then would not the funds of your father have made so much the difference? Yes, perhaps saved the revolution."

"Wash!" Bodine said. "They were cutting up the pie, and Yü here was left with an empty plate. Sun Yat-sen was never the real boss of China—he was the window dressin' for the round eyes."

65

Marshal Yü ignored him. "My control was mined-under by treacherous persons, bribed by the Japanese and misdirected irredentists. When the bad days came, the reactionary schemers crept in—young Communists. I barely managed to escape with meager personal belongings and make my way to Shanghai, where I have been forced to live in exile."

"Get your hankies out," Bodine said.

Adrian exploded. "*Damn it all!* I don't understand you people! Why didn't you just come forward? My God! All this subterfuge! Going around in circles! I've been trying to find you for weeks!" Adrian felt all the frustration and anger of someone playing a game where the rules change constantly and he isn't informed.

"I told you why," Bodine said. "He's Chinese."

"That at least is accurate," Marshal Yü said with some humor. He remained impassive to Adrian's outburst and Bodine's cynicism. He looked like the bemused scholar rather than the warlord who had won Sian.

"Yeah, and as far as all this banana oil about what went on in Sian, there's another version. The Chinese reds have got a grip on the Northeast now, and Chiang has pulled the Tungpei army south to Honan. Leavin' the locals, like Yü here, holdin' the bag."

"Badly untrue. The Generalissimo and I enjoy relations of the best. He has assured me, privately, he surely supports any move that would return me there."

"I'll believe that when I read it in the Bible."

"*Look!*" Adrian said sharply. "I don't care about any of this! Mr. or Marshal Yü, or Min or whatever—why didn't you come forward so we could discuss the disbursment of the Sun Account?"

"My agent at the bank informed me of your arrival, Mr. Reed Junior. I chose to wait until I could gauge your intent. Was that so unwise?"

"In the meantime he put the arm on your girl friend and her monkey, just to hedge his bet."

Adrian shook his head wearily. "My intent is simple. I want to come to a speedy agreement, divide the money, and go home."

Yü rolled the stub of the cigar in the circle to the corner of his mouth. "Ahhh, sadly no, I must decline to divide, no."

Both Adrian and Bodine looked at him. "No?"

"Oh, yes, no. This is the rock your father, Mr. Reed, and I stuck upon. I must decline to divide this money. I need the *entire* sum."

"What!"

"Look out!"

"Mr. Reed Junior, there is still a robust irredentist movement in Sian. The old guard of the Tungpei Army would welcome me back—indeed implore me back! I need these funds, all of them, to finance a return—to go home."

"Oh, boy," Bodine said, whistling through his teeth.

"Here is the offer I made your father, Mr. Reed Junior. Let us use this money together—you and this humble self in the great patriotic cause as General Grant or Pershing might. We know the Japanese are the enemy, let us stand against them at the top of my country!"

Bodine was now whistling "The Stars and Stripes Forever," but Yü went on. "When we have gloriously won, I will return all monies to you at twice the amount! You will receive three million! Oh, yes, plus the rights of minerals— unlike the so unfortunate Dr. Sun, I can deliver. This is the offer I made your father."

There was a long pause, a sigh, and Adrian heaved his shoulders up, then sank back as far as the rigid chair would allow. He had not really been listening. "Marshal Yü . . . I'm not a revolutionary. I just want to conclude a business deal. I can't involve myself in any coup . . . obviously my father had second thoughts about it. . . ."

Marshal Yü stood and bowed. "I respect your decision. My car will deposit you at your hotel."

Adrian looked up. "You won't discuss an alternative? Certainly we can compromise after twenty years!"

"Ah, that's it, isn't it?" The sweet smile. "After not coming to an agreement with your worthy father for twenty years—does it seem like I would now with his son? I will wait."

"He's got you, kid," Bodine said. "He can wait—but can you?"

Another pause while Adrian pinched the bridge of his nose. Then, "Tell me, Marshal Yü—are those secret Japanese books mentioned by Dr. Sun with the money in the bank vault?"

"Oh, yes, Dr. Sun received them from military parties unknown while in Japanese exile. They are there."

"If . . . I agreed to this . . . adventure, would those books be turned over to me?"

"On the instant of our together plans."

"All right, all right . . . where in the hell is Sian?"

Bodine answered, "It's the capital of Shensi Province, way the hell 'n 'gone up in the mountains, smack up against Inner Mongolia with the Great Wall separatin' it from the Odors Desert. Full of wild-assed bandits, hard cases, Muslims, and God knows what. If they aren't all starvin' to death in the annual famine, then, by God, they're shootin' each other's butts off. Sian is the only part worth a hill of beans, and Yü here is right, he once ran it like his own private preserve. He was the resident warlord—the big wazoo—they used to call him the 'Big Marshal.' Ask him who's runnin' the shop now."

Adrian looked toward Yü.

He lowered his eyes. "My son."

"That's right, kid, they call him the 'Little Marshal,' Chan Chow-ki—color him red."

"A disgrace!" For the first time the amiable host dropped his polite manner. "A stone on his father's heart! Raised among foreigners and bad influences! He was corrupted by my foul enemies, opium, and, I confess, my indulgence! He is a puppet dancing at the strings of notorious grafters and seriously unscrupulous persons! As a Westerner, you cannot know the infamy of a Chinese son who would disgrace his father!" He had leaned forward, spitting the cigar ends out in this vehement denouncement. Then easing back, he regained control. "Forgive me."

Adrian could not help but think of his own father's disgrace and his attempt to restore his name. He made up his mind. "We will have an agreement then, Marshal Yü. I will commit myself—God help me—to backing your return to Sian. In return you agree to return the money twice over—and give over the Japanese books. Is that right?"

"So agreed." They shook hands.

"Now, if you don't mind I would like to be taken back to the hotel. In the morning we can meet and go to the bank."

"Please, no, allow me to say it is too late. Stay here the night as my guests. We will go to the bank together so, at the morning."

Adrian was taken aback; he knew this was not an offer but a command. He looked over his shoulder at Bodine, who raised his eyebrows.

"This is Grandma's house, kid, and Yü here is the wolf." It was then Adrian really understood that anything Bodine had said about the Marshal was an understatement.

TEN

SERGEANT I. M. "MAX" Masaki came from that most unfortunate of all Japanese castes, the dispossessed samurai. His forebears had pledged their swords to the Lord Saga on the southern island of Kyushu and, it was said, crossed the Tsushima Strait in the sixteenth century to invade Korea. That was ancient glorious history. When Japan entered the modern world in 1868 with the Meiji Restoration, the feudal lands of Lord Saga were committed to the Emperor's "safekeeping," and samurai were forbidden to wear swords. Worse, they had to go to work.

Saga was one of the poorest provinces in the Empire.

The samurai class had once lived an austere life of *Hagakure* by choice: "A samurai lives in such a way that he will be prepared to die." Now they lived this way because they had to.

It was hard times, and, being redundant, samurai were reduced to poverty and even begging. Some struggled to change. His grandfather was one of these, and Max grew up on the small family farm hearing stories of the great days, while he and his five brothers and sisters worked at mean, grinding labor every daylight hour. It was a brutal, back-breaking life, dull and relentless, providing barely the necessities. There were two ways out: education or the military. Although Max was bright, first in his class at the government primary school, it required private funds to go on to a university. There were none.

At sixteen he joined the army and found himself in the cavalry. If he thought farm life was brutal, his life as a recruit was a sadistic nightmare. Discipline was severe in the extreme—not just the cuffs, slaps, and punches that accompanied the slightest infraction—but regularly the entire barracks would be turned out, kicked and dragged from their cots, made to bend over, and were beaten with clubs on the rear end twenty, thirty times. The slightest moan or cry of pain started the whole thing over again. It was called "paternalistic punishment," and it reduced them all to mindless robots ready to obey instantly.

But Max survived and, because he was good at handling horses, he advanced. By the time he was twenty-five, he was a lance corporal making ten yen ($2.30) a month. Then it was his good fortune to come to the attention of Captain Sato.

Tetsho Sato was everything Max was not: the modern Japanese, the big city man from a wealthy industrial family, who was indulged and allowed to finish his education abroad. Enjoying the reputation of a sportsman, he traveled in the United States during the 1928 racing season with his jumper Niji, winning the Hunt Trophy at Madison Square Garden.

In New York two things happened that changed his life. He was called "dirty yellow Jap" to his face. Not by some yahoo in the street, but by a beautiful, drunken lady at 21. Like many Japanese males, Sato had an arrogance of country and race, and it would have never occurred to him for a moment that anyone was his equal, let alone his superior. It came as a shock to find that others might actually think differently. This minor event triggered a fierce hatred of America that shaped his life. At that time the second thing that profoundly affected him was Homer Lea. He read his book *Valor of Ignorance* and was galvanized. Here was an *American* warning that Japan had the military power and will to advance across the Pacific and, unless stopped, would sweep in a great tide over Western civilization! Sato vowed to make this a reality. His days as a sportsman were over.

When he returned to active duty in Japan, he found a nationalistic spirit in the wind: *Hakka Ichiu Kodo!* One Family All Loyal to the Emperor! Racists like Dr. Okawa advanced the theory that, because Japan was the first state in existence, her Divine Mission was to rule the world. The military agreed, and Sato aligned himself with the extremists. Newly graduated from the Staff College, he joined the Tokyo Army Club and the secret Sakura-Kai, Cherry Society. Their aim was army rule, military expansion and an end to the "Manchurian problem." Japan governed leased territory in Manchuria through a "mandate" of the South Manchurian Railway. This included control of police, taxation, education, and public utilities. A special army, the Kwantung, was stationed there to enforce their law and protect Japanese settlers. It was a situation unmatched in any other nation of the world—but it wasn't enough. The Army wanted to occupy *all* of Manchuria by force.

The Cherry Society set out to implement this. In the next years two Japanese prime ministers were assassinated, and in March 1930 a *coup d'état* came close to success. It was clear that the officer clique was now stronger than the government. At about this time Sato came under the wing of General Tojo, who was looking for a bright young man who could fit into the social life of Shanghai and gather information for his Kwantung army and the Cherry Society.

In late 1930 Captain Sato was transferred to Kwantung HQ at Hsinking, and Max went with him, assigned to a Saber Company of a reconnaissance regiment. Like most nations at the time, Japan had no central intelligence-gathering branch. The military police, *kempei*, handled the field work, but at high level spies were recruited by each military arm to its own purpose. Because of his background, Sato was sent to Shanghai under cover as an agent. He would act as military attaché to the consul and infiltrate the social life of the city. Max would act as his aide and handle the routine field surveillance work. Both men would feed information from their segments back to Hsinking for evaluation and pave the way for future military action.

In the following year very little of interest was transmitted other than statistics and the indiscretions of consular secretaries. When Marshal Yü had approached the dancer at Frisky's, they knew in advance and Max was immediately alerted. The Marshal was on the list of "transient warlords" to be watched. His home base, Shensi Province, bordered on Japan's Manchurian sphere of influence, and any shifts in power were viewed as crucial to policy-making. Captain Sato ordered Max to watch Frisky's and to monitor the comings and goings to the *Melodious Bird Song*, Yü's junk.

Now, as he drove up Bubbling Well Road in the captain's Ford roadster, Max nursed a sore cheekbone from last night's altercation with the Marine, Bodine. However, he was sure he was unknown, that their security was not compromised. He had absorbed some of the captain's fervent nationalism. Dealing with Westerners had become offensive, and he was only sorry that he had not been able to hurt the Marine seriously.

As he spun along toward the Shanghai race course, the road was crowded but negotiable. If it had been during the three-day Spring Race Meet, his progress would have been impossible. Then the road was jammed with cars, rickshas, pedestrians, and erratic bicycles. Progress was so slow that the beggars kept pace and tapped on car windows. All along the way vendors attracted attention with gongs and duck rattles. It was a frantic time of horn-honking, shouts, and grinding gears, so congested that rickshas and Yo-Yo carriers had to take to the sidewalks. But now, with the summer heat, the taipans were in their cool mountain retreats and the road was passable.

At one time, the Race Course and Recreation Center had marked the western edge of the city. Then the march of Shanghai progress had crept up and passed it, until it was surrounded with modern buildings, a green island in the midst of department stores and towering apartment houses. Ahead, the road kinked around the clubhouse, its bars, lounges, and verandas stretching out to an empty track where the ponies ran clockwise in season.

The Shanghai Race Club was one of many bonding associations of white foreigners in the city that did not allow Orientals to become members. This was interesting since the big betting on the races was generated by Oriental money. The Chinese were desperate gamblers, and each race was a sweepstake, with merchants in silks and coolies in rags risking all on a single outcome. Because of their fervor the club survived and profited handsomely.

Max carefully parked the Ford near the stable block and walked around the corner to an arcade along a row of box stalls. As he did so, he heard angry voices. Two men and a groom stood by a pony under the shade of the arcade roof. One was Captain Sato, the other a big florid man he recognized as the British secretary of the club. He had been a major in the 11th K. E. O. Lancers (Probyn's Horse), and an early member of the Shanghai Otterhounds, a drag hunting group that rode to the hounds across the local countryside, with little success and a lot of crop damamge.

"You deliberately choose to misunderstand me, sir!"

"I understand you most perfectly!" Captain Sato replied. He was tall for a Japanese, wearing a crisp polo shirt, riding breeches, and beautifully polished boots. Max knew the pants and boots well. He and Sato were the same size, and to save the captain bother, his clothes were fitted on him and the boots worn until broken in. Sato had told his friends that because of this, Max was indispensable as an aide and he would overlook any shortcomings this side of treason or sodomy. It was also one of the reasons for Max's smooth progression up the ranks.

The major dropped his voice. "You have been asked politely to move your animal to the stalls provided for nonmembers!"

"What you mean is nonwhite. Although a gentleman of breeding, education, and a family a thousand years older than any here, I am excluded, insulted to find myself in less proper quarters!" Although he was speaking in a cool, detached manner, Max detected the signs of repressed fury. Captain Sato had an arrogant aristocrat's head, beautiful skin (now blotched with red at the cheeks), and the flaring nostrils of a fierce warrior. It was *he*, the scion of a merchant family, who looked the samurai. As for the family being a thousand years old, Max doubted that. He slowed and stopped respectfully

72

several yards away, where the captain's tack leaned against the stall. He waited for the explosion.

"The rules and bylaws of the club were established for the mutual benefit of all! They are *our* position and therefore not negotiable!" The major was barely under control, veins standing out, fists clenched. "You will find the guest quarters on the south side of the quad. I ask you again kindly to remove your animal there!"

"The south side is, of course, in the sun. I will not allow my most valuable animal to be in discomfort."

The animal they spoke of was a "griffin," a new pony as yet not entered in a race. Max was familar with it. Captain Sato had shipped it down from Manchuria to compete in the fall season. With close-coupled bodies and short, thick legs, Mongol ponies were not usually graceful, but this one obviously had a strong Arabian strain, a throwback to the Mongol conquest and the plunder of blood mares. He was a stud, with a small elegant head, arched neck, and high plume of a tail. His finely made legs tapered to small hooves, and as he shifted nervously, there was a satisfying spring to his pasterns. The color of the coat was a marvelous blue-dun and had been brushed until it shone. He was unsaddled, and as the *mafu* held his bridle snubbed off, his eyes cut back at the angry words of the major.

"I tell you one last time! Move that horse!"

Sato's head shifted slightly toward Max. "Bring my kit."

"Sir!" Max snapped to and, picking up the bag, trotted to Sato, holding it out at chest level.

"Open it."

"Yes, sir!" He unbuckled the brass catches and folded back the flap.

"Now take out my side arm." Max dug in, removed the 8mm Nambu from its holster, and passed the gun over by its wooden grip, so as not to mark the bluing.

The major's eyes got big. "Here now! What's this?"

Sato thumbed the safety off, raised the gun in the major's direction, then shifted it to the right, placed the barrel against the pony's head at just the right point, and pulled the trigger. There was a muffled explosion, a scream from the animal as it reared and plunged sideways, slamming into a water barrel and overturning it. The *mafu* jumped aside just in time as the pony hit the ground, legs kicking, shuddered, and was still.

In the stunned silence Captain Sato put the safety on and handed the gun to Max, who replaced it in the bag.

"Now, Major, *you* can move him."

Max picked up the rest of the tack and, passing the shaken major, followed his officer down the arcade toward the parking lot.

Adrian Reed met with Marshal Yü at nine-thirty Monday morning in a private room provided by the Hong Kong-Shanghai Bank. Of the twenty or more top companies in the city, this venerable octopus of an establishment was held in most awe. Beginning with the commercial invasion of China a century before, in the battle to get the better of and more money out of the Chinese, it had led the attack. Almost half of China's trade was carried on in Shanghai, and the H&S was second to none when it came to grabbing its share. The bank's officers had long ago mastered the Chinese art of seeming to waste time and exchanging irrelevancies while talking business—then striking at the last possible moment. Cotton millionaires and warlords were treated with the same British civility and attention to profit.

In a long day of negotiations, paper shuffling, and maddening legal translations, Adrian realized he was bargaining from a foregone conclusion; without Yü's signature he would get nothing, neither the money nor the "crates of documents." He had spent a sleepless night deciding how to handle this disadvantage. In the end he knew he could not passively accept it. He had to mount the tiger's back. Before the final signing he sat with Yü in very private offices. He asked that the lawyers and witnesses be withdrawn. There were raised eyebrows, but this was done.

He took a deep breath. "Marshal Yü, there is one thing I must ask. If I am going to invest my father's money—my money—in this undertaking, then I must ask to go along and act as observer, I must be part of the spending of that money"—he smiled—"and life." Adrian had waited until the last possible moment to spring this on him.

If Yü was surprised, it was evident only in a second's hesitation. "Ah, Mr. Reed Junior, very admirable, yes, oh, yes. But as the civilized man, surely you would not wish to go the soldier's way—no, no." He shook his head. "Stay here at the Palace Hotel. You are not the military man."

"True. Captain Bodine has agreed to act as my military adviser. He suggests also a staff of several other officers—specialists in their fields—who can evaluate our progress."

This was going down hard with Yü. He clucked his tongue, no longer smiling. "Oh, too bad, these are no doubt—Western military men who believe that as Chinese we are not so likely to conduct a good war."

"Not at all—informed observers whose language I speak, whose information will allow me to comprehend our little war—good or bad."

"Yü shook his head. "It is not suitable that as marshal I be monitored. No, no."

"These will be my people, Marshal. They will instruct me—not you—in our progress. Those are my final terms."

There was a silence and they sat, the filtered light from a parabolic arch falling on the polished table, shadowed outlines of many mullions crossing the two.

"Alas," the marshal said, "forgive me, but I am not sure this arrangement is possible."

"Well, then," Adrian said, pushing back in his chair, smiling his own version of the sweet smile, "you will have to wait another twenty years to negotiate with my son." It was a reversal of last night's speech by Yü.

There was another pause, then Yü chuckled. "I see you have your father's head, after all—you understand bargaining. Very well, I am impressed by your resolve. I agree."

The lawyers were called in and the signing took place. The million and a half was now free to be spent in the pursuit of war. The irony was not lost on Adrian that he was committed to exactly the same high-risk military adventure his father had underwritten twenty-three years before.

At the conclusion Marshal Yü was his usual affable self, offering a benign smile and trumpeting to the "continued cooperation of Chinese and American interest for mutual success." It seemed to be spoken with perfect sincerity. That was what was so maddening. Adrian found Yü's character impossible to gauge. Viscous, it slipped through your fingers, clinging but slippery.

One thing they both insisted on: an inspection of the funds. After all this time, each man wanted to be sure the money really exsisted. They were taken to impressive underground vaults and shunted in an electric cart along narrow tracks to a gated alcove. The gate was unlocked, and stacks of rough oak boxes bound with straps were visible. One was pried open, and both Adrian and Yü leaned over. Large coins, each wrapped tightly in rice paper, lay out in long rows, dozens and dozens, stacked eighteen inches high in each box. Adrian reached down, fished one out, and unwrapped it. It was an American gold double eagle. He turned it over and inspected its proof mark. It showed the head of Liberty on one side, the eagle on the other, and was stamped "Twenty Dollars." Its actual weight in gold was slightly under one ounce. Adrian replaced it and turned to the bank official.

"I'd like to see the Japanese books."

He was led to two long, flat cases, and the lid of one was angled up. Taped to the first book was a careful typed notation:

1. Orders of mobilizations of the active army and navy of all Japan.
2. Orders of coast defense.
3. Active orders of high command during war.
4. Regulations and orders of telegraphic corps in battlefield.
5. Regulations and field orders of sanitary corps in battlefield.
6. Regulations and orders of field artilleries.
7. Regulations and orders of general telegraph corps.

8. Important schedules.
9. Details of regulations of the lines of communications.
10. Orders of the chief inspector of military training.
11. Orders for regulations of the lines of communication.
12. Orders for heavy artilleries and seige guns.

This was the inventory for this case. There was the other.

Adrian looked at the book. It was large, the size of a ledger, bound in scarlet and embossed with Japanese characters. Inside, the pages were covered with neat Japanese calligraphy.

"Do you read Japanese?" Yü said behind him.

"No, of course not. I can only hope these are not records of a bathhouse."

"I can assure you of fidelity," Yü said seriously. "Dr. Sun transported them around for many years."

It was a moment Adrian had rehearsed. He knew exactly what he would do. When he left China, the books would go with him to Washington, there to be handed over to the highest possible official and be properly orchestrated. He did not want them buried in the State Department; he would make sure they understood that his father's patriotism had never been in doubt.

He replaced the book. "All right, let's finish our business."

As the Ford roadster returned from the racetrack, Sergeant Masaki made his report to Captain Sato. If the captain was disturbed over shooting his cherished pony, he did not show it. The Marine Bodine was the topic. Masaki said he had picked him up twice with Reed now. The American had been highly visible from his arrival, actually advertising for Yü. (They shook their heads over this.) The Sun Account had been common knowledge in intelligence circles for years, and a discreet inquiry by Captain Sato at the H & S bank, plus some of the Emperor's good yen, had gotten results. The $1.5 million in the account had been placed there in 1910 by Hugh H. Reed, a California oil man. This was confirmed. Was the son in Shanghai to activate the money for a plot hatched by Yü? Bodine indicated this possibility. They knew him as a career Marine, married to a brothel keeper, and a minor underworld dabbler—was he now being recruited as a mercenary? Good question.

There was another. "Masaki, what about this dancer with the monkey?"

"She seems to be as she appears, a performer, sir. All inquiries indicate this."

Sato wasn't so sure. He had a weakness for convoluted schemes. He did not trust anything that seemed too simple on the face of it. He took out a note pad and scribbled on it. "Have this translated and delivered to Madam Bodine. Let's see if we can stir things up." Sato had his little sense of humor too.

At dusk Max Masaki parked the Ford a block from the Dragon's Tail on Kiangse Road. Shouldering his way through the streetwalkers, he paused at the vermilion gate. As he did so, a painted child reached out and gripped his crotch.

"Oh, sir, you are most heavenly blessed!"

He struck her hand away with a blow that brought tears to her eyes. She clutched her wrist and shrank back.

"You know the person of Madam Bodine?"

"Y-yes."

"Take this note to her!" He pressed the note and a coin in her hand, and she turned and ran through the gate. Max loved children and fiercely hated a people who would prostitute them. He was sorry he had hurt her.

Madam Bodine received the note in stunned disbelief. She read it twice.

> Madam Dragon's Tail,
>   Do you know your salty husband, the Marine, spent the night with a lady and her monkey?

"What!! A lady and monkey!!" She crashed out of her sleeping room in such a fury that the lights flickered, shot through the beaded curtains, and approached Bodine's quarters, tilting forward at an alarming angle, arms pumping.

Bodine lay on his back, head supported by a silk pillow, softly snoring. He was dead tired after yesterday's exertions, bruises still vivid on his neck and shoulders. The covers were thrown back, and he wore his T-shirt and shorts, legs crossed and hands folded on his chest. Madam Bodine jumped on the bed with a noisy compression of springs and, standing, straddled him. "You dirty dogsbody!" Pulling up her tight skirt, she began to urinate on his chest.

"Geee-zusss!" He came straight up, reflexes working, and grabbing her by the ankle, spun her off the bed. She hit the slick floor and slid into the aperitif table, throwing off a shower of watermelon seeds. He swung off the bed, eyes puffy with sleep, and stood up holding out the wet T-shirt. "What in the holy hell!"

Twisted over, she bit him on the bare ankle, a bright ring of lipstick circling the mark. Yowling, he jerked her up by the hair and propelled her through the doorway with such force that the beaded curtains came unstrung, exploding in a thousand bright dots. He lost his footing on these and they both crashed to the floor, upsetting the portable metal fountain in a flood of water and blue celluloid balls. As they tumbled over, she got a grip on him, fingernails digging in, legs kicking, trying to drive her knee into his crotch.

The occupants of the house were quiet as the two struggled on the floor, thumping and grunting in open hand-to-hand combat. They had all been through this before and kept a low profile.

Bodine had been through it before, too, and knew what was needed. He managed to get on top and pin her arms over her head with one hand. Livid, she shouted up at him in a shower of saliva, "What's the matter, chicken red hair? Not get enough at home? Go after monkey lady?" With his other hand he pushed her legs apart, jerked open his shorts and, erect, entered her, thrusting forward. "Oh, no! No sweet talk!" She bucked backward, but he hung on, riding her as she tried to twist away. "Oh, no! Oh . . . no . . . ohhh . . . ohh . . . big boy!"

After he'd showered, hair slicked back and in a black robe with embroidered dragons, Bodine walked to the vermilion gate. He spoke in Chinese to the painted child. "Red Bud, you brought that paper to Madam?"

"Yes, honored sir," she said shyly, showing him the bruise on her wrist. "He did that!"

"As fast as a whip, sir . . . but he paid me."

"What was his face?"

"Different, the same, you know, islanders."

"Japanese—how did he come?"

"By a shiny new machine with wavy windows."

"Son of a bitch!" Bodine said in English. "The gink in the Ford!"

ELEVEN

A NAKED MAN lay on newspapers spread on a bare bed frame. Legs crossed, head resting on a rolled-up rug, he squinted at a tiny ad in the *North China Daily News*. He moved it back and forth off center, finding just the right focus until he was able to make it out. Nearly bald, with ginger hair combed neatly across the top of his head, he had a disconcerting face; pronounced pop eyes were the prominent feature. One of these, obviously false, remained in a fixed position, clear and resolute. The real eye was easily distinguished by being bloodshot. His skin was dead-white, with the exception of his face, which at first seemed a healthy tone of pink, but was actually established from a network of exploded veins that built to a burgundy climax on the nose. Under the nose was a bristling mustache that gave the impression that it might at any moment throw off quills.

The ad read:

> Seasoned Army officers interested in well-paying, adventurous job with oil company, please contact C.C.P.O 1002.

A pounding on the door continued in erratic tattoos, then increased its tempo. The naked man retrieved a bottle of Tiger Bone Whiskey from the bedside and took a long draft. He put down the bottle, hefted himself up, and, barrel chest out, walked on bird legs across a mean room to the door.

Opened, it revealed a very dark Indian in gold-rimmed eyeglasses. "This will not do, Colonel Gibb! You have been ordered to leave these premises on this day!"

"Really?" the colonel said. "I didn't hear that. Can't imagine why—you got my chit."

"Chits are no good! You must pay in money!"

"That's damned inconvenient—very well, I'll get on to my clerk." He moved to shut the door, but the Indian bent forward, livid.

"No! You get out! Out! There has been no pay for these rooms for many months! I command you to leave!"

"You command nothing, nit!" Gibb said, expanding his chest and slamming the door shut with it.

From the other side the Indian screamed that he would return with the police. Gibb had no doubt he would. He went back to the bed and took another draw on the whiskey, finishing the bottle. Then pulling a large port-manteau from under the bed, he rummaged in the bottom until he found his last Mills Bomb. Going into a tiny W.C. that contained only a pull-chain toilet, he stood on the wooden seat and hooked the handle of the grenade over the lip of the overhead tank. He tied a long stout string to the pin and secured the other end to a heavy brass curtain ring. This he dropped out the narrow window, letting it down until he was satisfied it was the right distance above the alley. Then he went in and dressed.

When the Indian returned with a bushy Sikh policeman, they found the colonel immaculately dressed in a silk pongee suit, regimental tie, and bou-tonniere. Cigarette at a rakish angle, he held a bamboo cane in one hand, portmanteau in the other.

"What's this?" he said through yellow teeth, examining the two. "The wog parade?"

Spotting the portmanteau, the Indian shouted, "You will not take personal items until the bill is paid."

"Do you know British territorial law, nit? Do you know that a British sub-ject may carry away what is hand held?"

The Indian hadn't heard of this and hesitated, then pointed to the only decent piece in the barely furnished room—a handsome campaign chest bound in brass and showing a complicated lock. "That will stay! You will not receive it back until I have payment of the rooms!"

"Room," Gibb said, "and a damned *shabbo* one at that! Very well, I will leave my property—but, by God, if it's tampered with, I'll be back and snap your nackers off!" The chest was filled with nearly a year's editions of the *London Times*. Saying this, he pushed by the man and descended the stairs, the Sikh behind him. They parted amicably in front of the worn steps and went in opposite directions. Gibb walked up the street and turned in the alley next to the building. Coming under the brass ring, he hooked it with the crook of his cane and jerked hard. The string exited the third-story window, bringing the pin, and as Gibb reversed, he rewound, and tucked it in a pocket. Stepping out smartly, he crossed the street to the trolley stop.

There was a muffled *whomp* and the side of the building exploded out at the third story, sending a lazy shower of bricks, shattered flooring, and dust into the alley. When the window lintel gave, the roof support cracked and the tiles slid off, clackling to the cobblestones in an almost orderly procession. On the roof itself electric wires stretched and snapped, falling against metal gutters to begin sparking. This impressive opening act was followed by a cascade of water from the sheared-off main. It flooded down from the opening, splashing on the parched stones, then continued down the alley in a vigorous stream. Beggars ran under the waterfall, holding heads back, mouths open, while children raced and laughed in the first real wet in ten weeks.

As the trolley accelerated from the stop and came by the front of the building, Colonel Gibb tipped his Panama and had the pleasure of hearing the anguished wail of his landlord.

For Adrian and Marshal Yü, the bank had another valued commodity, secrecy. A dummy corporation was set up, called Sino-Cal Oil Ltd. and after their signatures, funds from the Sun Account were transfered into it to be drawn on by Yü as president and Adrian as comptroller. This was necessary to avoid suspicion during the provisioning of the military expedition. With a small staff and office carrying the company name on the door, business could be funneled through an established front.

As for the bulk of the gold double eagles, they would remain in the vault. Adrian and the Marshal were presented with different keys. Both would be necessary to open it.

It had been Adrian's decision to take offices in the Palace. It was expensive, but he wanted to be close to day-to-day activity and thought a Western hotel a more likely front for the "company." When he worried aloud about their high visibility, Bodine said, "There's nothin' secret in this town, kid. At least if we're in the Palace our credit will be good."

The Palace Hotel overlooked the Bund with a broad view of the Whangpoo River and was almost in a direct line with the capital ships tied up at the Man of War Buoys. Between them and the passenger jetties, a tangle of junks and sampans were in constant motion, crawling with waterborne humanity, some of whom seldom touched the ground. In contrast, the vehicular traffic on the Bund flowed twenty-four hours a day in a well-directed pattern past the great hotel's door.

To reinforce his stand on frugality, Adrian had withdrawn just 500 Mex in walking-around money and had taken a tram. Getting off in front of the hotel, he crossed the stream of traffic and entered the lobby. It was tea time, and above the rattle of cups a Viennese string quartet played "Baby Face" with determined verve. He threaded his way through American Naval officers (toughing it out with charming companions while the wives summered at Tsingtas), businessmen of all stripes, and the ubiquitous tourists, Kodaks clutched, queueing up behind caparisoned guides. The ornate cage elevator took him to the fourth floor, and he walked to the end of the hall, pausing in front of a paneled door. On a polished brass plaque engraved letters stated:

SINO-CAL OIL LTD.

He shook his head and entered. Inside, two large connecting rooms were filled with the bustle of young men working at desks. Marshal Yü had insisted on personally hiring the staff, and these turned out to be thin young men, students, translators, and literary stylists, who, he said, would create the necessary smokescreen of legitimacy for the company. One clerk was dedicated to creating felicity in an ideograph. When Adrian asked what that was, it was pointed out that a well-chosen "chop" on a calling card could make all the difference in intent; an endeavor could very well fail because of its poor selection. Bodine explained that this was the Chinese way of business. If nothing else, Yü's office staff looked as if it had been in place for years, and Adrian went along, vowing to keep an eye on the books.

This was not easy. Finding his way through the financial byways laid down by the Chinese clerks was tricky, and he wasn't always sure he followed the right turns. All the military items—weapons, uniforms, the hundreds of sundries the small army would run on—had been contracted for C.O.D. Nanking. This was the staging area. Yü's junk the *Melodious Bird Song* would take them upriver when all was ready, and the contractor would then be paid off in hard coin. From there the expedition was to proceed on to Sian by leased train.

So far the majority of the bills were being run up by Marshal Yü. He insisted on a suite at the Palace, so he too would be close to the operation. It was staffed, and he set a lavish Western table with nothing but the finest wines and cuisine. All this was charged to the hotel, paid out of "company" funds. It made Adrian furious, but there was little he could do, as the agreement between them had stated the "oil company" would foot all personal expenses while in Shanghai.

As for the actual army, Marshal Yü reported his Tungpei agents in Nanking were having no trouble enlisting Manchurian volunteers in exile. There was no way to check this as it was conducted underground—however, Bodine was attempting an appraisal through contacts in the U.S. military in the area.

Their own enlistment of observers was nearly closed. The blind ad placed in the English language papers had brought more response than they could have asked for. There was no shortage of at-liberty military personnel in the city. This was the business of the day. They had already selected a German engineer whose speciality was fortification and siege. He had served in China before the German concessions were handed over to the Japanese in 1917 and 1918, and he knew Sian. The other choice was a retired U.S. Navy Chief Radioman, who, Bodine said, was the original "Sparks." Nothing would be more crucial than a communications expert. "And this guy has ears that can hear a frog fart."

Now they were to interview an even more senior candidate: Marian P. H. H. Gibb, former colonel of a Nepal Gurkha Brigade and commander in the Lahore Division during the Great War. His record was impressive. Among dozens of decorations: the Victoria Cross at Ypres in December 1914 with the Fourth Gurkhas and First Highland Light Infantry. His bent was armor and heavy artillery. On the down side were hints of erratic behavior. Reading between the commendations, transfers and lack of promotions, ending with an early medical discharge—Adrian thought it possible to see a pattern. Alcohol. Bodine scoffed at this, saying he never heard of a combat officer, including Grant, who didn't booze, and remember what Lincoln said about him.

They had gathered in the "war room": Adrian, Bodine, and Yü. The Marshal had asked to be present at the choosing of observers, and there was no reason to exclude him. When Colonel Gibb came in, he was not as expected. He was about the same height as Bodine, with powerful shoulders and the square build of a laborer, in no way resembling the typical British officer Adrian had expected; a Douglas Haig, say, or an Allenby. He had been provided with Marshal Yü's battle plan to be read on premises. This was a classic formation of two flanks swinging to enfold the city while an attack group fought their way to the enemy HQ. A straight-ahead confrontation. With it was included projected plans, Sian troop strength estimates, maps, and a timetable.

The colonel stood drawn up, cigarette ash hovering, fixing the three plotters with that one baleful eye. Despite his poorly arranged features and workingman's physique, he had presence, size. They sat below him, expectantly waiting for his considered opinion on their planned *coup d'état*. Flopping the folder noisily on the table, he pronounced judgment.

"Hard cheese, gentlemen, hard cheese!"

Adrian looked at the others, but they continued to stare at the colonel. He went on. "Even if what's left of your Tungpei chums are twice the strength you say they are, Marshal, in combat readiness, an' you have the old boy network greasin' the slides, and the damn reds stay put, and Chiang gives his pope's blessin', and everthin' ticks off like bloody Big Ching, it will be dicy, very dee-damed-dicy." If Gibb didn't look the British officer, he sounded like one with a plummy accent compounded with some sort of regional slang. "It's the war chest, lads—on that kind of knicker you can't expect to field a respectable force—it would be pure char!"

Adrian didn't know what "char" was (charade?), but he felt his father's money was called into question. "Are you saying one and a half million dollars is not enough to raise an army?"

The colonel smiled with yellowed teeth. "Reed, is it? My dear old son, we shot off more than that in brass cases in one afternoon on the Western Front, just probin' for position. War's an expensive business, if you haven't heard. Even with the Mex exchange rate you're not going to buy much in the way of an army for your million and a half."

"He's right," Bodine said.

"Then what are we talking about?!" Adrian was annoyed.

"Army's the wrong word," the colonel continued, "much too rigid. What's called for here is somethin' entirely different, m' dear." He suddenly slammed his hand down. "*Dazzle! Noise! Bloody bravado* and a bit of the old eye-wink! The Chinese aren't nearly as impressed by killin' as they are with the noise it makes! Give 'em a big *bang*, say I!" A large map of China was spread on the table, and as the others pulled their chairs closer and looked down, he took a flask out of his inner pocket, tilted his head, took a swig, and replaced it, quick as a flash. It happened like an involuntary tic, and only Adrian caught it out of the corner of his eye, a subliminal flicker over before he was sure he saw it.

"The railroad's the thing," Colonel Gibb said, punching the map halfway up the coast at Lien-yu-kang. "The Lunghai line's the one to take . . . it cuts across the main Peiping–Hankow line at Chengchow and follows the Yellow River through that bottleneck pass to Tungkwan. The extension to Sian was finished last year—nice timing for our side, I say."

Marshal Yü looked up at the colonel, smiling as usual. "It was our intention to take the trains."

"I hoped we weren't goin' t' hike it," Bodine said.

"Not *the* trains, old sons, *our* train. The thing to shop around for with your budget is *speed! Bloody, rapid forward movement! Speed!* Now—say we make up a military train, and it proceeds at maximum speed! *Zip! Zip! Zipper!* Stoppin' only for coalin' and water. Bloody blasts straight through to Sian and *BLAM!* We're onto the buggers before they can get their peckers up!"

"That surely can't be done? The railroad won't give you clearance on the line?" Adrian's experience with riding trains had not been without delays.

"With enough squeeze, we could have the whole coast moved over a few feet, bunkie," Bodine said, "but the question is, do we want to?"

The colonel winked, which was an unnerving experience as the glass eye rolled skyward. "We supply our own bloody clearance, Captain. We run another gang ahead of the main train, armed to the canines, and they damned well clear the track, open switches, and blast any fud of a slow freight off the line if need be! *Boom! Blam! Speed* is what we must have!" He leaned in, eyes protruding like lobsters, unnerving his audience. "All bloody right, what do we need in the way of warm bodies? A thousand ill-humored fellows, honed to ice-pick-points—hounds, hungry for a bit of rape and booty, each chap with an automatic weapon, not those damn antique broom-handle Mausers, but something impressive like a bloody big American Thompson! *Pow! Pow! Pow!* Somethin' that's goin' to make noise and big holes, forget about the marksmanship! Something the wogs can cuddle, rub up to a shine, oil and look swinish with.

"Now, here's the important thing—we take along enough lorries to move these fellows off the train once we get there and into Sian on the old double! Mobility is what I'm talking about—lightnin' strikin'! *ZAPPO!!*" Colonel Gibb was a fanatic for movement. After the battles of attrition that had bled "trench" armies in the Great War, he had avidly followed his old boss General J. F. C. Fuller and even the Frenchman, De Gaulle, on the theoretical battlefield possibilities of all-out mechanized war. Get there first! Roll over the buggers! They were talking about tanks, but his mania was for speed! You got the troops to the objective before the enemy was ready even if you had to shoot the sots out of the end of a cannon.

"*All right!* Say they're onboard, the train is rollin', movin' through that nasty devil of a countryside, *faster! Faster!* Down all the filthy side-twistin' curves, past empty fields, farmers afraid to show their knobs, deserted stations, miles of wild, beastly mountains, gorges with damn shaky trestles over 'em, and then—finally, the last tricky bit of esplanade before Sian—a steamy *toot!* The train slows, skids to a halt, wheels locked up, *sparks, squeals,* the boxcar doors flap down, KABLAM!!" He pounded his fist, and they all jumped. "Ramps are lowered, the lorries cough, fire up, *kapuk! kapuck!!* Engines revvin', waitin'! The troops hop down from their boxcars, surly, querulous, ready to go, chop heads! They pull back the bolts on the Thompsons, *clack!* Form up, and climb aboard the lorries. Each vehicle has a ring-mounted Vickers on the cab roof, keen-eyed gunner behind it. The trucks stand by ready to roll, officers hack their watches, they wait . . ."

There was a pause.

"For what?" Adrian asked.

"What's wrong? What's needed here, old sons?" He crooked his hand, coaxing them.

Adrian looked at Bodine, who smiled, enjoying the show. "You tell us, Colonel."

"*Noise!! Impressive intent! The long arm of fear!* The one thing that turns civilians t' puddin' and troops t' deserters."

"Artillery," Bodine offered.

"*Right!* Captain Bodine, do you remember a gunner imported by Marshal Sun during the trouble in '27?"

"Baron Whank?"

"He was neither a baron nor a Whank—just a petty officer in the German navy—a master gun layer. But no matter, the fellow had a genius for large bores—jerked the lanyard on the thirty-eight-millimeter 'Paris Gun'—Big Bertha, I mean, gad! That was the high-water mark of trajectory—*sixty bloody miles!* At any rate, he showed up here in China, brought over by the late Marshal Sun to manage a recycled naval gun he'd had Skoda mount on a railway car."

"Hell, everybody knew the Baron," Bodine explained to Adrian. "He was got up in a Prussian uniform with the monocle screwed in his eye and a Kaiser Bill spiked mustache—he looked like he'd seen one too many Von Stroheim pictures."

"Excessive fellow, but, gad, the eye on the man! Now here's the thing, that gun—a nine-point-two bore—big as a bloody ashcan, is sittin' on a sidin' in Nankin'! Saw it m'self!" Colonel Gibb twisted his topheavy torso toward Yü. "Sir, if you have the old pipe to Chiang, then it is entirely possible that you may be able to lease that piece of extraordinary artillery. It's under the Generalissimo's control. Could you chat him up about it, do you think?"

Yü bobbed his head. "Yes, he has been most encouraging—we had dinner recently and discussed our little expedition in some detail. Yes, oh, yes."

"Well, by gad! If you can requisition that . . . I doubt that there are more than a dozen shells left to fit it—but damn me, that should be too many by half. Have you any idea, any dim conception, what the horrific impact of a nine-inch shell is like?" He looked at the faces of his audience. Only Bodine, whose expression had remained whismical throughout Gibb's recital, looked like he might. The colonel went back to his story.

"All right—there we are! The train has stopped—only this time—*twenty miles* from Sian. Dawn is bustin' out, the air is full of exhaust fumes, the lorries vibratin' with power, beggin' to come unstuck, *rummmm! Rummmm!* The troops hunch in the back, each man-jack clutchin' his big Thompson—and each ready—positively quiverin' to pull the old triggo, let loose a stream of bullets into the other chaps, *anybody!* But first—first the bombardment!

"The gun will be in a converted gondola on a Vavasseur mount, the barrel projectin' out like a bloody smokestack laid on its side, and the whole thing painted in the sinister jig and jag of camouflage. Now it begins to elevate, slowly inchin' up—our faux baron, behind the sight—eye squintin' down the mil scale, doing his geometry and the mysterious mumbo jumbo gunners use to find their aiming point. This one is twenty miles away and that smokestack of a barrel is inclined up at almost a forty-five-degree angle now, visible for miles around, like some obscene gesture. The baron makes minute adjust-

86

ments, twirlin' this, screwin' down that, an evil warlock, stirrin' the brew, droppin' in the last nasty potions, then he's ready! He gives the signal! We clamp our hands over our ears and it goes off! *KA-BLOODY BLEWIEE!!!* Liftin' the whole damn train several inches off the ground. *The whole bloody train! Engine and all!* The sound is like bein' inside a vacuum pump and havin' the air suddenly sucked out. Nobody will hear for hours.

"At the other end of the line, *twenty miles away*, they hear a rumble. Storm clouds? Thunder? And it's true enough, the thing has been known to conjur up rain. Then here it comes, followin' the baron's trajectory like a tiger leapin' on a lead—a shell the size of a rubbish can filled with high explosives whooshin' in! Next an imperceptible wail, *Waaaaaaaaaaaaaaa!* A cleavin' of the air that builds up to a rushin' sound like the approach of a freight train! Some poor devil may even see the final arc of the shell, a brief brilliant flash as it descends . . . then in the next instant a searin' light brighter than a star! An earth-movin' tremor, *WHOOMPA-RHOOMMMPHH-KA-BLABLOOOMMM!!* Billows of choking dust and smoke, then the real sound of the explosion, a hollow pop that will break every eardrum in a quarter of a mile and a wave of concussion that will flatten everythin' the shell hasn't already bloody pulverized!"

He stopped and they all looked at him, trying to concentrate on the good eye. After a beat he went on, voice softer. "But that won't be the worst of it. No, the real terror will begin after that first shell has hit. . . ."

There was another pause, and Adrian finally had to ask, "Why is that?"

"Because they will be waitin' for the second one."

Bodine scraped his chair back. "Colonel, you are some yap dazzler."

Later that same evening a small closed van made its way through the tangle of streets north of Soochow Creek into the Hongkew District of "Little Tokyo." The shopkeepers here were all Japanese, and it was common to see kimonos and hear the clack of *geta* on the pavement.

The Chinese driver of the van and his helper had been chosen for strength and discretion. Both were members of a powerful Triad that prided itself on purveying to the most perverse taste. This trip was one the driver made weekly and was thoroughly familiar with. As the van turned up a narrow cobblestone lane and around mungo pines to the sweep of a private drive, the cargo in the back shifted slightly.

Sitting on a red litter in the dark interior, it might have been mistaken for a painted figure in shocking costume. Then, as a knife edge of light from the door seam cut across the face, the eyes blinked and the scarlet mouth was moistened by the tip of a pink tongue, preparing . . .

TWELVE

WHILE CAPTAIN SATO waited, he went over business on hand, ticking off what he now knew. It was developing into a conspiracy more far-reaching than he had first imagined. It was surely the biggest thing that had come his way in the service—a career windfall. Before the report was sent in he had to be careful to get it right; as it was, it would open old wounds in the Department of the Army.

Sato's contact in the Hong Kong-Shanghai Bank had come up with a shocking piece of news. When the Sun Account vault was opened, something else was found stored away: *two cases containing* thirty *highly secret Japanese mobilization and war plans.* The man had personally been present and had seen the American, Reed, examining the contents. There was now no doubt in Sato's mind that Reed was an American agent. At the moment those secret books were still in the bank vault, but how long would they stay there? His government must act.

First he must have corroborating evidence. To that end Sergeant Masaki was to get into Reed's Palace Hotel room and search it thoroughly. As for himself, he would search the dancer's room later tonight. He still could not believe she was not connected to the plot.

Was that them? His head turned sharply, responding to a sound from outside. He went to the window, inched open the shoji screen. The narrow cobblestone lane appeared empty.

He pushed back the kimono sleeve and looked at his watch. It was nearly the hour, and they usually brought her early. Where was she? Had something happened? He bit his lip and paced back across the room. It was the exact size of eight interlocking tatamis, furnished in the most austere *Daisenin* style (with, however, a stocked bar and running water). He maintained this hidden *pied-à-terre* on the far side of the Hongkew District, "Little Tokyo," a heavily populated Japanese enclave that had even elected their own "major" (in a preview of things to come). He felt anonymous here, well away from his bachelor rooms near the Japanese Consulate on Whangpoo Road.

Trying to reconstruct the Sun Account, Sato remembered a friend of his father who had been in the foreign office during the 1900-1915 period. It had been an inspiration. He wrote him in Kyoto and received a disturbing reply. Sun Yat-sen had spent many years in exile in Japan, taking refuge there as early as the turn of the century. He had close friends among the ultra-nationalists and moved in radical circles. The Japanese encouraged this and sought to use him for their own purposes, but Dr. Sun in his endless manipulation of every possible source to serve China had turned the tables on them. It was unthinkable, but somehow he managed to get hold of the highly important Japanese documents—cases of secret and sensitive papers.

The loss had been hushed up at the time, and the indication was that a foreign power had never received them, and the hope was that they had been lost or destroyed. Incredibly, the government had done nothing about changing the plans! They were still operational! Yü obviously had received the authorization to sign for the account before Sun died, and must have known about the plans. The other curious connection was Homer Lea. Sato couldn't help wonder at his knowledge of Japan's intentions in his book *The Valor of Ignorance*. Had he had access to the plans when he wrote it? Adding it up, Sato was more than ever convinced that Reed was an agent of the American government, probably an army officer, and that his connection with Yü and Bodine had to do in some way with high-level U.S. military espionage.

There was the suggestion of a sound at the door, perhaps the passing of a fingernail across the wood—he was right! Somebody had been in the lane! As usual they moved silently, as per instruction. The door was unlocked, and he stepped quickly into the tiny kitchen area, his back to the entrance, so that when they came in, each was hidden from the other. There was the whisper of silk as they carried her in, then the fragrance of an erotic scent.

As he waited for them to position her, he shook with excitement, so stiff against the silk of his kimono he had to shut his eyes, call on his Zen training and concentrate—will himself—to hold back. Then, the click of the latch as the carriers stepped outside to wait. Using breath control, he managed to calm down enough to walk to the sleeping room. His movements were like those of a mechanical man, or as he believed, the rigid stride of a samurai. He took a deep breath and slid back the door.

The layers of *futons* were squared exactly in the room, rising in its center like a plump platform. Posed on this traditional Japanese bed was a traditional Chinese "bride" in the position of a fallen leaf. She was a limp, acquiescent shape, a flow of a figure that might have been poured liquid on that pouf of quilts. Her head lay against her slender right shoulder, arms forming a graceful bow that extended down, seemingly disconnected to the tapered fingers completing the curve. The whole effect was as though her backbone had been severed, releasing all extremities from further service. It was a pose of total subjugation, acceptance to whatever fate offered. Compliance was the aphrodisiac.

She was dressed only in a bride's headdress of red to ward off the devil, its full veil falling to her shoulders, obscuring the face. Below this her nude body had been whitened and creamed until it appeared luminous, punctuated by rouged nipples and tiny crimson slippers. As Captain Sato, stiff-legged, tumescent, strutted toward her, one thing compelled him, one sexual drive he had been unable to satisfy any place else. He kept his eyes straight forward until the last possible second, then suddenly dropped to his knees, kneeling at her feet. Finally he looked down.

Foot binding had been part of the Chinese culture since the eighth century. The rendering of young girls immobile by deliberately maiming them was a kind of sexual satisfaction that took a special civilization to devise. It was begun very young by pulling the heel and toes together, until the toes were turned under. Bones that resisted were broken with the blow of a wooden mallet. The pain was constant and continued for years until the feet went numb. This was endured because a girl's desirability was determined more by the size of her feet than by the beauty of her face. Matchmakers asked, "How small are her feet?" Not "Is she beautiful?" This developed a teetering, swaying walk that was regarded as a mark of sexual appeal. In extreme cases like this one, the recipient was unable to walk at all and had to be carried. The perverse idea was that this object had been made helpless for *you*. She could not move, stayed where you put her and would *serve you in any way you wished*.

Sato began his ritual by removing the crimson "night slippers." These feet were the ideal: chubby, soft, elegant—and *three inches long*. Two fingers could be inserted in the cleft between the front of the foot and her heel. This was the focal point of his desire. He would not touch another portion of her body. As he caressed her dwarfed feet, beginning with the ankle and moving to the heel, arch, and finally the turned-under toes, his hands explored tarsal, metatarsal, phanges, until his excitement reached a crescendo. Pulling the sash on his kimino, he let it drop and placed himself between the curved arch of each foot. Seconds later he exploded in climax.

This occurred twice more in identical episodes until, drained, he retreated into his minute bathroom. In a precisely timed manuever the two carriers silently entered and, covering the lady with a cape and hood, lifted her from the *futons*. Carrying her out, they went down private stairs to the back of the building. In the old days she would have been borne away in a red lacquered sedan chair, but given the captain's need for anonymity, there was no question of that. So she was bundled into the back of a small, closed van parked under the pines and driven off. As the van turned at the end of the lane, the side panel caught the light and faded Chinese characters announcing "Laughing Lotus Laxatives" could be read.

Adrian's romance with Lola had gone badly off the track. He could trace it to the night on Yü's junk. When they dropped her off the next day on their way to the bank, she pecked the Marshal on the cheek, squeezed Adrian's leg, and hopped jauntily out, dragging Ramon. She had apparently recovered from the overkill of brandy. But when Adrian rolled down the window and called after her, "Will I see you tonight at Frisky's?" she replied, "If you buy a ticket."

That had set the tone. When he went around to see her, she'd been just as breezy as ever, but put him off: she was too tired to go out, Ramon was cranky, and so on. Adrian got mad and swore to himself he wasn't coming back. After all, he'd been interested only in going to bed with her, and if that was going to be a problem, forget it.

He couldn't. There had been something so bizarre, so sensual about her gliding across the stage with that damn ape, face pressed against its hairy head, that both repelled and attracted him. From the minute he had seen the poster outside of Frisky's, he had been caught up in their drama.

The truth was, Adrian had never known anyone quite like Lola. It would have been impossible in San Francisco or Los Angeles, given his friends—his prejudice—even to be seen in public with her. She represented the kind of women and life that was not accepted socially by the people he knew. He could not imagine, for instance, taking her into the Mark Hopkins. That brassy-dyed hair, those hints of dresses, the way her body moved would have given it away. Everyone would have known exactly why he was with her. It was 1931 and times had changed—but she was not a girl you took home to Mother—or for that matter to the maître d' at the Biltmore. He believed he was tolerant, and he had had his share of easy ladies on the polo circuit, but again they had all been in his narrow circle of society. He couldn't imagine any of them using her language. He had never heard the word "fuck" used by a woman other than a whore. It amused him but also would be embarrassing

91

in public. It had never occurred to him to think of her as anything but a sexual object. Now he did.

First, he missed her good humor; outside of the brief tiff at Yü's he'd never seen her moody or mean. She was funny—a rare quality among the girls he knew—and she was honest. She hadn't played games. When he thought about it, she had never asked him for a single material thing. What bothered him was the anxiety he sensed beneath her easy manner. He had never poked at this, drawn her out, afraid she would suddenly dump all her problems in his lap and he would be responsible for her. Now as he got along without her, he had the constant feeling of emptiness, that he'd missed a meal. *Was this love?*

Knowing her schedule, he showed up at the boardinghouse in the late afternoon before she went to Frisky's. When she opened the door a crack, he smiled, trying to be casual. "Hi, Lola."

"Hey, Ramon! Guess what? Frank Buck is here!" She laughed, closing the door. "Wait a minute." When she opened it and let him in, Ramon was chained to a waste pipe by his alcove. He swayed back and forth, hooting, upset at Adrian's arrival.

"I always did have a way with animals," Adrian said.

"He's cranky today, getting old, I guess." She was in a worn, thin kimono with fuzzy slippers on her tiny feet. The ironing board was set up, and she went back to it. "Long time no see—Hey! How about that? My Chinese is getting better."

He sat uneasily on the bed, laughing with her. "Yes, well . . . that business deal I told you about suddenly dropped in my lap, and it's been hectic trying to put it together. I've been meaning to co—"

"Yeah, Charley told me you two were running a chow mein factory or something." She ironed with choppy strokes, head down.

"Charley?" He felt his stomach drop.

"Charley Min."

"Marshal Yü?"

"Charley."

He badly wanted to ask her where and when had Yü said that, but he held back. "Well—what are you doing?"

"Ironing, see?" She held up the iron. "Leave it to me to end up in a place where there's twelve zillion laundrymen and I iron." She wore no makeup and had piled her hair up, tying it with a bright purple string. He could see the red roots plainly.

"Are you letting your hair grow out?"

"What? No—it just needs a touch-up job.

"Why did you bleach it in the first place?"

"Oh, I don't know, trying to look modern, Harlow, that kind of thing."

"I like the color. I bet you were a terrific redhead."

She raised her eyes. "Irish is what I was. With these freckles and a carrot top, Ramon and I would have to start clog dancing." It was true, the freckles were very visible in this light. It was an Irish face—a very elegant one. It occurred to him for the first time that without the dyed hair and makeup, dressed differently, she might very well fit in. . . .

"Shit!" she said, jerking the iron up. "I damned near burned the fuckin' thing!"

Ah—but what could you do with that mouth? Or with what she thought or read—or rather didn't read. No. She could not be changed easily into what he wanted others to see. He'd have to take her as is. He noticed for the first time a large bouquet of yellow roses on the floor near the window. He hurried on. "Lola . . . I thought maybe I'd stop around after the show tonight and we'd go out to eat."

"To the noodle palace?"

"Well, I . . ."

"Thanks, cowboy, but I think I'll pass."

"But why?"

"Why not?"

Adrian jumped up, suddenly angry. "Damnit, Lola—I miss you!"

"What you miss is nooky."

Adrian was shocked, knocked back. "That is a lousy thing to say! It's—"

"True. Right?" She laughed. "Come on, what else do you miss? Name one thing."

"Why . . . well, you're funny. . . ."

This did not go down well. "Funny? *I'm funny?* Fanny Brice is funny. Benny Rubin is funny. Tell me I'm leggy, tell me I've got tits like snow cones, tell me I'm a jazz baby, but don't tell me I'm funny."

He moved close to her, resting his hand on the ironing board. She ironed toward it. He picked his hand up and put it around her waist, feeling a trigger of electricity. "I *like* being with you, Lola, I look forward to it—there was never a time I didn't feel glad, just because I was going to see you."

"Bushwa."

"Are you telling me the time we spent together wasn't great? Are you saying you don't want it to happen again?"

She stopped ironing and looked at him. "You're beginning to sound Irish—you've got the bullshit for it."

He threw his arms up. "Damn! You're a hard woman! Come on, admit it! We go together."

"No, we don't. The only thing we've got in common is nothing in common. Look, cowboy, I like you, you're okay, even with the high heels and funny hat, but where's it going to get me, besides to the noodle palace and back home to my own bed? I have to tell you I'm bored with that. . . ." She held the iron up. "No! Let me finish—I've been in this Paris on the Whangpoo for three months now—you've been coming around—what? One? And I haven't been out once, really out for a big evening. Not to a swell café or nightclub—the only dancing I've done is with Ramon. This is not what a young girl dreams of."

"And whose fault is that? Tell me! I'll take you out this minute—tonight! I'll get a reservation at the Astor, we'll have a midnight champagne supper, and we'll dance till dawn." He lifted her chin up from the ironing. "But—we have to leave Ramon home—apes are not welcome tangoing among the swells."

"I can't do that . . ."

"You want to go swanking around? You're going to have to park your monkey, lady." He knew he had her.

"Well . . ."

"Tell you what, I'll wear my white dinner jacket."

"You've got a white dinner jacket?"

"I'm rich, aren't I?" he said, smiling.

She smiled back. "You finally said something romantic."

After he left, she sat in the alcove, back to the wall, drinking a beer with Ramon.

"Well, I finally did it, I played him like a poor fish—now all I have to do is reel him in." She had once told herself she would never stoop to using sex as bait to get a man. Oh, well, she sighed. By holding out a couple of weeks she had goosed their romance along. If she could just keep her legs together a couple more—who knew? Things were looking up. There was even another possibility. It wasn't one she wanted to dwell on, one she believed she would not need, but if she did, she would.

At ten-thirty Captain Sato saw them come out and get in a cab. It was the first time he had seen Lola, and he was startled by her appearance. The white skin and vivid makeup was not unlike that of his Chinese "bride." When she bent over to get in the cab, he very clearly saw the full shape of her breasts. He had always been shocked by Western women's flaunting of nudity on the street. He guessed this one to be a whore.

Crossing over, he went through an empty hallway and straight up the stairs. He wore a double-breasted linen suit with a Panama hat cocked at a rakish angle and made no attempt at concealment. He felt it was beneath the dignity of a samurai to skulk around even as a spy.

He had taken the precaution of buying a passkey from the night man and now opened the only door on the top floor. It led to a large, messy room. The flags of women's clothes flew from poles stretched across the beams, and under them an ironing board held more silky squares of folded underclothes. At another angle of the room a shaky card table was laid out with a partially worked jigsaw puzzle. Sato looked at it: the Grand Canal in Venice.

A small scarred desk in front of the window seemed to offer possibilities, and he carefully went through it. There were dozens of crossword puzzle books carefully filled out in pen. It occurred to him they could be ciphers, and he tore off several pages and added them to his pocket. The other scraps of paper, scribbles of odd numbers, were unrewarding. Several were stuck together with some kind of candy, and when he opened a balky bottom drawer, he found a plate with the rigid remains of God knows what kind of food stuck to it. Disgusted, he stood up. Western women were filthy pigs. He knew from his tours. Wads of lipstick-smeared paper floating in toilets, hair combing at the dinner table, dirty necks and twisted stockings . . . the last one he'd pillowed with hadn't even bothered to get up and wash after they'd finished.

He stood in the center of the room and looked around. To his left was an unmade bed, under it several cases of Peking Five Star Beer. She was a drinker. Next to a curtained alcove at the back, an enormous trunk stood half closed beneath a bright, bare bulb. He approached and shoved it open. Inside, dresses hung on varnished hangers, and fabric-covered drawers filled the whole of the right section. He opened one. It was packed with tiny shoes that might have been made for a doll; patent leather, beaded, silk, alligator . . . fluffy pompoms, scuffies, bright slippers . . . soft leathers, ridiculous high heels. He reached down and picked up one of the pumps, a red satin one edged with brocade. He pushed his fingers inside, twisted them into the toe area, then put the shoe to his nose, inhaling deeply. As he did, there was a rustle of curtain behind him. Before he could turn, something sprang on his back and sank long, sharp teeth into the fleshy part of his shoulder above his collarbone. He began to scream for the first time in his adult life.

When they came back at dawn, both a little drunk and silly, they found the room a shambles. "Damn!" said Lola. "Oh, damn!" She had put Ramon on the chain, but it had a long lead, and he had managed to tear up everything in his reach. "I knew I shouldn't have left him alone!"

"I'll help you clean up," Adrian said, seeing his vision of a tumble in bed vanish.

"No, no, I've got to calm him down. You go on. It will be easier if you're not here."

He paused in the doorway. "I'm sorry, Lola, but we did have a marvelous time. . . ."

But she wasn't listening, backing Ramon toward the alcove, rubbing his neck. "It'll be all right now. Come on, baby. . . ."

As Adrian went down the stairs, he noticed blood, but he didn't think anything of it at the time.

95

THIRTEEN

WHEN ADRIAN $CAME$ into the "war" room of Sino-Cal on Monday, Bodine sat with his feet up on the map table, dragging on a bottle of Tiger Bone. He tilted the bottle toward Adrian. "We just got our marchin' orders, kid." Gibb sat holding a telescoping metal cup, chair angled back against the paneled wall. He was immaculately dressed as usual.

Adrian frowned. "What?"

Bodine tapped a sheath of papers. "Orders just came down from on high." He pointed the bottle toward the ceiling. "The Marshal reports his Tungpei agents in Nanking have been overwhelmed with Manchurian volunteers. Enlistments have been closed out at two thousand, which, he says, will give us a comfortable margin to select our crack force from."

"A crack is something one falls through," Gibb said.

"You were going to check that out?"

"Well, my man in Nanking—at the Standard Oil pontoon—says there has been movement north of them in the exile camps, but it's hard to say whose. No one had advertised himself as recruiting for a glorious quest to Sian. But they wouldn't—that's Chiang's country, and Yü would have to have his okay."

"Yü said he had Chiang in his pocket."

"What he meant was, old dear," Gibb said, "that Chiang had both hands in Yü's pocket."

"You got that right," Bodine said.

Adrian sat down. "What about the railway gun?"

"There's nothing laid on about it."

"Damn!" Adrian had been impressed by Gibb's very visual description of the big gun and seized on the idea. After the weeks of weapons talk and military nomenclature, Adrian, like most dilettantes, quickly grasped the surface jargon and began to feel there wasn't all that much to military science, after all—applied brutality. He felt that with the sheer power of a large bore threat—"You do what I want or else!"—the enemy would cave in without a fight.

"Didn't expect Yü would get on to the Generalissimo, Reed," Gibb said. "He's going to do it his way. That's what these fellows are about."

"Gibb's right," Bodine said. "Yü is not gonna take any advice from us round eyes—if we have a battle, it's going to be to keep *us* from knowing what *he's* doin.'"

Adrian picked up the orders and read: "'All Shanghai personnel and attached observers will leave at 0800 on the morning of the third . . .'" He looked up. "That's next Sunday!"

"You got it."

Adrian went on. "'. . . they will be assigned quarters and the *Melodious Bird Song* will sail, arriving in Nanking on the sixth. From there they will be transported to a staging ground up-country, where troops are already billeted. Training will begin on the tenth and continue for six weeks. . . .'"

They were leaving Sunday! Adrian had to admit he had enjoyed the process of putting forces in motion that would disrupt the politics and status quo. Military madness. The euphoria of the preplanning stage, talking of battles and heroics without the surcharge of death and casualties. "But," he said, "are we ready?"—the classic wail of the military virgin.

Both Bodine and Gibb enjoyed this, laughing. "Well, we damned better be. We gotta put our assholes where our mouths, are or vice versa," Bodine said.

"Being ready for combat is like being ready for the dentist."

"Exactly."

"If it's any consolation, bunkie, remember Chinese generals are famous for not movin' until ready. Yü wouldn't commit himself until he was sure he had the edge."

Adrian got up. "Why don't I go up to his suite and talk to him?"

"You won't find him."

Adrian paused. "Why?"

"He's downtown layin' on the party."

"Party?"

"Gala," Gibb said. "Damn decent, I thought."

"He's invited half of Shanghai."

"What?" Adrian kept saying. "What?"

After he had adjusted to the idea of the party, Adrian calmed down. It made him furious that Yü would conceive and implement this huge, visible party to be paid for, again, out of his father's funds. But he guessed that in terms of morale it might make friends. Yü certainly seemed to be the man about town—Shanghai—and knowing him to be very intelligent and what was more, canny, he chose to believe it made social sense.

That night (Monday) he stopped by Frisky's to ask Lola to go. He thought this was a positive gesture on his part, to invite her to a party of his peers. He believed he had come a long way from being uneasy that anyone he knew knew he knew her. He fidgeted backstage at Frisky's until she came off after the second show, then sprung it on her.

"Lola, Marshal Yü is throwing a formal party this Saturday night. . . ." She snapped the chain on Ramon, then sat down at the dressing table, stripped down the top of her dress, sponged the caked makeup from her marvelous springy breasts. This caused him real anxiety. "I thought you might like to go." That was simple, straight to the point.

"Thanks, but I'm going."

"Going?"

"Charley already asked me. Listen, cowboy, you wanna ask a date to the big prom, you better get up early."

Captain Sato's bachelor flat on Whangpoo Road was done up very much in the Western style; Mission furniture, fumed oak by Gustav Stickley, and bare floors. There were a lot of books unread on shelves, but Homer Lea's well-read one was on his nightstand. The library, the focal point of the rooms, was dominated by Japanese heroes. A large painting of Admiral Togo hung over the inglenook fireplace, flanked by a slightly smaller one of General Nogi. Below them, centered on the mantel, was an autographed photo of Sato's mentor, Colonel Hideki Tojo.

Sergeant Max Masaki faced these titans as he read his notes to the captain. Togo especially intimidated him. The piercing eyes seemed to watch him, the mouth turned down behind the snow-white, clipped beard. Admiral Count Togo, victor of Tsushima, destroyer of the Russian fleet, every Japanese schoolboy's hero, "the Togo Boys," preceptor of the Prince Imperial (now Emperor Hirohito), the only man (with the Emperor) to hold the Collar to the Grand Cordon of the Chrysanthemum, and as Chief of the Imperial Staff, the only man with the rank of Field Marshal (gensui). He had retired now to his house in Kajima-Machi; it was hard to imagine him "Grandfather" Togo, puttering in his flower garden with his grandchildren, but there he was, as evidenced in current newspaper photos—still extant after fifty years of glorious service!

It was easier to relate to Colonel Tojo. Max had seen him many times, in Tokyo and Hsinking, aggressive and all business as he advanced up the ladder in the Kwantung Army. His own boss, Captain Sato, sat at right angles to the fireplace on a hard bench in the inglenook. It wasn't actually a fireplace, really a tiled niche with a gas heater for the cold days of winter. Right now the temperature was in the nineties, and the only breath of air came from the river, through a window above the captain's head. Sato was in his kimono, the shape of a bandage showing on his right shoulder blade, his arm in a silk sling. He had actually volunteered the information that he'd been bitten by a large dog. Max didn't ask what kind.

Max had made entry into the Palace Hotel room of the American, Adrian Reed, as ordered. This had revealed no information, hidden or otherwise, that indicated he was a military person. Other inquiries confirmed that Reed was a well-known polo player, that his father, Hugh H. Reed, had died the previous year, that Adrian Reed worked at no established job. On his passport he was listed as a "horse breeder" and gave his reason for visiting China as "touring." As a horseman, Sato was interested in the polo background, but still would not be convinced Reed was not working as a spy, military or not.

Max went on, rattling off his report on the doings of Sino-Cal, Marshal Yü's front. Max had had no problem gathering the information. Several informants had been anxious to supply it for a fee. He had a list of all the observers' complete supply, disbursement, correspondence, train arrangements—even the uniform designs. The only gap was on troops recruited in Nanking. To get that, the Tungpei agents would have to be personally bribed.

Captain Sato listened to the lists without comment; his mind was elsewhere. The humilation and terror of the ape attack had left him shaken. He had known that the dancer had a trained animal—Max had told him about the act at Frisky's—but it had never occurred to him that it would be in the hotel room. He assumed it would be kept in a cage at the theater. What a mistake that was! When it had jumped on his back, the shock, the sheer terror had been a complete surprise. The bite was serious and the pain most severe. The doctor had told him the shoulder muscles had been badly damaged and that he could expect atrophy and some permanent stiffness after the wound healed. Staggering through those rooms with the horror of that thing locked on his back had panicked him, and there was real fear. Later, he had no idea why the ape had finally let go or even how he himself had gotten out of the room and onto the street. He was still running when he finally got control of himself.

He had run away! It was unthinkable in a samurai! It was cowardliness—there was only one way to wipe it out. He would have face that ape again and destroy it.

". . . October third."

Sato looked up at Max. "October third?"

"Yes, sir. That is the date Marshal Yü's junk will leave Shanghai with the mercenaries. It will arrive in Nanking on the sixth."

"All right. Get over to the consul and have this lot encoded for Hsinking. Include a message to General Honjo's office indicating that, if agreeable, we will take the train to Nanking on the fourth to intercept and continue surveillance. Ask for confirmation and contingency instructions."

"Yes, sir. Is that all?"

"You are sure this Reed Junior is going along with the military personnel on Yü's junk?"

"That is what I was told. The day after the party, Sunday morning, they will separately . . ."

"What party?"

"Marshal Yü has announced a party for Saturday night, the second. He has engaged the entire roof garden of the Wing On Store."

"Why didn't you tell me this before!"

"It is a social event, and . . ."

"Never mind! How many people are going to be there?"

"More than a hundred. It is said to be a dinner in honor of Marshal Yü as a great humanitarian."

"*Ha!* The man has a sense of humor at any rate." There was a pause. "I want you to get me an invitation."

If Sergeant Masaki was surprised, he held it in nicely. "Of course, sir."

It had been an instant, intuitive response from Sato. For weeks now Sato had followed the dossiers of the principals: Reed, Jr., Bodine, Yü, and the woman. Now he suddenly had to see them, up close; they had to emerge from the paper reports to the dimensions of real people. He wanted to evaluate their personalities, have a firm, visual picture of whom he was dealing with. He would observe them, discreetly of course, and why not? He was known as a man about town, a sportsman; they had no idea of his military connections.

He convinced himself it was a sound idea. Immediately he felt better, lifted out of his depression. He shook off the sling and stretched his arm, clenching his fist and lifting it toward the painting of Admiral Count Togo. The admiral's expression didn't change, but then it hadn't when faced with the Russian fleet at Tsushima Strait. He had ordered immediate attack, signaling, *"I answer for our success."* Captain Sato felt the same way.

FOURTEEN

SEVERAL BLOCKS WEST of the Bund, three large department stores lit the night with polychrome neon. In the evening diners gathered in leafy restaurants on the upper floors. The view was expansive, and these places were popular for weddings and parties.

At the Wing On Store roof garden, the Roy Fox Band, touring from London, mounted the latticed podium at nine and tuned up, trying out "Easy Come, Easy Go." Waiters and busboys serving tables watched the first dancers slip and slide to the insinuating rhythm; the evening began.

At ten-thirty Marshal Yü arrived with his retinue, Lola on his arm. Dressed in the starched armor of his immaculate set of tails, he led the way to a center table reserved for his party. Lola was seated on his left, Adrian on the right. The military observers and their ladies next, with Colonel Gibb at the bottom of the table. Bodine had not arrived yet.

After champagne had been served, the Marshal rose and offered a toast. "Exceptional work demands exceptional men. A bolting horse may become an exceptional animal. A man who is detested may accomplish great things.

"As with the insufferable man—it is simply a question of training. Search for brilliant and exceptional talents to be our generals and horses."

He sat down to a nice tinkle of silver against crystal. Colonel Gibb rose in the uniform of the Fourth Gurkhas. Like all Indian rigs, it was exotic, topped by a pillbox hat with a chin strap. His decorations ran to five rows beginning with the maroon of the Victoria Cross, a tone that nicely matched the exploded veins of his nose. He lifted his glass, both eyes tracking. "Gentleman and ladies, I give you Marshal Yü:

> "A man who will not flee will make his foes flee.
> Foot firm, and faith fast,
> He will stand till storm past.
> 'Tis to the virtues of such men, man owes
> His potion in the good that heaven bestows."

Glasses clicked. "Marshal Yü!"

When the salute died down, Lola leaned over to Yü. "Charley, what's all this military stuff? I thought you boys were in the oil business."

"Ah, forgive us, princess, men and boys love to play at being soldiers."

"The ones I know would rather play doctor." She smiled at Adrian, expecting to get a rise, but he was talking to the fat-ass wife of the German. Then the food arrived.

Dinner began with freshwater lobster, sea urchin, salted prawns in the shells; then squab in oyster sauce, steak globules, and nine friendly vegetables. With it were served half a dozen wines and a serious champagne. As they ate, guests arrived, and by eleven the room was filled with an ebullient, elegant mob.

Probably no place in the world had quite the exotic blend of expatriates as Shanghai that summer of 1931. The International Settlement, diplomatic corps, and the military were stirred together with Chinese connivers, retired warlords, and rascals of all flags. They made a concoction that would have gone down hard in even the most liberated capitals. In a city famous for its sinful excesses, those worldly sophisticates at the top of the volatile mix were certainly not going to carp about anyone's style of life. Live and let live. If you could accept as your dinner partner the Eurasian result of a Russian-Czech, Uighur-Golok union, or a respected banker who kept a stable of chubby twelve-year-old boys, or if you could live in a city where the number of resident prostitutes was greater than the entire population of Toledo, Ohio, then you were on your way to understanding the social tone of Shanghai society.

The guests enjoying Marshal Yü's bounty were certainly not the elite; the big rich and people of leisure were summering at Tsingtao, the Cannes of the Far East. These were the second-level consular people, inveterate party-goers, the wild young crowd, and ubiquitous deposed Russian aristocrats.

They were a raffish bunch, adventurers, opportunists, people on the make, but nevertheless, or perhaps because of it, an attractive, exciting combination. Even the four-flushers and deadbeats were turned out in full dress, their ladies painted and primped, hair bobbed, dressed in slinky Paris copies run up by Chinese dressmakers on Yates Road. Together they spun around the dance floor to music punctuated by the popping of champagne corks.

The ballroom had been built in the style of a trellised garden house, consisting of framing arches and pillars in a crosshatching of lattice, called *trellage* by the decorator. Potted palms and hothouse plants swayed and climbed up the lattice, dripping down like an arbor, an occasional exotic petal drifting onto the heads of the celebrants. It was charming, and if few knew and even fewer cared that the food had to be carried up three flights of narrow back stairs by sweating waiters—well, that was to be expected.

One of the nicest features was the terrace outside overlooking the river. Live boxwood had been trimmed into topiary shapes and bisected by gravel walks that covered several acres of rooftop. Here, at a table in a far corner between the hedges, Ramon had been placed out of harm's way. Lola had put him on a short chain and fed him. She would check on him every half hour or so. He was quiet now, fascinated by the movement of the ferries gliding across to Whangpoo Road. The lights of the city shimmered in the placid river, and the sharp bark of the ferry horns carried over the traffic noise five stories below.

Lola was enjoying herself. This was her idea of a good time: everybody dressed to the teeth, sipping bubbly and acting silly. She was wearing a paillette gown that fit like the paper on the wall. It was one she didn't wear onstage, because Ramon had once snuffed one of the beads up his nose, dancing. The only fly in the ointment was a Frenchy across from her who kept talking about animals. She was the friend or something of the big guy in the sailor suit who didn't say two words.

"I'ave thees beeg doggy, ey wolfhound, but he is naughty, too, he geets on my bed an' does thees . . ." She made a jerking motion with her hand, laughing. "I tell Eed, you better watch out zee doggy has a betear one." She had a short manish haircut, and as she leaned over, the dress gaped, showing one small tit. Lola wondered if she was a dyke.

"I luv eeps. Have you eever seen a Mandreel? No? Ees balls are blue and za peckare red! True! And all za time doeeg thees!" Another hand gesture. Lola tried to catch Adrian's eye.

"Do you know za Goreeia? No? I am told he has thees leetle tinee one, thees beeg." She held up her little finger.

Lola hated this. It was not the first time someone, women mostly, had gone on about animals and sex, trying to find out about Ramon. It disgusted her. She finally caught Adrian's eye. He smiled. "Dance card filled up?"

They stepped to the dance floor as Roy Fox segued into "How Could We Be Wrong?" "Oh, I love this!" she said, following Adrian and bending in his direction. He wasn't a very good dancer, just a bit off the beat, but his body was superb and he held her firmly, easily breaking a path through the mob. He leaned down suddenly and kissed her on the nose.

"Hey, you're going to expose a freckle."

"You look terrific—you're letting your hair grow out."

"Not really." But she was.

"Lola, all I've done is think about us . . . you. . . . I made a decision—"

"You're going to order from column one instead of column two the next time we go to the noodle palace."

"I'm serious! There's something special I've got to say to you!" Her heart jumped. "Let's go out on the terrace." As they did, the band went into a reprise of "Isn't It Heavenly." *Boy!* she thought. *Boy!*

He pushed open the double doors, and they stepped out onto the terrace. The night was superheated with the fragrance of flowers and the river.

"Lola, I . . ."

"Wait a minute, cowboy," she said, breaking away. "I want to check on Ramon." Adrian knew better than to say anything, and he waited patiently until she came back. While he did, he got his speech ready. He was determined to get in bed with her tonight.

"He's okay—watching the boats."

Adrian took her into his arms and pulled her to him in a long kiss, hands cupping her behind. She gently broke off and stepped back, adjusting her dress. "Hoooeee! Easy, cowboy, you're going to unstring my beads!"

"I want you, Lola."

"I guess I can believe that."

He took her in his arms again, this time tenderly. "I mean it's been hell without you!"

"Poor boy, still suffering from lackanooky."

Adrian winced. "Damn it! It's more than that—listen! I want to talk to you, seriously. I want to ask you something important."

Suddenly Lola knew exactly what was coming next. He was going to ask her to marry him! It had worked! Just like they said: if you want something bad enough from a man, all you have to do is button up your drawers and he'll come around. Maybe she should feel cheap about pulling an old one like that, but what the hey—you had to go after what you wanted in this old world.

"Lola, are you listening?"

"Yes . . ."

"I told you I might have to go on a field trip with the oil company—remember?" She didn't. "Well, it's come up. I'm not sure how long I'll be gone—only a few weeks, I hope, maybe a month. This is sudden, I know, but we're leaving Monday . . ."

104

Five minutes ago if anybody had told her she would be getting married, she would have given them the horse laugh. She'd been married once when she was sixteen—or thought she was—to a good-looking guy who sold Pan Time. They had honeymooned at the Somerset Hotel in New York City. It adjoined the entrance to the Palace Theater—about as close as she ever got to the place. It turned out the rat had a wife and kids. . . . What had he just said?

"Leaving?"

"Sunday, tomorrow. I know it's unexpected, but I didn't want you to worry."

"What would I worry about?"

"Well, it's a little more than just a routine job." He was enjoying this, experiencing the heady sensation of bidding farewell to a ladylove as he went secretly off to war. "That's why—before I go I wanted to ask you . . ."

"Yes?" She started to smile.

"I want you to be waiting for me when I come back. I want you to be my girl."

When he didn't go on, she said, "Be your . . . what?"

He blundered ahead. "My girl . . ." He started to pull her in closer, but she jerked out of his grip.

"That's really it then? I'm going to be your 'girl'—like in college or something. Do I get a fucking frat pin? Are you going to carve our names on a fucking tree?"

"Lola, I want us to . . . to get to know each other. What I want is . . ."

"I *know* what you want, bud, you want a sure piece of tail when you come back!"

"No! I . . ."

She spun around, slapping her beaded thigh. "Boy! Am I dumb! Look at the dummy! You want to know how damn dumb I am? I'm so damned dumb I thought you were asking me to marry you!"

Adrian's mouth dropped open. "What . . ."

"Yeah, that's right! Miss Dummy! Ha! Ha! Ha! And let me tell you it had me worried! Yeah, that's right, ace, I mean you're all right, you've got a nice hairline and you keep your fingernails clean, but just between you and me, you're about number nine on a list of ten great lays. Me wait around for you? Cowboy, I don't wait around for nobody!" She turned and walked toward the French doors. "Good-bye and goodie!"

Adrian was stunned. "Lola! What . . . was that all about?"

"You figure it out, Einstein."

When she came inside, she ran into Bodine. He had arrived late and slightly drunk. He was wearing his dress set of liberty blues and looked spectacular: blue jacket, white pants with the wide red stripe, brass buttons, and a

105

chest full of decorations. He had seen Lola on Yü's junk, but they hadn't spoken. "The monkey lady, I believe?" He was smiling.

"What are you," Lola snapped, "the bellboy?"

Bodine laughed. "Wanna dance?" A tango had struck up.

"Don't tell me you can dance too?"

"Listen, has Garbo got big feet?" She recognized one of her own. They stepped to the floor as Adrian came in from outside. Bodine winked at him over her shoulder.

Lola knew from the instant they touched that he was a superb dancer. They stepped out in rapid steps, she walking ahead, spinning, only fingers touching, then the pause, the dip, and they swirled off again, his feet stepping intricately between hers. Other dancers stopped, moved back, and opened a circle in the center of the floor. An amber spotlight was redirected, found them and held, the pailletted gown sending off flashes of light, celebrating every nuance of her body.

This is it, she thought, *there is nothing better. To be held, moved by someone who anticipates every move, to have him invent and you follow, then reverse. To move with total confidence, know you're very good, be admired. The thrill of connecting, reconnecting, interlocked, perfectly matched.*

She had forgotten how much she loved it, how it was to be caught up in familiar, sensual music, swept away by insistent beat, wanting it to go on . . . and on, never stop; wanting to freeze time, now! Have everyone else fade away. To be alone and dance together.

Bodine was behind her now, and she pressed back against him, shoulders up, arms held straight down, fingers entwined, moving slowly. Their eyes were lowered, and the spotlight cast heavy, mysterious shadows. As the compulsive rhythm accelerated, she turned, spun, and they walked side by side, feet arched at each step, arms extended, cheek to cheek. At the center of the floor she turned again and locked her arms around his neck as the tempo peaked in a crash of cymbals and abruptly ended. Bodine dipped and bent her to the floor, arm supporting her waist. She hung suspended, the line of her back forming a half circle, neck thrown back, eyes closed, curls touching the floor. In that second the spot blinked out.

There was a moment's silence, then applause from the other dancers. Adrian sat at the table watching and felt miserable. What had happened? He had never, never, said a word about marriage! Not a hint! My God, he had finally talked himself around to being seen with her, introducing her to his friends! He'd thought she would be delighted, grateful! He had to admit he did not understand women. If this was not original, for the first time it seemed at least profound.

"Lovely thing," Colonel Gibb said. He sat directly across from Adrian in his Indian uniform, like some absurd figure out of Kipling. One eye below the pillbox hat was at half mast, the other, the false one, was alert.

Adrian knew the colonel had been living in the Sino-Cal offices, sleeping on the map table, but said nothing about it. He had offered him an advance, but had been politely turned down. According to contract, the military observers would not begin pay until they reported for duty onboard the junk Monday.

The heavy German lady leaned over. Her husband had vanished. "Vat do you think ouf our new chancellor, Adoff Hitlar?"

"Who?" Adrian said.

"Fellow's a damn char!" Gibb said.

"Jar?" she said. "Jar?" Puzzled.

"Enlisted, for God's sake. The man's an enlisted, a corporal—I mean next it will be a pearly, won't it?"

"He vas a hero in der var!" She was getting heated.

"The Iron Cross, y'mean? My dear old thing, they gave those out for rollin' bandages."

She snorted and got up. "The fellow looks like Charlie Chaplin to me, can't see how anyone would take him seriously." But she was gone. "Hate a damn German, got my gob full of them in '16."

To Adrian, Gibb was a repository of every known prejudice. He also began to believe the colorful slang and sound effects were a private joke, a leg pull.

"Tell me, Colonel," Adrian said. "I can't place your accent. What part of Britian are you from?"

"Haven't lived there since I was a tad, Reedo, can't really remember—lots of half timbering as I recall, thatched roofs, of course, and lanes, marvelous bloody lanes. Accents?" He paused. "None of us could ever understand the other, y' know, grunts got to be refined, and nods—nods began to take on accents—nothin' quite as meaningful as a sincere nod. I nodded my way right into bed with many a roadside flower . . . ."

Adrian realized he would get nowhere. "I'll bet."

"We were speaking of the Miss Ryan—lovely, yes. Reminds me very much of a Bengal lady I had the acquaintance of in the Malay States. . . ." As he talked, he seemed frozen, rigid, like a ventriloquist's dummy, only his mouth worked. A full tumbler of whiskey sat in front of him. "Big as a minute she was, a regular Queen Mab, a fairy princess—from the best family, of course, never cared for those bloody dark lascars m'self, black tongues put me off— no, she was white as you and I." He picked up the glass and, to Adrian's astonishment, drained it, setting it down again in a smooth motion. "Had the damnedest trick she'd get up to. Used to climb aboard the old nob and spin on it like a bloody propeller! Whizzo! I mean, on my word, sittin' or standin' she could whorl on it like a spinner! Damned clever little thing . . . last time I stopped around they told me she had been eaten by a croc . . . can't been much of a meal for the fellow. . . ."

Adrian pushed back his chair and got up. The colonel may have been the shining example, but everybody else at the table was feeling no pain. They had arrived at the stage of good cheer, revealing their innermost secrets and ambitions, pledging brave companionship in the battles to follow. They were all drunk. All but Marshal Yü, who smiled sweetly and raised his glass, and Adrian, who felt totally sober. Working his way toward the bar at the back of the room, he planned to remedy that at once.

Captain Sato watched him. He sat at the far end of the bar under the swag of a palm frond. Cigarette clamped in his teeth, eyes squinted as the smoke curled up, he wore his most arrogant expression. He was convinced he could hold his liquor and had been knocking it back all evening. The more he drank the more surly he became. They were exactly as expected: a room full of useless, empty-headed Anglo-Saxon trash. What was needed was a great cleansing war that would forever clear these silly cavorting asses out of the Orient. Would they have allowed such Japanese goings-on in an American restaurant or a British one? Hardly. How dare they presume to export their corruption and filthy greed, spreading disease and debilitating civilizations that had been in full flower when these idiots painted themselves red and swung from the trees!

The dancer, Lola, had spun by with that Marine only a few yards away. She had the delicate childlike body of a *kokeshi* doll and a bold face that signaled adult pleasures. Baby feet perched on the stilts of high heels, a child playing the woman. A thought struck him: had she brought that ape with her?

He shifted as the American Reed moved down the bar to an empty stool near his. It was an excellent chance to examine him. Sato's first impression was that he'd seen him before, then he realized that his features, the sharp hairline and profile, were the ones that looked out from Western magazines—men in shirts and high collars, or standing in front of huge motorcars in golf clothes. He was what they believed "ideal"—tall, fair, and broad-shouldered. This one no doubt had played football at an expensive school—that would account for the scar across his nose and his size. After graduation he took up polo and now with inherited wealth did nothing. This season, bored and rich, he was playing war.

"Have we met?"

Sato realized with a shock that Reed was speaking to him. He had been staring. He bowed. "Please forgive my presumption, sir, I thought so, but it was my mistake." Sato slid off the stool and, bowing again, moved away.

Adrian watched him go, thinking he was tall for a Japanese and good-looking, with long hair, nice manners, and a way of wearing clothes that suggested money and breeding. He turned back and ordered another stinger.

Sato was shaken at having been caught, but reassured himself that Reed would never remember him. He had heard many times that foreigners believed all Orientals looked alike. Straightening, he opened the terrace doors and went looking for the ape.

Lola and Bodine, breathless and flushed, came off the dance floor. "You're very good, Red."

"Thanks." He was pleased. "That's somethin' comin' from a professional."

"I mean it, where did you learn?"

"Oh, I spent my youth in dance halls tryin' to make it up to the dollies. It helped if you could dance."

"On-the-job training."

"I still go over to the Frisco a couple times a week. You know that place?"

"Frisco?"

"Yeah, it's a big dime-a-dance hall advertisin' 'Girls of All Nationalities.'"

"What nationality do you like?"

"You name it—every color includin' green."

"I'll bet." She looked toward the table. "We'd better get back."

"C'mon, I've seen enough of those birds." He steered her toward a small table near the doors to the terrace. "Let's flop here and cool off. I want to talk to somebody pretty."

"Yeah, well, do me a favor, don't ask me to marry you."

"It'll be tough."

"Work on it." Lola looked toward the main table. She couldn't see Adrian and didn't care if she ever did.

A waiter passed by and Bodine whisked a bottle of champagne and glasses off his tray. "I'd just as soon have serious booze, but this will hafta do." He poured their glasses and held his up. "Here's to the sweetest pair of cakes I seen in a long hitch."

"You're real bashful, aren't you?"

"No, I'm a Marine."

"Is that what it is?"

"That's what it was. I'm out now. Lookin' for the main chance, as they say."

"Like what?"

"You want to know what I'd really like—my dream?"

"I'm not sure."

"It's clean, I'd like to have one of those big dance halls like the Frisco— girls of all nations—me walkin' around the place in a box-back suit with a dollar cigar, givin' the nod to my favorites, protectin' those little darlin's, tryin' out new steps with a different one every night . . ."

"Just a rooster in a hen yard."

"You got it."

It was easy talking to a guy like Bodine, somebody you didn't have to watch your p's and q's with. She'd grown up with people like him. Looking at his face, she saw her father, Billy. Pale lashes and too-bright eyes. Boozers. She was willing to bet he was like her old man, drinking day in and day out, without a sign. No staggering or slurring, able to carry on, make decisions, full of jokes—then *BLAM!* Explode into violence, punch you up or worse, be sorry the next day—a dangerous drunk.

"Who's got you down—the polo player?"

She realized she'd been drifting off. "Nah, it's my fault. I always go for the pretty boys. Show me a hairline and I'll roll over."

"He's an okay kid, he's wising up."

"Kid, that's what he is all right—a kid at what? Twenty-five weighing in at one-eighty?"

"Well, he needs some of those smooth edges roughed up."

"Yeah, with a hammer."

Ramon had been dozing and woke to see a dark figure moving toward him down the path between trimmed boxwood. Backlit by the tall glass doors of the garden room, the bright glare behind it sent off shafts of disturbing light. It confused him. His nose twitched, but he depended on his eyes for visual contact. He rubbed them, twisting his head this way and that. Then the light was blocked briefly and he saw it was female. But it wasn't *his* female.

The French lady, wearing the briefest wisp of lavender silk and trailing a scarf, undulated along the path. Very drunk, she compensated nicely, shifting her weight just before each stumble. As she went she called softly, "Ramon! . . . Ramon! . . ." Reaching his chair, she stopped and, canting her leg seductively, spoke in French. *"Ah, Monsieur Ramon, mon charmant bête . . ."*

Ramon began shifting nervously, his eyes dilating. He made half-complete facial expressions—threat signals and instinctive behavior buried under the years of training and human imprinting. The lady lowered herself slowly and knelt at his feet. Then, putting elbows on his knees, she rested her chin on clasped hands and looked at him. Rhinestone bracelets on her wrists caught the light, and the effect was extraordinary. Her face had a feral look, and a lock of short bobbed hair, cut and parted like a boy's, hung over one eye.

"You're very beautiful," she said softly. *"Très magnétique d'aimant!"*

Chained and trapped, Ramon began rocking from side to side. The strap of her gown had slid off one shoulder, and the light picked up the gleam of one small alabaster breast.

"Ahhh, Monsieur Ramon, do not be afraid. I come to you as another animal . . . can you give me absolution with your wild spirit? I feel such . . .

impudique ennuyer . . . monotonie . . . can we touch across the gulf of human and animal? Could we, I wonder, couple? Ahhh, what would that be like? To have those dark pilose limbs locked around me? To be entered by another species, to push through, to break the wall between woman and beast." She slid her dress up and pressed the cross of her body against his leg. He jerked back in a spasm. Then she moved her hand up his thigh and, lifting her face toward his, scarlet lips parted, she put out a moist tongue.

Ramon had moved back as far as he could, straining on the chain. But she pursued him, and when their faces were inches apart, he drew his own lips back in a low, awful snarl, the fearsome canines as sharply defined daggers. He had only suffered her this long because she was female. Now the gleam of teeth against the red gums, white of eyes against the black muzzle formed a hideous, ferocious mask. The sound was an ominous signal preceding mayhem, a split second away from attack.

She jerked back with a little gasp, fell hard, got up, stumbled, and, lurching down the path, hiccupping in terror, made for the oasis of light. Her scarf lay where she had dropped it.

Captain Sato witnessed the whole perverse tableau. He stood behind the topiary shapes, hand resting on the hilt of an *Aikuchi* dagger tucked in his waistband. Should he attack the animal now? He might not get another chance. Nothing could be simpler than slipping up behind it, slitting its throat, and tossing the body over the parapet into the stream of traffic below.

FIFTEEN

"*THAT'S ABOUT IT,* Red. My life story's been a bunch of three-a-day vaudeville stints and layoffs, stuck in one-horse towns, being kidded along by guys like you. I never played the big time—the Palace or the Paladium. My folks did, but that was all over before I came along. I could tell you different, and on a good night I might." Somehow she had poured out all this to Bodine. She couldn't imagine why.

"C'mon, kid, you make it sound like it's all over—you're what, twenty-three or -four?"

"Twenty-six. It's not me—I'll make out—it's Ramon. I'm scared he's going to get sick on me or die. It was a terrible mistake to bring him on this tour—selfish."

"Look, I like animals too, but after all he *is* just an animal."

"No, no, he isn't. For damn near forty years he supported my folks, now me. I owe him." She laughed. "What's a girl and her monkey to do?"

Captain Sato debated on how he should attack the animal. He decided he had to face it, it was the only honorable thing to do. The memory of that thing on his back was very vivid, and it was with reluctance he slid the blade out of the black waxed scabbard and went forward.

Lola got up. "Speaking of Ramon, I'd better check on him."

"Sure, I'll go with you." Bodine pushed the door open for her, and they went outside. "Not any cooler, is it—"

"*Listen!*" There was a high-pitched scream just audible above the traffic sounds. "Ramon!" They ran toward the sound at the far end of the terrace. The rooftop was nearly empty, and Bodine sprinted ahead on the path, legs pumping, arms going, kicking up gravel. In the nightclub the band struck up the "Tiger Rag," and it was impossible to hear anything else. At a distance between hedges Bodine could see a man bending over something, his back blocking the view.

The minute the ape saw Sato it let out a piercing shriek, but Sato did as he'd decided he would: approached him face to face. The dagger seemed a small advantage over those terrible teeth. The animal was crouched in the chair, upper lip drawn back and puffy, jaw jutted forward, teeth exposed, swaying back and forth, snarling. It was unnerving, but Sato forced himself forward. Would it suddenly leap on him? He held the knife ahead, thumb on the flat edge of the blade. There was no guard on an *Aikuchi*, and he used the fencing position. If attacked, he would strike up under the top rib toward the heart. Was the configuration of ribs the same as in humans? He didn't know. The animal stayed where it was, and Sato changed grips, moving forward to cut its throat.

"*Hey, you!*"

He turned and saw a man in uniform running toward him. Police? He quickly pushed the dagger into the scabbard, tucking it under his vest, and stepped back. In the next second he recognized the Marine, Bodine. Before he had adjusted to this, he was rudely pushed backward.

"*Whatta you up to, jack?*"

Captain Sato did his best to remain calm. He must not expose his position. "Please excuse me, I was interested to see the animal."

"Yeah?" Bodine pushed him. "Lookin' for ancestors?"

"*Do not put your hands on me again, sir!*"

Bodine gave him a stiff-fingered jab. "*Like this?*"

Lola ran up, and Ramon immediately clutched her, making small chirping sounds. "Ramon! Are you all right?"

"Is your monkey okay, sugar?"

"I assure you, sir, the animal was not touched."

Bodine shoved him again. "Who asked you?"

"He seems all right, Red, just scared . . . who is that?"

"A Jappo, all teeth an' bows."

When Sato spoke, his voice shook with emotion. "If you mean to insult me, sir . . . then as a military man, meet me in a duel—time and place of your choice, but not in this public place!"

113

Bodine laughed. "A duel? What kind of dumb shit is that? A duel—Jee-zuss!"

Sato tried to maintain his dignity; holding his head up, he was almost the exact height of Bodine. "If you are a gentleman . . ."

"A gentleman? I ain't no fuckin' gentleman, you asshole! I'm a *Marine!*" Up to this point Bodine had been amused by the Japanese and the monkey; now triggered by "gentleman," his personality changed. He went over the line from drunken insults to violent intent.

Lola saw this. "C'mon, Red, it's okay. Ramon's probably just tired. Let's go in."

Bodine stretched his neck up, holding his face close to Sato's. "Oh, no . . . we got a real wiseacre here. The bird says he wants to fight a duel—he thinks he's a fuckin' gentleman . . ."

"C'mon, Red, I'll buy you a drink. . . ."

But Bodine wasn't listening to anyone now. Smiling, teeth showing, he spoke in a hoarse whisper, pressing his face even closer. "You know what I'm gonna do, gentleman Jappo? I'm gonna kick your yellow balls up around your fuckin' ears!"

Sato's hand shot to the hilt of the dagger. Before he could really grip it, Bodine's hand was on top of his. They stood face to face now. Pushing down, Bodine kept the knife in the scabbard, and despite Sato's efforts to draw it, he could not. Bodine, with his sloping, powerful shoulders and absurd muscular arms, had hustled easy money arm-wrestling in cabarets and bars all over the Far East; this was exactly the kind of contest he excelled at.

As Sato strained against him, he felt the stitches let go in his shoulder and the soak of blood against the inside of his shirt. Neck muscles standing out, he willed himself to lift the knife and cut the belly out of his detestable enemy. As he bent forward, braced, trying to push him off the mark, he was only inches away from Bodine's chest and could clearly see the Navy Cross, actually make out the tiny engraving of a caravel in the center circle, smell the brass polish, the body sweat, and that disgusting odor particular to meat-eaters. The pain was excruciating, a throb that ran down his shoulder and arm until he could no longer feel his hand, could not move Bodine. "Bastard! Bastard—" His voice broke, and he was near tears with frustration and rage.

Bodine suddenly released his hand and stepped back. "You wanna pull that? Okay, go ahead! That's right! Try it—go on! You wanna duel, I'll duel you American style! King of the mountain!" And he laughed the crazy laugh that had alarmed Adrian the first night they met. "The winner throws the loser over!"

Sato was backed against the low wall at the roof's edge. Five stories below the traffic streamed along, the sound of Klaxons and ricksha bells clearly heard. "You got the balls for that, monkey man?"

Sato flexed his hand, trying to get some feeling back. The shoulder and arm were numb now, with a deep pain that made him tremble.

Bodine quickly took off his white dress belt and wrapped it around his right fist, gripping it so the embossed brass buckle faced out over his knuckles. "Come on, gentleman Jappo! Come and get it! You think you're as good as me? Prove it!"

Sato knew he would have only one chance. The first blow must be decisive, and it would have to be one he had the remaining strength for, *shimo-tatewari*: bottom vertical split—bringing the blade up between the enemy's legs and slicing through the lower bowels. He got set and suddenly lunged forward with a shout, "Kiiii-yaaaaa!" His right foot slapped the gravel in approved samurai style, and he brought the knife up with everything he had.

His timing was badly off, and Bodine easily sidestepped and slammed his fist into Sato's left cheekbone. It was a shattering blow, and as the brass buckle came away, it left the embossed eagle design stamped on Sato's cheek. The knife clattered to the roof, and Sato's head jerked sideways, spraying saliva. He reeled back against the parapet, and for a minute it seemed he might go over, but he stayed upright, dazed and disoriented. Bodine stepped lightly between his feet and struck downward, being careful not to scratch the buckle on Sato's teeth; he smashed into the jaw below the left ear, unhinging it. This time Sato literally spun around, rolling along the edge of the parapet. But again he didn't go down; instead he stood, head sagging to his chest, eyes glazed as he tried to find his face with his good left hand.

"*Stop it! Stop it!*" Lola was horrified. She couldn't believe the guy had done anything to deserve this. My God! The awful thing was, she knew Bodine was showing off for her. His fighting was like his dancing, quick, precise, and showy. And he wasn't going to stop; she knew that too.

As Sato stood swaying, in shock, Bodine hit him again and again, but he still wouldn't go down. He took the blows dumbly but remained on his feet. This seemed to infuriate Bodine, and in a sudden deft movement he grabbed Sato around the waist and hoisted him up in a fireman's carry. Putting one foot up on the low wall, he grunted and, giving himself a push with the other foot, mounted the wall.

People coming out from the dance floor heard Lola's screams and pushed cautiously forward. They saw a man standing on the wall five stories above the street, rocking back and forth, trying to get his balance, then begin to press another man over his head. The band had stopped playing and all at once the sound of heavy breathing was audible above traffic sounds. One man was limp, unresisting, and the other straightened his arms and got him overhead, then slowly swung the body around until it was parallel with the building. As he bent his knees slightly, it appeared he was ready to throw him over.

"I wouldn't toss the fellow down there, old son." Colonel Gibb stood a few feet away, holding a drink and casually drawing in on one of Marshal Yü's cigars.

Bodine twisted his head around, straining under the weight. "Yeah? Why not?"

"He might fall on a white man."

There was a second's pause, then Bodine laughed, wavered precariously on the ledge another second, and finally stepped down, giving Sato a rough shove. Sato fell, tearing out the knees of his dress pants on the gravel path, but got up at once and, without looking back, stumbled off through the crowd toward the brightly lit glass doors.

Lola had left minutes earlier in near hysterics. What a horrible, rotten evening! My God! First Adrian, then that crazy, murderous Marine! As she came through the doors, Marshal Yü was waiting. She fell into his arms, bawling. "Oh, Charley . . . it's so awful. . . ."

He put his arms around her protectively and led the way across the crowded floor. Ramon trailed behind, holding on to Lola's hand. If it was a bizarre scene, the sophisticates in the room took it in their stride, giving Ramon's appearance a little round of applause.

Stopping at the table, Marshal Yü put Lola's scarf around her shoulders. "Not to worry, please, princess," he said. "I will take care of you, oh, yes." Those were the nicest words she'd ever heard. Then with the Shensi bodyguards leading the way, they went through the bar on the way to the elevator. As they did, they passed Adrian, slumped on one of the bamboo stools, head on the bar, out cold. It was coming up three o'clock.

At five Adrian jerked awake as coffee was pressed on him by the bar manager. Trying to focus, he saw that the place was nearly empty. Busboys were clearing the tables, and sweepers pushed brooms around the remaining drunks and diehards. Adrian got to his feet and shuffled toward the elevator. He had to be at the docks and aboard the junk by eight.

Back at his hotel, he navigated through a lobby full of early morning tourists, a raffish figure in his full dress suit among the bright faces and sensible shoes. He took the elevator to his small room and after a shower and more coffee actually didn't feel too bad, still coasting on the booze in his system. The real hangover would come later. He got together gear, most of it left over from his polo years—boots, tough twill riding pants, and some khaki military shirts he'd bought at the army and navy store. His trunk would be stored in the hotel, and he was taking along only a duffel and a kit bag. He gathered up his shaving things and his father's heavy pocket watch and chain.

116

It was the only personal thing of his he had, and looking at the Masonic fob reminded him how proud the old man had been inducting him in the lodge.

Going out, Adrian left the door ajar. He wasn't coming back to this hotel. Enough of trying to be the tightfisted businessman. It wasn't his style. If the expedition was successful, he would take the best suite in the Palace—if not, he would work his way home on the first boat.

The black cloud of his misunderstanding with Lola still hung over him. He sighed and guessed there must not be a woman alive who didn't expect to be proposed to. Lola had seemed a woman of the world, a sophisticated lady who took her pleasure where she found it, no strings. Their casual bedding seemed to suggest that. Certainly the girls he was used to took more persuading, but he had been wrong. Like her sisters everywhere, Lola was interested in tying the knot: marriage.

He was confident of winning her back; it was just a matter of changing his tactics. He wrote her a funny note about his proposal, saying he would be back like a "bad Mex" and hoped she would forgive and forget. He mailed it at the desk and went out.

Driving down the Bund was peaceful. The snorts and whistles of the cranes of the docks were quiet, and the ships in the roadstead dozed. It was Sunday, and thanks to the *fanquei's* "Number-one God," the coolies had a day of rest. As they passed Kiukiang Road, Adrian heard the bells of Sir G. G. Scott's Gothic Cathedral summoning those who weren't sleeping it off to early service.

Marshal Yü had insisted the "observers" arrive separately and at intervals, a distance from the junk. That way they would avoid suspicion at their departure. Adrian had the cab stop a block away, paid, and got out. Squinting against the morning sun, he could see the huge Chinese godowns shielding the junk from sight. Hoisting his bags up, he started off toward them. It was already hot, and he began to sweat as he walked.

It was when he turned into the alley between the buildings that he got his first unpleasant signal. *The junk wasn't visible at the far end opening to the river.* He began to jog, then run. He was on time . . . early . . . had it moved to a new berth out of his line of sight? Breaking into the open area of the dock, he stopped, unable to accept what he saw; the space was empty.

Where that massive vessel had been only yesterday was now an open stretch of water. Bits and pieces of jetsam moved sluggishly as the tide slapped at the dock.

The *Melodious Bird Song* had left without him.

SIXTEEN

AFTER ADRIAN GOT over the shock of the empty space where he had expected the junk to be, he began to reason. Why had it been moved at the last minute? A nautical problem? Tide, wind, weather? Had Yü's son, the "Little Marshal," gotten hold of their plans in Sian and dispatched agents, or even assassins, who sent Yü to cover? A lot of unexpected events might have caused Yü to pull out ahead of schedule—a quirky crew, an outbreak of cholera (notorious in Nantao every summer). It had to be something like that, a rational explanation; the *Melodious Bird Song* had slipped downstream for some perfectly valid reason he had yet to come up with. It was no doubt hidden, waiting until the others could be contacted and regrouped—after all, this was a secret operation, not a commercial sailing; one could not expect smooth departures.

He walked down the wharf through the tangle of rusted-out oil drums and mushy, rotting planks, looking for some neighbor along the riverfront who spoke a bit of English and might have seen the junk leave—it *was* an enormous vessel and highly visible. At a distance, through the irregular shapes of native craft, he made out two black stacks and the flap of a British ensign. By the time he got close enough to see that it was a gunboat, he was panting in the 100-degree heat from the exertion of dragging the heavy duffel bag. The kit bag sawed at his shoulder, the boots were tight, and he was soaked through with sweat.

The H.M.S. *Cockchafer* was anchored at the end of a long causeway of overlapping, shaky boards. The decks above the sag of its hull looked empty, and only the thinnest wisp of smoke rose straight up from one slightly askew stack. He began to despair. Then on the afterdeck, under a faded canopy, he saw a man sitting in a deck chair reading the Sunday papers. Adrian dropped his bags and shouted over. "I wonder if you could help me!"

The man, tousled and wearing a beige bathrobe, got up and walked to the rail. With the low freeboard of the gunboat, he was elevated only a foot or so above Adrian. He appeared to be eating prunes out of a glass dish. "If you're looking for Maurice, he's gone for a rubber of bridge on the *Bee*."

"Ah, no . . . I was looking for a particular junk. Did you happen to see the *Melodious Bird Song* sail?"

"You're not Richard, then?"

"No, sorry."

"My error, old man," he said, spitting a prune pit into the dish with a *plink*. "*Melodious Bird Song*? Hmmm, I don't know that one. What's she look like?"

"A huge junk—five masts . . ."

"Oh, you must mean the *Yangtze Queen*. She's a Foochow pole junk, a great behemoth of a thing."

"Are you sure?"

"Oh, I say, yes, she was anchored just down there all last month." He pointed with his spoon the way that Adrian had come. Then, turning, he shouted up at an open wheelhouse. "Hello, Leslie!" A blond man appeared and leaned on the pipework railing. "Did you see the *Yangtze Queen* stand out?"

"Righto, about five this morning. She was running on diesels."

The first man turned back to Adrian, spooning up a last prune. "That would be her. She's owned by Y and R—leased out for private cruises, larky things—you know."

Adrian couldn't believe it was the same junk, but he didn't want to offend his informant. "Do you happen to know where it was going?"

"Couldn't really say. Nanking, most likely, that's her home port."

"Thanks." Adrian laboriously picked up his duffel, shouldered his kit bag, and started off. "So long."

"If you see Richard, tell him Maurice is on the *Bee* at buoy number four, will you?"

"Sure."

Adrian found a cab with great difficulty, and stuffing the burden of his bags in the backseat, gave the Palace Hotel as an address. The rational thing to do was go back to HQ and wait for contact from Yü. As he reversed directions from this morning's expectations, the first really serious doubts began to seep into his brain, along with the poison of last night's intake.

He reached the Palace as Big Ching, in the neighboring customs house tower, struck ten o'clock. He towed the duffel into the lobby, turned it over to the bell captain, and took the elevator to the fourth floor. There the door to Sino-Cal Oil Ltd. stood open, and he received his second shock of the morning.

The place was cleaned out. Desk drawers and files stood open; the floor was papered with a tumble of useless correspondence. Anything of any value that could be carried away had been: the expensive American typewriters and office equipment, down to the last pencil. Adrian stood for a moment as the impact hit him. For the first time, he realized just how shaky the whole business had been; the offices suddenly looked like an unimaginative stage set that had been struck after a flop. On the paper underfoot he could make out the ideograph, the "chop" that had been so carefully selected for the right impression. That seemed particularly prophetic.

He went out in the hall and took the elevator to Marshal Yü's top-floor suite. The door there was open. It was, as he expected, emptied. Closets bare, personal effects removed (and, he guessed, some of the hotel's). Wherever Yü had gone, obviously he wasn't coming back.

Adrian returned to the office and, passing the open door of the war room, stopped short. A body was laid out on the top of the map table, arms crossed in the formal position of a corpse at a wake. In the half light it took Adrian a minute to adjust to detail, and he had the unpleasant image of remembered funerals, passing by open coffins, his father's waxy effigy as he'd stood looking down at the old man for the last time.

He recognized the figure on the table; it was, of course, Colonel Gibb, still dressed in his Indian rig, pillbox hat in place, booted and spurred. His chest moved as he snored lightly, obviously sleeping off last night's drunk. So much for the exponent of speed, movement, and lightning attack. Suddenly Adrian got very mad. Stomping across the room, he grabbed him by his madras sash and began to shake him viciously, rattling his medals.

"Wake up you silly, damn fool! ZAP! BLAM! BLOOIE! What about some of your rapid forward movement! FAKER!"

The colonel opened his good eye tentatively. "Haloo, is it tea time?"

Adrian shoved him back and went out of the room in disgust. He found a working phone and dialed the home number he'd been given for their personal banker at the Hong Kong-Shanghai Bank. After some time the man came on, diffident and wary. "Webbshaw here."

Adrian swallowed to keep the frustration and fury out of his voice. "This is

Adrian Reed, at Sino-Cal Oil. I'm catching up on a bit of work at the office. I wonder if you could give me the current standing of our account?"

"Why . . . it's closed out as instructed, Mr. Reed. There are several small outstanding statements I will forward on to . . ."

"When . . . when was that?"

"What?"

"The account closed out?"

"Yesterday, sir, Saturday. Considering the amount of gold to be moved, it was thought best to transport it after banking hours. At five in the morning, to be precise. By eight o'clock the shipment and necessary paperwork were complete. It went very smoothly, if I do say so."

"Why wasn't I informed?"

"I have no idea, sir. That came under the province of Marshal Yü. As president of Sino-Cal Oil, it was his option to inform whom he pleased." This was said stiffly. "Also, two keys were necessary to open the vault—both were presented."

The key! Adrian felt in his pocket. Yes, it was there on the chain with others; he could feel its particular shape. How then? He had been careless; the keys lay on his dressing table every night. Had they taken it, made an impression, and put it back? No doubt. Probably done by the "sincere" ideograph expert.

"If there is anything irregular, sir, I suggest you get in touch with . . ."

Adrian did his best to keep his voice level. "There were two cases of personal papers in the vault my father had deposited. Were they moved?"

"Everything listed in the Sun Account and transfered to Sino-Cal Limited was shipped to Marshal Yü's junk."

"I see . . ."

The banker caught the warble in Adrian's voice, and his own firmed up. "I have a statement of final expenditures for transportation and armed guard—it comes to some four hundred and twenty-four U.S. dollars. Shall I send it to your offices at the Palace?"

"Yes . . . yes, of course . . . why not?" Adrian hung up.

Well, there it was. There was no longer any doubt about what had happened. He had been swindled.

Marshal Yü or Charley Min or whoever he was was also a con man. That Adrian had accepted the man at face value, along with the junk and comical bodyguards, now seemed incredible. With his scholarly appearance and polite ways Yü certainly did not look like a con man. But they never did. In the States, given the kind of money involved, Adrian would have never accepted anyone at face value; he would have checked him out, investigated. But this was China, and what did he know of warlords and Sian? He had also believed Bodine when he confirmed Yü's claims. Bodine was his "military expert." Yü had no doubt bought the claim on the Sun Account for so much on the dollar, maybe even from the real Marshal Yü—then patiently bided his time until Adrian showed up. Very slick. The greedy bastard had not been satisfied with his half, but had gotten Adrian's too.

The thing about this con (like all successful ones) was that the suckers thought they were involved in an illegal operation and would not go to the police or government. A lot of good it would do anyway. Adrian had signed over the account willingly; the gold had legally been Yü's (or his) to use. All Yü agreed to was that "if" the coup was a success, it would be paid back double. (Who was greedy?) The party was Yü's crowning glory, all highly visible, the very night before he would sail off into the sunrise. Everything— the hall, the band, the food, the gallons of booze, even the tips—had been paid for on credit. In fact, almost all the expenses run up in Shanghai were charged—yet to be paid for. Yü had been very careful not to dip into the Sun Account.

In the next hour the German engineer, then the ex-chief radioman, showed up, still toting their gear. Where was the junk? What had happened? As Adrian suspected, the inside men included only the Chinese staff—Yü's students (relatives?). There had been no "Tungpei Army agents" recruiting in Nanking; that had all been window dressing. All the tons of military equipment—enough to outfit two thousand men—would be sent to Nanking C.O.D. where it would sit on some dock waiting to be picked up. Arrangements made with the railway line for transportation, trucks that were ordered to be put on flatcars, all the complicated threads of military procurement they had woven in the last weeks would come unwound. When they did and the creditors knew the extent of the swindle, they would come looking for Adrian.

The two observers were already suspicious and were asking questions he couldn't answer. Once it was obvious that the marshal had done a bunk, they began to blame Adrian. He was a partner in the operation, he had sat in on interviews, hired them; he was their boss. They were "observing" for him. He was equally responsible. Like most people swindled, they still couldn't quite believe it had happened; they were sure there was still something to be salvaged. It was probably only because of this that Adrian wasn't personally attacked.

And he couldn't blame them. They had made arrangements, left their wives with great expectations, refused other propositions. Worse, told that they would be paid when they boarded the junk at the beginning of the operation, they had put out their own money for uniforms and even handguns. They were furious as the picture became clear. The racket finally woke up Gibb, and he came in, uniform still immaculate, pillbox hat framing the ruined face.

"By gad, why wasn't I roused! Captain Bodine said he'd be here at 0700, the dog!"

Bodine! Adrian thought. *Yes, what about Bodine?* He was the only one not here!

Adrian shoved his way to the door and took the elevator to the lobby. As the cage door opened, the Finnish manager of the hotel was waiting for him. He was a pleasant man renowned for his beautiful daughter. "Excuse me, Mr. Reed, but I wonder if I might have a word with you?"

"I'm in rather a hurry—can it wait?"

The manager lowered his voice. "It concerns the Marshal's suite—room service, telephoning, the hiring of cars—those kinds of things. I am afraid the chits have got quite expanded. Then too, sir, your office rent will come due Monday. I'm sure you would want to bring it up to date." His smile was pained. The word was out, something was rotten in Sino-Cal Ltd.

"You're right, of course. Why not send that to our bank and let them deal with it? Ask for Mr. Webbshaw."

"Whatever you say, sir." But the manager looked unconvinced, and Adrian knew he wouldn't dare show his face around the Palace again. Indeed, he had an idea that by tomorrow there would be few places in the city he could. *Damn! Damn! Damn!* Not only was he skinned, broke, but Yü's creditors would be down on him like a ton of bricks! He was now literally trapped in China without even the return boat fare.

Adrian took a cab to Kiangse Road, and as he went, the enormity of the wrongs done him expanded in his mind until he was ready to explode. When he found the address, he slammed out of the cab, kicked the gate open, charged through the narrow yard, bounded up the stairs, pushed his way into the vibrant green hall, bellowing, "Bodine! Bodine!" He was convinced he now knew what had happened. Bodine had "steered" him to Yü. They were in it together. As Adrian pounded down the hall, his anger accelerating to blind fury, the singsong girls and old ladies ducked for cover.

All, that is, but the Dragon's Tail. She shot out of the beaded curtains and met his charge with one of her own that stopped him in his tracks. They were both yelling at the top of their lungs and, curiously, saying nearly the same thing at the same time.

"Where is he?! Where's that bastard!!"

"Where he go?! Where that damn crook, sneak too!!"

"Tell me!"

"You tell?"

"What?!"

"What did you say?!"

She began jabbing him in the chest, forcing him backwards. "You smelly crook's friend, you better, by God, tell him. I bite off his worm of a pecker when I catch him!"

"He's not here?" Adrian said, finally catching her drift.

"Not here! Dumb, short, son of a sea shit gone with my money! You got him? You got him?"

She continued shoving him until he was in the doorway. "No! No! I don't know where he is, damn it! I thought he was here!"

"Not here! Bastard steal my money and run off with lady and monkey!"

"*What!*" She gave him a final push and he skidded on the grease-slick top step and had to catch himself to keep from falling. The porch loungers jumped for their lives, and beer bottles rattled down the steps. By the time Adrian got his balance near the bottom, the door had slammed and it was mercifully quiet.

A ricksha took him to the theatrical boardinghouse and he found Lola's room empty. The bamboo poles lay in the hall along with trash that included the dead yellow roses. The Chinese manager said she had moved out late Saturday night. Men had come and taken her trunks away. He had been paid.

Adrian stepped out in the street, waved off the ricksha boy, and began to walk aimlessly. In the early afternoon the pungent smoke from the food vendors' cooking fires curled around the faces of customers, drifting up through the jumble of awning and signs, rising to shimmer in overheated heat waves. The sun beat down, and he shifted his Stetson over his eyes. Depressed and drained, he began to feel the queasiness of his delayed hangover. As he walked, the crowd parted, watching him, giggling at his "cowboy" hat. Small children scampered across his path, holes cut out of the rear of their pants in the traditional Chinese solution to the diaper problem. It was a noisy, friendly street, packed with Sunday strollers, sidewalk entertainers, beggars, whores, and gunboat sailors. Adrian saw none of them, moving straight ahead, going over it. He now believed they were all in it.

Lola had known Bodine before; that was obvious from the way they danced together. She and Bodine had steered him to Yü. That whole business of her going to dinner on the junk had seemed very odd at the time. It had probably begun with Ansel O'Banion writing to Bodine and tipping him off that the sucker was on his way. There was no way Yü could have put the thing together without them. Adrian had believed Yü, because Bodine told him he should. When they were playing war, he depended on Bodine to guide him. He could see now that people like Gibb were a joke. It all added up: Bodine's wife saying he'd run off with a lady and a monkey—and finally, Bodine was the *only one* who hadn't showed up at Sino-Cal and raised hell about being swindled. What really hurt was Lola's going off with him. An aggressive, cocky bore twice his age—well, they deserved each other.

Focusing, Adrian found he had walked himself into an odd, wedged-shaped street and was lost. He had started to turn back when a large car cut the angle of the corner and stopped, blocking his way. Moving to one side to go around it, he was pushed violently from behind. At the same time the rear door of the car swung open and he was projected inside. In the next instant a rough bag was jammed over his head, his arms were tied behind him, and he was beaten to the floor. It had happened in a blur of Chinese faces, and he had no clear image of the human, but the mechanical rang a bell. There was something very familiar about the car. As it moved away at high speed and he heard the supercharger cut in, he knew for sure. It was that big Horst phaeton that had chased them from the noodle palace, the one Bodine had "killed." Obviously, it had just been wounded.

The hospital was across from the London Mission and near the Central Police Station on Honan Road. Max had brought a single perfect pear, wrapped in tissue. As he sat in the tile corridor, he cradled it in both hands, rotating it slowly to keep his perspiration from dampening the paper. A doctor came by, paused, and walked back. "Are you a relative of"—he looked at the chart— "Mr. T. Sato?"

"Associate."

"Pardon?" The doctor leaned closer.

"Friend, please."

"Ah, yes, Japanese, then?" The doctor found the difference annoying. "Well, yes, your friend is doing nicely. I understand after the accident he hailed a cab and had himself driven here. Remarkable."

"Accident?"

"Yes, damn bad business, apparently he was hit by a motorist. The fellow didn't stop. Rotten!" He checked the chart. "Nasty contusions, must have taken a fender in the face. A lot of swelling and some damage to the malar region—cheekbones—but the worst of it is his jaw." He waggled his own to illustrate. "Broken just below the external acoustic meatus"—he tapped the spot—"hinge. We've got it wired and he's doing fine. Be up and about in no time."

"May I see him, please?"

"Of course, my dear chap. You may find him a bit thick from the morphine, but by all means go in."

Max padded into the private room and bowed before the bed. He was wearing his conservative hand-me-down Tokyo-made suit. Hands at his sides, he elevated his eyes slowly and was shocked. Captain Sato, illuminated by a southern exposure that flared the window mullions, was unrecognizable. His face was a puffy mass of vaselined surfaces and bandages, culminating in a boxed-in affair that protected the wired jaw. Max was distraught; he bit his

125

lip in compassion and waited until his voice was steady. "Sergeant Masaki reporting, sir."

There was no answer, but a hand came up, wagged, and seemed to indicate awareness. Max moved closer and placed the perfect pear on the surface of a table next to the bed, twisting it slightly so that its best profile was outlined by the light. He knew better than to refer to the accident or even suggest they were in a hospital. Flopping out his notebook, he began his report in Japanese. "As ordered, I positioned myself on the dock at midnight last. At five—five this morning, Sunday—Marshal Yü's junk left under power, turning upstream toward Nanking at full steam. This was three hours earlier than previous information indicated. 'Observers' did not appear, nor did the American, Reed Junior, until eight o'clock after the junk had departed. Each came alone and all expressed surprise, then anger, at the absence of the junk. I waited until one o'clock afternoon time and reported to the consul, where I was informed of Captain Sato's location. . . ." He paused, choosing his words. "Train reservations have been made for Nanking. I await ongoing orders. . . . What shall I do next?"

The hand fluttered and Max stepped closer. He flipped his notebook to a clean page, put it firmly in the captain's left hand, the pen in his right, and waited while Sato held it close to his swollen face and scribbled a single word.

Max gently took the notebook back and examined the word.

BODINE!!

Bodine? Bodine what? He looked at the captain, but he had drifted off. He leaned closer; yes, his eyes were shut. Then he saw something very odd on the captain's cheekbone. Under the vaseline was what looked like the imprint of an eagle.

It sat on the mound watching the car approach. A size somewhere between that of a badger and a wolverine, gray on top and black underneath, with matted fur that somehow looked disheveled, unpleasant. Zoologists called it a ratel, but the Chinese disagreed, saying it was an unknown species inhabiting only graveyards, dining off the dried flesh and bones of the old dead. It was true that nobody remembered seeing *these* ratels anyplace else. Certainly nobody ever trapped or hunted them, and, ratel or not, these animals were left strictly alone. The habitat of this particular one was just outside Shanghai proper in the Puto District. The graveyard was a series of mounds, some twice as high as a man's head, looking like natural formations from a distance. Actually, they had been created by burying the dead in coffins above ground and piling dirt on them. Over the centuries they built up in layers and became "terraced steps to heaven."

126

It was from one of these heavenly heights that the animal saw a car turn in through an opening in the low stone wall that contained the graveyard. The car came to a halt in a dusty valley between the humped shapes.

Adrian felt the car slow and stop, the door click open, and the rough thrust of hands as he was shoved out on the ground. He landed on his knees, sending up a cloud of powdery dust. Hands went through his pockets, slapping and grasping, taking everything he carried. After a shuffle of feet and muttered instructions, the hood was jerked off and his head was held rigid, forcing him to look down at only the narrow circle of dirt in front of him.

"If this is a robbery . . . or kidnapping, you people are out of luck. . . ."

"Where is Captain Bodine!" This was said in good English with Chinese overtones, and from the hollow sound, it might have come from the backseat of the car.

"Bodine? I . . . I was at his place earlier—"

"We know that! We were watching it! You are his filthy accomplice! Where is he now?!"

"Damnit! I don't know! I was looking for him myself!"

There was the singsong of Chinese, and Adrian's hands were untied. Had he somehow said the right thing? Did they believe him? His left hand was pulled forward, arm held in a vice grip, fingers shoved under except for the little one. He began to sweat.

"You know where that dogsbody is! Tell!"

"I'm telling you! I don't know!" Adrian's head was beating like a hammer, and he kept asking himself what was happening, how in hell had he gotten into this. If he just had the chance to explain, if he could look somebody in the face, talk to them . . . Then, as he watched in horror, a tube of bamboo was slipped over the end of his little finger and pushed up tight to the first joint. His head was held in such a way that he saw only his own hand and the hand and arm holding the end of the bamboo.

"Where is he!"

"I don't know, damnit!" His head was twisted slightly upward, and the lower arms and legs of a man came in view, wearing the loose jacket and wrapped pants of a coolie. The man's hand went slowly behind him and reappeared, holding a *da boa*, the traditional Chinese beheading knife, a broadsword really, about two feet long and looking a bit like a bolo knife or a machete. No respectable bandit was without one, and in Chiang's Nationist Army "the Yellow Arrows," so called because of their arm brassards, had the power to mete out summary execution with them on the spot. The weapon was carried in a sling on the back, so the user could reach over his shoulder and bring it rapidly into play. The owner of this example twisted it slightly, until the blade took the sunlight, flashing.

"*Where!*" the disembodied voice shouted.

127

"*I don't . . .*" The blade swung in a precise arc, the wielder controlling its path in a wrist action not unlike that of a golfer. Adrian's little finger was neatly sliced off at the first joint below the bamboo guide. He gave a startled grunt.

He didn't really believe they would do it! The shock was worse than the pain . . . the man holding the bamboo quickly tied off the stump of the finger with green thread, stopping the worst of the bleeding, then just as quickly shoved a slightly larger tube of bamboo up to the knuckle joint. They were going to take off the next one! He remembered what Bodine had said about the green thread; they were going to keep cutting until nothing was left but the big pieces. Adrian was no stranger to pain—he had suffered plenty of it with polo injuries—but it was not something you got used to. He would have gladly told them where Bodine was if he knew—he would have lied, but he didn't know enough about Shanghai to be convincing. My God! To be slowly sliced up! He began to feel faint.

Then he heard something so startling, so out of context, that he couldn't believe his ears! The voice was repeating an ancient ritual, and when his turn came to give the response, he answered the second part automatically.

After a pause the voice asked, "You are a Freemason?"

"Yes . . . yes, that's right . . ."

There was a flurry of Chinese, and Adrian was untied, brushed off, and helped to his feet. The executioner and the man who had dealt with his finger gently guided him past the others, who stood with their heads bowed. At the car Adrian stumbled on the running-board step, was caught and gently passed onto a jump seat.

Here he found himself sitting opposite a young Chinese in a mandarin gown. Adrian recognized him at once as the one he had wrestled with on the floor of the noodle palace—his ear was still bruised where Adrian had elbowed him. He was also the one with the chrome-plated automatic who had shot and killed the young Chinese girl.

His father's watch and chain with the Masonic fob was handed back. "This is yours?"

"Yes."

"I am also a brother, one of the *Chin kung-tang*, Chinese Freemasons."

"Is that right."

The young man snapped the rubber band around the bundle of Adrian's private papers and passport. "There is a letter here, from Dr. Sun Yat-sen to General Homer Lea . . . you knew them?"

"No—my father supported Dr. Sun's revolution."

The young man shook his head, making an odd sound in his throat. "This is so sad, such a terrible mistake. If only I had known."

"Well, nobody asked me, did they?" Curiously, Adrian felt little anger against this man, rather a profound relief that he had stopped cutting him up. All because of the watch fob and Dr. Sun's letter. Amazing. The only reason he had had the heavy watch and bundle of papers with him was that when he'd left this morning he had believed he was going on a trip. Otherwise they would have been in a drawer in his room at the hotel. Amazing.

"You must please forgive me, but of course when we saw you with this man Bodine at my father's house, we assumed you were his accomplice."

"Hardly. I met him for the first time the night we visited your house—I had no way of knowing what he was to do there."

"Ah, yes, of course. We should have known."

"That was rotten about the girl."

The young man frowned. "This was nothing. There are many girls. I hope you do not think we caused all this to happen because of a girl?"

Adrian was disturbed. "Well, I . . ."

The young man's face was angular and very smooth, delicate, almost feminine, suggesting the aesthete, perhaps a poet, certainly not the torturer. He must also be something of the *bon vivant*, as he leaned forward, Adrian could see French cuffs under the wide Chinese sleeves.

He looked earnestly at Adrian. "This girl was a concubine of my father, an ungrateful creature who had accepted his protection. But worse—she ran off with a *foreigner*, a white man who insulted us. Insulted us! It was decided in family council that it would be better to send another white man after him into the French Concession. We hired Captain Bodine to find and kill him. He agreed, but did not do this, *no!* Only beating the man. Worse, he said he killed him. This is what the silver was for. He meant to cheat us. This has to be revenged."

Adrian kept quiet. He found it difficult to comprehend Chinese morals. He also found it difficult to believe he'd been snatched from the butt of this revenge by the Freemasons and Homer Lea. He said this.

The young man lowered his voice conspiratorially. "The *Chin kung-tang*, the Freemasons, are a part of one of the most powerful secret societies in China. Our lodges overseas funnel money and men to our cause. They supported the overthrow of the Manchus and were behind their fall in 1911. My uncle, K'ang Yu-wei, was a great leader in that movement. In 1900 he sent a cable to the San Francisco lodge asking for money to be sent through Singapore to aid the revolution. Homer Lea was selected to carry it and subsequently sailed on the S.S. *China* from San Francisco, taking sixty thousand dollars to the rebels. His passage was paid by the *Chin kung-tang* in Los Angeles, because, of course, Homer Lea was a Freemason of that lodge."

Adrian shook his head. Amazing.

"It was in China during the Southern Revolt in the Yangtze Valley that General Lea made his name known to my people. He won his dragon sword

129

at the battle of Po Lo. When I went to Stanford, I found many people who remembered him."

"*You* went to Stanford?"

"Class of '21."

"My God! You were a freshman when I was a senior!" It hit Adrian with heavy irony that here was a modern man, a Freemason, a college alumnus, obviously highly intelligent—a man who minutes before had ordered his finger cut off. A man prepared to slice the rest of him up like baloney. Why? For not revealing the whereabouts of a scruffy ex-Marine who had been paid to kill the lover of his father's concubine. The laughter welled out of him, a kind of relief after this black comedy. The young man smiled, then joined him. The others, hearing them, took it up. The Chinese love a good joke and they understood instinctively that that was what had just happened here.

They were still laughing while they piled into the car, jamming in the front and back, two standing on the running board. The Horst picked up speed, and as it turned out of the graveyard, the ratel, perched on its personal mound, cocked its head and listened to the sound. It was curious but not frightened. It never had anything to be frightened of.

They dropped Adrian off at the Palace about dusk. The young man shook Adrian's good hand warmly and presented his card. Adrian noted the felicity of the ideograph and thanked him. "It's been, well . . . interesting. I suppose every experience in life teaches you something."

"It is said, 'the best of friends may be enemies in the dark.' I am in your debt. You must allow me to erase my humiliation—of not seeing in the dark. If at any time you need assistance, you must trumpet your brother."

"Thanks—and by the way, I was telling the truth—I have no idea where Bodine is."

He looked hurt. "Of course I believe you! You are a Freemason." As Adrian stepped back, he received one last memento: a bamboo tube. He didn't look, but he was sure the tip of his little finger was enclosed.

Crossing the lobby of the hotel, he felt like Napoleon returning from Waterloo, or at least Moscow. Fortunately, after leaving his room with the firm resolution that he would return only to finer things, he had neglected to inform the management; he hoped he wouldn't meet them and that the room was still his. He took the elegant elevator to the fourth floor and plodded up the hall. His door was still open. For a minute it made him uneasy, then he remembered he'd deliberately left it that way in the morning. But when he stepped into the tiny sitting room, a man was sitting in the one comfortable chair, smoking a cheap cigar and reading a year-old copy of *Captain Billy's Whiz Bang*. He looked up at Adrian.

"What kept you, bunkie?"

SEVENTEEN

A*DRIAN WAS ACROSS* the room in one jump, slamming into Bodine. He hit him with such force that when the chair tipped they skidded along the floor together for another ten feet before crashing into the wall. The cigar, liquor glass, and the magazine Bodine had been reading seemed for a split second suspended in air, then fell into the complicated tangle of arms and legs. Bodine squirmed to the top as Adrian's fist clipped his nose. "Bastard!" Adrian shouted. "Crook!"

"Christ!" Bodine yelled, grabbing his nose with one hand and Adrian's right wrist with the other. "Knock it off, bunkie! Fun's fun!"

Adrian swung with the other fist, and as Bodine fended off the blow, Adrian struck the freshly cut end of his finger on his elbow. "Ohhh! Jesus! Ohhh!!"

"*See?* You're gonna hurt yourself! What in hell's the matter with you?"

"You're what's the matter with me!" Adrian said, fanning his little finger. But the action was over; this was the high-water mark of the scuffle. The fury of his pent-up anger and frustration ebbing, Adrian realized that if Bodine was in his room, then some of his conclusions were wrong. "What are you doing here anyway? Answer me that!"

"What are you talking about, for Pete's sake?" Bodine asked. He had drawn back, too, but eyed Adrian warily as he sat on his chest. "I been waiting here for you! What in hell do you think I'm doing? You dumb bohunk!"

"Why didn't you come back to HQ at the Palace? Answer me that if you can!"

"You think I'm stupid or somethin'? When the junk wasn't there, the last thing I was gonna do was go back to that hotel and have the rest of those yo-yos and bill collectors on my ass. I hope you weren't dumb enough t' show up?" Bodine slowly raised himself off Adrian's chest.

"Of course I did! Damn it! Nobody told me this was going to be a con job to separate me from my share of the Sun Account!" Adrian pushed himself up, holding his little finger out gingerly. "I believed that damned silly story of a coup! I believed Yü when he said he was a warlord, a friend of Chiang Kai—what's his name?—and all the rest of the bushwa! Hell, I believed everything! Which only goes to prove Barnum was right! There really is a sucker born every minute!"

Bodine had picked up his cigar from the floor and, brushing it off, relit it. Puffing the fractured end up, he put the chair on its feet and sat down again. When he was sure the cigar was going, he retrieved the glass and poured it half full from a whiskey bottle on a tray. Only then did he look Adrian straight in the eye.

"That makes two of us that got took, bunkie. He had me fooled too." There was a pause as their eyes held, and Adrian noticed that not only was Bodine in the most comfortable chair, the bottle of whiskey sitting on the tray obviously had to come from room service. He got mad again. "You see this?" He held up his little finger, still tied off with the green thread. "You see this! Your friends from the noodle palace chopped it off because I wouldn't tell them where you were!"

"What!"

"That's right! And they were getting ready to cut the rest of me up into little pieces! Thanks to you and that insane business with the girl!"

"And you didn't tell them?"

"I didn't tell them because I didn't know! Believe me, I would have told them in a minute if I had!"

"Lemme see that." Bodine got up from the chair and took hold of Adrian's wrist.

"Don't touch me!" But Bodine dragged him into the small bathroom. He took the thread off and ran water on the wound, scrubbing it with soap.

"Jeee-zusss!" Adrian howled. "Damn! Damn! Damn! It didn't hurt that much when they did it!" Bodine tore a towel into thin strips and expertly bandaged the wound.

"Soon as you can, have that looked at. You can catch an infection here quick as the clap."

132

"You know why they did this?" Adrian said, even angrier because of the pain. "Because you cheated them! That's right! They paid you in silver to kill whoever took the girl, and you didn't do it!"

They walked back into the small sitting room, Adrian holding his finger aloft.

"Of course I didn't! Would you kill a man because he'd run off with some rich old bugger's cookie?"

"I . . ."

"*And get this!* I didn't tell the silly slits I'd kill the bird for them either! I said I'd punish him—and that's what I did, bending him a little outta shape. They assumed I'd kill him, of course, because that's what *they* would have done. Now, I'm damned sorry they came down on you, but as I remember it, you went along on your own two feet."

They sat down, Bodine once again in the comfortable chair, Adrian in a rigid straight-back. There was another long pause and Adrian made an effort to calm down. Finally, he said, "Why didn't you tell me Yü wasn't a warlord?"

Bodine relit the green cigar and looked up through the foul smoke. "What are you talkin' about now? They invented the name 'warlord' for that bird. He is the *gen*-uine article. He ran Sian for years with a gang of ex-bandits—those Tungpei 'patriots' he was always talkin' about—he was *it*, the big wazoo! Ask anybody, look it up."

"Are you telling me he's not a con man?"

"Well, he's that too, isn't he?"

"Why would he go to all that trouble—pull an elaborate con job? Why not go through with the coup as we planned?"

"Sometimes I wonder about you, kid—because he wanted *all* of the money! *Jesus!* This way he got it without sharin' a dime with anybody—like you and me. Also, it was complicated, double-crossin' and tricky—all the things dear to a Chinaman's heart."

"But what about all that business of his knowing Dr. Sun, Chaing, the disgraced son, was that true?"

"Well . . . the part about Sun was—he had to deal with a lot of people like Yü during the early days of the '11 revolution—those babies are what finally did him in. As for Chaing, yes, he outfoxed Yü, pullin' his troops out of Sian and leavin' him open for the kid to take over."

"I can't believe this son who was supposed to be so dissolute—on opium, a weakling—could have done that—taken over."

"You're wisin' up. That's where Yü switched things around. It wasn't the son that went overboard for the nags and bimbos—it was Yü. He was a glutton for anything he could shove in his mouth or up his ass—a gobbler. The mistake he made when he was ridin' high was sendin' the kid to Oxford, thinkin' he'd follow in the old man's footsteps. Instead, the Marxist's got a hold of him, and when he secretly came back to China, Chiang put him through his Whompa Military Academy. Those were the days when he was playin' footsie with the Bolshies himself. Later I heard the kid went to Moscow."

"If you knew Yü was corrupt, and the boy was the straight one, the reformer, why didn't you warn me?"

"Would it have made any difference? I didn't get the idea you went into this thing for any high moral reasons. I thought you came in for the money, like the rest of us."

"But you must have suspected this was a phony military operation—recruiting out in the open, in the Palace Hotel for God's sake! People like that fool, Gibb, and the rest of those so-called 'observers'!"

Bodine took a long tip-up on the whiskey glass and slammed it down on the tray with a rattle of ice cubes. "What did you think we were gonna get, bunkie?! The graduatin' class from West Point? You think those guys were a bunch of oddballs? You should see the ones we turned down! You think mercenaries are gonna be your average sweethearts of Sigma Chi? Come on! Wise up! And don't sell Gibb short. He knows what he's about. He may be a little odd—but hell, he's English."

He moved forward in his chair, pointing the nasty cigar at Adrian. "Let's get somethin' straight right here! There's not much I won't get up to, an' I've cut some close corners in my time, but by God, when I give a man my word, that's it! I told you I'd help you, and I meant it! Yü pulled a fast one on both of us. I thought I had the old bastard figured, but he was a little too cute for me. Sure, the military operation was sloppy, but it was also Chinese and it's the same thing. You gotta remember I came out of this like you—with a goose egg. No, the bastard outsmarted us. You gotta give him credit, though—it was slick as seal shit."

Bodine relaxed back, trying to puff up the faulty cigar. For a moment the wheeze of his resuscitation was the only sound in the room. Adrian got up and paced, pressing his pounding head. There was something left he had to say. "I went by your place today on Kiangse Road. . . ."

"Business or pleasure?"

"Your wife was shouting the place down—she said you took her money and . . ."

"Jee-zuss!" Bodine laughed. "How's that for a woman! I took her money! When she wants something, it's our money! I dip into the cookie jar and all of a sudden it's her money. Kee-rist!"

"She said you had run off with Lola."

"What!" He broke out laughing. "That is funny! My God. The first time I talked to the woman was last night's bash." He looked carefully at Adrian, still smiling, the gap between his front teeth especially visible. "You ain't serious, bunkie? I can't believe you'd think I'd go off with your sweetie."

134

"She moved out of her place last night and didn't leave a forwarding address . . . or even a note."

Bodine rolled the dead cigar in his mouth, cutting his eyes up to where Adrian stood still clutching his forehead. "In that case I guess we know where she is." Adrian jerked his head up, frowning. Bodine nodded. "That's right. Yü."

"But why? Why would she do it?"

"Why?" Bodine chuckled. "Because he's got the money and you haven't."

"I just can't believe she would go away with that . . . old man."

"Believe it. Yü's a ladies' man. He's been knockin' over the dollies for years. He's got a reputation as a real cocksman—hung like a horse. He's what the Cantonese call wet salt—amorous." He caught Adrian's look. "Yes, that old man—sorry, but that's the way it is. I've seen him myself with some rare beauties. He's got half a dozen wives and, I'm told, had an honest-to-God harem up in Sian. Now that he's also got plenty of Mex, he sure won't have any trouble gettin' laid."

This was tough, and Bodine knew it, but it was time this smart-ass polo player stopped griping about everybody trying to do him in, and wised up. It was his own damn fault if he got took, and as far as the dollies, it was time he learned a thing or two there.

"I just can't believe Lola was like that," Adrian said again.

"Like what?"

"She thought I was asking her to marry me! I had no intention of marrying her!"

"Yeah? Well, you're gonna hang around girls, kid, you gotta offer 'em more than a pretty face and some pork. They like intentions, they wanna know what you can do for 'em, they're big on futures. They'd rather have you lie to 'em and tell 'em somethin' than be honest and say nothin'. Honesty is not a good policy in romance. They like presents, goin' out a lot, and sweet talk. What do you ever give her?"

"Why . . ." Adrian said, flustered, "a windup Victrola . . ."

Bodine laughed. "Jesus. You wanna give something they can wear an' show off to their buddies, somethin' small an' expensive. Cash is always good too."

"I guess I just don't understand women."

"Who does? The idea is not to understand but get in bed with 'em. Do you have to understand a horse to go for a ride?"

Max looked at the paper for a long time and eventually it spoke to him. Like most Japanese, he was familiar with the symbols of calligraphy. The old style of writing, *kanji*, with its thousands of ideograms meant for scholars, and the newer *kana* (ninth century) developed as "letters for women" (and used by the modern army), were both picture writing. Their characters stood not for sounds but for words, and the important thing was how they were rendered. A beautiful, cursive style brushed delicately on the paper with ink could subtly alter the meaning if laid down in bold blocky strokes.

Like the language, Japanese intent wasn't always evident on the surface. Suggestion by abstract wording or even unspoken inference was often carried on without either party's issuing a command or obeying an order. No sensitive person spoke of "love," "death," the Emperor, or asked outright for a favor—just as no one ever suggested that a dishonored person should commit *sepuku*—it was understood, and they did it.

There were clues in every twist and turn of the brush, and like Marshal Yü's "chop," if they weren't interpreted correctly it could be embarrassing or even dangerous. Max now applied this ingrained ability to translate the pen strokes of Captain Sato's one word message:

BODINE!!

Why it was written in English was obvious: it was outside official channels, addressing Max privately. That it was a name and in capitals announced its importance. What it said was: there had been no "car accident"; that the Marine, Bodine, had caused the captain's distress. The exclamation points were the crucial thing. The first indicated that the attack had been cowardly, an insult. If it had been otherwise, Captain Sato never would have written the name in the first place. The second exclamation point was very serious. There could be no other interpretation except the need for immediate action.

Max was honored that the captain had asked him to intercede; no matter what his rank he *was* samurai, and the captain knew it. For Max there was only one form of action: to kill your enemy. That was what was required of him now, and that was what he set out to do.

He began by using the telephone. He sat in his crowded room at the back of Captain Sato's apartment in a space stacked with file cabinets and cardboard boxes filled with "research"—statistics, evaluations, long memoranda on the consul and military staff of the other treaty powers. There were the names and rank of the Shanghai Defense Force and a complete diary of warship movements. He dialed the Sino-Cal offices at the Palace Hotel.

An angry voice came on the line, and when Max inquired after Captain Bodine, began questioning *him* sharply. Something must have gone wrong with the Sian coup. He hung up quickly and sat for a minute thinking. Should he go to that filthy Dragon's Tail and confront Bodine's wife? No, first he'd try Reed Junior's hotel again.

This time a desk clerk was congenial and freely offered information. Max hung up and smiled.

Reed had gone up to his room around five—earlier, a pug-faced man with red hair had also gone up, saying he was expected.

What incredible fortune! It had to be Bodine!

Max changed into Japanese wrap-around pants and jacket, tugged on split-toed *tabis*, and twisted a cloth around his head. This is what he wore on surveillance; fading into the background, he was easily mistaken for a Chinese. He unlocked his metal army trunk and carefully unwrapped a *katana*: a long sword. This was not his family's estimable weapon, The Mountain Hag Cutter, a legend in Kyushu. It had been sold piece by piece before he was born. The sword furniture went first: scabbard, hilt, ornamental *menukis*, in the lion and peony design, then the openwork *tsuba*, and finally the blade, made and signed by the great Kunihiro in 1585. No, this was an inexpensive modern weapon made for the common soldier, a *gunto* with a metal hilt imitating sharkskin, and a blade that was sturdy if not pure. Nevertheless, it was sharp enough to sever a man's head with a single whack. Max tucked it in the back of his sash, pinched off the lamp, and went out.

Bodine suddenly held his hand up, pointing to the door. Adrian heard something too. My God! Had that bunch in the Horst followed to check his story? Bodine reached behind the chair into a green duffel Adrian hadn't noticed, and withdrew the trench-cleaner. Then moving to one side of the door, Bodine jerked it open.

Colonel Gibb stood in the opening, smiling, at a slight cant, still resplendent in his Gurkha finery. "I wonder," he said, "if you might have the proper potable to top this up." He held out the same enormous tumbler from the party.

"Jee-zuss, Gibbsie, we thought you were the point for a gaggle of slopes." Bodine uncocked the pump shotgun.

"Sorry, Captain Bodine—just the bum-end of the Praetorian Guard, a wounded faun in search of a beaker of dew in a bloody forest of wogs." He crossed the room with unerring direction and picked up the whiskey bottle, poising it over his glass. "D'ya mind?"

"By all means," Bodine said, as if he were the host.

"I see you're ready for duty." Adrian was still abrasive.

"Rather. Damn slow start, though. That fellow Yü was not to be trusted, knew it when he ordered the pink champagne—no, a gentleman wouldn't have done that." Gibb tossed back the contents of the glass. "*Kanpei!*" then looked at both of them, the glass eye examining another corner of the room. "You're goin' after him, of course."

"There is that possibility," Bodine answered.

Adrian couldn't believe his ears. "You *know* where he is?"

"Headin' for Sian, I should think." Colonel Gibb filled his glass again. "That's my guess."

"Sian? You mean he still plans on going through with the coup?"

"That's exactly why he's goin' back, bunkie. Yü was tellin' it straight when he said his son dishonored him. There's no way he's gonna let him get away with that. The only difference is how he's goin' about it. Instead of usin' us—troops and guns, to shoot his way in—he's gonna use your money and *buy* his way in."

"I guess I don't understand the Chinese," Adrian said.

"Look, the old-time Chinese don't like to fight. To them a soldier is scum, beneath contempt. He has no honor. Way the hell back, they let the Manchus take over their country without a struggle, then gave 'em everything they asked for until they got fat and harmless. The Manchus allowed *themselves* to be put inside walls—boxed up in places like the Forbidden Palace in Peking. They've done that with all outsiders, includin' us, in the International Settlement—we may think we're keepin' them out, but the truth is *they're* keepin' us *in*."

"Take a sight at the Great Wall," Gibb said. "A singular structure, m' boy, greatest length of fortification ever constructed. *Whizzer!* More than fifteen hundred miles—they say it's the only man-made object that can be seen from the moon—don't know about that, but it's a bloody big piece of work. Done up by those old fellows to keep out the enemy. The thing took hundreds of years to build—and why wasn't it a success? Why didn't it keep out the other chaps? Because the minute it was finished and the last door locked, *ke-lunk!*, the general on one side, *zip!*, sold the keys to the general on the other. *Zap!* You might keep out warriors, old son, but you can't keep out greed."

Bodine said, "The Chinos have made a fine art out of bribery, bunkie—look at Chiang. He moves his troops around a lot, but he'll only fight when he really has to, and then only against the Commies. He hasn't taken the Japs on once—he stays in the saddle buyin' warlords and playin' one off against the other. That's what Yü will do with your old man's money—he'll buy the officers an' troops out from under his son."

"But can we catch him?" Adrian asked. "What about that bunch of bodyguards?"

"If we can't handle three or four of those pancake eaters, we ought t' turn in our balls. As for catchin' him—we know the junk went upstream early this mornin'. Most likely it will stop at Nankin'—wouldn't you say, Gibbsie?"

"The old boy is goin' to have to take the chug to Sian, and the main terminus for the Teintsin-Nankin' railroad is there."

"All right," Bodine said. "I got a hundred in Mex—how about you two?"

"About seventy-five U.S. dollars and change," Adrian said.

"A pound or two. I'm afraid like the other chaps I was countin' on Yü's baksheesh to float me," Gibb said. "As a matter of fact, my portmanteau is in the hall."

"Well, it ain't a hell of a lot of spondulicks to launch a campaign on, but we'll make do."

"Wait a minute, let me get this straight," Adrian said, looking closely at both of them. "The chances of catching up with Yü must be slim, and getting any of the money back even more so. Why do you two want to go after him? It has to be dangerous, time consuming, and uncomfortable. Surely there's an easier way to make a living than this. Look—if it's because you want to help me . . ." This bothered Adrian. He was not going to accept charity.

Bodine smiled. "I'd like to tell you that was the reason, bunkie, that we were a couple of do-gooders, lookin' out for your end, but it'd be wash. Then, too, I could say takin' a trip would be smart. Besides those boys from the noodle palace, this town's gonna be full of unhappy bill collectors, mean-ass wives, and sore-loosin' suckers. No, it ain't none of those, it's a simple reason everybody can understand, the thing that will send an Es-kemo to the Congo. An honest, old-fashioned, solid reason."

"Revenge," Gibb said.

"Right. After all the jawin' I've done about the white man's load out here, I sure can't let no Chinaman get the best of me."

Revenge and racism, Adrian thought, but he understood. To him it was shocking that a white woman—Lola—would take a Chinese as a lover. He had tried out several Chinese girls since arriving in Shanghai, but that was different.

"Before we get all lathered up and go chargin' outta here, like Barney Google's horse Sparkplug, maybe you better tell us why you're going, bunkie."

"Me?"

"I sure hope it's not to catch up with that dancer. She don't owe you nothin', and I can't believe she knew Yü was pullin' a scam."

"No, I wouldn't have anything to do with her, not after Yü."

"That's good, 'cause I'm not goin' on any pussy expeditions chasin' after some other poor sucker's love life. Forget her. There are plenty of other little darlins around."

Adrian considered telling them Yü had taken the Japanese code books—his determination to clear his father's name—but it would sound sentimental, idealistic. Instead, he said, "I came out here for the money, remember? I'm not going back without a good run at it."

"That's the talk!" Bodine said, slapping him on the back. "You gotta keep the old eye on the doughnut, kid, and not on the hole. Next to revenge, money is the best reason in the world to do anything. A real mover. Now let's get on with it and head for Nanking, chop chop!"

"How, old son?" Gibb said. "With the cloud we're under, Yü's creditors are goin' to be snappin' at our backsides. Don't think we'd better shag the public transports."

"True."

"What then?"

Bodine snapped his fingers. *"Fat Minnie!* By God, I think it's her time of the month!"

Bodine came out of the hotel at dawn carrying the long green duffel and wearing a faded Marine shirt with the faint outline on the sleeve where sergeant's stripes had been removed. A campaign hat of the "Montana Peak" variety was cocked over his eyes, and it still had the brass Anchor and Globe Marine Corps device screwed to the front.

Max recognized him at once and pushed up from where he'd hunkered down during the night with ricksha boys. He adjusted his sword and moved swiftly into the street, staying out of sight. When Bodine reached the curb, Max would step out from concealment at the far side of the closest car and strike a lightning blow, then disappear in the traffic. He put his hand on the hilt of the *katana* and tugged it loose from the scabbard.

At that moment Reed Junior appeared next to Bodine, joined by a second man in a stylish pongee suit and Panama hat. They stood talking a moment as Max waited, poised only a yard away, concentrating. He willed Bodine to step off that curb so he might strike and kill him on the spot—avenging his captain.

Max had to act with the sure chance of success. If he missed—or worse, got caught—it could jeopardize Captain Sato's security and embarrass the Imperial Army.

A cab pulled up, and, bunched together, the three men loaded their gear, climbed in, and rode off. There had been no safe moment to attack, and after they had reached the end of the block, Max tucked the sword away, got into another cab, and told the startled driver to follow.

EIGHTEEN

FAT MINNIE *SAT* knee-deep in the dirty water, her skirts barely clearing the tide of garbage. Big and white, she seemed nearly as wide as she was long, her canvas sunshade presenting a kind of downward droop that did nothing to trim up her shape. However, she was well-stacked, and topping her complication of stays and bulges were two rather pert projections with scorched tips. If she had an over-the-hill look, it was because she was well-used. Her admirers spanned several generations of Latin, then Yankee sailors who treated her with affection and dismay. It was from the latter that she had received her nickname.

Like many of the American gunboats on the Yangtze Patrol (*Panay, Leyte, Mindanao,* etc.), she had been named after a Philippine Island—Mindora. Built in Manila in 1898 and commissioned in the U.S. Navy after the Spanish-American war in 1902, she had been shoved bodily into the twentieth century, like it or not.

Warren Bodine had been introduced to her through her captain, Lieutenant (j.g.) Wally Hamm. They were shipmates when Bodine came to China and had shared many a hairy run down the Yangtze as volunteer guards for the Y & R. steamers, with Hamm still a young ensign (he had been on board the *I'Ping* when Bodine ransomed the reluctant missionary's wife in 1928). Later

141

Hamm took command of the *Mindora*, and after Bodine retired they kept up the Navy-Marine give-and-take.

As the cab carrying Bodine, Reed, and Colonel Gibb came down Ferry Road to *Fat Minnie's* anchorage, they could see she was preparing to get under way; a great plume of smoke, enlivened by sparks, poured out of her stack. "There she is," Bodine said. "*Fat Minnie.*"

Adrian was not impressed. "Either she's on fire or leaving."

"You're right, old son—she's standin' out," Gibb said. "It doesn't look like we're goin' to make it."

"Don't you worry," Bodine said. He gave the driver instructions to pull up at the sampan wharf. "There's no need to hurry. The old girl takes a long time to raise steam—she's got to show an optimum one-twenty-five on the gauge or she won't go at all." They stopped, offloaded the bags, and after Bodine haggled with the coolie poleman, climbed aboard. As they proceeded leisurely toward the gunboat, Bodine explained. "The *Minnie* goes up to Nanking once a month—her 'monthly,' as they say—mostly just to see if she can still make it. Hell, she should have been sectioned out when Dewey liberated her thirty years ago."

The poleman crossed the flats and expertly maneuvered the sampan next to the *Minnie's* port gunwales. Hopping across to her low freeboard, Bodine was met by Wally Hamm.

"Come out to say good-bye, Warren?"

"No, came out to bum a ride to Nankin', Wally."

Wally looked closely at the two passengers climbing aboard behind him. "You people must be desperate. If Bodine hasn't told you, *Minnie* is like fresh pork—she doesn't travel well."

Bodine introduced the others and explained that they were after Marshal Yü. He left out any reference to the Mex or coup, and instead suggested he had made off with Lola and Ramon.

"Well, it's a sad story," Wally agreed. "It's not every day a man loses both his girl and his monkey. You're welcome aboard—come on up to the con." He led the way under the canopy, past sailors and coolie deckhands getting her under way.

"How's the old girl behavin'?" Bodine asked.

"Strictly geriatric. Her boilers can't keep up a full head of steam for more than three minutes running at full speed—clearance between the cylinders and walls is something like three thirty-seconds of an inch—and she's getting senile, sometimes forgetting her firing sequence." They went up a ladder to the open bridge. "The main engines and throttles have leaky valves, one air pump had a broken piston, and the port circulating pump has been frozen since 1918. About the only thing that holds the old girl together is her paint. If I put a chipping party over the side, she'd sink straight away."

"Is there still time to get off?" Adrian asked, smiling.

"Not a thing to worry about—of course the radio won't operate, but that doesn't matter, because they housed the antenna in years ago and we haven't got a sparks rating on board anyway."

"You better jump for it, bunkie, while you can still wade ashore."

"Don't listen to Bodine," Wally said. "She's got a fighting heart, and as the Navy says, she's in damn fine shape for the shape she's in." They came into the tight confines of the conning bridge, sharing the space with the Chinese quartermaster and pilot.

Wally gave the command, and the anchor engine began to wheeze, hauling up two rusty appendages. Adrian stepped back three paces to be out of the way, and gave a howl as his rear end was burned on a bulky piece of machinery.

"That's the steam-powered steering engine," Wally said. "Being on the bridge makes it handy to check and see if it's running—but we usually do it with a wet finger."

The anchors were up now, but the steam expended had sent the pressure down to a hundred pounds. Wally rang the main engines ahead, and the pressure began to drop further as they crept out into the roadstead. Maneuvering through the tangle of harbor traffic, they lost headway against the current.

"We have a choice," Wally said. "Either we make enough turns to stay ahead of the current, in which case the pressure will drop until water comes over the engines and we could blow a cylinder head—or we slow the engines, maintain pressure, and go nowhere." It was obvious the latter was taking place and they were drifting backwards. "Let go anchors!" Wally shouted.

Immediately the Chinese pilot began to scream. "No, anchor! No allowed! No anchor here! Very blad! No anchor!"

"Must anchor, chop chop! *Fai Tee!*" Wally shouted back.

By then the steam was completely played out, and the anchors came rattling down. "What do we do now?" Adrian asked. "Wait until we make more steam?"

"That's right, but in the meantime dragging the anchors will probably mean locked flukes. Then, before we can get under way again we'll have to raise and lower them until they shake loose—by which time the pressure will be gone and we'll have to start all over again. I hope you're not in a hurry."

Max watched the *Fat Minnie*'s lack of progress from the shore. What should he do? What *could* he do? There was no way to follow them upriver by boat, and certainly no way he could sneak aboard if he did. He got back in the cab.

Driving off the dock, they passed by the U.S. Navy communications shack: COMYANGPAC. He had the driver stop and got out, positioning himself by the screen door, waiting patiently until somebody noticed him. Finally a chief yeoman pushed open the door. "What do you want, boy?"

Max bowed low, doing his best to be humble. "Oh, please sir! My officer leave on puffing boat!" He pointed.

"The *Minnie?*"

"Have most important sea chest suppose to deliver!"

"Well, you've missed 'em, boy. They're off for Nanking, God willing. Your pigtail's in the wringer."

"Is there not some way I make up way to catch alongside and deliver chest? Please, sir, no find, lose job."

"Well . . . they'll tie up to a spar for the night. If you can get transportation, you might catch them at Ching Chaing, upriver. Lord knows, the *Minnie* is slow as a bad debt."

Max urged the cab to all possible speed over the Garden Bridge, across Soochow Creek and up Whangpoo Road to Captain Sato's flat. He paid off the cabby, unlocked the garage door below the apartment, and pushed it back to reveal the Model A Ford roadster. Working frantically, he put an extra tire and tools in the rumble seat, positioned two five-gallon cans on the running-board tie-downs, and looped a water bag over the headlight bracket. Then, unlocking the gun case, he selected an Arisaka 7.7mm sniper's rifle and its companion scope. He slipped them into a canvas sheath and tucked it and his sword under the front-seat well.

He backed the car out, relocked the garage, and drove off. They had used the car many times to reconnoiter the countryside around Shanghai, and Max had a good idea of the lay of the land. It was noon, and roughly two hundred miles to Nanking. Ching Chaing was almost halfway, and even with the bad roads—or none at all—he thought he could easily make it by dawn.

The *Fat Minnie* proceeded up the Whangpoo River out of Shanghai and turned left at the river gate junction. This was the mouth of the Yangtze where it flowed into the Yellow Sea, and the river was stained by the heavy burden of silt carried 3,500 miles from its source in Tibet. It was this buildup that created the vast alluvian plain on which Shanghai (*City Above the Sea*) had been built.

As the *Minnie* puffed along, each propeller was driven by a two-cylinder reciprocating engine, and at each stroke a squirt of water from the condensers shot high above the surface of the river. Because of this, she was known locally as the "Yangtze Sprinkler."

Every three hours or so, she had to spar moor to clean the fires and give the strokers a blow. There were no ash hoists, and when the fireroom hatches were open to manhandle the buckets of clinkers on deck, the forced draft was killed and the fire lost its go. That meant the fire had to be built up from scratch. Another long wait. Adrian, Bodine, and Colonel Gibb sat on the afterdeck watching this. "My God!" Adrian said. "We're never going to get anywhere!"

"I didn't promise you the Dollar Line, bunkie. You gotta remember we're guests of Uncle Sambo."

"I find it most pleasant." The Colonel was lounging in a folding deck chair, Panama over his eyes, and a half-full tumbler of whiskey clutched in his right hand. "Too damn much zip-zippin' about these days, anyway. Not enough layin' back, I say."

Wally came up. "We're going to chow-down while the coolies blow the fire up. If you'll follow me, gentlemen."

They went along the squeeze of a passageway to the tight rectangular space of the wardroom. The old mainmast ran straight up through the center, and at a table built around it two ensigns and a chief gunner's mate sat drinking warm UB beer, waiting for chow. "Sorry about the beer, but the fridge hasn't worked since 1920 or '21," Wally said as a messboy poured.

Adrian shook his head. "This is a real shock to a taxpayer. Our Navy is suppose to be the best in the world—what happened to those great big ships I used to see plowing through the waves in Movietone newsreels?"

"China is the end of the line for every worn-out crock in the fleet," an ensign named Fred "Pop" Porter said. He was balding and looked near forty. "The *Minnie* is a chicken. You should have been aboard the *Monanock*. She was a Civil War monitor, for God's sake—the first ironclad to round Cape Horn."

"When I was on the *Quiros*," Roger, the younger ensign, said, "she was so terminal they posted a sign on the bridge with rules: one—she shall not be towed; two—she shall not fire a shot; and three—she shall not steam where there are heavy swells." They all thought this was funny.

"Come on," Wally said, "you're going to give these civilians the wrong idea. We have some new boats out here—the *Guam* and the five others of her class that were laid down in '26."

"Yeah, but they still can't get it right," the chief said. "They've got a six-foot draft—what we need is a boat that will float on wet grass." The "wet grass" gunboat was the dream of all river sailors.

At this point the messboy came in with trays of food. The small wardroom had no pantry or galley, and he had to carry their meals up a ladder from the crew's galley across the deck and through the passageway, beating off the flies along the way. The food was put down, and immediately a groan went up.

"Jee-zuss!" Pop said. "Not friggin' pheasant again!"

"On the same lousy piece of toast!"

Adrian tasted the meat. It was delicious. "You're not complaining about pheasant?"

"We have that or wild duck every damned day!" Pop said. "The crew has

145

lost about half their teeth on shot. We're gonna have to start checkin' for web feet next. Shit!"

"We don't get much red meat," Wally said. "No cold storage. The lakes around here are full of pheasant and migrating birds—what the Chinese call fly-fly ducks."

"Give me a good old barnyard walkee-walkee any day," the chief said. "Ever taste one of them black chickens up at Chungking?"

"How do you bag this game, chaps?" Gibb was forking in a breast section, eating with delicate bites.

"With a three-pound salute gun loaded with BB shot."

Gibb looked up. "I say—with a cannon?"

"A cannon?" Adrian laughed.

"We've gotten as many as fifty of our feathered friends with one broadside," Pop said.

"It's not something you'd want to brag about at your local hunting club, but around here it's hand-to-mouth. Wednesday is our big night—we get baked beans."

"You ginks have been out here too long," Bodine said. "When the dogs stop barkin' at you, it's time to go home."

"I can't afford to go home," the chief said, "not as long as Haig and Haig is ninety cents a bottle."

"Hear, hear." The colonel raised a toast. "To the drinkin' man's Valhalla!"

"The wife and I have a full-time houseboy for fourteen U.S. a month, and we belong to three clubs ashore," Pop said, picking at a wing.

"It's even better if you're not spliced." Roger smiled with obvious satisfaction. "You can get your ashes hauled three nights out of four and recuperate on the fourth with duty aboard."

Everybody agreed it *was* good duty. All those poor bohunks were in the breadlines at home, selling apples, mooching, there were no jobs, and the damn Wobblies and Reds were stirring up trouble—here the Navy took care of its own.

There was a surge of motion, and the dinner plates set up a rattle as the engines turned over. Wally pushed his chair back. "Sounds like the mighty giant has stirred herself. I'd better get topside to stand by for the next failure."

After a long, slow day Adrian stood with Bodine at the bow as the *Minnie* turned from the mainstream and maneuvered close in shore. The spar buoy was put over, and they tied her up. It was just about dusk, and the light was fading.

Adrian looked up. "How come we're stopping here?"

"This Navy doesn't travel at night on the Yangtze, bunkie. The *Minnie's* only got a little gasoline generator, good for maybe an hour's light, then it's candles. When it gets dark around here, everybody climbs in the rack."

"Where are we?"

"We passed Ching Chaing a couple of miles downriver. We're about halfway to Nanking. They stop here 'cause it's quiet and we're upstream from the garbage and shit."

Adrian looked up at the cliffs only a thousand yards away. From this angle, he could see the fringe of tough saw grass and the top of what looked like a ruined stone tower. It was a lonely spot. "I hope we're not going to have to sleep below. My God, there's no room down there and not a breath of air."

"Naw, we'll bunk topside."

They were issued canvas hammocks, and Adrian tied his between two of the stanchions at the lower deck railing. "This isn't half bad. It's a lot cooler than Shanghai."

"I'm gonna sling mine topside behind the stack," Bodine said.

Colonel Gibb strolled up. "I'll join you, old son." He was still in his suit and tie, Panama hat at a rakish angle, a drink in one hand, the hammock draped over the other.

"I'm going to stay down here."

"Suit yourself." And they went off to the ladder leading to the third deck.

Adrian took his shoes and socks off, set them on the hatch cover, and hung his pants and shirt neatly over the railing. He climbed into the hammock in just his shorts; it was surprisingly comfortable. They were out beyond the mosquito line, and the gentle rocking of the boat with the water lapping against the hull next to him lulled him to sleep almost at once.

On the bridge, Quartermaster 2nd Class Randall Voss had the watch. He was a bulky boy from Bridgeport, Connecticut, who had been tattooed at the Danbury Fair and subsequently thrown out of the house by his mother, who was convinced that only degenerates and sailors got tattooed. He joined the Navy. Tonight he wore a webbed belt and a holstered .45 automatic that was called the "target pistol" because nobody had ever hit anything with it. He was reasonably alert, but not riveted. There was no moon at all, and it was very dark, with only the suggestion of where the sky met the shoreline. Peering over the bridge railing, he couldn't see the water two decks below. For a minute he thought he heard an unfamiliar sound, but put it down as the *Minnie* shifting her bulk.

Adrian was totally sunk in sleep. The hammock hung like a peapod at the rail just over the water, enclosing him in a snug cocoon. Then in one tiny section of his brain an alarm sounded. Something cold had just touched his foot and was proceeding up his leg. He was dreaming and had the impression of a large snake. When it reached his shorts, his eyes fluttered, snapped open, and he let out a piercing scream. On the bridge Randall straightened up so fast he slammed his head on the pipe canopy. Fumbling out the .45, he snapped off the safety and jumped down the ladder.

In Adrian's frantic convolutions to escape the hammock, it swung wildly, closing in on him like a clam shell. He could not seem to get his leg out to make contact with the deck, and as in a nightmare, time seemed suspended.

Randall Voss came thundering down the deck with the target pistol in one hand, an acetylene light in the other.

Beaming it over the side, he picked up a boatload of Chinese. They had glided silently up to the *Minnie* and in the pitch black, reaching for a grip with a boat hook, had shoved it into Adrian's hammock. It was caught now, and as the boatman pulled at it he rocked the hammock violently, preventing Adrian's escape. In the bow an unpleasant-looking Chinese with rotten teeth and a scraggly mustache swung up a *da boa* and Randall fired. He missed, but the man wasn't striking at him, and in an easy arc hacked the rope holding one end of the hammock to the stanchion. It fell, releasing the boat hook and slamming Adrian's back and head against the teak deck.

By now there were a dozen men topside, but the Chinese and the boat had disappeared in the night. Bodine, holding the trench-cleaner at the ready, helped Adrian up. "Ohhhhhh!" Adrian moaned, holding the back of his head. "God! That hurt!"

"You shouldn't have strung your hammock down here, bunkie."

"Well, why in the hell didn't you tell me that!"

"You're gonna have t' figure out a few things for yourself—this ain't a lecture tour, y' know."

Wally swung a wet cloth in the breeze and handed it to Adrian. "You all right?"

"Thanks." Adrian laid the cloth against the back of his neck. "I guess I'll live—who were that bunch? Pirates?"

"Nothing so romantic—probably just poor farmers. They row out at night and steal anything that's not bolted down. We've had them reach into portholes. It can be pretty unnerving to have a hand come crawling across your face in the middle of the night."

"It can't be any worse than having a boat hook shoved up your shorts!"

"It could have been a lot worse," somebody said. "He could have gotten a grip on your nuts."

That was hard to argue with.

Max proceeded straight up through the Chapei District, then across the flat, boring Shanghai countryside. In the distance, off to his left, patient drone mules circled wells, drawing water for irrigation. Beyond them in the fields many backs bent at work. He passed a gray-walled temple with monks sitting in the shade delousing themselves. From the burial mounds behind them, he could smell the casually buried dead responding to the heat wave.

By three o'clock he was following the river road along the Yangtze. It was not paved, and as he went, dust plumed up in his wake. He made an effort to pass around the larger concentrations of population, and where he couldn't, his passage was slowed by the congestion of carts pulled by ruined horses. Mangy dogs snapped at his tires, and the beggars seemed determined to throw themselves under the wheels. For Max, a tidy, immaculately clean Japanese, the Chinese were an enigma. The foul streets, lack of sanitation, and utter filth appalled him. As he passed small shops and homes, he could see in through the open doors to rude tables and stools, straw beds and primitive cooking conditions. It wasn't just poverty. There was no attempt at simple decoration or modest celebration of beauty. None.

It was the same in the open countryside. Driving along next to the Yangtze's muddy path, he would glimpse ahead what seemed lovely streams feeding into it from bright green fields and the umbrella of trees shading thatched-hut villages. When he arrived, he would find the streams polluted, the river's edge packed with pitiful boat people, living like animals on wretched, verminous craft. The villages swarmed with flies from open garbage dumps, and with all the sweet country air, huts would be dark and windowless. The ground around them beaten flat by thrashing and without flowers or anything deliberately planted to relieve the utter dreariness. Max set his mouth and put it down to laziness and lack of national spirit. These were character flaws that the Japanese had dealt with successfully.

By nightfall the lack of road signs or even roads slowed his progress considerably. Asking directions was impossible; he spoke some Chinese, but it didn't matter; the people hid from his approach. Even this close to Shanghai, everyone was wary of bandits. China had suffered from these irregulars since the failure of the 1911 revolution had turned the country into armed camps and spawned that Oriental curse, the warlord. In the north the armies of three field marshals had been involved in fighting around Hopeh Province, and in a final decisive battle on the alluvial plain west of Tiensin, the Fengtein Army of Chang Tso-lin had emerged victorious, decimating his enemies.

It was the shattered remnants of defeated armies, leaderless, hungry, desperate men who had formed into bands that ravaged the countryside, exacting squeeze and taking hostages. There was no real central government to speak of, and the locals were left to the fortunes of war. Chiang Kai-shek, the strong right arm of the Kuomintang, the emergent political party, stayed in the south, biding his time, playing off his own generals, and fighting the Communists. The foreign garrisons did their best to protect nationals in the concessions, and visible gunboats patrolled the rivers. If you were smart in the China of 1931, you stayed home.

At some time after three in the morning, Max located the feeble lights of Ching Chaing. Skirting the town, he turned in on a rough path a mile down the road that he calculated led to the cliffs overlooking the Yangtze. He parked the Model A with difficulty in the ruins of a stone barn, where he hoped it was concealed. There was no way to tell; it was dark and impossible to make out landmarks. Without the headlights of the car he might have very well missed the cliffside completely and gone over the edge. He looked at his watch. Because he had followed the twist of the river (like the gunboat), it had taken him nearly fifteen hours to make a trip the train did in four. He wondered if that Navy chief had given him the right information. Was the gunboat here?

Taking a battery flashlight and the rifle, he made his way along the cliff top, looking for signs the gunboat had tied up offshore. A good mile from the car he finally made out the swinging speck of lantern light at what appeared to be mast-top height. He estimated this was the approximate position, but was it the American gunboat, a junk, or his imagination? He would have to wait until morning to find out. Dead tired, he lay down in the rough saw grass and promptly fell asleep, his head resting on the canvas carrier containing the sniper's rifle.

Max woke to a shrill, piercing trill. It carried across the water, and he jerked up to find dawn breaking. There, only a hundred meters offshore, was the gunboat. The sound he heard was the bosun's pipe as the morning watch came on. At this range even their features were visible. The sun was behind him, and its vivid rays illuminated the homely shape of the *Fat Minnie*. The sag of her deckline was enlivened now as the Chinese "crew" began a clean sweepdown fore and aft, and cooks set about breakfast. The bosun's pipe next announced the "smoking lamp was lit."

It was perfect. He had stayed on the northeastern shore of the river to give him the right shooting light, and from this elevation on the cliff he could aim directly down into the open bridge. Max was well concealed on the grassy field and could make out no house or man-made obstruction in his line of sight. He slipped the rifle out of the canvas carrier and once again checked it. This particular model, the Meiji 38-year type, had been modified into a sniper's rifle by careful attention to manufacturing and rechambering from 6.5mm to 7.7. Its best feature was a special telescopic sight the captain had insisted on. Max attached this to the left of the receiver, screwing it in opposite the turned-down bolt handle. Snapping out the wire monopod under the fore end, he rested the rifle on its support and braced his shoulder to the stock, eye to the scope.

Bodine and Adrian had coffee in the crew's quarters and went up to watch the *Minnie* get under way. Colonel Gibb was sleeping in, and as Adrian passed him, they saw he had removed only his coat, hat, and shoes. His legs were primly crossed over still-neat trousers, creases razor-edged, and above his folded hands the regimental tie was correctly knotted. As usual, the glass eye remained gazing at the sky while the other slept.

They went up the ladder to the bridge, where Wally Hamm and the quartermaster, Randall Voss, were going over the charts. "I hear you turned in below for the rest of the night, Reed," Wally said, smiling.

"That's right, and if you had a cellar on this tub, I would have gone down there too."

"You can't let these Chinos get you down, bunkie. They're just playful. If that bird had wanted to, he could have taken your head off last night, rather than just choppin' the hammock stay."

"Their concern was lost on me at the time."

"Mr. Bodine's right," Randall said. "Those slopes are sure death with them hog hackers, but give 'em a gun an' they can't shoot for sour owl shit."

"That's encouraging."

"It's got somethin' t' do with their eyes, I think—they just don't see right for shootin'."

"It's not that. The dumb bastards don't know how to lead a target."

"Let's hope they don't learn," Adrian said.

The stokers began to build up steam, and as the ship's company bustled about, Bodine and Adrian stepped to the starboard side of the bridge. Leaning on the pipe railing, they looked at the rise of the cliff at the shoreline. "You couldn't go ashore here if you wanted to," Adrian said. "There are cliffs like this all along the river."

"That's because the river's dropping. It does that even this far down. Hell, from October to April up at Hankow the water will drop fifty feet, near a hundred at Chungking. That's one reason the *Minnie* parks out here. You don't want to be tied up ashore when it falls out from under you overnight—it can be embarrassin'."

"I guess."

"In this country it's one damn extreme after another. In spring with the meltin' snow and monsoons the river will bust loose and rise fifty feet in a few hours. It comes roarin' down from the mountains, tearin' everything up, sendin' out great surges of water over the dikes that back up sewage—Jesus, what a stink! At that point the whole valley is one big lake, and you have to navigate by the rooftops of villages."

The magnification of the scope was 2.5X, the field of view 13 degrees. He not only could see Bodine clearly, but he could actually make out the anchor and world emblem on his campaign hat. Max had waited patiently until Bodine came on deck, then followed him up on the bridge. At any time in the last few minutes he could have gotten off a shot that probably would have been fatal, but he wanted to be absolutely sure. With Bodine facing him, looking into the rising sun, it couldn't be better. Max was a good shot, excelling in the handling of weapons as if to reinforce the image of himself as a samurai, a man at arms. He snapped in the five-shot clip, cocked the rifle on closing the bolt, and took off the safety by pulling out the mushroom-head knob and turning it to the right. He was in the correct prone firing position. He was ready.

"Why stay in China with all its troubles?" Adrian said.

"Why? Hell, I love this country. The States are full of radio-talkin' politicos, money grabbers, and weak sisters. Here it's like you turned the times back a couple of hundred years. There's somethin' to push against, t' get your teeth in." Bodine laughed. "If we could just get rid of the damn Chinese, it would be near perfect."

Adrian believed him. He was a throwback to Social Darwinism and Manifest Destiny, trumpeted by adventurers like Homer Lea, Teddy Roosevelt, and now the Japanese.

They would make China into a better place if they had to kill the Chinese to do it.

Max was holding his breath, letting it slowly out, eye against the rubber ring of the scope. The graticule pattern provided for drift and windage and was calibrated for a maximum range of 1,500 meters. The aiming reticle was zeroed in on Bodine's cap device. Max moved it down in minute increments until it steadied between his eyes, then began to squeeze the trigger.

Squinting, Bodine raised his arm, pointing to the cliff. "Do you see . . ."

"What?" Adrian looked in that direction, startled in the next instant by a sharp crack followed by a whine. Still looking toward the cliff, he saw a white puff of smoke. When he heard a commotion behind him and turned, Bodine was sprawled on the deck. The campaign hat was gone, and his head a mass of blood.

Max lowered the rifle. He had kept his eye to the scope until he got the shot away and had seen the bullet hit Bodine square in the center of the forehead.

The captain's honor was satisfied.

NINETEEN

EVERYONE WAS SHOOTING at once. Colonel Gibb appeared on deck and fired Bodine's shotgun, Panama hat in place, tie straight, pumping the empty shells out in a blur. Randall Voss was banging away with the "target pistol," its blued barrel lifting his hand spastically at each round. Below, Adrian could hear a catalogue of detonations, from the woodpecker chatter of automatic weapons to the thump of what must have been the salute cannon-cum-bird gun. The racket was horrific, and with the acrid smoke and noise it was impossible to tell if anyone was firing back from the cliff. He had remained in a half crouch, as if arrested in the first motion of a dive for cover. The truth was, there was no cover in the open pipework and canvas of the bridge.

Wally Hamm knelt over Bodine, shielding him from view, and Adrian was thankful. He hated the sight of blood. He had seen plenty of it during his polo years and avoided the inadvertent viewing of injuries other than his own. He did not want to look into what had been, minutes before, a healthy, animated face and find the mouth slack and the eyes glazed. He did not want to look on death.

Max backed away from the cliffside, crawling flat on his belly and pulling the rifle after him. Over his head the air was alive with the zip of bullets, each announcing its own caliber by trajectory and loudness of intent. He could actually hear them cut the tough saw grass. There was little chance of being hit from the angle of fire, but nevertheless he didn't rise for a good twenty yards, then got up, running at a crouch, sliding the rifle into the canvas bag as he went. There was a possibility that the gunboat would put a landing party ashore, and he wanted to clear the area as quickly as possible. Ahead was the outline of the ruined barn where he'd hidden the car. It was a tumble of uneven, worn stones, obviously built in a time when the soil along the cliff was fertile. Every stick of wood and usable thing had been carried away, and only the corner end of the building stood upright, forming a "tower" by default. Max stepped over the rubble, picked his way around a crumbling angle to where the car was parked out of sight—and stopped short.

A half dozen Chinese stood around the car. One actually sat behind the wheel; another hunched down, busily cutting up the spare tire into what looked like shoe-length sizes. The others sorted through tools and supplies tossed on the ground. At his appearance, they stopped and looked up. All were poorly dressed in ragged mismatched clothes, and although Max could not immediately detect any firearms, each man carried the wicked beheading sword on his back. They were obviously not farmers, and certainly couldn't qualify for even a marginal military appearance. Were they *ni-zku*—bandits? Had they seen him shoot Bodine?

The sporadic firing from the gunboat was still echoing loudly up the cliff; they could hardly miss that. There was a movement, and Max was aware of another man standing slightly behind him, holding what looked like a percussion shotgun. That made seven.

The Chinese behind the wheel smiled with rotten teeth. Ragged as the rest, with matted hair and a scraggly mustache, there was a slyness and hint of intelligence in his face. He pushed the corner of his eyes upward with dirty index fingers, then pointed to Max. "All time Nippon fella." The others laughed. "You bring one time ridee-walkee, cumshaw?"

He had a sense of humor. He was suggesting that Max had brought the car as a present. In pidgin English words were treated as Chinese characters, and a great deal of the country spoke it. One advantage was that only about three hundred words were needed to carry on a conversation. Max now tried to remember a few of them. First, he had to establish firmly ownership of the car. "Ridee-walkee blongee plenty number-one soljer boss!"

Eyebrows went up and tongues clucked. The leader raised his hands and mimicked shooting a rifle. Another man put his finger to his forehead and crooked his thumb. "Nippon all time soljer?" They had seen him shoot Bodine!

He hesitated, then said, "All-proper soljer!"

"Ai-ee! Hao-hao!" They seemed to approve and looked at him with new interest.

Max calculated his chances. He still held the rifle case at his right side, and there were four shells left in the clip. Could he unlimber it in time to get into action and make a run for it? No. He *was* a soldier and could not abandon the captain's property to them under any circumstance.

The leader had been watching him carefully. *"Ai-ah!* Nippon fella!" He waggled the steering wheel. "You come alongtime! Savvee makee ridee-walkee?" Max squared his shoulders and walked to the car. Holding his eyes on the leader, he very deliberately shoved the rifle case under the front seat, then pushed in beside him behind the wheel. The Chinese smiled and pointed ahead. "Wantchee longside, chop chop!" Max turned the ignition key, bobbed the choke, and the engine fired. While he did this, the others threw the tools and tire sections into the rumble seat and clambered aboard. He flopped the Ford into gear, let the clutch out. It groaned and they moved away.

The *Minnie* continued upriver at her snail's pace, "sprinkles" fanning out in a fine mist. Bodine had been carried below, the blood hosed off the bridge, and Adrian and Gibb stood under the canopy looking back at the cliffs. At the rail, ship's company still held their weapons, the deck littered with spent shells.

"No chance of duckin' ashore?" Gibb asked. "An' trackin' the fellow down?"

"I'm afraid not," Wally said. "Comyangpac is sticky about landing parties. Only where the 'lives of U.S. nationals and noncombatants are in imminent danger is Navy personnel to effect direct action on Chinese soil. . . .'"

"I see," Gibb said, uncocking the trench-cleaner.

Everyone was still in shock. Not so much from the attack, but from the fact that it had been successfully carried out. "Jesus!" Pop said. "That's the first time the bastards ever really hit anybody. I mean, God! I can't believe it! They got him square in the forehead—that was some shooting!"

"It had to be an accident, dumb luck!"

"Hook doesn't have anything that could shoot that straight—a bunch of old rabbit guns. I heard that baby, *zee-wow!* It sounded like a Springfield."

"I don't think so." Roger doubled as gunnery officer and was the boat's ad hoc ordinance expert. "A thirty-ott-six makes a lot more noise."

"Maybe it's not Hook then."

"Who's Hook?" Adrian said.

Wally swung around, pointing. "Just up ahead five or six miles is a tight bend in the river—the hook. It's the squeeze concession of a small-time bandit we call Captain Hook. He shakes down the locals, and his boys fire off a few rounds when we go by. They've never hit anybody before, and he knows the Navy won't pay off, so it's really kind of a charade. Up to now it's been a joke, harmless."

"The thing is," Roger said, "the river narrows down to a place where we have to pass them practically eyeball to eyeball. Now—up on the bluff they've got this old Maxim seventy-five field gun . . ."

"Is that big?"

"Well, think of a high-explosive shell about the size of a fireplug."

"What!"

"That's right—it's a big mean-looking old devil. We think it's just there for show, and as far as we know it's never been let off—but on the other hand, if it was, they could hardly miss. And I'll tell you, that fireplug could knock some hole in the *Minnie's* rusty ass."

"Wait a minute!" Adrian said, gesturing at the sturdy gun mounts fore and aft. "You've got all these big guns!"

"Shall I tell him?" Roger said.

Wally smiled. "He's a taxpayer."

"For her size, the *Minnie* has probably got more armament than any other ship in the Far East Fleet." He held his fingers up, ticking them off. "We have four four-inch rifles and four six-pounders—eight big pieces of ordinance. But none of *us* has ever seen any of *them* fired. We've never been issued shells, and if we were, it would be tricky. These are real museum pieces with fixed iron sights and cranky three-shift breech blocks."

"I don't believe this!" Adrian said.

Wally patted him on the arm. "Nothing to worry about, Adrian—remember, the bandits don't know that. When we steam the hook, the crew will man the guns just as if they worked, and we'll point them in their direction anyway."

"That's right," Roger said. "The bandits probably don't have any ammo for their gun either."

Adrian wasn't that sure.

Max was directed across open fields of saw grass. He could tell by the loop of the river that they were taking a shortcut across a point of land. In the distance the brown snake of the Yangtze straightened out. The car labored painfully in low gear under the combined weight of his passengers, and he kept his eyes straight ahead, doing his best not to appear nervous. Jammed into the front of the roadster with two others, the man with the bad teeth was pressed against him, giving off disturbing odors. Max knew if he turned his head he would find him staring.

They rode this way for perhaps twenty minutes, then as the river came closer, the car dipped down into a depression and he could see the smoke and

156

clutter of a ragged group of huts. Coming up the rise, an advance guard of yapping dogs and dirty children ran out to meet them. He slowed, stopping the car on the upswing of the hill. There seemed to be forty or fifty individuals; men in the same poor clothing armed with knives, *da boas* and a scatter of antique weapons. Women peered out from doorways, babies clutching their legs. The old hunkered together, and it appeared more a poor village than an armed camp. Around them the grass had been beaten flat; piles of garbage, seeping sewage, and rotting discards traced the perimeter of the compound.

The car was swarmed over, and Max had the feeling they regarded it as a captured trophy. The bandit leader got out ceremoniously, and beating off the most persistent of the welcomers, took Max by the arm and walked him toward the cliff edge. Through the crowd, Max saw an object with tall spoked wheels, low wooden carriage, and the projection of a heavy iron barrel. They stopped in front of it, and he bent down to read the brass manufacturer's plate:

MAXIM-NORDENFELT M. 1897

It was a popular design originally sold to the Transvaal government and used by the Boers during the 1899-1902 South African War. In the interim it had probably changed hands a dozen times before being stolen from the old Republican Army warehouse at Nan-t'ung in 1928 by "Captain Hook." Since then it had sat on this cliff top, an ominous beacon, without anybody able to fire it.

At this moment Max knew exactly *why* they had taken the effort to bring him here. Turning toward the river, he could see the speck of the gunboat rounding the hump of land and steaming toward them.

Adrian watched uneasily as two Lewis machine guns were mounted on the upper deck. Forward, Roger and the gunner's mate were issuing more weapons: an assortment of sub-machine guns, Springfield rifles, shotguns, pistols—something for everybody. On the bridge Wally cocked back the bolt of a worn hunting rifle, and Colonel Gibb adjusted the sling on one of the Springfields. "You going to be okay with that?" Wally said, indicating Bodine's pump shotgun. "It doesn't have much reach."

"He's right, old son, it's a bit short-ranged."

"Well, you told me we were going to see the whites of their eyes, didn't you?"

"True." Wally smiled. "If they get real close, I could also let you have a cutlass or a boarding pike. We still have some aboard . . . if you can believe it."

Adrian believed it.

"Hook comin' up!" the bosun shouted from the bow. Along the starboard railing, behind projections and bulkheads, the ship's company pointed their eclectic weapons toward the cliff top. The gunner's mate walked the line, underlining instructions.

"Now remember the drill, you people! No sustained bursts! And, Voss, for Christ's sake, watch that Thompson! The last time you ejected four hot cases down Cookie's shirtfront!" Somebody laughed. "It ain't funny, assholes! We had duck soup for a week!"

Adrian heard the gunners on the upper deck cock the Lewis guns and the shuffle of feet as they got ready. Below, the fires were clean, and the stokers bent into it to give maximum speed past the danger spot—about on a par with a fast jog.

On the cliff top Max had the two boxes of ammunition pried open. The shells lay in their original excelsior packing, and although the brass cases were corroded, they seemed sound. The fuses were something else. If powder-filled, they would be sensitive to humidity and temperature and, being exposed to the elements, as these were, useless. He took one out of its cradle and examined it. It had German markings and was mechanical. Good, its only drawback was a possibility of lost tension if it had been stored too long. The only way he would find that out was by trying it. He screwed one into the top of the cleanest shell and set the calibrations for nearly point-blank range.

To arrive at the rank of sergeant, Max had taken a series of written examinations. One of them included ordnance, and he tried to remember it. Stepping up to the gun, he tentatively tugged the cam lever back several times and got the breech open. It was a screw mechanism, with a block mounted eccentrically to the bore's axis. He looked up the barrel and could not see light. The bore cleaning brush was still strapped in a leather holder on the side of the carriage, and he got this out, shoving it up the length of the barrel and dislodging several bottles and what appeared to be a nest.

Around him, the bandits were pushing and shoving like excited children. The entire camp had gathered at the cliff edge: nursing mothers, toothless hags, dogs by the dozens, and giggling girls in shapeless sacks. A communal shout went up and fingers poked him, pointing. The gunboat was clearly visible, rounding the hook about a mile off and approaching the squeeze in the river. Max looked up. When it reached a position where a clear shot down the angle of the cliff was possible, it would be in sight for probably less than a minute. He would have only one chance.

His audience was hopping up and down, screaming with excitement in anticipation of noise and destruction. Lifting the armed shell gingerly, he maneuvered around babies and old ladies, aligned the nose with the bore, and inserted it, rotating the block to swing its solid section into place behind the cartridge case. The gun was pointed in the general direction of the river, but

158

the barrel tilted up at the sky. Max twisted the elevation screw up as far as it would go, but the barrel still wouldn't depress enough to reach the river.

He shouted at the Chinese. "Pushee upside! Chop chop!" indicating they were to lift the tail piece. A dozen instantly fought for the honor, knocking each other down to get a grip. With a communal grunt they lifted it, and he shoved the wooden ammunition boxes under the towing eye. Sighting it again, he realized the trajectory was still wrong. This time he had them push the gun to the very edge of the cliff, turned at nearly a right angle to the river. He set the brake blocks and lined up the barrel, putting his eye to the rocking-bar sight on the left side of the carriage. Laying out an invisible mark the gunboat would have to pass, he manipulated the leveling wheel until the barrel corresponded with his line of sight. When it got to that marked-off section, he would fire directly into the bridge. The shell would be timed to pass through and explode in the engine room.

The shipboard comedians fell silent, and everyone on deck watched the spot on the cliff where the gun was visible. The *Fat Minnie* was committed to the squeeze, and the helmsman kept as far as possible to the opposite bank as the narrow bottleneck of the river would allow. On the bridge next to him, Wally fine-tuned his binoculars on the gun. "Jesus!"

"What is it?" Adrian said.

"They've manned the gun! Swung the damned thing around until the barrel is pointing down our throats!" He shouted into a megaphone. *"All hands open fire!!"*

As the boat approached his aiming coordinate, Max stood to the left side, behind the gunlayer's guard. Bracing himself, he held on to one end of the firing lanyard ready to jump clear of the expected recoil.

NOW!

He gave the lanyard a fierce jerk—and the rotted cord snapped off in the middle! The bandits, fingers in their ears, looked at him, mouths open. Without hesitating, he reached for the remains of the cord, looped it around his fingers, and jerked again. This time it went off.

Adrian heard the boom from the cliff top and in what seemed the same instant felt a buffet of air that passed directly overhead. The second's delay in firing, plus the *Minnie*'s forward speed, had thrown the shell's trajectory off by a scant yard, and the incoming round narrowly cleared the bridge target. Holing the ventilator on the top deck directly behind them, it proceeded in an almost perfect alignment, traveling downward between the lower deck railing and disappeared into the river with a modest splash. The spring in the fuse mechanism had lost tension, and the shell would not explode for another three minutes.

On the cliff top several unexpected things happened at the same time. The hydrospring recoil system that made the gun maneuverable also made it "lively" when fired. Going off, it recoiled, violently, upsetting the boxes elevating its tailpiece. As it did, twisting to one side, the heavy artillery wheel closest to the cliff edge dug in, rotated, and started to slip over. Lying prone two yards away, Max watched in horror as it began to go. There was nothing anyone could do to stop it; they were all hugging the ground as a curtain of incoming fire from the gunboat below shredded the cliff edge. Everyone had a good view as two tons of dead weight disappeared from sight.

Directly below, Randall Voss, isolated at the bow with the erratic Thompson sub-machine gun, looked up to see an enormous object hurtling off the forty-foot cliff and plunge straight for him. He jumped, but not quickly enough, and the trailing edge of the carriage clipped him as it hit, breaking his leg below the knee. The sound of the cannon as it broke through the teak deck was more impressive than its own voice and all the combined gunfire it proceeded to drown out. The splintering of wood was accompanied by dense, solid iron colliding with pipes, valves, deck framing, and the years of accumulated stores in the *Minnie's* chain locker. Its crashing, thudding rumble echoed between the cliff sides, and miles away, people looked to the sky for rain. The ship's company was stunned; the crescendo of the cannon's passage through the deck had stopped their own noisy gunfire as surely as the drop of a conductor's baton at the end of an impassioned movement.

The barrel had fallen in nearly a straight line and punched a solid hole in the *Minnie's* tender iron bottom. Its further descent to the river floor was arrested by the wooden wheels. As they met *Minnie's* bottom, their iron hoops were flung off, spokes shucked, and they fetched up to the hubs. The gun stopped dead.

There was a split second's pause as the astounded crew looked toward the awful hole in the deck, still reverberating with the sounds of falling pieces and groans of contracting metal. Then they jumped into action. Randall was dragged back. The bosun climbed down into the tangled space of the chain locker and saw at once that the gun barrel had penetrated the iron hull. Water was gushing in.

On the cliff top Max jumped up and ran for his life. The bandits still lay prone, staring at the vacant spot where their totem had vanished seconds before. With several dogs yapping at his heels, Max made it down the gentle incline to the Ford and leaped over the door onto the seat. Reaching for the ignition key in the nickle-plated trefoil, his hand closed on open space. *It wasn't there!* He heard a shout and looked up to see the bandit leader and two men running down the slope toward him. Kicking the door open, he climbed out and scrabbled under the seat for the rifle. *It wasn't there!* They had taken it and the key out of the car while he was struggling with the field gun. A high-pitched whine went over his head, and he knew where the rifle was; the leader had stopped and was firing it at him. The other two kept running, the first man reaching over his shoulder and unsheathing the bright blade of a *da boa*.

Then Max remembered—he'd put his sword under the seat well when he left Shanghai! Had they taken that too? He shoved the seat up and began searching frantically—was it there? Bent over, face pressed against the front of the seat, his hand explored blindly—then his fingers found it, pushed to the back under the jack. He jerked the blade free and turned as his attacker reached him. Expecting no resistance, the man was in full charge, *da boa* over his head when Max turned, and in a sweeping right-hand motion sliced through the thin cotton jumper and opened up his abdominal muscles. The man stopped with a small, shocked cry, took one step back, and sat down abruptly, hands clutched to his stomach, holding his entrails in.

Behind him the second man saw the sword flash and turned to run. But he was too late; Max brought the blade up and over with both hands and buried it in his left shoulder. The man went down screaming as another shot winged by.

The bandit leader struggled awkwardly to get the rifle in the proper position and aimed, but he had never handled a modern weapon and it was beyond him. As he fumbled with the bolt, Max bore down on him, swinging the bloody sword and shouting his samurai battle cry. It was a frightening charge, but the bandit stood his ground and got the next shell in place.

Max had been drilled that there was no excuse a Japanese soldier could offer for leaving his rifle in the field. None. Death is preferable. As he ran toward the man fumbling with his rifle, his determination was reinforced by the man's bad aim. As the third, then fourth shot sang past, he knew the clip was empty and it gave his charge extra impetus. "Captain Hook," unnerved, dropped the weapon and ran.

Scooping it up, Max reversed direction, ran back and leaped into the front seat of the car. This time he nudged the car out of gear, let off the hand brake, and began to roll backward down the gentle slope.

As he did, the entire bandit camp appeared at the top of the hill in full pursuit: ragtag irregulars, women, children, and the old—a dozen curs running in the vanguard, yapping their heads off. Rocks and sticks were hurled, then a blast from the percussion shotgun and buckshot rattled off his windshield. At that point the small incline began to straighten out and the car slowed, rolling a few more feet, then stopped.

The *Minnie* kept to her course downstream with a slight limp, as the river eddies detoured around the cannon barrel projecting from her bottom. But she was under way, and the leak around the barrel had been slowed. The bosun's working party had hammered a full roll of oakum into the leak with wooden wedges and mallets. The gun's carriage had been tied down to prevent it from shifting the plug of a barrel, and it seemed to be holding for the moment.

Ship's company, Adrian, and the officers stood looking down into the impressive hole, watching the desperate operation. They all had been awed by the cannon's dramatic appearance onboard.

"That is really something!" Roger said, shaking his head.

"Jesus!" the chief said. "I'll bet this is the only fuckin' ship in the entire history of the U.S. Navy that ever had a cannon *dropped* on it!"

They all had to agree.

"Wait until Bodine sees it," Wally said, smiling.

"Sees what?" Bodine said, pushing through the crowd.

NANKING,
FALL
1931

TWENTY

SOME TIME AFTER midnight on the fifth of October 1931, a procession of vehicles moved across the northern edge of Nanking. Two Packard touring cars, tops up, side curtains snapped in, preceded four chain-driven Rio trucks, all tightly covered with tarps. As the convoy left the huddle of the town, a new moon, bright, unclouded, washed over an abrupt change in the landscape. Stone bridges crossed clogged streams to nowhere; the tangle of wild briers tracing the hump of building foundations and the faint grid shape of city blocks were cast in dark relief. By the side of the overgrown road the flutter of game birds rose with the passage of the convoy's headlights, and at a distance, enclosing the ghosts of dead populations, was the shadowy impression of a great wall.

In the backseat of the lead Packard, the blur of a small face appeared in the stitched square of an isinglass window. Distorted, the twist of red-blond curls bounced under a cloche hat.

"Christ! What happened here, Charley?"

A portly Chinese gentleman leaned over and caressed her shoulder, moving his fingers under a fox scarf. "A thing not for you to worry about, princess. Yes, it was trouble long ago, distant."

Nanking had seven times been the capital of regional empires (twice before the birth of Christ), four times the seat of more "modern" governments, and once the capital of death.

The *Taiping Tein Kuo* (Heavenly Kingdom of Great Peace) captured it in 1853. These religious fanatics led by a despot, a self-styled "Little Brother of Jesus," set out to put others on the "Right Path": common property, abstinence, and destruction of landlords. It was a popular cause (not unlike later communist aims), but intolerant of dissent. Before their defeat by the mercenary armies of Charles Gordon a decade later, twenty million Chinese had been killed. In Nanking alone, a population of one million had been cut in half. Now, seventy years later, the Packards and Rios traveled past empty fields where streets had once teemed with life and the buildings of a city had stood. Beyond, the great wall circled the survivors and the melancholy reminder of the missing.

At one of thirteen gates, the vehicles exited to the edge of the Yangtze. They were ferried across to Pukow on the north shore where the convoy made its way around the main terminus of the Tientsin-Nanking Railway. Lights on dim, they bumped over the tracks to a fenced junction on the outskirts of the yard. On a siding behind barbed wire the dark shape of a private railway train picked up the shine of their incoming lights. Behind the locomotive was a baggage car and an elegant dark green parlor/sleeping car. On the railing of its rear observation platform a name could be read: EMPRESS OF THE EAST.

The lead Packard stopped at the gate, and Marshal Yü shifted, looking past the shoulders of his driver and personal bodyguard to a heavy car, a Minerva, parked inside the wire. The gate was opened by soldiers, and the Packard entered, stopping alongside the other car. For a long moment it seemed there might be an impasse, a problem in protocol; then with the clack of a latch the rear door of the Minerva swung open.

The Marshal sighed and eased himself forward. As he did, he spoke softly to his companion. "It would be most considerate if you allow me to conduct business, just the minute."

"Take your time, Charley," Lola said. Patting her silken leg, he got out.

He crossed between the cars behind his bodyguard, bowed, and stooped into the backseat of the Minerva. There, lounging against the right side of the seat in a gray silk Nationalist uniform, he recognized Dai Chung-hsi, the Generalissimo's Chief of Staff. The man had a scarred face like mended crockery and a wayward mustache that reminded Yü of cats' whiskers. They exchanged greetings, a litany of admiration for the other's honesty, bravery, and good taste, then launched into a neutral conversation about mandrake roots. Actually, the deal had been agreed on months before. It was simple venery; one third of the gold, some two hundred thirty-nine thousand in U.S. dollars was to be paid in advance for the nod of the Genera-

lissimo's shaved dome. It was a shocking bite, a squeeze of imperial propor-
tions, but the Marshal understood and accepted it. There was no way he
could continue without an unspoken agreement that they supported him
against his son. Getting down to business, he tried to squeeze another concession.

"There is the unimportant possibility that I will be followed here by those
who do not wish me well."

Dai smiled. "I cannot imagine any who would wish to do you harm, dear
sir."

"It is sad—malevolence in the world exceeds belief—still, those who walk
with heads high must often tread on trash."

"So true."

"These may be foreigners—Americans—and as such out of bounds by our
laws."

He pushed the right button. Dai brushed at his whiskers and commented
without concession, "Foreigners—Americans included—have no rights here
other than what we choose to give them." In 1927 when Chiang's Cantonese
troops had taken the city they had roughed up American nationals, attacked
the Standard Oil compound on Socony Hill, and forced the evacuation of the
American consulate in what was called a "shocking violation." The American
government had been forced to swallow the insult like a fur ball. Dai took out
a gold Waterman pen, a cherished possession given to him by Herbert
Hoover when he worked as a young engineer on the Kallan Mining complex
at Chinguang-tao. He poised it over a tidy notebook. "Please give me the
names and descriptions of these persons." While he took them down, the
soldiers began unloading the trucks.

In the backseat of the Packard, Ramon slept fitfully, his face pressed in the
corner of the mohair upholstery. He slept a lot now that they were no longer
working Frisky's. Lola had not even bothered to tell the management they
had quit. Fuck 'em.

Yü had made her an up-front offer the night they drove away from that
insane party. Sixty-eight thousand dollars in gold to travel with him for the
next year. She couldn't say yes fast enough. It would be presented to her in a
"dowry" chest that she could keep under the bed if she liked. Here was a guy
who understood women.

So I've sold myself for an old man's gold. And that old man was an eyeopener in the sack. He had some new moves. Once you got used to the
tubby shape and slick skin, he could take you over the hurdles. Better, he was
sweet, generous, and treated her like she was important, fragile as an egg-
shell. She felt secure, taken care of. As for Adrian, she hadn't given him two
thoughts since her "honeymoon" began.

* * *

Bodine rotated the campaign hat, glad to be alive. He had been doing this for most of the day, sitting with Adrian, Gibb, and Wally Hamm under the canvas canopy at the stern of the *Minnie*. Luggage was piled around them, and Nanking was coming up. "How much do you figure the *Minnie* was movin', Wally? Up and down?" Bodine had asked this same question a dozen times.

Wally answered it the same way each time. "It was smooth as a duck pond at Ching Chaing, Warren. Couldn't have been more than a few inches' vertical movement."

Bodine stopped the hat's motion and examined the anchor-and-ball Marine Corps insignia screwed to the front. It had been distorted into a twist of metal, and above it an ugly hole pierced the "Montana peak" of the crown. "I figure that bozo was zeroed in between my eyes. He had the wind drift and yardage just right, but didn't calculate the *Minnie*'s up-and-down movement— she looked steady as a platform, right? Then when he pulled the trigger, she dropped that couple of inches and the bullet hit this cap device—deflected it." He rubbed his fingers over the brass. "It saved my ass."

"What saved your ass was a head like boiler plate. You couldn't penetrate that redheaded knob with a twenty-millimeter shell." Wally had made this joke before, but they laughed again. It wasn't funny. It had been a close thing; the bullet had traveled upward along Bodine's scalp, plowing a furrow four inches long, one quarter inch deep. The pharmacist's mate had taken twenty-three stitches to close the wound. Bodine's red hair was shaved straight up the front, and a bandage, reinforced by a wide band of tape, was anchored to his nose. To Adrian, it had the look of a Greek helmet. It was also likely both of Bodine's eyes would be black.

"I wonder who he was," Bodine said for the umpteenth time, not raising his eyes. What he didn't add was, "Why me?"

"Pilot comin' aboard, Mr. Hamm!" Voss shouted from the con. They got up and walked to the rail. It was late afternoon, and in the fading light the city of Nanking could be seen about a mile upriver surrounded by a high wall. Between it and the shore was the commercial sprawl Hsia-Kuan, an artificial "island" created by a canal jammed with junks and sampans. The Yangtze was nearly 4,000 feet wide here and choppy. Ahead in the roadstead were two American destroyers, the *Noa* and *Preston*, tied up with a dozen other warships, British, French, Italian, and Japanese. As they came by the outboard *Noa*, there was a noisy whistle toot and good-natured insults exchanged by deck crews.

"The *Noa* was up here during the trouble in '27," Wally said. "They were the first to open up on Chiang's Nats."

"You mean they *fired* on the Nationalist Chinese?" Adrian said, amazed.

"That's right, along with the *Preston* and the *Emerald*—a British destroyer.

168

When Chiang's Sixth National Army moved in and kicked out the old war-lord, they started knocking the local population around. There was a lot of looting and they attacked the foreign consulates—shot the Japanese consul in his own bed. Our man, John Davis, finally got the missionaries to move, and they retreated up there." He pointed to a wooden signal tower just visible on the north shore. "Socony Hill. Hobard, the Standard Oil manager, let the Navy build that tower. When the Chinese attacked, they signaled the de-stroyers out here and the barrage began. Later, landing parties were put ashore and everybody got out."

"I don't understand this," Adrian said, shaking his head. "At home they think Chiang Kai-shek is some kind of hero—America's friend. Wasn't he Sun Yat-sen's disciple and married to one of those Soong sisters who went to college in the States?"

"Wellesley. He retired the old wife and kids and married Mei-ling Soong in a Christian ceremony—her father, Charley, publishes Bible tracts. She speaks English with a southern accent."

"When you've heard that, you've heard everything," Bodine said.

"Well, the Kai-shek part of his name means 'between two rocks,' and he has got it rough. Staying on top out here is a real tightrope act. Feeling is run-ning strong against foreigners, Adrian, and being a better politician than he is a general, Chiang plays on it. It's a dangerous time for round eyes. When you go ashore be careful."

"Oh, sure," Adrian said. "Being careful with Bodine around is like wearing a condom with the end cut off."

"You're beginning t' talk like me, bunkie."

"It's a disease."

"Halloo!" Colonel Gibb shouted. They had forgotten him. Snoozing as usual in a deck chair, now hat over his eyes, he pointed with a whiskey tumbler, and they turned and followed its tilt. Through the drab tangle of masts and sooty stacks, the *Melodious Bird Song* swung at anchor, a butterfly among moths.

The train due that morning from Shanghai arrived in Nanking that afternoon. Like many Chinese institutions, the railways were run without an eye on the clock. A current travelers' guide warned:

> *There are no recognized hours at which trains come or go . . . as a general rule the first train arrives about daybreak and leaves an hour or so after . . . [there are] sometimes four each way a day but oftener eight [and occasionally none] . . .*

Although a bird flew only 160 miles from Shanghai to Nanking, it was 193 miles by rail and could take four, eight, or twelve hours—or a week. When it did arrive that October fifth at the terminus of the Teinsin-Nanking Railway, it was met by an avalanche of helping hands. Alighting passengers had to run a gauntlet of coolies, porters, and hotel guides. One man waited for the tide to subside, stepping down a half hour later from a private compartment.

He wore a Borsolino hat, brim snapped down hard over the circles of indigo sunglasses, and a raincoat thrown over his shoulder, arranged so that its collar concealed his neck and lower jaw. Foot poised above the platform, he braced himself with a slender cane and moved in a way that kept his head held at a constant level. Below, a servant bowed but did not offer to help.

"At your command, sir." Sergeant Masaki bowed once more and picked up two Gladstone bags. "The motorcar waits in front." He then led the way, careful not to set too brisk a pace and cautious not to suggest the captain wasn't up to one. Outside the train shed, he held the car door open and Captain Sato entered, body lowered to a sitting position in stiff increments. Max had carefully washed the Ford and touched up the dings and scratches but had been unable to find a spare tire, and worst of all, the windshield had been pitted by buckshot and snippets of telephone wire fired at him by the bandits. The captain didn't seem to notice, or if he did (and to Max this was more disturbing) said nothing. Max stowed the luggage in the rumble seat and got in.

As he connected the ignition wires, Captain Sato said two clenched words: "You're sure?"

"Yes, sir, I personally saw the bullet hit him." The car started, and they moved off toward the Nanking ferry.

When Max had found himself at the bottom of that hill after the car had rolled to a stop and the bandits roared down on him, he had been resigned. He once more took the sword up and, standing on the seat, prepared to go down fighting in defense of the captain's Ford roadster. Then a remarkable piece of timing occurred. A muffled explosion boomed up from the river. The bandits, convinced the American gunboat was opening a barrage on them, broke off the chase and went to cover. Max grabbed a handful of ignition wires under the dash, frantically pulled them apart, and hot-wired the car. It started, he backed around and tore off across fields until he found the river road.

Afterward he guessed at what had happened. The shell he had timed and fired at the gunboat had missed and gone into the water without exploding. Later the faulty spring had made contact—and *boom!* That is what they heard and what had saved him.

Arriving in Nanking that same evening without further mishap, he went straight to the Japanese consul, and a coded telegram was sent to Captain Sato.

In the Shanghai hospital Captain Sato, sitting up and taking nourishment through a straw, had been coming along nicely. In the three-day interval while Sergeant Masaki traveled to Nanking, his condition improved. Then on the fourth day he was galvanized by two telegrams that arrived within hours of each other. The first from Masaki indicated he had arrived in Nanking after "most successful shooting." The other was a brisk communiqué transmitted through the Japanese consulate and routed from General Hojo's office at Kwantung HQ, Hsinking.

MOST SECRET *information passed from agents placed in Kuomintang state* CHIANG KAI-SHEK *has given go-ahead to* MARSHAL YÜ *coup*/NATIONALISTS *will allow* MARSHAL CHAN CHOW-KI'S *garrison to be suborned*/THIS MUST NOT SUCCEED/*repeat*/THIS MUST NOT SUCCEED/*proceed to* SIAN AT ONCE *and offer* OUR ASSURANCES OF SUPPORT *and continued military advice*/
I.S.H./H.T.

Sato looked again at the counter signature. General Tojo personally initialed it!

He got up at once, and over the protests of his doctor, dressed. He allowed himself to be fitted with a neck brace and left for Nanking on the morning train.

As he sat next to Max, leaving the station, head held rigid against the movement of the car, the change in his appearance was startling. The elegant head of the aristocrat had resolved into a grim profile with all the subtlety of an ax. The bandages were gone, but the stitched cuts and purple bruises remained along with the curious "eagle" imprint on his cheek. The most brutal alteration was the wired jaw, now held prominently in an undershot position, pulling the lips back in a grimace, teeth exposed. It was necessary for the captain to make a constant sucking sound to stem the flow of saliva. Looking straight ahead, he spoke with a minimum of mouth movement and a maximum of spray. "Sian?"

"I have booked a compartment on the Tientsin-Nanking for the Lunghai connection. You will transfer to the Peiping–Hankow line at Hsuchow. The train leaves tomorrow afternoon. Until then rooms await in Nanking at the Yangtze Hotel."

When Adrian and Bodine were rowed over to the junk, they found a caretaker crew and a British leasing agent from Y&R who had just arrived on the "morning's" train from Shanghai. The agent was furious—Marshal Yü had departed in the middle of the night without paying the one month's rental on the vessel. Not only that, valuable fixtures were missing, including a complete flush toilet, pipes and all. Sometime around midnight dozens of heavy crates, furniture (even a grand piano), had been off-loaded into sampans and ferried ashore. There, as near as he could surmise, everything had been put into trucks and driven off. Very bloody mysterious, Adrian and Bodine agreed. When the agent grew suspicious, they explained they were creditors on his trail. There was commiseration and they departed.

Now, after a farewell to Wally Hamm and ship's company of the *Minnie*, they rattled along in an ancient Renault with an open landau back. Luggage was piled around them, and Bodine was summing up. "Look, we know damn well Yü took the train. That's where those trucks were heading last night, loaded with your old man's gold."

"Plus furniture from the Palace Hotel and a flush toilet," Adrian said. "The gall of that man is outsize."

"He's got a lot of nerve too."

"Is there a pub around here, old son?" Gibb asked.

"That's just where we're headin'."

"Why not just go straight to the train station?" Adrian said, annoyed.

"The Sian train don't leave until tomorrow. You wanna hang around till then?"

"No, and I don't want to hang out in a bar either!"

"Bunkie, easy—a little recon won't hurt. Yü's a tricky old bugger; he may still pull a switch. We'll investigate." Adrian knew that Bodine's idea of investigating was to conduct a survey in the first bar they came to.

"Solid thinkin'," Gibb agreed.

The streets were nearly empty by Shanghai standards, without foreigners, glossy shops, motor cars, or visible public transportation. Adrian asked why.

"There are no foreign concessions in Nankin' or anything like it. Worse than that, the damn place is fulla missionaries—there's more Americans here than any other place in China, and ninety-nine percent of them are missionaries. It's a friggin' missionary monopoly. They run the university, all kinds of schools, a hospital, and even a Chinese YMCA—if you can believe that—and to be real sure they don't miss anybody they got 'Prayer Centers' set up around the city to catch the rest."

"Come on, Bodine!" Adrian said. "Just because you have it in for the missionaries doesn't mean they don't do good work out here—what about all those schools and hospitals?" Adrian was getting tired of Bodine's personal prejudices, recited as though carved in stone.

"So they can get the moral squeeze on the poor devils! It's pretty hard to resist a Bible thumper when somebody's shovin' an enema tube up your ass. And there ain't nothin' worse than some superior peckerhead tryin' t' blackmail you into believin' what he does 'cause God's personally given him the word!"

"Wait a minute! They're not all like that! My mother was an ordained minister and . . ."

Bodine turned and looked at him, eyes wide. "Your mother was a missionary?"

"No! She was a Pentecostal evangelist!" It was out before Adrian realized it. Not that he was ashamed of her, but the flamboyant preaching and faith healing had been an embarrassment for a young man growing up in what he thought of as sophisticated company. Certainly the last thing he wanted was for these two to know it.

"Well, I sure ain't gonna speak bad of a man's mother," Bodine said, shaking his head. "No, sir, I wouldn't do that. Besides, it's not your fault if your mother was a missionary."

"She wasn't a missionary!" Adrian said through his teeth. "But it wouldn't have made any difference if she had been! She totally believed in what she was doing—she gave it everything she had, trying to lift mean spirits out of dull, dirty lives. As a kid I saw people react to her—they were changed, enlightened! Damnit, I don't care about the words she used or even what names she invoked—she made people feel better about themselves! So don't talk to me about faith and religion!"

Bodine smiled. "You know, bunkie, sounds like there's a little of the preacher in you."

"*What!*"

Bodine held his hand up. "I ain't talking about religion anyhow—I'm talkin' about missionaries. I been around these people out here for twenty years, and they treat anybody who ain't one of 'em like they got the plague, and the military—who's here to protect 'em—like they got V.D. Yes, sir."

Adrian gave up. Nothing would change Bodine. It was a waste of time trying.

"Remember old Feng Yu-hsiang, the 'Christian General'?" Gibbs asked. "Used a fire hose to baptize his troops—always thought that was a nice touch."

Bodine went right on. "Missionaries have ruined this place! It is one lousy town. There's nothin' t' do—no cabarets, first-class cathouses, and damn little high-daddy hilarity. Outside of some beer on ice up at the Standard Oil compound, the hotel we're goin' has got the only decent bar in town. The place is as dead as a congressman's ass!"

"Or your head!" Adrian said, getting in the last word.

The taxi stopped at a rambling building about a half mile from the old city gate. They paid the driver and went up wide wooden steps under a sign that read YANGTZE HOTEL.

Leaving their luggage at the desk, they crossed a musty lobby to the bar. It was dimly lit by globes of murky Bent Art Glass and hung with beaded fringe.

The vague illumination showed complicated woodwork, long gone black from varnishing, and a curious contraption. A series of paddles attached to a belted shaft ran the length of the ceiling over the bar. It looked to be a cross between the front end of an airplane and the rear end of a riverboat. Rotating to the wheeze of a cranky motor, it turned slowly enough to be able to count the revolutions of the paddles. A sign explained its function: CONDITIONED AIR MOVING BREEZE BAR.

If the setting seemed morose, the clientele wasn't. At six o'clock it contained most of the sundown drinkers, a lively bunch that greeted them like long-lost friends. Obviously intrigued by Bodine's holed campaign hat and the curious bandage, they listened to the story with several new variations, adding their own versions of "Hook" folklore. It seemed he was a landmark, a cherished local villain.

As the evening wore on, the offshoot of the investigation actually produced several clues. An eyewitness swore he'd seen a convoy of chain-driven trucks behind a touring car moving through the city late last night toward the ferry. Also a passenger on the morning's afternoon train had heard talk about a warlord's private car on the line.

About midnight at the bar they ate a dinner of shark fin in thick white sauce. Gibb thought it tasted like shredded ray, only "springier."

"Whatever it is, it's terrible!" Adrian said, putting his fork down. "Rotten!"

"Here." Bodine took walnuts from a bowl, smashed them on the bar, sprinkled the pieces of nut on top, popping the last nut in his mouth. "Now try it."

Adrian took a forkful and spit it out. "My God! That's worse!"

"You don't drink enough, old son," Gibb said, forking up his own helping. "That's the problem. Marvelously improves the appetite, j'know."

"That's right," Bodine said, digging in. "It's suprisin' the muck you can get down once you're well oiled."

"Not only that, but drink is good for the health. You should really try to develop the habit—especially out here with all the pesky bacilli friskin' about. Look what quinine did for us British. Wouldn't have lasted a fortnight in Injah without, j'know."

"Quinine isn't alcoholic," Adrian said.

"Yes, but how could you get the filthy stuff down without gin?"

"I don't know about the medical shit," Bodine said, "but booze is a great civilizer. After you been drinkin' awhile even the Chinese don't seem too bad. And I'll tell you this—booze has saved more marriages than sex." He took a long drag on his glass, shuddering. "Can you imagine married life without drinking?"

"Hardly."

"You married, Gibbsie?"

"No, no, I say, no. Almost had a run at it once, but got so spiffed the night before couldn't make the ceremony."

"There's one good reason for drinkin' right there."

"Righto. Saw the lady years later, and she had a goiter the size of casaba right under her chin. Terrible—looked as though she'd been bobbin' for the thing."

"That reminds me of a bimbo I boffed once who had three tits . . ."

Adrian pushed his plate back. "If you two don't mind, I'm going to turn in. After that hammock on the *Minnie* I'm looking forward to a real bed."

"Sure," Bodine said, "but don't you want to hear about the dame with the three tits?"

"Not on an empty stomach." Adrian waved good night to the cheery crowd and walked to the desk, where he checked in. There were only two floors in the hotel. He was led upstairs and down a hall, then to a balcony around the square of an open courtyard. An ancient porter brought their bags, and the minute he left, Adrian undressed, flopped on the bed, and was asleep.

Directly across the courtyard in a room nearly in line with Adrian's, Max was sleeping on the floor. He preferred it; taking the extra bedding, he made up a kind of *futon*.

In the next room he could hear the labored breathing of Captain Sato. Because of the danger of choking with the wired jaw, he had to sleep propped up in the bed. With his hat and clothes removed, the captain's altered appearance was even more startling. The long Western-style hair he had affected had been cut within an eighth of an inch of his scalp, giving his head the stippled look of a monk or military ascetic. The facial expression was the most disturbing. The parted lips and bared teeth had the eerie effect of eighteenth-century Japanese face armor, those highly stylized pieces forged to look like a frozen battle cry.

The captain had never been one for an excess of words, and now he talked in a kind of shorthand. However Bodine had contrived to work the injuries on him, it had obviously produced a severe trauma. Max didn't want to speculate on its effect on his ability to proceed with the assignment.

Just as he began to drift into sleep, sudden sharp detonations sounded, like erratic gunfire. He jumped up instantly, sword in hand. It seemed to be right in the room. *There it went again!* Fully awake, he realized it was coming from directly below them. He could tell now it wasn't gunfire—he'd heard enough of that lately—*but what was it?*

Downstairs in the bar, Bodine had discovered that if he lobbed a walnut at just the right angle into one of the slow-moving paddles of the Air Breeze machine, it would whack it across the room into the opposite wall with a resounding crack. This caught on at once, and everybody had to try. More walnuts were produced, and it developed into a game.

Max listened to it for a half hour. Unable to sleep himself, he could hear the captain's uneasy movements. At a final growled *"Max!"* he jumped up, put on his kimono, and slipped out the door to go down and complain. He padded around the open balcony to the single set of stairs leading to the lobby, then stopped suddenly, pulling back. Three soldiers in Nationalist uniforms went by at the bottom of the stairs. He watched as they approached the desk, questioned the clerk, then disappeared toward the bar. The last thing he wanted was any confrontation with the Nationalists; they were the enemy. He began quietly to retrace his steps.

The noise dropped off as the Nationalist officer entered the bar. Leaving at the door two soldiers carrying rifles fitted with bayonets, he came across the room. There was sullen disapproval from the drinkers. In the "old days" it would have been unthinkable for any Chinese other than a servant to come into their bar, but they had all witnessed the brutality of the Cantonese soldiers, and no one felt ready to protest. The officer, a young lieutenant in a rough uniform with native slippers attached to puttees, looked them over and stepped directly up to Bodine. Bodine leaned on the bar, hat cocked forward, popping walnut shards in his mouth. The wide tape anchored to his nose gave his eyes an odd look.

The officer consulted a piece of paper. "Red hair . . . you Boorine."

"Not me, pal, you got the wrong customer."

"You Boorine!" He looked around. "Where Grib and Ree?"

"The name's Hoobert Heever, chump—ask anybody."

"You come!" Then the lieutenant made the mistake of reaching for Bodine's arm. Bodine smacked it away in a fast, stinging blow. Startled, the lieutenant jumped back, holding his numb wrist, and fumbled open an angular wooden holster, unlimbering the ubiquitous broom-handled Mauser. As he raised the gun, Gibb, slumped at the bar, apparently asleep, reached up behind him and with a grip like a lobster's claw, pinched the spinal nerve at the back of his neck. The officer jerked convulsively and dropped the gun. As he half turned toward his attacker, Bodine hit him quickly in the Adam's apple.

Confused by the sudden motion and unable to see their officer clearly through the crowd, the soldiers at the door hesitated, then finally advanced, bayonets held forward. It was perfectly quiet for a minute, everyone frozen; then Bodine casually tossed a walnut into a revolving paddle and it struck the opposite wall like a burst of gunfire. The soldiers fired back without aiming and brought down one of the Bent Art globes in a shattering crash of glass. At this, the soldiers turned and ran for the lobby.

The bar crowd decamped in a body, slamming out a back door behind the bar that led into the courtyard. Bodine and Gibb finished their drinks and followed.

Returning to his room, Max was startled to see a mob of men suddenly explode into the courtyard below him and make for a center door leading onto the street. For just one instant he thought he saw a campaign hat and a flash of red hair.

Exiting onto the street, the drinkers ran directly into a detail of soldiers. Rifle bolts were cocked back, bayonets thrust forward, and they were effectively trapped.

In his room Adrian was roused by the noisy shouting in the street. He got up to shut the window. Looking down, he was surprised to see Bodine and Gibb along with the others from the bar being herded roughly together by soldiers. He leaned out the window.

"Bodine! What in hell is going on?"

An officer looked up and shouted to several soldiers, who made for the hotel entrance.

"Run for it, bunkie!" Bodine shouted.

Adrian dashed back through the room, picking up his boots, hat, and pants. As he got to the outside hallway, he could hear the soldiers pound up the only staircase. He hopped into his pants, put on his boots, and climbed over the balcony railing. He let himself down and hung suspended until he heard the footsteps pass above him and go into his room. Then he dropped to the courtyard and crouched in the shadows under the balcony. Where could he go? He could hear soldiers through the door open to the street, and the only other door led back into the bar room. Ducking low, he moved along the wall, then crept through it and behind the bar. As he did so, he saw the crude wooden handle of a large handgun lying hidden under a pile of broken glass. He picked it up and cocked it.

As he squatted on the floor, tucked between barrels and bottles, the smell of shark fin sauce came up strong, and he thought he might be sick. Then there was a choking sound, a scrape of feet, and a hand appeared on the edge of the bar rail, not six inches from his face.

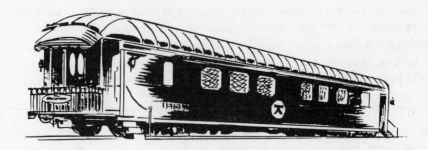

TWENTY-ONE

WHEN THE HAND appeared, Adrian pulled back sharply, holding the gun handle so tightly that his fingernails cut into his palm, index finger crooked around the trigger. Inches away, the back of a head rose above the bar as a man levered himself up. As he did so, a horrible gagging sound continued—long gasps, fighting for breath. Getting to his feet, the man staggered toward the lighted square of the lobby door, the crunch of broken glass marking his passage.

After he was gone, Adrian asked himself why had he run? Why was he hiding? Because Bodine told him to? He had done nothing. Why didn't he show his passport, demand his rights as a U.S. citizen? But he knew why. The stories of atrocities had worked on him; the shooting of the Japanese consul in his bed, barbarous acts, Wally's warning to be careful. Soldiers were erratic, arbitrary, and without restraint; no one knew what they might do.

Adrian shifted the gun, wondering if the safety was on. If that soldier had discovered him, could he have shot him? Pulled the trigger at point-blank range? No. It struck him just how foolish it was to have taken up the weapon. If he was found with it, they would no doubt shoot him out of hand. Had he picked it up because he thought that was what Bodine would do? Bodine said he was beginning to talk like him—was he also beginning to think like him? He had to smile. God forbid. Bodine was one of those individuals who acted instantaneously no matter what the consequences—was that the stuff of heroes? Fortunately, or unfortunately, Adrian had too lively an imagination—he could clearly visualize the consequences: if he pointed that gun at someone, there was a good chance they would react by trying to kill him in return. Holding it gingerly by the broom handle, he lowered it into a crock of what smelled like pickle brine. It bubbled to the bottom.

As he waited, crouched behind the bar, things seemed to quiet down and he could no longer hear the soldiers in the street. Should he take a chance and go back to the room? A noisy burst of conversation interrupted his indecision, and two men appeared at the entrance to the bar. He recognized the desk clerk and the Nationalist officer. Recovered now, the officer angrily slapped his wooden holster, and Adrian realized they'd come back looking for the gun.

Adrian didn't wait. Tugging down his Stetson, he duck-walked out the open back door. Keeping in the shadows, he crossed the courtyard. As he looked up, he could see the arms of a guard leaning against the balcony railing outside his room. The street door was still ajar, and no one was in sight. He went out and quickly walked away from the hotel.

With no idea of the city layout, he decided to head in the general direction of the river. If he could find the docks, he could get back to the *Minnie*. It was very dark, and the streets were confusing as they twisted through a rabbit warren of houses. At nearly four in the morning the houses were closed and shuttered, doors bolted against night enemies. He met no one, and the sound of his own footsteps made him increasingly anxious. "Alone and afraid in a land I never made . . ." who said that? He had no idea, but whoever did had it right. There was no worse nightmare than being alone and afoot in the dead of night in a strange, hostile city, where no one spoke your language, knew you existed, or cared.

Then, miraculously, a pinpoint of bright light appeared off to his right. It seemed a beacon, and hurrying forward, he was cheered immediately by a clean whitewashed building, surrounded by dark and ominous structures with the look of a stage set when a scrim is lowered. Even more astounding, a single electric bulb illuminated Chinese characters and, below them, in English, it read:

PRAYER CENTER
Come unto JESUS

For the first time in his life the words had meaning, and Adrian went through the open door smiling. He came into a long, narrow room with many folding chairs. At first he thought it was empty; then at the far end he saw a man sitting at a bare table reading a book. Above him on an otherwise blank wall a large picture of Jesus Christ looked cloudward, a sunburst of golden rays streaming out from his crown of thorns. In the pained anguish of

179

his expression, Adrian felt a kinship. It was very quiet, with the exception of the hum of an electric generator. "Excuse me," he said, his voice sounding hollow.

The man looked up, frowning. Middle-aged, with a scrubbed face and hair shaved clean over his ears, the dust of talcum powder was visible on his neck. "You will find a bar at the Yangtze Hotel."

Adrian was taken aback. "Why, I . . . I just came from there. My name is Adrian Reed. . . ."

"You're not welcome here."

"What?"

"Please leave." The man went back to reading.

Adrian realized he must look like a wild man: two days' beard and wearing the sleeveless undershirt he'd slept in, wrinkled pants, and beat-up hat. He wondered if he also smelled of gin. "Forgive my appearance, but there's been trouble at the hotel, and I need some help. . . ."

The man didn't look up. "I'm sure. You people are always in trouble. We don't want you here. Leave."

"Wait a minute!" Adrian said, getting mad. "What 'people' are you talking about? I'm a fellow American! What kind of Christian charity is this?" He made an involuntary gesture toward Jesus.

The man slammed the book closed. "Our charity is reserved for those who need it. Do you think you're the first drunken sot to stumble in here? We get dozens every week when the ships are in—'fellow Americans,' sailors looking for a handout or directions to the bar—they make me ashamed to be an American. We will rejoice when you all sail away for good and leave China in peace!"

"I'm not a sailor, but I'll say this, you should thank God they're here! Just who do you think will protect you while you go around converting the population to psalm singing? The next time you have a knife at your throat and some bandit or rotten soldier is climbing aboard your wife, I'm willing to bet you'll be the first one to scream bloody murder for Uncle Sam—and it will be one of those 'drunken sots' who risks his life to save your self-righteous ass!"

"*Get out of here!*"

Adrian stomped away, then at the door felt foolish about his outburst. "I'm sorry. Tonight has been hell. You'll have to forgive me." There was a pause, and when the man didn't answer, Adrian said, "At least tell me which way the river is."

The man turned his back on him, lips compressed.

Bone weary, Adrian walked on, hopelessly lost. Taking several wrong turns from the mission, he continued until the buildings fell away and empty lots stretched into fields. He was startled to find himself in an odd, disturbing landscape with unnatural humps and irregular shapes overgrown with wild vines. Beyond, the sway of cattails and reeds stretched off to darkness and the ominous shape of a wall. Finally he slumped down, putting his back against the cut stones of what appeared to be a ruined bridge. Below its arch the base was choked with wet plants, and the smell of decay and stagnant water rose up. He intended to rest a few minutes and then turn back toward town, but he fell immediately into an uneasy sleep.

When he woke, the sun was up, and as he shifted his body, he realized with horror that something large was snuffling at his hair. Jerking his head up, he looked into the tiny, greedy eyes of a large pig. Alarmed, he rolled over and tried to get to his feet but slipped instead down the slope into the slime under the bridge. He reached out frantically and got hold of one of the pig's rear legs. Slithering to get a footing, he managed to pull himself back up on firm ground. The instant he grabbed it, the pig set up a terrific squealing, and as Adrian lay panting, still gripping the thrashing animal, he very slowly became aware of a pair of felt boots, long legs, and made out a tall figure standing above him. As he squinted into the sun, the features were blurred against the sharp light, and he wasn't sure, but they seemed to have rounded edges.

"Hey, you!" a voice said. "You're getting my pig dirty!"

The fracas at the Air Breeze Bar of the Yangtze Hotel was developing into an international incident. The patrons had been roughed up and bunched into a truck, then driven to the Nationalist compound at New Gate. There they were held overnight. Fortunately for the round eyes, the American consul was in town and, following a get-tough policy adopted since the humiliations of '27, he went into action.

After the Opium War had been provoked and won by the British in 1840, one of the "unequal rights" demanded at the Treaty of Nanking was exemptions of British nationals from Chinese law. In subsequent treaties most-favored-nation status was established for U.S. citizens that allowed them to be tried in their own consular courts. The consul pointed this out and threatened a new breakdown in U.S. relations with the Kuomintang government. Word came down, and the bar patrons were released by noon the next day.

When Bodine and Colonel Gibb left the wire enclosure, the consul's car was waiting. They climbed in, all smiles. "Thank you, sir! I knew we could count on the good old U.S. of A!" Bodine said.

"Damn fine!" Gibb added.

"Didn't I tell you, Gibbsie, the slope-headed bastards bit off more than they could chew—"

"Kindly keep quiet!" The consul was not friendly. He was a spare man, a veteran of China service who had worked up through consular grades and had his eye on the Court of St. James. "Listen to me, both of you! I know exactly what you're up to, and let me state flatly that as far as I'm concerned, they can lop off your damn silly heads! But it will not be in my district!"

"Why, we're not . . ." Bodine opened his eyes wide, the nose bandage giving the illusion of their being slightly crossed. Gibb did his best to look hurt.

"Shut up and pay attention! Those Nationalist soldiers came into the Yangtze Bar looking for you specifically—do you understand? Someone has ordered your harassment—or worse. They're trying to tell you something, and you would do well to heed it. If it had not been for that riot, they would have taken you out of there and we might not have heard of you again. It was just luck that they had to bring the whole lot in and we were notified."

"It wasn't luck, sir—that was the idea of the riot."

There was a pause, and the consul turned away toward the window, watching for a minute the passage of light across the Tzu-chin Shan hills. When he turned back, his manner was slightly altered, although no more cordial. "I know you, Sergeant Bodine—I remember when that woman you ransomed upriver filed a protest through the missionary board." He paused again, but Bodine didn't comment. "I did not approve the decision resulting in your 'retirement'—but I also could not approve your actions—she said you made advances."

"Only held her arm, sir—leadin' her away from the forward zone." Bodine lowered his voice. "The woman had balls, sir—they damn well clanked. No white man in his right mind would have touched her. I think she was funny, sir—you know, a homo."

"I don't want to hear this! My only intention is to make sure you are on the next train out of Nanking! If you people cause me trouble here, I will see to it you are thrown completely out of the country! You have both been soldiers and, as such, know the law for involvement with foreign armies, fomenting coups or other such business. Be warned! You can face imprisonment if caught by us, and beheading if caught by them!"

"You got us wrong, sir. Our only idea's t' catch up with a bozo who owes us—"

"Absolutely," Gibb said.

"Spare me the details! In order to extract the other bar habitués with the minimum amount of bother, I have given my assurances to General Dai that you two will be on the next train out of Nanking, and that's damn well what's going to happen! I am personally going to deliver you to the station."

"Thank you, sir, that's just where we were plannin' to go, isn't that right, Colonel?"

"It's a bloody coincidence!"

The tall girl reached down and easily picked up the squealing pig, tucking it roughly under her arm. It squirmed and continued a pitiful wail, but she was strong and held it firmly, whipping a line around its rear feet. Then, without another word to Adrian, she turned and walked off, pushing through the grasses. He got up quickly, filthy from the slide into the muck, and shouted after her. "Excuse me, but you speak English—perhaps you could help me."

"I do doubt it," she said, and kept on going.

"What's the matter with people around here! Damn it! Just tell me which way the river is!" He followed her as she plowed along the indent of a trail, the sharp branches snapping back against his arms and face.

Finally they came into a flat place with low scrubby weed and the shards of pots on what once must have been a tile floor. There were signs of a recent camp, and several Mongol ponies stood nervously switching flies with their tails. Packed up ready to go, they were held by an enormous old man who reached for the curve of a rifle stock protruding from one of the saddles. Two rough-coated dogs the Chinese call *wonks* immediately ran out, snapping and growling, circling Adrian. Kicking out frantically, he managed to land several solid blows, and the dogs backed off, snarling. The girl paid no attention. She threw the pig over the back of one of the animals and tied it on.

"Here is a man in the middle of China, and he does not know which way is the river. He must have dropped from a bird, like a squirt of shit." She said this to the old man, who watched Adrian carefully, hand still on the rifle butt. They did not resemble other Chinese Adrian had seen. They looked not unlike American Indians, large and broad-faced, with clothes bright and tattered, long duffel robes and the tips of boots that turned up in the Turkish manner.

The girl was even more of a puzzle. Powerfully built and nearly as tall as he, a bit bowlegged and burned brown from the sun, she moved with an assurance not seen in Chinese women. No bound feet for her; the felt boots looked to be size 12 triple E at least and were planted on the ground like anvils. She was dressed much like the old man; the long robe pulled in at the waist by a heavy belt done up with bright carnelian stones, the plaited handle of a quirt tucked under it. Her face was like his, wide and flat, with sharp cheekbones and hooded eyes. Her hair, pulled severely back, was knotted into a thick braid that hung down her back.

She was not beautiful in any Western sense, and the odor of horse and God knows what else clung about her strongly. But she had size and presence, and no one could fail to notice her in a roomful of fragile beauties. She swung up easily on the horse. "You kind of people should stay home."

Sawing at the reins, she had started to turn away when Adrian had an inspiration. "I'm looking for a princess and a dancing monkey."

She pulled the horse up. "What did you say?"

"She was stolen away by a fat, evil old man, who is returning to his kingdom to kill his only son."

She looked at him sharply, then laughed. "You're a crazy man."

"It's true! I was on my way after them, traveling with a redheaded man and another with a glass eye when we were separated by soldiers and I got lost."

"That surely is a sad story. Get yourself a begging bowl and sit here telling it—soon you will be rich." But she was obviously intrigued. "A dancing monkey? What kind?"

"Show me the way out of here—take me along and I'll tell you a story about it." He smiled.

"Crazy man, I don't need any storytellers. If you were to tell me you were on the run for murder and rape, I might take up your case. In this country what a person looks for is reliable villains."

He laughed. "Well, some may say I qualify. Come on, take me along and I'll tell you more about the dancing monkey." He pointed to the extra horse tied behind the old man. "Let me ride that horse."

She spoke quickly to the old man, and they both laughed. "If you can ride that pony, you can surely come along."

He saw what she meant. The pony looked mean and wild with a coat that was coarse and had white streaks on it from the Mongol colic treatment. Its fetlocks were dung tangled, and worse, there was no saddle or pack of any kind, just a rough bridle and reins—a bad sign. As Adrian approached, the pony rolled its eyes up, showing the whites, and began to shy, pounding small, sharp hoofs into the hard-packed dirt covering the tile floor. This created a noisy clatter, and the other ponies reacted by snorting and pulling away. The *wonks* picked it up and began barking, forcing the girl and the old man to dance their ponies sideways, beating around them with the butts of their whips until the dogs were cowed and driven off.

When Adrian reached for the reins, the pony twisted its head around, lips puffed out, and tried to bite his hand. He reacted instantly as he had in all the long, tough years of breaking polo ponies. Taking the reins in one hand, he swung with the other fist and hit the animal square in the nose, as hard as he could. The pony snorted, staggered back, and before it could recover, Adrian grabbed its mane and vaulted aboard, locking his long legs around its belly. The animal immediately backed, nearly sitting down, but Adrian forced its head up, kicking in sharply with his heels. When the pony jumped forward, all four feet leaving the ground, Adrian kept his seat and let it out. They raced through the weeds, hooves muffled in the padding of grasses, the rattle of dry reeds sending the wild birds fanning out in sudden flutters.

Adrian worked the pony back and forth in tight patterns, letting him out, pulling him in. They slipped and fell several times on the wet, irregular ground, but Adrian was up and back on him at once, and each time the pony resisted less. Finally, worn down and dominated, it was under control.

The Chinese girl and the old man watched incredulously. If there was one thing they knew it was the ability of riders, and this man was as good as any they had ever seen.

At the end of a long run Adrian pivoted the pony in a showy turn and galloped straight for them full out. When he came pounding past, he flicked the rump of her pony with the end of his reins.

"Let's go!"

She dug in and followed him, the old man bringing up the rear.

The crush at the main terminus of the Tientsin-Nanking railroad began early. As the most direct connection to Peking and all points north, it was extremely popular. Like its opposite, the *Blue Express* that left Chien Mên for Shanghai, it was a favorite of foreigners as well as affluent Chinese and traveling merchants. It ran a combination of baggage cars, third and second-class coaches, and a single first-class car with compartments. Since he knew Chinese trains were always overcrowded, Max had staked out a position on the platform that would allow him and Captain Sato to be the first to go aboard when the train was made up. The captain was sitting now on the incline of a shooting stick, and Max stood close by to fend off anyone who might jostle him.

A crowd already packed the station, some coming just to watch, others burdened with bundles and bags, babies riding mothers' backs. Pulling this way and that, the crowd pushed and shoved with the squawk of shouted directions, plaintive wails, and a dozen dialects. Noisy hucksters badgered them, and as the shuffle of hundreds of feet built up, the sound hovered under the corrugated shed roof and reverberated.

The passengers waiting for the first-class car had the advantage of a low picket fence and a railway guard between them and the masses, but nevertheless, Max kept a close eye on the captain's privacy. He seemed stronger today, the cane had given way to the shooting stick Max carried for him, and although Sato still wore the neck brace hidden by his raincoat, his movements seemed less stiff. As Max watched the crowd, a nagging worry persisted—a recurring dart of an image that spoiled any anticipation the trip might have for him. A brief glimpse of a campaign hat and red hair in the hotel courtyard the night before had shaken him. He had been unable to sleep the rest of the night. He *knew* it couldn't be Bodine. There was no way he could have survived the shot Max fired. He had seen it hit him. Still, like a continuous film, it kept flipping over in his mind until he expected to see Bodine in each face in the crowd that passed.

The consul's car pulled up in front of the station, and his driver got out and opened the rear door. Their luggage had been picked up at the hotel, and he unbelted it from the rack, setting it on the curb. As they stepped out, Bodine saluted the brim of his campaign hat. "Thanks for the ride, sir—and the advice."

"Very decent of you," Gibb said.

"If you two are smart, you will take the first train back to Shanghai."

"You're dead right, sir, that would be the smart thing to do."

"Absolutely," Gibb echoed.

The door was shut, then at the last minute the consul rolled the window down, passing a small card through the crack. "Oh—Engvick asked if you'd give him a call when you got back." Bodine took the card, and the car moved off.

"Why, that hypocritical old fart." Engvick was an intelligence officer working out of the American High Commissioner's office in Peking. His speciality was the Northern Tungpei Army and particularly Sian.

They plunged into the crowd, elbows working, and bought two third-class tickets. "C'mon," Bodine said, "I ain't ridin' with a bunch of bohunks packed in them sardine cans. Let's try the baggage car." As they pushed their way down the platform through the surge of frantic passengers, they bought foodstuff from vendors who ran along after them. There was no third-class dining car, and they would have to make do with what they found in the stations along the way. Colonel Gibb passed the solids, stocking potables in the shape of two five-gallon jugs of Tiger Bone Whiskey.

In the yards, cars were switched with the clang of couplers, and a big French 4-6-4 compound-locomotive moved them into position along the platform, the hiss of its escape valves throwing a fog of steam across the last-minute passengers shoving forward as the cars stopped. Survival of the fittest was the order; only the physically fit would find choice seats. In the first-class pen Captain Sato moved forward with stiff dignity as Max broke the way. The Gladstones were passed up, and as the captain mounted the steps, Max locked his arms on the handles at both sides of the doorway behind him to prevent any pushing. His head was twisted to one side, and he had a clear view as two men charged along the platform and disappeared with a stream of vendors in their wake. There could be no doubt this time; one was Warren Bodine.

Bodine and Colonel Gibb fought their way to the baggage car, pushed their luggage through the open door, and climbed up. The baggage master

186

screamed that it was not allowed, but Bodine shouted him down and slipped him some small silver. The space in the rough framed car was taken up by trunks, boxes, and crates of all sizes being shipped up the line. There was even a caged toucan, a bird with an enormous bill one-third the length of its shiny black body. It cocked its head and watched them with a bright BB of an eye as they arranged their gear in front of the open door. Colonel Gibb stretched out and uncorked the Tiger Bone for a stiffener before his nap, while Bodine hunkered down at the edge of the doorway.

He positioned himself to fend off others who might have the same idea as they and to have a view up the platform if Adrian appeared. A whistle cut through the crowd hysteria for one brief blast, the cars lurched as the driving wheels slipped, gripped, and the train moved forward. Bodine stayed at his post, rocking back and forth with the motion of the train until they cleared the shed and were shunted through a series of crossovers and onto the main track. When they picked up speed and the thump of wheels settled into a regular pattern, he slid back next to Gibb, whose Panama was over his eyes, arms and legs crossed.

"Well, the peckerhead didn't make it."

"Too bad. Nice lad."

"A damn pain in the ass, a polo player, for Christ's sake! What in hell is a guy like that doin' messin' around China, anyway? Will you tell me?" He didn't give Colonel Gibb a chance to answer. "The first time I saw him I knew he was gonna be one of those scissor-bills who couldn't button his fly with two hands. He needs a mama, someone to hold his winkle while he toy-toys."

"Maybe we should have waited about a bit if you're worried . . ."

"Worried! Who in the fuck is worried? Am I his sugar titty? I couldn't care less. I quit stewin' over recruits at Blanc Mont in '18. You can't be gettin' into a sweat every time some dumb-ass boot doesn't show up for reveille. You know that."

"That's right."

"Besides, we didn't have any choice. The next Sian connection doesn't shove off until next Thursday, and by then Yü will be dug in."

"True."

"I'm not gonna worry about him."

"No."

"Why should I?"

But Colonel Gibb was asleep.

Max settled Captain Sato in the small compartment. Between the seats the space was filled by a large table made of the same highly varnished wood as the walls. The car had been built in the Nord works at La Chapelle, and the

187

windows were decorated with a true-love knot and a cluster of rosebuds painted on the glass.

He carefully arranged the captain's clothes and set out his shaving gear in the squeeze of a water closet. Finished, he bowed sharply. "At your command, sir."

He was ready to turn away, expecting no answer, when the captain said, "Did you read the Marine Bodine's service record?"

"Ah . . . yes, sir." Max was startled. From the minute Bodine had appeared on the platform, he had thought of nothing else. To hear Bodine's name spoken suddenly was alarming. Had the captain seen him? Did he suspect he was still alive? It couldn't be. Max was still in shock himself.

"He was decorated with their Navy Cross four times."

"Yes, sir."

"Four times." There was a pause, and Max wondered what the captain was getting at.

He was recovering, adjusting the facts in his mind to rationalize his ghastly defeat by Bodine. The captain's method was begun by grasping at the official evidence of his bravery in battle. It was no disgrace to be bested by a heroic warrior in battle. The *Kamakura War Tales* told of many such encounters. The code *Bushido* said that heroic death or even defeat in battle by a great warrior was a most honorable outcome. Although the Japanese had many decorations, from the Order of the Golden Kite to the Order of the Rising Sun, they were not given per se for bravery. This was expected automatically of all soldiers, and to suggest otherwise would be an insult. Nevertheless, the fact that his enemy, Bodine, had been shown to be brave comforted him, made his wounds worthy. Bodine had been killed in the traditional way by a samurai retainer avenging his lord. It was time to put it out of his mind and get on with his mission. He had mentioned the decoration to Max as a subtle suggestion of Bodine's bravery. This was his way of acknowledging Max's skill in killing him. He would not speak of it again. Bodine was honorably dead and the matter was closed.

When there was no further comment by Captain Sato, Max bowed once more. He opened the compartment door and stepped into the companionway. He stood for a minute to get his balance in the sway of the train and adjusted the captain's Nambu automatic in his belt, buttoning his coat carefully over it. He had taken it out of the bag when he unpacked. First he would find the porter and arrange for the captain's dinner; then he would find Bodine and kill him—again.

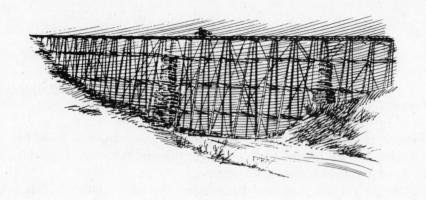

TWENTY-TWO

THE MATTHEW FLINDERS came up from Melville Island, passed through the Makasar Straits west of Borneo, and picked up 250 ex-U.S. Army remounts at Manila. Off-loading copper from the Mount Lyell fields in Tasmania, it proceeded through the China Sea and, turning west up the Yangtze, arrived in Nanking on Friday, October 12, 1931. Tying up on the south bank at the Hsia-kuan docks, the crew unloaded small stores for the Missionary Council and waited to get rid of the horses.

For the ship's master, it couldn't be quick enough. He had been smelling horseshit for two solid weeks. There was no place on the small coastal freighter you could get away from it. His morning eggs tasted of it; even tobacco took on its aroma. Now, on the wing of the bridge—downwind—he still smelled it. If that wasn't bad enough, the constant drumming of ten thousand hooves night and day was like being sandwiched between jackhammers. He expected the bottom of the ship to fall out any minute. When he saw the horse dealer ride on the dock, he smiled for the first time since they'd left Australia. He'd dealt with this one before.

Mavis Ming Billy. Coo-eeee! A big lummox of a bird, eleven stones at least, an Ordos Mongol from way-in-hell-gone beyond the great loop of the Yellow River. Up there they all were horse dealers, men and women, selling hides and skinning the taipans with polo ponies and griffins for the spring

189

races. Her missionary English was a howl, and he loved to jolly her along (as a matter of fact, she had starred in several of his sexual fantasies—he liked great big women).

As she got closer, he saw she was with that giant of an old man and a stranger, filthy dirty and looking like a larrikin. When they were beneath the wing, he shouted down, "Hey, Billy, is that your new cobber? I thought you were savin' that sweet thing you sit on for me."

The girl shielded her face from the sun and shouted back, "Your mouth is as filthy as your boat. I've come for the horses if you people haven't killed them all in the transporting."

"Horses? Is that what they are? Ready for the glue factory, it looks like to me. Ridden into the ground by those nigger troopers at Luzon." Laughing, he went down the ladder toward the gangway.

Adrian got off his pony and handed her the reins. "Billy? Is that your name?"

"Some of it."

"Well, thanks for showing me the way home, Billy."

"You didn't tell me about the dancing monkey."

"His name is Ramon and he wears a dress suit."

"Is that all? It's not very much to tell."

"It wasn't much of a ride, either."

"Where are you going?" She made no bones about being nosy.

"I've got to catch up with my friends. We're off for Sian."

"I go that way to Lintung. You can come along and tell me the rest."

"Thanks again, but it's a long ride, and I sure don't want to spend it on the back of a horse."

"You don't ride like that."

"Sweetheart, horses are my business, and riding them is what I like to think I do best, but as transportation they leave something to be desired—I'll take the train."

"We take the trains. When we unload here, we herd the horses across river and put them in the cars. I could use some help at this. I pay in silver—ten of your Mex for two weeks, meals included."

"That's very generous, I'm sure, but I'm in a hurry."

"Suit yourself," and she turned her back as the ship's master came down the gangway.

At the Navy landing, Adrian found that the *Minnie* had gone back downriver for repairs. He also heard the glad news that the Yangtze Bar fracas had cooled and all its patrons had been released. Hurrying to the hotel, he found his bags waiting along with a note from Bodine:

Bunkie—

Gibbsie and I are shovin' off for Sian on today's (Thurs) train. If you don't make it you'll have to wait a week—so forget it.

P.S. See you in Shanghai—maybe.

Bodine

Damn! They hadn't waited for him! And the next connection wouldn't be for a week! Depressed, Adrian sat down on the hotel front steps, an unnerving sight for the tourists who veered around him: a rough-looking character in a mud-streaked undershirt, tangled hair, two days' growth of beard, and a sweat-stained hat. An example of how far a white man could fall, going Asiatic. He didn't notice their disapproval, lost in his own dark thoughts. What now? Back to Shanghai? Nothing had changed. With no money he'd have to dodge creditors and somehow contrive to get home—give up on all the time and money he had put into this hard-luck project. Damn! And double damn! He picked up his bags and, furious, shouted for a cab.

Mavis Ming Billy stood with the ship's master, badgering coolies who were running a ramp up to the double doors in the freighter's port side. Adrian's cab drove on the dock and he got out, shouldering his duffel bag. She paid no attention, and he had to wait until she finished abusing the Chinese. Then, doing his best to smile, he said, "I'm going to Sian with you after all."

She didn't bother to look up. "In that case, it will cost fifteen of your Mex."

"*What!* You offered to pay me before!"

"That was before."

"Before what?"

"I asked you. Now you ask me."

Adrian laughed. She was getting hers back for his earlier refusal. "Okay, sweetheart, you got me at your mercy." He dug in his pocket and produced the wrinkled bills. "Here's your blood money."

She carefully counted it. "I will take you along because I am a Christian, but you will have to work too. This is not a tour."

"I'm going to have to work, and still *pay* you?"

"Take it or leave it."

"All right! All right!" Adrian was agitated by her one-way, humorless attitude.

She mounted her pony. "Don't expect to be standing about if you want to travel with me—and don't curse. Jesus doesn't like it." With that, she kicked the animal ahead as the first of the remounts came pounding down the ramp.

191

"By God!" Adrian said. "What a damn nerve!"

"She's got that," the master said. "She'll take the gold right out of your teeth if you're not careful, cobber. It says something that her people choose to send her down here to do the dealing. She's the sharpest of the bunch, and they're all as mingy as gypsies."

"Where did she learn to speak English like that?"

"The missionary school at Murkden—they shipped her down there as a kid so she'd have the trade language to beat down the foreigners. And I'll tell you something else, those nuns taught her to keep her legs together, so keep your fly buttoned—you won't be needing your dobber this roundup."

"I'd as soon mount a moose," Adrian said. This stung the ship's master, who would have liked nothing better, horse smell and all.

"Hey, you!" Mavis Ming Billy shouted from her pony. "Get on that horse you ruined and move! I don't carry the lazy!"

Biting his tongue, Adrian rummaged in his duffel bag and pulled on his army-and-navy store shirt. Then he tied the bag on the pony, mounted, and rode into the confusion.

The horses were to be driven down the ramp and herded along a narrow alley to native barges at the river's edge. There they would be ferried across to the Pukow side and pens in the freight yards of the Tientsin-Nanking. To do this were four Filipino handlers who had come with them, the girl, the old man and Adrian. Although it was a drive of only a few miles, the nightmare was getting them on and off the barges and across the river (at its widest here). These were full-sized cavalry mounts, not ponies, and the confinement of the long voyage had made them skittish. Released from the dark hold of the ship, they charged off the ramp half blind, snorting in terror, and it took everything the riders could do to turn them toward the barges.

Flapping his arms, Adrian cut back and forth, working them toward the chute of the alley. Then he plunged in with them, galloping along with one leg skinning the side of the building, the other against their bony ribs. Lashing out with the end of the reins, he fought to keep up with the tide, ducking the projections of signboards and wooden awnings. Above him, Chinese leaned out windows, shouting and enjoying the show.

At the river the horses were funneled aboard the barges and packed twenty-five to the trip. They were not tied together for fear that if one went over it would take the rest, and only a bamboo railing, twisted together with rattan, separated them from the water. Those who took them across stayed mounted, and the Chinese poleman did the best he could.

As the afternoon wore on, the barge decks became slippery with wet manure, and they began to lose animals. The bark of a steamer whistle or any other sharp noise would set them off, and skidding and slamming together, the outside animals would crash through the flimsy railing into the water. The pull of the river was swift here, and floundering for shore, many didn't make it, disappearing to be dragged ashore farther down and chopped up for food. The girl was being paid per head on delivery, and they spent hours searching the banks, trying to recover the swimmers.

Adrian shook his head at the poor management and horse handling. Mavis Ming Billy stayed on the railroad docks on the far side of the river, well away from the water, shouting instructions. Apparently fearless in most areas, she was wary of the water. For Adrian, the muddled, distant orders, hollered out in Mongolian or whatever it was, gave the operation a bizarre Marx Brothers direction, and if the work hadn't been so hard—and dangerous—he would have found it amusing.

Coming across with the last load, Adrian and one of the Filipino handlers had almost reached the dock when the barge was caught by the expanding wake of a river steamer and slued sideways. In the sudden shift the horses on the outboard edge of the barge slid through the railing and with a shattering crash of bamboo went over. Adrian and the handler desperately tried to hold their own horses back in the stomp and scramble that followed, but when the barge dipped in the second surge of the wake they were carried along. It was Adrian's experience that staying with a falling animal was safer than a midair dismount. The Filipino believed otherwise and jumped off at the last minute. Sliding on the wet manure, he fell backward, slamming his head with a sickening thud on the deck. In the next minute he had disappeared over the side into the water.

Adrian hung on, legs straight out, and they hit with a terrific splash. The pony surfaced, head up, legs flailing the water, and struck out for the shore. Adrian caught the brief bob of the Filipino's head out of the corner of his eye and, afraid the thrashing hooves might strike the man, he pushed off from his pony and swam to the spot. The water was oily, foul tasting, and the pull of tide compelling. Fighting against it and trying to locate the Filipino seemed a losing battle. Although the river was filled with sampans and power craft, no one made the slightest effort to offer assistance, and, in fact, their movement threatened to swamp him in each surging wake. Choking on the filthy water, he was ready to give up when he saw the tint of color and realized it was blood. He ducked down, got hold of the man's clothing, and began swimming laboriously toward shore, tugging him along.

He reached the dock, and the usual cluster of Chinese gathered immediately. With no help from any of them, he got the Filipino up on the rotting planks and found he was alive. Dazed from the nasty head wound, he smiled foolishly and actually tried to get up. Adrian pushed him back gently. "Easy, friend. You better rest a minute—let's find something to wash that cut with."

There was a clatter behind them, and Mavis Ming Billy rode through the crowd, scattering old and young. She was furious. "Why did you let them get away!" She jabbed with her whip toward the river. When the horses had fallen from the barge, they had been only a few hundred yards from the Pukow side, but the terrified animals had turned and swum toward the middle of the river. There, caught in the current, they were swept away. "You're not going to be any good to me if you keep losing horses!"

"Are you out of your mind?" Adrian shouted back. "Didn't you see this man fall in? He was drowning!"

"That's his business! Your business is to watch my horses! You'd better be careful or I'll leave you behind!"

Before Adrian could think of an insulting enough reply, she rode off, the tail of her pony tossing. He caught his own horse, helped the Filipino aboard, and walked him to the freight yards.

By nine o'clock the last animal had been squeezed in the pens, and in the final count they had lost fifteen. Adrian lay down next to the pens, oblivious to noise, flying manure, and the spray of urine. Putting his head on the duffel bag, he slept like a baby.

At dawn he was startled awake by Mavis Ming Billy banging on a tin can next to his ear. Twisting over, he grabbed for her boot, but she easily avoided him. "What in hell do you think you're doing!" By God, he'd had it with her.

"If you lie around all day, you won't go with us. Sloth is the enemy of progress."

"No kidding? Did Jesus tell you that?" The morning was not a good time for Adrian, and he got up in a foul mood. It had been a week since he'd had a proper bath, and his beard was beginning to crawl. He took his shaving gear out and walked to where the others were hunkered down, eating. The Filipinos—small dark men in straw hats—wore the odds and ends of old U.S. issue, wicked-looking bolo knives tucked into webbed belts. They shared what looked like fried cakes with the girl and the old man. Adrian looked at the man he had saved from the river, but there was no answering expression. Apparently he'd already forgotten about it.

The yard around them was noisy, echoing the snort and slam of horses against wooden pens, and beyond, the heavy breathing of a donkey engine making up the freight train. The early morning light was hazy with the smoke of charcoal fires and dense white puffs that rose from the engine's funnel. Adrian heated some water in the tin can, washed his face, and combed the snags out of his hair. Taking out a shiny chrome Rolls razor, he stropped it back and forth in its own case. Then, unscrewing a shaving brush from a celluloid holder, he lathered up from a sliver of soap.

While he did this, the others ate noisily and watched. When he began the delicate business of shaving under his nose, Mavis Ming Billy said with a smirk, "Did the monkey shave too?"

Adrian paused, holding up his nose. "That's right, he was very careful about personal cleanliness."

This was lost on her. "Where did this monkey dance?"

He paused again. "In a theater in Shanghai—Frisky's."

"By himself?"

"No."

"With who?"

"A lady named Lola."

"Lola?"

"Lola."

"Was she paid to do this dancing?" This consideration was always at the front of Mavis Ming Billy's mind.

"Yes."

"If she and the monkey did the dancing, what did you do?"

"Nothing," Adrian said shortly.

"Were you married to this lady?"

"No."

She slapped her leg. "That is slick as glass! Living off a girl and her monkey! I've heard of men living off girls before, but never off monkeys!" She poked the old man and repeated it in Mongolian. He began to laugh, and the Filipinos took it up.

Adrian got mad. "It wasn't like that! You don't understand a damn thing!"

"I understand enough not to get lost a mile from the river, and I know enough not to miss a train—and don't curse. Jesus doesn't like it."

"I don't care what He doesn't like! Who are you to be a big know-it-all! A damn dumb horse honker who smells worse than they do, selling broken-down remounts!" It was a poor comeback, and he had lost his temper.

"You think you know something about horses? You are the one who lost most of them yesterday." She said this with such pompous contempt that Adrian wanted to hit her.

"You may find this hard to believe, sister, but I happen to value human life more than a bunch of ratty plugs!" He leaned in close to her face, spitting the words out, furious.

She reached up and pinched the tender skin he'd just scraped clean. "I will say that you are surely pretty. I can see why the girls and monkeys like you." He slapped at her hand, but she grabbed his wrist and, twisting hard, threw him sideways to the ground.

He scrambled up, knocking over the shaving water. "What in hell do you think you're doing!"

"Come on! Come on! I'll wrestle you!"

"What?" He laughed. "You're the crazy person."

"In my village it's a thing we all do—men and women. I can beat most at wrestling. I can beat you."

"Well, that's interesting, sister, but in case you haven't noticed, I'm not a Mongol and I don't wrestle women."

He took a step back, and she suddenly jumped forward and grabbed him. Putting a foot behind his leg, she threw him with a hip lock and jumped heavily on top. Rolling and scuffling on the ground, they sent up a cloud of cinders while the *wonks* circled, barking and snapping. The old man kept on eating, apparently unconcerned, and the Filipinos shouted encouragement in Spanish. For whom, it wasn't certain.

Adrian spotted her ten or twenty pounds, but she was strong, with powerful arms, and an obvious skill at wrestling. Elbows and knees working, they slammed and pummeled each other. She had immediately gotten an armlock on him, and panting with the exertion of straining against this grip, he was slowly forced down. His arm was twisted up with such force that he realized she meant to break it. This contest was not going to be played against any rules, except the savage one of maiming your enemy.

Why she had decided he was the enemy, Adrian was unable to fathom. He was used to women liking him, and this hurt his pride. There was no doubt in his mind that she had deliberately chosen to provoke the fight, and it was an unsettling revelation to be physically threatened by a woman. He was not about to let her win even if it meant hurting her. At the moment that seemed remote.

He gave way under the grip until both knees were on the ground, but as he did, he moved crablike in the direction of the fire a few feet away. She kept up the pressure on his left arm, forcing it up until his hand very nearly touched the back of his neck. The pain was electric, then numbing, and he knew that if he relaxed for one instant she would snap the arm up and break it. She tried to stop his movement by the plant of her feet, but he succeeded in forcing a shift in her position until she stepped into the fire. She quickly hopped out, but lost her leverage, and he rolled, pulling her with him. She kept the grip locked on his arm, but he was able to swing up and hit her under the chin with the palm of his right hand. He struck with such force that he could hear her teeth clack together. She sat back, stunned, and he twisted out of her grip.

As he stood, trying to work the kink out of his arm, he watched her warily. Her mouth was bloody where she'd bitten her tongue, and she seemed dazed. Then, shaking her head, she made another move for him. He was ready for this and stepped cruelly on her calf with his boot, pressing down hard. Leaning in, he put his large fist in front of her face. "Enough!" he said. "If you start up with me again, I'll really hurt you!" As they looked at each other, faces inches away, he wondered if he could do it. He decided he could.

Max had been unable to find Bodine aboard the train, and in the end he gave up looking, convincing himself that Bodine had taken another line to Shanghai. Still, as they rattled across Honan Provence for the next two days, it nagged at him. Marshal Yü's private train was just ahead and it made sense that Bodine would be after him. He hadn't brought himself to report Bodine's survival to the captain yet, rationalizing that it would cause a setback in his recovery. As it was, he improved daily, no longer wearing the neck brace; his movements were more assured, and although the jaw still jutted forward in the grip of the wires, speech was clearer despite the necessity to constantly suck in saliva.

He did this now, sitting in front of the window as the last of the Honan countryside flashed by. Climbing out of the lowlands, loess hills rose in terraced levels, precise and beautifully molded. The cluster of villages strung out along their base were dun-colored like the fields, and the occasional farmer he saw dressed in black stood out sharply. This was the beginning of the North-West, real yellow earth country. The temperature had already dropped twenty degrees and a cold wind was blowing down from distant mountains, their hard edges traced by a snow-covered ridge line.

Behind the captain, Max went about the business of packing. Late tonight they would get into Changchow, there, the trunk line of the Lunghai Railroad cut across a loop of the Peking-Hankow and they would change trains for the final connection to Sian. Following the Yellow River through the bottle-neck pass at Tung-kuan, it should arrive a day and a half later.

Captain Sato went over in his mind what he knew about the Sian situation. In the hospital he had digested the near kilo of data fed him by Hsinking HQ, and it boiled down to confusion, or as they put it, fluidity. The cartographers had given him an updated set of maps locating possible troop placement, and this was his most valuable tool in guessing at Yü's intentions. They now knew he was not going to attempt the coup by force; local commanders would be suborned, and Sato believed the key to thwarting this was their positions around the city.

"Bring me my map case, Sergeant."

"Yes, sir." Max immediately put down what he was doing and went out into the companionway. The awkward leather map case was stored in the trunk and would have to be retrieved from the baggage car. Max found the porter and, as he expected, the man whined with all kinds of excuses: the baggage car was twenty cars back on the end of the train, he didn't have the authority to take him there . . . and so on. But Max was not a sergeant for nothing,

197

and when everything else failed, he threatened the porter's health, and with that, they set off.

This was not the first time Max had traveled the length of the cars. He had done it three times before, looking for Bodine, first discreetly checking the occupants in the first-class compartments, then walking through the second- and third-class coaches. Now as he began the routine again, passing down crowded aisles, he once more looked carefully into each face.

Despite the dramatic drop in temperature, Bodine and Gibb sat by the open door of the baggage car. "Smell that whiff of mountain? That's the first noseful of fresh air I've had in a month of Mondays."

"Brisk."

Bodine had pulled on a battered forest-green Marine-issue overcoat. It had been shortened to the hips and lined with the fur of a Himalayan goral. After eleven years it still smelled of goat and had been known to clear a space for him on public conveyances. This, along with wool socks under laced-up boots, was his concession to the weather.

For Colonel Gibb, nothing would do but a complete change of wardrobe. Opening the capacious portmanteau, he removed twenty-weight tweeds, cuffed and complete with vest, which he laid out on a crate. He took off his pongee suit and folded it neatly away. Then, standing in long silk underwear, he began to dress. The sway of the train caused some difficulty in catching up to pants legs, but he managed and went on to knot his regimental tie and buckle on gaiters over stout brogans. Cap in place, he tugged on gloves and was ready for the change of seasons.

Stretching out next to Bodine and uncorking the Tiger Bone Whiskey, he poured off a full portion in a telescoping cup and offered it.

"*Kanpei!*" Bodine said, tossing it back. "Whiskey always tastes better in cold weather."

"Can't say I observe a seasonal preference for drinkin'. Got one for weather, though, been nurtured in sultry climes, j'know."

"Then get set to freeze off you're knackers, Gibbsie. The mountains around here are mean. Some of 'em—the Tapa Shan and Tsling—have got peaks up to fourteen thousand feet. When you cross those babies you'll think you were with Peary. I was stationed in Pekin' in '23, and we used to chase missionaries up in the high country, and I tell you it was colder than the Pope's pecker."

"That cold."

"A friendly word of advice: Put that glass eye in your pocket until spring."

"How's that?"

"When I did this hitch in the Legation Guard . . ."

"Was that the Horse Marines?"

"Oh, hell, no! All the Mounted Detachment was good for was sunset parades and wearin' funny hats—nah, I had a machine gun company, serious business. Anyway, this other gunney, a sergeant named Houston, told me a story about a Scandahoovian, Thorkidsen, who was a horse trader north of Inner Mongolia. Had his eye shot out in a brush with bandits up at Suiyuan, and bein' young and vain then, bought hisself a glass one. It was a great success with the Saratsi girls, and he wore it everywhere. Then one winter he got caught in a blizzard above the clouds on the Tsling snowfields. Summer up there lasts about fifteen minutes; it starts snowing in July. Well—now get this—it was so fuckin' cold that his glass eye split! It shattered in his eye socket!"

"Damned hard cheese!"

"Worse than that, it was downright inconvenient. You're not gonna find any eye doctors lurkin' around that neighborhood. No, sir, the poor bastard had to ride nine hundred miles to Pekin' to have the pieces picked out. After that you can believe he carried it around in his pocket when the temperature went below eighty. Now that's just t' prove how cold it can get."

Colonel Gibb leaned forward and in a deft motion removed his false eye. He buffed it up on the silk square of a pocket handkerchief and passed it over. "Don't have to worry, old son. It's not glass, j'know."

Bodine took it gingerly. "Why, it doesn't weigh nothin'." He looked at the painting of the eye on one side, beautifully rendered right down to the hint of red veins. "They sure got the look of an eye right."

"Injan work. The chap could put the charge of the Light Cavalry Brigade on your shirt stud."

"What's it made of?" Bodine asked, rotating it.

"Guess."

Bodine held it up to the light. It was a silvery white, lustrous and translucent. "It's a pearl! A big fuckin' pearl!"

"Right you are. A *mohar*, most likely from the Gulf of Mannar in Sri Lanka."

"Jumpin' Jesus! It's gotta be worth a fortune!"

"I should imagine, weighs in at three hundred and thirty-three grains—something like twenty-seven karats."

"Woo-ee!" Bodine handed it back carefully. "I know! You got it out of a forehead of a idol, right? One of those kind with about a dozen arms stickin' out like you're always readin' about in the dime novels?"

Gibb smiled. "No, sorry, nothin' like that, I'm afraid. Actually it was durin' the Bengali tip-up in '11. Old King George had let it out at his Coronation *durbār* that the capital of pukah Inja was to be switched from Calcutta to Delhi. Well, that got the wind up everybody's tail. The New Party radicals went starkers, and riotin' broke out. Then when Lord Hardinge, the new viceroy, came loppin' along on an elephant durin' his regal state procession, KABLAWOOEE! A bomb damn near done him in, and the fellow that chucked it got clean away. I was brought in with my Gurkha lads 'cause they were to be trusted, and we went on the hunt. Never officially found the bomber, but we got onto the ringleaders on the sly, a pair of *bhadralok*— respectable people, intellectuals. A man and wife, both of them barristers and Tilak militants. There was no doubt about it, they'd done it, but we didn't have the proof. The two of them were rich as Lot, with a big palace outside of Delhi and plenty of chums in Congress. So I was ordered to take a few lads out there in mufti and chop them."

Bodine looked at him.

"Yes, that's right. We did things like that in those days. Caught them in bed and my Gurkhas chopped the man straight away with their *kukris*. But the woman was beautiful, and she begged me not to let them use their knives and spoil her face. Saying this, she put the pearl in my hand. I have no idea where it came from before that."

"An' they didn't use the knives?"

"No, I carried a little rim-fire pocket gun, and I pressed the muzzle tight up against the caste mark between her eyes and pulled the foldin' trigger. It was very neat."

"Damn!" Bodine said. "That was hard!"

"Yes, but they *had* bombed the Viceroy, and we couldn't let that go by— then, too, she was a wog."

There was an uneasy pause, and they both sat looking out the square of the open baggage door, past the blur of near objects, to shadows lengthening on the landscape as early darkness fell. In one corner, between crates and trunks, the baggage master cuddled up on mailbags and dozed. The toucan, observing them from its cage above, gave an earsplitting blast that sounded like a puppy being stepped on. Bodine jumped.

"Jee—zuss! Somebody oughta cut that damn pelican's throat!"

"Didn't lose my eye until later on," Gibb continued, caught up in a compulsion to retell the story. "Had no idea then I'd be usin' the thing to plug a hole."

"Well, it makes a handy container to carry it in, all right."

"That's what I thought. It was a responsibility to tote about, the first piece of real goods I ever owned. Came from a good family, j'know, all on the right side of the blanket. But damnme, we were poor, and silly twit that I was as a lad, I had my heart set on the army. In those days it was impossible to get into a fashionable regiment without real nick—bought your commission, of course."

"You mean you paid *them* to sign over?"

"That's right—old Tommy Brudenell, that dim fellow who led the Light Brigade into the Russkie guns at Balaclava, paid forty thousand pounds to become their colonel. Then, too, the really splendidly turned out ones like the Second Life Guards hadn't seen action from Waterloo to Tel-el Kebir—sixty-seven years. They were stationed in London or Windsor, prancin' about between teas and such. And here I was snortin' to be a Caesar, a hero—so, I wrangled a commission in the Injan army where you could find a bit of action and they actually paid you. If you lived like a bloody monk you might exist on your pay out there."

"That wasn't the regular army?"

"My dear, no. Before the Mutiny in '57 it was the private property of the East Inja Company—after that the Injan Government took it over. Then too there was the 'army in Inja,' regiments of regulars who were rented from the Crown."

"Rented?"

"We British have always been fond of the commercial thing—that's what the army was for—to protect the merchants. So it only stood to reason the fellows should pay for it. Naturally, we liked to think of it as a gentlemen's club—you know, a keen interest in huntin', horses, and hoors. In the end I picked the Fourth Gurkhas because it was a sound regiment and had a reputation for ferocity—I thought highly of ferocity in those days."

"Didn't we all."

"Got on fine with the Gurkhas. Marvelous little fellows, mercenaries from Nepal, j'know. No foreigners were allowed set foot there. Did all the recruitin' themselves. Never heard a bad word about 'em. The rest of the lot, Injans and such, were not allowed to come into our tents or barracks with their shoes on. Had to show the brutes they were inferior. But we all accepted the Gurkhas as damn near equals.

"When the Great War for civilization came along, we all went mad with delight. Kiplin' said a soldier should refrain from gettin' drunk more than necessary, obey his superiors, and pray for war—and my God, we did that. All of us were young and full of ginger, convinced that the world was made for our pleasure, and to us, war was the greatest pleasure of all."

"It wasn't your bunch alone," Bodine said. "When we went over in '17 we all thought it was gonna be a lark, a dustup. Those that came back had their minds changed for 'em."

"Yes, as the civilians say:

> "God and the soldier we both adore
> When at the brink of ruin—not before.
> The danger over, both alike requited,
> God is forgiven—the soldier slighted."

"Ain't that the truth."

"At the time, the only thing that marred my pleasure at the thought of

201

death and destruction was a fellow I shall call Birdie. He was a captain in the First Highland Light Infantry. At division, we were billeted with the Highs, and it was tradition that we fight together, so I saw a lot of Birdie at mess. He was a regular send-up, wispy as a feather with battin' long eyelashes and tossin' hair. He flitted about doin' bird imitations, shoutin' out, 'Caw! Caw!' or the occasional 'Tweet! Tweet!' He was a silly damned fool but amusin', affectin' the inability to say his r's' like the old-time cavalry officers; 'It's a weal wegiment and so wugged!' That kind of thing. We all knew he was not for the nautch girls, but he was tolerated, bein' a good officer. The odd 'Nancy' was not all that unusual in the army. Why, it's said Chinese Gordon himself preferred young boys, and Kichener, the very fellow who was goin' to command us all in France, would never have a married man on his staff. That's true. This is not to say they indulged in any kissy-kissy—God forbid! No, the army had its clique of dandies, Pimpernels; brave men who pretended to be delicate and effete. He was one of those.

"And by God, if he didn't get on to me! Can you believe it? Started hangin' about with little favors, bringin' me momentos, and I'll be damned if he didn't bake a cake on my birthday! I was mortified. The Gurkhas began to smile about it, and I tell you if the fellow had laid one finger on me, I'd have done him in on the spot—but he didn't. Then we went to France.

"It was late in '14, and I was sent with a squad t' the west side of Wy-tschaete, a village the Huns had succeeded in holdin' during the tip-up for Ypres. I was t' meet a gentleman ranker from the Highs, and we were to coordinate an attack on the Huns through a nasty piece of wood called Petit Bois, to the southwest of the Maedelsteed spur. The fellow was Birdie, of course—he had wangled the assignment. 'Mawian, m' deaw,' he says, always callin' me by my first name, 'what a supwise! I thought you would be in the south of Fwance!' Everybody thought he was a howl but me. Well, we needed a bloody laugh.

"The weather was filthy, thawed out just enough so that the ground was waterlogged, and we sunk into mud at every step. There were about a dozen of us in the send-out, and as we sloughed into what was left of shell-pruned trees, ZEEWOOOWW!! Shells were zippin' high overhead and breakin' in the rear where the regiment had formed up. I remember thinkin' how lucky we were when I felt a light hand on my arm, and turnin', saw Birdie smile his silly grin and go down. My own legs went out from under, and I pitched into a gouge of a hole. Bullets had shattered both of my shinbones, stitched across them almost parallel. As I sat up and reached forward, unable to comprehend it, another struck my eye, knockin' me flat. As I lay on my right side, the blood from the holed eye ran into the other and I was sure I was blind. Then, curiously, I heard the machine gun fire for the first time, the muffled slappin' of the bullets thuddin' into that wet ground, like a baker kneadin' dough.

Around me were the awful sounds of the others, callin' out, thrashin' about in the mud, all cut down. I don't believe we returned one round. . . .

"I must have passed out, and when I came about I heard Birdie's voice. He lay with his arms tight around me, shielding me with his body. 'Don't cwy, Mawian, it's all wight, I'll get you back.' I realized I must have been cryin', and asked him if he was hit. 'Not bad, in the funny bone and ankle, I think, hawdly use them anyhow.' He actually giggled. The firing had stopped; the others around us were finished. I don't know how long we lay there. I seemed to pass in and out of consciousness, confusin' the real with the unreal. Through it all I could hear Birdie whisperin', comfortin' me, tellin' me I'd be all right, not to worry, think of it as a cleansin' experience, that I'd look marvelous with an eye patch and that after this we'd be like brothers. With his good hand he mopped the blood from my face and pressed his hand-kerchief against my eye. Shock had passed and the pain was ghastly. I lay there, shakin' and whimperin', wishin' t' God I'd never seen the army. About dusk we heard a single shot, close. Then another. Birdie raised his head, laying his finger across my lips. 'It's nothing—snipe shooting,' he said, but I knew what it was. One of the Huns was walkin' among the fallen, makin' sure they were dead. Stoppin' by each one for the *coup d' grace*. There was a shot just off to our left, and we knew we would be next.

"'Good-bye, deaw Mawian,' Birdie said, kissin' me on the forehead, then crawled out of the hole. For one horrible minute I thought he'd done a bunk, run off and left me—then I heard him shout, 'CAW! CAW!' Hoppin' on one leg, flappin' his arms, he was doin' that 'wounded' bird imitation, leadin' the Hun away from me. The fellow emptied his pistol into him and, frightened half to death, ran for his life. A minute later the machine gun opened up. It was so close I could hear the retainin' pins click and the water in the jacket guggle as they shifted it. They got me once more in the shoulder, and Birdie was chopped to pieces . . . but I swear t' God in that second of silence after the gun stopped, I heard the silly damn fool whisper, 'Tweet, tweet . . .' Tryin' t' be funny right up t' the last. . . .

"The Huns pulled back and the stretcher bearers found me in the mornin'. I was in the hospital, out of it, a week later when the Lahore and Meerut divisions went up against Givenchy. The First Highland and Fourth Gurkhas took two lines of the Huns' trenches with almost no casualties. They were jammed in 'em, shoutin' their fool battle cries when the Huns set off mines they'd laid. The Fourth Gurkhas were blown t' hell, *all of 'em*! Not a bloody son was left, except me, of course. At that moment the outfit ceased to exist. When I went back to duty in '16, I was seconded to the Lahore Division and did my best to spend m' life, but only succeeded in bein' made a colonel and pinned with the V.C."

He suddenly turned, and Bodine was shocked by the anguish and fury in his face. "What right did that damn silly fool have t' do that! Who asked him t' put himself in front of those guns for me! The rotten bastard! The damned prancin' Nancy! I gave him nothin'! An' the dirty dog gave me his life. . . ." His voice choked up, and the good eye filled with tears. "And the very worst, the terrible thing that I will hear all my life, is so silly . . . so foolish . . . pathetic . . . the last words of the only true hero I've ever known . . . 'Tweet . . . tweet'. . . . My, my God . . ."

There was a long, silent spell, punctuated by the clack of the train wheels. It was dark now outside, and then suddenly a disrupting pounding was sounded on the connecting doors between cars. Complaining, the baggage master roused himself and unbolted the latch, first peering through a crack, then opening it. A porter came in, followed by another man. Bodine thought he looked Japanese.

TWENTY-THREE

ADRIAN STAYED AT one end of the boxcar, practicing with a Yo-Yo. The Filipinos had brought a couple with them from Batangas Province, south of Manila, where they said they were invented. Staying clear of the Mongol girl and the old man, he had made friends with three of them, using his "Mexican Spanish" picked up in California. The fourth man was older and had been with Aguinaldo during the Insurrection in 1902. He claimed to speak only Tagalog and made no bones about hating Yankees. The five sat in their half of the car, dozing and playing cards, separated from the girl and the old man by a communal cooking stove, cases of canned food and horse medicine.

What Adrian enjoyed about the Yo-Yo was its ability to annoy Mavis Ming Billy. Sitting with his back to the rough wooden slats, legs crossed at the ankles, he spun out its circular wooden halves on the long string, kept it "sleeping" until she looked up, then jerked back and repeated it. There was something satisfying about the gesture.

She was annoyed, but only because the men weren't working. For her, they had been brought along like a shovel or hoe to do a job, and she resented it that they had to sleep and eat and actually just lie around. She worked with a small abacus, proud of her skill with it, zipping the wooden beads up and down until they clicked with their own rhythm. She went over and over what the profit on the horses would be, figuring how to cut their feed even closer and still deliver them alive. This job had been bad joss from the beginning. Her people, the Ordos Mongols, were used to dealing only with their own animals: shaggy ponies from the plains of Gwei Hua, sold to idiot polo players and gentleman jockeys at Peking.

They thought she was crazy to journey to *Murui-usu*, the "wrong river," as they called the Yangtze, and deal with *Meikua* horses—who would be so stupid as to bring long-legged misfits into a country where they didn't belong? She had become rich by taking these chances and using her English to traffic not only in horses and hides, but a sideline of Tibetan rugs, beaten silver jewelry, and carnelians. In fact, she had become too rich; there was a problem in finding a husband who could count and was as tricky as she was.

She met the Tungpei agents from Sian in Saratsi, a wild frontier town out toward the western terminus of the Peking-Suiyual railroad, and because they were desperate for the American remounts (why, she wasn't able to find out), she drove an even harder bargain than usual. The problem was, except for her half-blind grandfather, none of her own people would go with her to Nanking. So in the end, she had to hire the Filipinos and the surly American. After the horses had been loaded at the yards and the train got under way, they all lived together in the last boxcar, cooking over a dangerous wood stove and sleeping in their clothes on the dirty straw floor. Ahead, the animals were jammed in a long line of rickety cars, the dregs of T&N rolling stock. The trip was by turns arduous and boring, with long, tedious stops in switching junctions, relieved only by the endless routine of watering and feeding the animals. The old man acted as horse doctor, culling the sick ones and dosing them with foul-smelling brews. When one died, it was left by the right-of-way for the locals to fight over.

Adrian despaired of ever getting to Sian. As far as he was concerned, he was aboard the original slow freight; crossing Honan Province, it was a full two days behind the passenger train.

They stopped the second day out at a remote crossing with only the mud-colored square of a small building, painted with huge Chinese characters, to suggest the possibility of a "station." The landscape was drab, with no sign of habitation, and a warm wind blowing from brown fields fanned through gaps in the boxcar, sifting dust into everything. Adrian climbed down and, looking toward the engine ahead on the curve of track, made out several figures peering into its running gear. God knew what was wrong or how long they would be here.

He saw the shine of water and crossed the tracks to a nearly circular pond. In the absence of a water tower, it had been dug into the bare ground to supply locomotives. A rusty pipe drained into it at one end, and the surface was murky with a slight haze of oil. He pulled off his clothes and, taking the last sliver of soap, went in.

It wasn't bad—tepid and smelling of sulphur. The bottom sloped down until he was nearly up to his neck. He soaped up completely for the first time since leaving Shanghai. Ducking his head and coming up, he shut his eyes and luxuriated.

At that moment a small rock hit him sharply on the top of the head. He howled and dropped the soap.

Still wearing the same duffel robe, dusty boots, and long greasy braid, Mavis Ming Billy stood on the track embankment. "Hey, monkey's friend! Don't you know water is bad for you?" Then she threw another stone, barely missing him. This was obviously her idea of humor, the first she'd shown.

"You ought to try some on that big fat ass of yours!" he called. "Even the horses are beginning to hold their noses when you come around!" This time a stone hit him hard on the shoulder. He had finally offended her.

"Dirty mouth! Dogsbody!" She came scuffling down the slope, cinders flying. She picked up a stone that took two hands and hoisted it over her head. When she looked up, Adrian had disappeared. She stopped, rock poised, and waited for him to come up, and when he didn't, she was puzzled. Her life included no experience with water or swimming, and like the rest of her people, who were brave and reckless of their lives on horse and on foot, she was terrified by water and its mysteries. She had been raised in a place where it would be unthinkable to go into the icy, swift rivers. Folk tales were filled with the terrible things that lurked below its dangerous flow.

Still, she went tentatively toward the edge of the pond. Lowering the rock, she peered over. It was hard to believe that anyone could stay under that long, and leaning farther out, she searched the opaque top. At just that moment there was an explosion of water, and Adrian burst to the surface, honking like a seal. She dropped the rock and turned to run, but it was too late. Her legs were jerked out from under her, and flopping down heavily, she was dragged back and pulled under.

Standing waist deep, he held her face down while she flailed and kicked, churning the water white. He could feel her strength, but he hung on, one leg between hers, fingers tightly gripping her upper arms. He kept her under for nearly a minute, and when he finally did release her, she surfaced in an eruption of water. Her arms windmilled, and she gasped for breath, mouth working in hollow, choking sounds, eyes rolled back in terror. Jerking her around by the anchor of the robe, he shoved her forward, intending to deposit her on the bank. Instead, they both slipped on the slope, and he landed on top of her in shallow water. The robe was above her hips, and his face smacked up against the bare ass he had impinged—two glistening, plump globes, dimpled and for the moment highly provocative.

He was aroused instantly. Pushing her head under, he stood, thrust forward, and entered her roughly from behind. She bucked, choking, and tried to crawl up the bank, but he had her tightly. Leaning forward, he clamped his teeth on the thick braid at the base of her neck, jerking her head up. Holding her like that most abused of sexual partners, the female waterfowl, he pumped away, the slap of wet flesh counting the beats. She managed to get her head twisted to one side, mouth just above the shallow water. Gulping air, she thrashed and hunched, fighting him, but he kept on, hands kneading the handles of breasts. Finishing in double time, he nearly sawed through her braid with his teeth.

They lay together a long moment, quiet, dragging in breath, the water lapping their bodies. Then, feeling guilty and very vulnerable, he pulled out and stepped away. Splashing backwards up the bank toward his clothes, he kept an eye on her, ready to run, but her expression was dumb, neutral. Lying in the water, pushed up on her arms, she watched him, eyes flat, mouth hanging open. Adrian heard a sound off to his right and turned. The old man was coming down the track bed, moving fast, and there was no doubt at all about his expression.

He had his rifle, and as Adrian stood, riveted, he raised it and aimed.

Coming face to face with Bodine in the baggage car, Max had been stunned. There he sat on the floor in front of the square of open door, back against a crate, hat cocked forward, looking squarely at him. The odd bandage down his nose and his two black eyes formed a kind of *T*, suggesting a startling piece of calligraphy. The campaign hat was still vividly fixed in his mind, crossed in the scope's reticle, and now the damaged Marine Corps device and holed crown told him where he had gone wrong. He had aimed three inches too high. It was at least a relief to know the reason for failure.

Bodine did not recognize Max from their brief dark encounter at the junk. Bodine pegged Max, dressed in a conservative suit and tie, as one of the many Japanese salesmen who canvassed the back country.

Max regained his composure and bowed. "Please to forgive the intrusion, gentleman. I must remove an item from my so large trunk."

"You tellin' us or askin' us?" Bodine said, surly as ever around the Japanese.

Max bowed again. "Asking your kind permission, sir, of course."

"Well, then get on with it!" And Bodine turned away.

Max located Captain Sato's trunk, unlocked it, and took out the outsized leather map case. As he did, his mind raced. What should he do? The other man with Bodine appeared to be asleep—and the baggage master had curled up on the mail sacks, head bobbing on his chest. Could he take the chance?

In the end, what made up his mind was the thought that if he didn't, Captain Sato might discover Bodine was alive. Max couldn't face that wretched possibility. Handing the case and some small silver to the porter, he said, "Take this to compartment 4A. I will follow." The porter, delighted with the unexpected windfall, took the coins and the case and let himself out of the baggage car.

Max fussed in the trunk, trying to work out an attack plan. He no longer was carrying the captain's pistol, and at any rate its sound would wake the others. His main advantage was that Bodine had his back to him. He was searching for a weapon to strike him when Bodine pushed himself up and walked to the open door. Unbuttoning his fly, he began to urinate into the darkness. Max snapped the trunk shut and moved at once.

The train was proceeding at a good clip down the grade, and Bodine teetered on the very edge of the open door. Rocking with its rhythm, legs spread, watching the pattern of his effort whip back in the slipstream, he was intent on the business at hand, without the slightest hint that a single soul in the world wished him harm. Behind him, Max took three steps, arm poised to give him a chop behind the ear and push him out.

However, as he passed the toucan's cage, the bird let out one of its piercing screams and Bodine half turned. Max lunged, but as Bodine met the blow, he was still urinating. Ever fastidious, Max hesitated a split second. It was his undoing. Reaching across with both hands, Bodine locked up his arm and, spinning him, kicked his left leg out from under him. Max went very cleanly, without a sound, swallowed up in the night as though sucked out by an invisible force.

Colonel Gibb was awake, arms still crossed. "I say, that was an odd thing to do."

"Why in the hell didn't you give me a hand!"

"Didn't think I'd have time to get my pecker out, old dear!"

As Mavis Ming Billy's grandfather raised the rifle and aimed at him, Adrian stood stark naked, convinced he was about to be shot for rape. Could he rush him? His only hope was that, being half blind, the old man might miss. Before he found out, there was a shout from the girl, an angry exchange took place, and the old man stomped away. Adrian didn't wait for the next development; he dressed rapidly and hurried back to the boxcar, hopping on one foot, then the other, putting on his boots. When he looked around, the girl was following.

That night as the freight train rolled on, actually making some speed for a change, Adrian sat on his side of the boxcar, warily watching the grandfather and the girl. The old man wouldn't look at him, and, worse, the girl wouldn't stop. This made him uneasy, and for the hundredth time he told himself what a damn fool he was. He still couldn't believe it—my God, he had raped her! Still, she had egged him on, asked for it . . . all that wrestling business. He did his best to justify it, telling himself that with her people this was the way it was done, the stronger parties always taking what they wanted. That she had made the first move. He looked at her. She was big, all right, but not bad looking. If only she didn't smell so bad.

The Filipinos had fashioned instruments out of dried gourds and five-gallon cans and were whanging away at one of their *Zarzuel* songs. It was cheery if not particularly musical. A bottle of something volatile was passed around, and Adrian drank with them. He suspected it might be one of the horse remedies, but it helped, and they were all feeling no pain in short order. Then suddenly, without warning, Mavis Ming Billy leaped up and began to dance. It was an erratic, uninhibited crash of stomps, twirls, and arm flinging without any connection to the music. They all shouted encouragement, and she did a reprise, ending up flopping next to Adrian. "You see, I can dance too!" she said, flushed.

"You had me fooled, Billy—you're a regular Danilova."

After this high point the party fell off, the single oil lamp was put out, and with yawns and noisy wind-breaking they all settled into sleep. All, that is, but Mavis Ming Billy, who tugged at the material of Adrian's crotch in the dark.

"Give me some more of that thing!"

"Cut it out, Billy! Not here with everybody else . . ."

But she wouldn't take no for an answer and, shoving her hand into his fly, popped the buttons and roughly began hauling him out. "Easy! Jesus!"

"Come on! Don't waste time! Let's do it!" She turned over and pulled up her robe, obviously believing "it" had to be done from behind.

They went to it and, try as he might, he couldn't keep her from thrashing about and crying out. Mercifully, most of the sound was drowned out by the acceleration of the train. As he hung on for dear life, banging into the canned goods and rattling the stove, trying to stop her from bouncing them across the car, he asked himself what bizarre fate had placed him in this filthy boxcar of a decrepit train, filled with starved horses and wretched people, lurching its way across God knows where in China, scuffled around on the floor making "love" to a dirty, wild Mongolian girl in the company of four Filipinos and one half-blind relative. He also wondered for just a fleeting minute what his friends in San Francisco were doing. Probably sitting at this moment in the elegant Mark Hopkins Bar, sipping scotch old-fashioneds and perhaps discussing Sinclair Lewis's winning a Nobel prize or Martha Graham's "Lamentations." He wondered what they would think of this. He had to smile.

210

The junction at Cheng-chou presented a station done in the French style with iron spikes, like *chevaux de frise*, running along the ridge lines, and a town square directly across the way that was filled with noisy blackbirds in the daytime. Now, after midnight, they napped as the train passengers debarked into a confusion of conductors' whistles, shouted instructions, and the babble of other bewildered souls asking directions.

Captain Sato had by stages been annoyed at Sergeant Masaki's absences, then angry, and finally disturbed. He questioned the porter, who described the visit to the baggage car for the map case and his return alone. When they arrived at Cheng-chou, the captain had the porter lead him along the platform to the baggage car. There the baggage master, awake and engaged in supervising the unloading, could tell him nothing more. He assumed the Japanese gentleman had left with the porter. He had seen no one else but the two English travelers riding with him in the car.

Captain Sato compressed his brow and considered his options. Whatever had happened to Max, he dared not report it and get involved in red tape or worse. The sergeant was mentally agile, and if he was missing, it must be for a reason he was unable to communicate at the moment. Sato had no choice; he would have to wait and see. Turning away, he stopped as a thought nagged him. "What did the two English look like?"

"Like all others, sir," the baggage master said, showing a hint of humor, "except perhaps for the smaller man. He wore a curious plaster on his face and had most red hair."

"Red hair?" Captain Sato repeated.

Toting their own gear, Bodine and Colonel Gibb ferreted out the correct track for the "Great East-West Trunk Line" of the Lunghai R.R. (traveling to Sian via the industrial cities of K'ai-feng and Loyang). Unlike the cars of the T&N that would take sleek internationalists on to Peking, the Sian train was geared to the intrepid and cost conscious, with no fripperies like compartments; only coaches.

They found the baggage car guarded by a sullen Nationalist soldier, who actually refused their bribe and gave them the first hint that something very special was happening on the line. Resigned, they forced their way through a badly fitting door into a dim little third-class car. Three rough benches ran lengthwise, and at each end were two puny stoves, cold at the moment. The interior paneling gaped and had been patched inside with sacking. However, as Bodine ducked a nickled oil lamp, he read: ANGLE MFG CO, N.Y. on the wick wheel. Home sweet home.

They bucked several others down the back bench and settled in, piling

211

their gear on the seat in the Chinese way of taking up as much space as you can get. They had already dozed off when the engine gave a lurch and, heaving itself forward in steamy spurts, cleared the station and passed into the night landscape.

In the only first-class coach Captain Sato had pre-empted a double seat for himself, and it was unlikely that anyone looking at his face, with a jaw wired into a permanent snarl, was going to intrude. As the train picked up speed, he was preoccupied with the puzzle of Sergeant Masaki. He could not conceive that he had been misled about Bodine's death—and yet the captain had the sinking feeling that something was very wrong. The description of a small man with red hair in the baggage compartment shook him. He guessed there must be others who fit it—still, that, combined with the sergeant's disappearance, made him very uneasy. He had tucked the Nambu pistol in his waistline, and he checked again to see if it was secure. Once everyone had settled into sleep, he would personally check the cars from front to back. Yes.

For Adrian, the trip had taken on an unreal quality. After his initial sexual encounter with Mavis Ming Billy, she had pursued him relentlessly. Not satisfied with their late-night joltings in the boxcar, she tracked him down at each stop and they coupled anyplace that was handy, and several that were downright dangerous—once actually standing in the corner of one of the horse cars, dodging the stomp and shift of the animals. Discovering it could be done in ways other than from the rear, she insisted on innovations. Adrian had tried to introduce just a bit of foreplay—caresses and even kisses—but she was not interested in anything but one-to-one body contact, the rougher the better. Eventually he came to the conclusion that for her it was a form of competition, like wrestling, and she was determined to get the best of him, wear him down. She was succeeding. He had forgone bathing and was doing his best to keep up with her, but it was not easy.

Sitting with her and the old man in their end of the boxcar one night, Adrian tried to probe their relationship. Across from them, the Filipinos smirked and made in and out gestures with their fingers. Adrian ignored them. As the train lurched along and he watched Billy run up and down the abacus, he asked her a question that had been bothering him. "Billy, you were a virgin—had never been with a man—before we met. Why did you wait so long?"

"It was the nuns in that school." She kept on clacking the beads, not looking up. "They told me bad things about men. They said if I let one touch me, it would be like a snake in a mousehole, the pain would be terrible, I would bleed and be ruined by an unclean act. If I wasn't married, I would be a bad woman who spent disease, and if I was married, then I should let my husband near me only when I wanted a baby, otherwise it would be a sin and I would go to hell."

"My God! That's terrible!"

"It discouraged me. I loved the baby Jesus and did not want to offend him. But what those barren women told me was wrong. When you did it to me in the water, I found it did not hurt that much; in fact there was a good feeling about it, like horses must have, locked together. I decided I liked it, and it made me mad to think I had missed so much of it."

"Well, you're not going to believe this, but in the West it's connected with love . . . ideally, two people lie together only if they're in love."

"That is stupid. I don't understand you people always talking of 'love.' I love the baby Jesus because he looks down from heaven and protects me. You men talk of love when you want something for nothing. What you do with your thing has nothing to do with love. You do it to feel good in your body, and so do I. What has that got do with love? Does a stallion love a mare?"

"There are some who like to think it sets us apart from the animals, Billy—it's called romantic love, and because of it a man and a woman are suppose to find better things in each other. Poets like the idea too." He quoted Tennyson:

"As you give love, you will have love,
A loveless life is a living death.
'Tis better to have loved and lost,
Than never to have loved at all."

"What kind of talk is that! I will choose a husband because he is strong and can defend me, or rich and support me. Or—like you, he overpowers me and takes what he wants. I understand that. A lot of kissing and sweet talk will get you nothing. Love has to do with God, not men."

Adrian shook his head. "You're a tough lady, Billy. What about your grand-father?" The old man still scowled whenever their eyes met. "He obviously doesn't like you and I doing it."

"That is not what bothers him. He told me long ago I should take a man." She smiled, in a rare show of humor. "In fact, he offered himself as teacher. He does not like you because you are white and a stranger. He says it is beneath me to take someone as inferior as a white man and let him have pleasure from me. But I don't listen. I do what I want.

"Now shut up, I'm busy."

Adrian had learned a lot about women from Billy. All this time he had believed himself the predator, the dirty dog. Those early girl friends, his first serious love in college, the easy ladies on the polo circuit—he had felt smooth and slightly wicked seducing them into bed or so he thought. Each swore she did it only for "love." When it came right down to it, they had used sex to manipulate him, deliberately setting out to make him feel that because they "gave" themselves, he owed them. They had used him to get at his father's money, his name, and the bit of celebrity he had. He knew, of course, real love was supposed to change all that. Look where it had gotten him with Lola.

At least Billy treated it for what it was—pleasure entered into during a brief surrender between two selfish individuals with very different ideas of what sex meant, a contest of pleasure given and pleasure taken. He decided that Billy had advanced his opinion of women by being the first to treat him as a sexual equal.

There was a frantic wail on the locomotive's whistle, followed by a sustained squeal as the brakes locked up. Then a jarring, bumping lope, as the train skipped down the tracks to a final sudden stop. Everything that wasn't bolted or tied down changed ends in the car. They tumbled together with the canned food and stove parts, and it was a near miracle that nobody was brained. Piling out of the car, all were convinced a major train wreck had occurred, but when they looked down the tracks, the train was intact and no other was in sight. Only an exhausted belch of smoke dotted the sky above the heaving engine.

In the cab the French engineer mopped his brow. *Merde!* He had been proceeding along in the usual fashion—half speed—nursing the abused engine up a four-degree grade, when a man appeared directly in front of his eyes! Not five hundred yards down the track! *Merde!* This was nothing new, of course, in China the peasants preferred the nice straight tracks to their muddy roads and traveled along them like highways with entire families and livestock. No attention was paid to whistles or even the nudge of an engine. When some were killed, the relatives screamed and wailed, demanding compensation. It got to be a racket; people drew lots to see who would jump in front of the trains. The railroad solved this by establishing a flat payment of one hundred coppers (68 cents) per victim, and the market dried up.

It was the engineer's habit to blast the whistle, and if that didn't clear the track, to keep on going. Usually they got out of the way, but this one had stood firm and at the last possible minute the engineer had to hit the brakes. What convinced him to take this drastic step was the suit and tie. If you were French you simply did not run over somebody in a suit and tie.

The man was led limping along the right of way by the conductor and introduced to Mavis Ming Billy. He looked terrible. His face was bruised and embedded with gravel, and he seemed to have lost some teeth. Although the knees of both trousers were out and a sleeve ripped off, his tie was still nicely in place. It turned out the poor devil had fallen from the passenger train last night and still desired to continue on to Sian. Could he ride with them?

"Do you have any money?" Billy asked.

TWENTY-FOUR

FROM THE ROOF of the third-class car, Bodine and Colonel Gibb watched the sun come up. The interior had become impossible even for old China hands. The train made several local stops before it began its course up the mountain, and the car filled with country people carrying rude bags of produce and live fowl. Nursing mothers squeezed in with babies, and the compression of breath, bodies, regurgitated milk, and baby shit finally drove them out. They stood for a while between cars, rocking on a narrow platform, and when even that got crowded, climbed the ladder to the roof. The train had begun its long, slow ascent from the riverbed, and they were able to lie on the flat roof above the ventilators and actually sleep, belts looped around vent pipes.

Morning had shown the bottleneck of Tung-kuan pass, a spectacular piercing of the mountains that bounded Sian north, south, and east; great ranges rising in a shadowy overlapping, peaks lost in the clouds. At this one place the mighty Yellow River, "China's Sorrow," roared and twisted in a wide Y of upper and lower tributary before the foot of the Y dwindled off to the little Ching Ho and went west. The train traveled along the south shore above the swirl of river traffic, hugging the base of the Hwa shan Mountains, then leveling off, crossed over into Shensi Province and entered the border town of Tung-kuan. Sian was still nearly one hundred and fifty miles farther on in the We Ho Valley, but with luck they would reach it tonight—then, as they approached the railway station on the outskirts of the town, it was apparent they would not.

To find soldiers in a Chinese station was not unusual, but today there seemed to be nothing else. Troops were drawn up along the tracks, and several ponderous armored cars of Great War vintage blocked the access roads. What bothered Bodine and Colonel Gibb were the uniforms.

"Southerners," Bodine said.

"Cantonese?"

"Chang's Nats—KMTs. And you can guess why they're here." When the train came alongside the platform and ground to a noisy stop, Bodine and Gibb flattened out. The passengers, alarmed by the show of soldiers, stayed in cars, chattering nervously and peering out the windows. Everyone held their luggage as if its possession announced respectability. The muddle of troops parted, and an officer strutted forward with a megaphone. He was nattily dressed in a high-necked uniform girded by a shiny Sam Browne belt. As he began to speak in the squawk of a Canton accent, Bodine did his best to translate.

"Somethin' about the train not goin' on . . . because of serious . . . internal trouble. . . . Sian's been cut off. . . ."

After the officer finished, there was confused mumbling from the passengers, most of whom didn't understand what he had said. The Chinese, speaking the Shanghai dialect or northern Mandarin, were as much in the dark as the foreigners. But they all understood bayonets, and when the soldiers began gesturing with them, they got the idea and poured out on the platform. Clutching bags and bundles, they were pushed into lines and asked to show papers.

On the roof Bodine and Gibb remained lying flat, hats off to reduce the profile. Gibb was on his back, legs crossed and hands cushioning his head. "Look's like they started the war without us, old son."

"Yeah, Yü must have got his ass in gear. My guess is the Nats are here to see no one horns in while he buys his way in."

"You think the Nationalists support him then?"

"It sure looks that way."

"What do you suggest now?"

"You got me."

"Did you notice the make of those armored cars?"

"No."

"Austin, I think. We used a lot of them at Abbéville in '16."

"Is that right."

For Captain Sato the stop at Tung-kuan came as a rude jolt. He had just gotten to sleep after a long night of prowling the cars looking for Bodine. He

216

understood enough of what the officer on the platform said to know that the train was being held and his mission was in peril. The Nationalists supported Yü against his own son because the son was said to be a Communist; conversely, the Japanese were determined that the son stay in power, because if he did, it would tie up more of Chiang's army. In either case, Sato was not likely to be well received this morning. At the very least they would prevent him from going on to Sian. He could not allow that. The other passengers in first class had gotten off in a hurry, and the car was empty now, but the soldiers would be checking for stragglers at any minute. He had to move. Where?

Then, in an instant decision, he abandoned his luggage, and taking only a military kit containing his maps, went out the rear door to the platform between cars. There he climbed to the roof.

The Sian train remained alongside the platform throughout the day. Orders from Kuomintang HQ in Nanking had been to hold all passenger trains and prevent any persons, foreign or nationals, from continuing on for a period of not less than forty-eight hours. This was to extend to all roads (one) leading out of the city toward Sian. What wasn't excluded was freight traffic. This proved to be a serious oversight. It was claimed later that it was done for humanitarian reasons. Actually, stopping the flow of commerce and its tax revenues had never been considered. Whatever the reason, it drastically affected the outcome of the next few days' events.

It was a curious juxtaposition; at the tail end of the train, lying flat above the third-class car, Bodine and Colonel Gibb waited patiently until dark, when they could move. At the other end, above the first-class car, Captain Sato did the same, and neither was aware of the other. All were soldiers and had experience with the discipline of waiting. The day was cloudy, and the sharp edge of wind continued to blow down from the mountains. Bundled up, they lay dozing, occasionally shifting to check the station for troops and the armored cars. Although both Sato and Bodine used field glasses, curiously neither looked along the *top* of the train toward the other. At last the light began to fade, and it was dark.

Gathering up their luggage, Bodine and Gibb let themselves down the side of the train away from the platform. Using the cars as a blind, they walked the adjoining track and paused at the last one, taking a sighting on the armored car they'd picked out. Both had observed it during the day with the colonel's glasses, shaking their heads over the sloppy soldiering. It sat at a greater distance away than the others, perhaps five hundred yards, pointed toward the opening of a moon gate in the old wall that surrounded the town. In the dark one half was lit by the feeble overhead lights of the station, and its silhouette appeared in sharp definition: slab sides of 8mm armor plate dotted with bolt heads, angular, simple shapes of squares surmounted by cylinders—or "two ash cans on a cheddar carton"—as they said at the Austin Works. The "ash cans" were its twin turrets through which the snout of Maxim machine guns were directed between the gate, down the egress of a dirt road.

Outside the circle of the moon gate, the crew had established themselves, bullying those who attempted to enter the station and showing off for the girls who squatted with other would-be travelers by the side of the road. Their job, as they saw it, was to close off the station from the outside, and that's where they were. One gunner was left behind in the cramped confines of the armored car, half of his body poking through the hatch of the port turret. At the moment he was investigating his nose with a sturdy forefinger.

The two watchers nodded to each other and Bodine swung wide on the dark side of the car as Colonel Gibb crept forward in a direct line with its back, keeping the machine between him and those on the road. Arriving at the rear hatch (open for ventilation), he eased himself in and, familiar with the interior layout, looked to his left. In the round of the turret the lower half of the gunner rested against a canvas sling, the double handles of the Maxim gun pushed to his right, the cartridge belt dangling to a container on the floor. The sling was taut, and the bulge of his rear end hung over. Taking off his gloves, Gibb reached up and grabbed him hard by both cheeks, digging in with his fingernails through thin cotton pants. As he did, he let out a believable snarl, *"AAAUUUGGGHHHRRRAAAA!!!"*

The gunner shot up through the top hatch, *"YYIIIIIIIIIIIIIYYYIII!!!"* He bounded to the hood, then the ground, fell, got up, and streaked for the gate. As he came past Bodine, hidden behind the door, his arms and legs were pumping and his companions outside looked up in astonishment. In the split second he went through it, Bodine slammed the gate and locked it. Sprinting for the car, he ducked through the front hatch, pulled it shut and found Gibb at the rear. The four-cylinder engine popped away, and he appeared to be sitting looking out the back hatch.

"What in hell are you doin'? C'mon! Get up here! Get this damn thing goin'!"

Gibb's hand smoothly engaged the gears, and as he turned, Bodine saw a second steering wheel. "Have to reverse from the rear, old son."

"Do what?"

"The thing is, the front wheels have to follow the rear, so you'll have to steer up there too. Do try to keep in sync—that's a good fellow."

"Two steering wheels? Of all the crazy, Goddamn, Rube Goldberg . . ." But he got into position behind the other wheel and they started off, backing away from the gate, both sitting at opposite ends of the car, twisting the two separate controls. This took some doing, and their reverse path was erratic.

At a distance the crew of the nearest armored car looked up from their evening meal as the other car zigzagged past at a jerky five miles an hour. But the Austins were notoriously difficult to reverse, and they went back to their rice cakes. Fortunately, the engine was making so much noise they couldn't hear the pounding on the moon gate.

Inside the armored car Bodine and Gibb were having differences about the escape route. Although the taking of the machine had been carefully thought out, it was obvious the eventual direction hadn't. As Gibb continued in reverse toward the tracks, Bodine shouted, "Where in hell are you goin'! The road's that way! C'mon! C'mon! Put it in forward and let's find it!"

"I shouldn't think we would want to do that, would you?"

"Whattaya talkin' about? We're goin' to Sian, right?"

"Rather, but the road is exactly where the buggers will look for us—and we can't tell if it's blocked ahead, can we?" They were bumping over the tracks now, broadside to the two main east-west lines running into T'ung-kuan.

"Look out! You're on the tracks! Jesus!"

Gibb throttled down and shifted into forward. Then, getting up, he ducked and slid into the front driver's position. "Do you mind, old son? Punched a bit of time in with these types, j'know."

Bodine moved over, complaining. "You're gonna get us fuckin' well killed out here in the middle of the tracks!"

"Don't think so. That wog ranker said they were cutting off all service to Sian, right? I'd say we had the tracks to ourselves." He cranked the wheel over and turned the five-ton machine up over the rail, lining it up until all six wheels (double in back) were straddling the track.

"Oh, Christ! Now you've done it! We're locked up on the tracks!"

"That's the point, m' dear. These models were made to run on railroad beds. They were sold by the hundreds to the Soviets from '15 on for just that purpose. Russian gauge is five feet, and the Chinese four eight, so it's a comfy fit. Our wheel base is six six, designed to ride the ties."

"If you say so."

Gibb shifted up, and they moved smartly past the Sian train at the station platform, accelerating to a top of 31 m.p.h. The tires made an odd bumping hum on the ties, but Gibb seemed to have no trouble holding the big machine in place. As they traversed the yards and came through the tunnel in the wall, he flicked on the acetylene headlights and they moved away from Tung-kuan.

Captain Sato had seen them go by, but assumed it was a Chinese scouting party and went back to waiting. Stoic and long-suffering, he was prepared to wait the night out. Two hours later he was rewarded. He saw the light coming down the line, and minutes later a freight slowed for the station. There

219

was a clanging of signals, lights turned to green, switches were thrown, and as the boxcars came past him at a crawl, he easily jumped from one roof to the other. After clearing the yards, the train picked up speed and plunged into the tunnel. As it did so, the captain was sure he smelled the familiar odor of horses.

At a little after four in the morning, Gibb stopped the armored car at the bottom of a long grade. The lamps managed a dim arc of a dozen yards or so, and, ahead, the track could be seen continuing on over a trestle. Several hundred feet below in the total darkness was the sound of the "little" Ching Ho as it swept on toward Sian. The colonel took a long pull on the Tiger Bone Whiskey and got out. "Might as well stretch the old pins and top up." He unstrapped one of the extra gas cans and began pouring it into the nineteen-gallon tank. The Austin had a range of 125 miles, which he calculated would just get them into Sian.

While he did this, Bodine walked warily to the edge of the drop-off and looked across at the spindly wooden struts of the trestle. It had a single, one-way track and because of its length looked incredibly flimsy, like matchstick construction. "We're goin' t' cross that?"

"Don't see any other way, old son, do you? Can't get to the road from here."

"I guess not."

"I'm sure it's sturdier than it looks."

"Wanna bet? The poor bastards down below have probably sawed off half of it for firewood."

"Let's hope not, shall we?" Gibb returned the gas can to its place, adjusted his gloves, and got in, reluctantly followed by Bodine. They both took another stiff jolt of the Tiger Bone, and the Austin was started. Gibb popped it gently into low gear and they started across. It was possible to see the roadbed actually sway in the headlights, and looking out on his side, Bodine felt his stomach drop. Because of the width of the armored car the tracks beneath them weren't visible, only black empty space, with just a hint of a shine from the river far below. It was as though they were crossing on thin air.

"Jee-zuss!! This is like tightrope-walkin' a fuckin' elephant!"

"Nicely put, but look at it this way—there are people who actually pay money for a bit of a thrill like this—whirlybobs and such circus traps."

"Not me."

"Couldn't agree more. Can't imagin' why anybody would want to get their—"

"Did you hear that?"

"What, old son?"

"That—listen! There it goes again!"

"Really, I don't hear a—"

"It's a whistle! A Goddamn train whistle!"

"Oh, I hardly think so. The fellow back there said the line had been closed."

"Closed shit!! I'm tellin' you it's a train whistle!!" Bodine twisted around in the seat. The back hatch had been chained open for air, and bending down, he looked out into the darkness, along the line of track to where it curved down from the top of the grade. At that moment the powerful light of an engine beamed over.

"And here it comes!!!"

"I say, are you sure?"

SIAN,
WINTER
1931

TWENTY-FIVE

AFTER MIDNIGHT A conference was to take place in the rail yards of the Sian station at East Gate. This area, like the town, had all but been abandoned; service had ceased yesterday; engines were cold; nothing was working in the signal tower, passenger terminal, or workshop—it was the ominous silence of busy places—factories and heavy industry, where the absence of sound was loudly heard.

At the right of these tracks, a private car had come to rest on a siding. Detached from its engine, it sat with the baggage car brimming with personal possessions. The *Empress of the East* had been built by George Pullman in his Palace Car Works in the town of his name, south of Chicago. Intended originally for Leland Stanford, it had gone the rounds of Washo mine owners and ended up in China, to be traded off to a host of pretenders.

In a wide center window heavy curtains were pushed aside and a man stood silhouetted briefly against the soft interior light. It was Marshal Yü, the car's current occupant. As the time neared for his appointment he looked off toward the glow of a fire. It marked a gate in the wall that surrounded the rail yards. Guards had been placed here for his protection—but he knew if he was not successful in his coup they would be his jailers or, more likely, his executioners. He had forty-eight hours to pull it off, and he thought it very apt that it was in this place that it all should happen.

225

A T'ang capital, it had been officially called Sian (Western Peace) by the Ming dynasty in 1368. But these were latecomers; a city had been here a thousand years before Christ, its splendor and extravagance celebrated by poets and travelers. Court life was urbane, civilized, and the pleasure quarter exceptional, exotic excitement reaching a peak in March when the peony blossoms opened and "the city went mad." Marco Polo described it in the thirteenth century, when the Kubla Khan's son sat on the throne, as a city controlling twelve others. It was a high-water mark.

With the collapse of Mongol rule, it suffered rebellion and disorder lasting for centuries, devastating and depopulating entire areas. It was as though an evil spell had been cast over a once great and gentle kingdom, reducing it to the whims of barbarians. Sacked and burned, built and rebuilt to suit the convenience of each succeeding despot, it finally settled into a rectangular plan of about six square miles divided into two inner cities and an outer city; walls within walls. In modern times it fared no better, lurching from one disaster to another; Taiping, Nien, Muslim, and after 1911 a war with the Chihli warlords that very nearly finished it for good.

If this wasn't enough, these years had brought drought and famine so severe that whole districts had ceased to exist and the country was a wasteland. By the beginning of the twentieth century at least five million had died throughout Shensi Province. Marshal Yü had been a colonel of the Manchurian North-East Tungpei Army in those days, and raised up by Sun Yatsen's expectations, had declared for the Nationalist Revolution. With Yang Hu-cheng, "Tiger of the Cities," they held off a besieging Northern Army under Liu-chen-hua, and seized control of Sian in 1926. When Yang went back to his native province, Yü was left in power.

He was by turns ruthless and benevolent, no worse than the long line of rascals that had stolen from the people, the only difference being that there was now much less to steal. It was said that he accepted his reduced squeeze with good grace and went on to womanizing and gambling on a smaller scale. Always the satyr, he made the mistake of romancing the exotic Eurasian, Helen Webb, in public. This went down hard at home. Local concubines and an excess of wives were one thing, blond hairs on the pillow another. This made it easy for the left "reform" party to put forward (secretly) Yü's own son, Chan Chow-ki, the "Little Marshal." He was smart, clean, and practically a monk. While Yü was on the Riviera, cavorting, son succeeded father in a bloodless coup. When this happened there was scarcely a ripple. The people, used to the shuffle of satraps, did what they always did: went undercover until it was over.

That's what had happened now. The city was shut down: shops closed, traffic stopped, and except for an occasional army truck, streets empty. All reasoning people were hidden as best they could in homes and huts, meager food stockpiled, numb to the consequences of this latest madness. The very atmosphere was hushed, as if everyone had agreed on a conspiracy of silence. The few visible soldiers were behind hastily flopped sandbags at banks and rich men's yamens. This made everyone uneasy. Where were the troops? Preparing to defend the city? Sent to the walls and ramparts to await the onslaught of enemy armies? Manning the battlements against attack? No, the loess cave dwellers who lived on the outskirts of town sent word back that no one was on the walls; they were deserted. Where then?

They were all locked in their garrisons, confined to quarters, forbidden to move, leaves canceled until orders came down from their commanders. Those commanders—majors, colonels, and general officers—had been bought by Yü for forty-eight hours—rented on a graduated pay scale, bribed in democratic deference to rank and influence. Not quite as cut-and-dried as that, these warriors and heroes would not be bribed by just *anybody*. They respected and liked Yü, and most were ready to see him take control again. However, only a fool would have gone along for nothing—their men would have lost confidence, suspecting senility or worse. Each had a private audience with the great man, as always affable, remembering wives and mistresses, asking after their health, chatting on about his favorite subject, the efficacy of the mandrake root. Then, at last, not offering squeeze but a reward for their loyalty in his absence, a small token from the vast treasure he had brought to upgrade the army to stand at the ramparts against the Red Menace. There it was, the reason.

He carefully took out and showed a letter from Chiang, an order making Yü Bandit Suppressor of the Northwest. They all knew what that meant: the Generalissimo was ready to launch a new annihilation campaign against the Communists, who were interchangeable with "bandits." It was the Word. War would be renewed against the Reds, who with the help of their Russian allies had crept out of the trap in the South and were forming up in the Soviet area—Southern Kiangsi and Fukien—with its capital at Juichin. It was time to choose sides for the coming battle. The letter was signed at the bottom with the title of his official rank; Wei Yuan Chang. It was for this that Yü had paid his two hundred thousand plus dollars.

The generals now sat in their quarters, sipping tea, and waited for word to come down from the usurper. His success would be theirs, but they would not actively intervene until he removed his son from power. As these venerable officers, all senior grades with years of service and the authority of rank, waited to hear from Marshal Yü, he sat with the key man to his coup, a twenty-four-year-old lieutenant with baby fat and the fuzz of a starter mustache on his rabbity upper lip.

The interior of the *Empress of the East* had been done to a turn with the finest of veneered woods, mirrors, tassled drapes, and plush ornate furniture, tucked and buttoned. Delicate goldleaf patterns were traced on a curved overhead and lit by the half-circles of transoms, set with zip-cut, beveled, and jeweled glass. The brocade upholstery and Brussels carpet were worn from the years of travel, and although Leland Stanford might have raised an eyebrow at its current occupants, the car was still the apogee of Victorian elegance and gave a certain grace and respectability even to them.

There were several compartments, and the two principals sat in the largest, the parlor room, Yü spread out on a couch by the curtained window, the young man in a swivel chair with a French curved back. Yü found it hard to like Lieutenant Liao. He represented everything Yü found repugnant in the young: self-absorption, misplaced confidence, and bad breath. This pup wore a gray-blue uniform of the Tungpei Special Service Regiment, but he wasn't even Manchurian, actually a student from Peking with that dreadful accent they all affected. His glasses were the new horn-rimmed type, and like everything else about him they emphasized the wrong thing, weak eyes. But he represented the wave of the future; it had been young men like this, mere students, who had toppled him before, and he was not going to be caught twice. They called themselves Communists, but to Yü they were just one more group chasing the same old dragon: power. As for Liao, he was a zealot, a fiery patriot, a maker of speeches about the poor and downtrodden, and a greedy little crook. Yü knew him, because it had been his money that had supported his education. He was the son of his sister's maid.

Liao's foot rested on the rattan basket Yü had just filled with cold coins. Actually, as bribery went, he came cheap—fifty thousand to sell out his beloved leader and best friend. Lieutenant Liao was in charge of the special bodyguard that his son, Chan, trusted his life to. It was crucial that they be suborned and go over to Yü. Tomorrow night at exactly eight he would enter the capital and announce his succession and his son's "resignation." At that moment the "Little Marshal" would be "neutralized" by Liao's Peking Guards, and the army would arrive with a show of force, reaffirming him. Once in power, the first thing to be done was the purging of overstepping worms like this one.

"What's happened to your uncle? Is he still healthy?" Yü said.

"Oh, yes, he is more active than ever. At the top now."

"I met him in Paris, June of '22. As I remember he was on a work-study program." Yü chuckled. "Called himself Chou En-lai." This was a subtle slur, the name being a Pin-yin romanization of *Jou* En-lai.

The nephew passed over it. "He's come a long way. This last April the Comintern invited him to address the sixteenth Congress in Moscow—an unprecedented honor for a Chinese Communist."

"Amazing the turns in a man's career—as I recall he was a director under Chiang Kai-shek at the Whampoa Military Academy."

Lieutenant Liao rose. "You must forgive me, but it is past time for my departure—I have detained you."

"No, no, dear boy, it's been a charming interlude." They walked to the car door, which was opened by one of Yü's four Shensi bodyguards. Yü bowed. "Until we meet as colleagues. My best to your mother."

Tugging along his rattan box, the lieutenant hoisted up its heavy load and tied it on his bicycle. Waving, he pedaled off into the night. A bicycle! Yü shook his head sadly. What had genuine rascals come to? He watched as the young man wobbled past the fires of the machine gun company at the gate and disappeared into the darkness.

"Done!" Yü said aloud in English, smacking his hands together. The last Mex had been winnowed out; he had bought himself a coup. He paused at the mirrored door to the bedroom. Dressed as usual in the height of fashion: double-breasted dressing gown of quilted velvet that came nearly to his ankles and spats buttoned over his favorite yellow shoes. He was ready for romance.

Lola had watched the kid bicycle away. Some kind of Western Union messenger, she thought. The whole place, the silent train yard, made her very nervous. It was her experience that when you arrived at a depot you got off the train. She couldn't complain about accommodations. It was her first experience with a private car, and it was great—elegant, but also very remote. There was nobody across the aisle who could tell what time you got in.

The ornate sleeping room was tented with her clothes. Overflowing from her trunks to every hook, they draped the room in a pastiche of fabrics and paillettes. Ramon had taken to the overhead luggage rack. God! All her life she remembered him sleeping on the floor in a nest made up of old rugs or bedding. Once on the train, he had retreated to the ornate rack that spanned one end of the sleeping room, and she couldn't coax him down. Sad.

It was as though in old age he were reaching for the trees. Trees he had never lived in; probably no one in his family had for generations. One arm dangled down, and his eyes fluttered. Was he dreaming? What could an animal that had spent forty years of his life traveling with vaudevillians dream about? Could it possibly be about the jungle? A free, wild life? Ramon never had a wild life or a mate. She found this terribly sad. No doubt the reason for his nasty temperament; frustration vented off first to her mother, now her. He would live and die never having known what it was to really be an ape. He had been protected, well fed, pampered—was it worth it? No. The minute you inserted yourself between a wild animal and its natural life, the animal was perverted, ruined. No amount of good intentions and anthropomorphizing would make it whole again.

There was a light tap at the door. Charley was so polite; he would never come into her room without knocking. He'd been very considerate, kind, the short time they'd been together. She knew very little about what he was

229

doing, what was going on here. Actually she wasn't sure she wanted to know. He said it was political, that he was back in his old home town to take over; to her it had all the earmarks of a gang boss muscling in on another guy's territory.

He came in, and after bowing, kissed her, affectionate as always. "Ah, forgive my absences, princess, but these are busy times, we mount a daring event." She was wearing her fox scarf over pajamas. He was instantly solicitous. "You're cold!"

"Well, it is a little chilly. What happened to the heat?"

"A momentary inconvenience, to be sure." What happened was the station had shut down its power, and cut off from an engine, the private car went cold. Fortunately, it had oil lamps that were self-contained. But nothing could be done about the heat until after the coup. There was no way he would move them into town now. He could not take the chance that Lola or, even worse, Ramon would be spotted before he was in a position to enforce whatever he liked.

"I know!" he said, suddenly struck with an inspiration. Like all his dealing, it involved a bribe. "Why not let me send to town for the most warm fur coat?"

Lola's eyebrows went up. "Fur coat?"

"Yes, the kind that is made from fur."

"Swell," she said, kidding. "Make mine mink."

"Oh, I am sorry, mink is not possible," he said, very serious. "Perhaps you would accept Russian sable?"

She smiled. "I guess."

He put his arms around her, and she could feel the heft of his belly. She knew exactly what he was after, and it was the last thing she wanted at this moment, but she owed him. "Thanks, Charley, but I don't need a coat. Why don't we just crawl in bed and get warm?"

As they did, Yü said, "What would you like to try tonight, princess?"

"How about good old missionary style?" They both laughed.

Later, Ramon suddenly woke and, disorientated, swung down from the rack, perching on the chair below. He pushed the tassles aside and looked out the window, but it was dark. Unable to see, he pressed his face against the glass.

One of the young machine gunners strolled near Marshal Yü's private car. He'd been told to stay clear, and he knew there were two bodyguards on outside duty, but he hoped to catch a glimpse of the great man. As he watched, the curtains were pushed aside and a face appeared at the lighted window. For a minute he couldn't believe his eyes; then he turned and ran back to tell his comrades.

*   *   *

Just outside the city, Lieutenant Liao pedaled his bicycle across the Pa ch'iao, the most famous bridge in China. It was very dark, and as the wheels bumped over uneven marble slabs between long railings of low balustrades, he had trouble keeping it tracking properly with the heavy load of gold riding the rear rack. But he managed, and reaching the guard post on the southern side of the Wei River, he stopped. It was here that the emperors of the old Ch'ens An used to bid farewell to their viceroys. Now a surly guard shone a light on his pass and waved him on. It was twelve miles of tough pedaling before he reached Lintung and the lanterns in the temple courtyard of Huachingkung resort, another famous place in its time, with lotus pools and hot springs. One of the baths still had a hollow spot worn in the marble, said to be from the fat behind of the great Chinese beauty, Yang Kuei Fei.

The place had been chosen because it was close to the city and isolated enough to precipitate a fast withdrawal—the tracks of the Lunghai Railroad ran not far away. When the "Big Marshal" had appeared and the generals withdrew their support from the "Little Marshal," he had been escorted here until the matter was resolved. He was really under house arrest, in the charge of Lieutenant Liao and twenty men of the Tungpei Special Group. They called themselves "Peking Guards," and like Liao they were made up of young Peking students, rabid Marxists. This is what had brought on the crisis; the "Little Marshal," Chan Chow-ki, had been rash and moved too fast in the Red direction. Alarmed, the irredentists, reactionaries, and old-line officers had formed up behind Yü and encouraged him to come out of exile. It had been a serious mistake not to kill the old man four years ago when they had had the chance.

The lieutenant stopped in front of the marble pavilion, unstrapped the rattan basket, and lugged it inside, nodding to his comrades guarding the front of the building. They had not been allowed to bring heavy weapons, only Mauser pistols, and it was not hard to read into this the future of the Guards, once the coup had gone in Yü's favor. He was led down an arcade by a boy with a flashlight and at an inner door entered a low-ceilinged room, built completely in marble like all the other buildings. At the far end of the room, a man sat studying in the light of a single oil lamp.

"Little Marshal?" Liao said this in an intimate tone, slightly mocking.

Chan Chow-ki stood up from his desk, and when Liao put down the basket, they embraced warmly. "Well, there it is," Liao said, and then stood on the basket. "Does it make me a bigger man?"

They laughed and, holding hands, walked over and sat together in the shadows of a windowseat. "He bribed you, then?"

231

"Yes, of course, he bribed all of us. I am to see that you are neutralized by eight tomorrow night."

"He said that? You are to *kill* me?"

"He said 'neutralized' with his mouth."

Chan's face went dark. "Oh, that evil man . . ." There was such fury and hatred in his voice that Liao was startled. Chan was very much like his father, stocky where the elder was fat, but with that same combination of sweetness and shrewd intelligence in the face. Yü was corrupt and capable of anything, but his face betrayed nothing. Chan's unfortunately showed everything. "Then we have lost the army's support?"

"Yes, once he announces your 'resignation' in his favor, they will come forward for him."

"All of them?"

"So it seems. The youth cadres and worker committees have been locked up." Chan looked up. "Last night . . . it is just as well; they would have been slaughtered."

"What about the Russians?"

"The horses still haven't arrived."

"Damn!" There were tears in Chan's eyes. At thirty-four, ten years older than Liao, he was still the baby. "I've written to Chou."

Liao sighed. "Uncle can't afford to help us, Chan—the First Red Army has its own problems. They're not going to give Chiang an opportunity to catch them out. The Cantonese are encamped at Tung-kuan now, just waiting to jump off." It had been a meeting with Uncle Chou last March that had begun the trouble. Again it pointed up Chan's rashness.

He had been a brilliant student and a gifted orator. Four years at Whampoa had prepared him for the military life, and his devotion and selfless duty to the party made him seem the perfect choice for the new man. A natural leader. And he had paid his dues. After Chiang's Shanghai coup in '27 had rent Chinese politics down the middle, the shaky illusion of a Popular Front—Communist and Nationalist together—dissolved, and moderates were rendered impotent between two extremes. In the pitched battles and firing squads that followed, CCP rolls had been decimated to a few thousand who were willing to be counted. Chan was one.

The great peasant revolt in Hunan-Hupe had been lost, and Chiang's "extermination campaigns" (like the one coming up) had swallowed up and annihilated regional support until the remaining Communist troops were contained in several small enclaves fighting for their lives. Still, Chan had persisted, and when the chance came to be used by his father's enemies against the old man, he had taken it—and managed to use them. They had expected a puppet, but he had outsmarted them. Then again he went too fast, rushing forward before the Red cadres could infiltrate the army. The

232

generals might be corrupt, but they were fierce patriots and had finally seen the specter of a hammer and sickle waving over Sian. Finally alerted, they had reacted before Chan's comrades were ready. Now it was too late.

"If you don't neutralize me at eight tomorrow, what do we do instead?"

"I thought we might start by shooting your father."

Chan's eyes widened. "Can we do that?"

"It is the only thing that will stop him now. If I don't act on your life tomorrow night, he will find others who will. If *he* dies, the generals will begin fighting among themselves again. They chose you before because they didn't trust each other."

"Is the station guarded?"

"One machine gun company—about one hundred and thirty men from the Seventeenth Route Army—and Yü's four bodyguards."

"And there are twenty of us with only pistols."

"Yes."

There was a pause and Chan looked up suddenly. "Did you hear that?"

"What?"

"It sounded like a train whistle far off—are the trains still running?"

The French engineer gave the cord another tug and began slowing as they came to the trestle over the Little Ho River. He didn't trust it and would have preferred keeping his eyes shut as they crossed. He pushed the throttle up another notch on the quadrant, and a hiss of steam jetted, as the pistons closed and the driving wheels slacked off. Then at a stately walk he began to go across the trestle.

In the armored car Bodine watched the train's progress through the open rear hatch. "Jee-zuss, Gibbsie! Goose it! Get this friggin' can motivatin'! The friggin' train's on the friggin' bridge!"

"Don't know if that would be wise, old son," Colonel Gibb said. Accelerating slightly, the armored car began to shimmy, and Bodine was sure the right rear tire went completely off the narrow bed.

"All right! All right!! I believe you!!"

"Never could outrun that engine anyway—our top speed is thirty on damned good tarmac." Gibb was right about this. At the moment they were doing 8 m.p.h., and even at its "walk" the train was gaining rapidly. At mid-trestle they had at least a quarter of a mile before they could turn off to solid ground. "I'm sure the fellow will see us in time. Don't worry," Gibb said, smiling.

"Screw that! I ain't waitin' until I get a locomotive up the kazoo! Oh, no! Not me! No, sir!" Bodine got up and pushed between the front seat toward the back.

"Hope you're not goin' t' jump, old son—that would be a bit stiff."

"I'm gonna do what I know how to do! I'm gonna shoot the fucker!" He worked himself into the half round of the starboard turret, poking his chest and arms up in the breeze. Supported by the sling, he swung the machine gun around. It was one of the early Maxims, a handsome piece, with shiny brass sections and a bronze water jacket. He checked the fabric belt to see if it was clearing into the take-up box, then pulled back the cocking lever. The maxium range was nine hundred yards, and he set the sights to use every inch.

The engineer and Chinese fireman, each with his head out on an opposite side of the cab, watched the track ahead, checking for any outrageous warp in the rails or missing ties. As usual, the whole structure set up a slight galloping motion under the train's weight, giving them a queasy feeling of riding on rubber. As he heard the fireman shout, the engineer saw what appeared to be the winking of lights. The sound was lost under the engine's noise, but he was aware of something out of the ordinary when sparks zinged up from the cowcatcher. Next there was an explosion of glass and the headlamp went out.

Reaching out with the line of fire, Bodine had stretched the gun's trajectory, and a dozen rounds chewed up the ties before he could elevate and zero in on the locomotive's light. When it went out, he could only wait. There was no way to stop an engine head-on with .30 caliber bullets. Some light from a sliver of the moon allowed him to see the front end of the locomotive as it expanded and grew larger.

Jesus! Would it keep comin'? Was it going to ram them? It would be a simple matter for the engine to butt them off the track. A tap and good-bye.

If the engineer *was* unable to stop the train (whether he wanted to or not), it *would* only take a tap of the cowcatcher to send them over the side and in a sickening fall to the river below. The ten-thousand-pound armored car would sink like a safe, and there would be little chance of getting out. Bodine reacted to this oncoming disaster as he did in other moments of stress in combat; he ignored it. Once satisfied there was nothing else he could do to circumvent fate, he stopped worrying about it. The train would hit them or it wouldn't.

Although the engineer had no concern about the car and its occupants, he was concerned that if they collided, the car might get tangled and dragged along and tear up the tracks. With a very sensitive handling of the brakes he was able to bring the engine down several yards from the rear of the car. It pulled away, still held rock-steady by Colonel Gibb, and a few minutes later reached the other side of the trestle, bumping off the track and down the side of the embankment. The engineer immediately pushed the throttle forward and the engine picked up speed, charging straight ahead. Light or no light, he was not staying around. For all he knew, he was dealing with bandits or in the middle of a war.

When the train slowed, Adrian woke and extracted himself from Mavis Ming Billy's plump limbs. Sliding open the boxcar door, he looked back in time to see a curious-shaped car by the side of the tracks. A head was poked out of what appeared to be an ashcan attached to one side.

Forward, on the roof of the first car, Captain Sato had a terrifying front-row seat. Looking over the top of the engine cab, he had seen the armored car before the engineer and fireman had. Clinging on with stiff fingers, he watched the entire event played out: the arc of bullets, striking sparks off the iron prow, the sudden dousing of the lights and the horrifying minutes in the dark as the train hurtled on—then braked down. He thought he recognized the car as the one that had preceded the train out of the station at Tungkuan. He found it hard to understand why anyone would be stupid enough to be on the line.

Near dawn the freight train followed a river valley between loess cliffs. The fields were deserted here, and the long shadows of graves began to appear along the right-of-way: ancient elaborate structures in clay and tile larger than local farmhouses. Eventually they gave way to the great pyramidal tombs, marking the road to Sian. At a distance stood the blue mountains and, closer, at the foot of the Lisham range, the rounded walls of Lintung. Across from Lintung was a cluster of temple roofs, outlined by ornamental pine—the resort of Huachingkung.

The train had begun to slow several miles before this and came to a steamy stop at a country town called Lantien. When the boxcar doors slammed open, and he heard the snort and clatter of horses, Captain Sato hurriedly consulted his maps. He found their position and estimated correctly; they were ten or twelve miles from Sian. It was obvious he would have to find other transportation. The horses were being unloaded to the left side of the train, so he climbed down the right. He brushed off his clothes, walked to a simple whitewashed station, and tried the door. It was locked. He looked around. The closest buildings were farmhouses, far out in the bleak fields. Paralleling the tracks, a dusty road seemed to lead to the distant shapes of temples at the first slope of foothills.

At one corner of the station an old man sat bundled up against the morning cold. There were several baskets of potatoes carefully arranged by his side. Mustering up his Chinese, Sato spoke to him. "Where might a traveler find transportation into the town of Sian?"

The man turned his head, and Sato saw that cataracts clouded his eyes. "You are a foreigner?"

"Yes, that is right," he said, annoyed. "I have business in Sian, important business."

"Perhaps you know the home of my potatoes? My grandfather told me they came from foreigners. A place that is green all over, and they hate the red-hairs."

Sato hoped to avoid getting into the kind of circular conversations the Chinese love. They could go on forever without touching the subject at hand. "I must find my way into Sian. Is there a car or ricksha to be had here?" He had to speak up; the pound of horses and shouts of the men herding them were getting louder.

"Oh, you haven't heard? The city gates are closed. Oh, yes, no one can go there. That's right, the great warlord, the one they call the 'ever-ready stamen,' is back." He chuckled.

"I have money," Sato said officiously. "Do you know of any who would guide me there? I can offer protection—I go to see Marshal Chan Chow-ki on urgent business."

The old man laughed out loud this time, slapping his thigh. "Well, that is a joke! Your joss is right!"

Sato struggled to keep his temper. "Why is that?"

"The only guide you need is my finger." And he pointed toward the temples. "Red star is at the lotus baths, they say."

"What?" If Captain Sato found this hard to take in, at that second several shots snapped sharply, echoing across the valley, and he involuntarily ducked down next to the old man. On a low hill across from the train, two men sat on horseback, nicely framed against the rising sun. It wasn't possible at this distance to make out their faces or uniforms, but he could tell by the way they sat their horses that they were not Chinese. One man carried a lance, a pennant drifting back from its tip.

"Cossacks!" the old man said, spitting.

"How do you know?" Sato asked.

"We have had them around our necks here for months. I know the sound of their noise!"

Yes . . . he was right! Sato remembered the detailed troop placement on his maps. There was a brigade of White Russian mercenaries stationed outside of Sian. Lancers, who acted as the "Household Horse Guards." It was all coming together. As he watched, the two men rode toward the train.

"Baby rapers," the old man said, spitting again.

TWENTY-SIX

RUSSIANS HAD BEEN in China since the days of sixteenth-century tea trade. By 1920 there were more than 200,000 in consulates, the concessions of Hankow and Tientsin, Monogolia, Manchuria, and the port cities. When the ax of the revolution fell, they not only lost their extraterritorial rights, but overnight were stateless. The last of the White armies had been pushed to the sea at Vladivostok, and thousands were on the run from the Red Terror.

The Japanese and Americans pulled out of Siberia in the autumn of 1922, leaving the Whites without further support, and ten thousand more were evacuated in ships to Wonson, Korea, escorted by the Russian gunboat *Manchuria*. From there they eventually made their way into China, many finally ending up on the Avenue Joffre in Shanghai. Half starved and penniless, they were forced to compete with coolies for survival. It was not unusual that summer to see white men pulling rickshas.

But some did what they knew best: killed.

The Cossacks, called in the Turkic *kazak*, meaning "adventurer" or "free man," had been used by the Russians for their own purposes for three hundred years; one of those purposes was to suppress revolution. In this last great suppression they had been divided, those in the south forming the core of the White armies. After defeat, survivors who broke out made their way into China by Manchuria and went on to become bodyguards for rich men and

237

mercenaries hired by warlords. The 10th Mukden Lancers belonged to this group. They fought once again on the wrong side with Marshal Wu Pei-fu at Wuhan, and in the aftermath (he being on the Japanese payroll and anti-Chiang Kai-shek), found work in Sian as "household mounted guards." Here a curious schism developed. Because of "Red Directions" and Moscow cant, the Little Marshal, Chan Chow-ki, was embarrassed by the White Russians in his bailiwick and had them shunted out of the city near the country town of Lantien. Then, when the crisis developed and the regular army was suborned, he was forced to go hat in hand and ask if the 10th would support him against Yü. They would. if paid in advance and remounted. It had been his agents who contacted Mavis Ming Billy in Saratsi and overpaid her to bring the horses up from Nanking in a hurry.

The "baby raping" reputation came from an infamous incident at Wuhan. A girls' school was overrun during the fighting, and the girls, all under nine or ten, were raped. It was never proved who was responsible, but the story had grown in the telling and they never denied it. Ferocity was the Cossack's stock in trade, and the blacker the mark the better. This eventually worked against them. Like all mercenaries, they were treated with fear and mistrust by their employers and at Sian were issued only sidearms and carbines. Mounted on their big horses in impressive uniforms, lances bobbing, they were trotted out as showpieces. Tame bears.

The leader, or *ataman*, was an enormous ruffian named Bohdan Razin, a Yaik from the middle Ural River. Illiterate and already six feet six at thirteen, he was chosen for the Tzar's guards. He made a success at soldiering and might even have made sergeant if he'd been able to read. After the revolution, with his size and natural aggression, he bullied his way to the top of the 10th and promoted himself to general. At forty, and a hair under six feet eight, he looked down at the Chinese with some humor and himself with none. It had been his ego that insisted they be mounted only on full-sized horses.

The horse he was on now was tall but bony, and he rode him like an extension of his spine, sitting high, with his back arched, reins held absently in one hand, the other cocked on his hip like a prince. His uniform was a dark green, almost black, with thigh-high yellow boots that merged into a wide stripe on the pants. A peaked cap, white with a shiny patent visor, was tilted over one eye, and from his expression it was obvious he was pleased with himself and out to impress.

Adrian was impressed. He knew a horseman when he saw one, and the rider looked to him like everything you had a right to expect in a Cossack: a bold satanic face, whimsical shrewd eyes, and a marvelous bushy beard. Behind him the other officer sported a gold *fouvrage're* over one shoulder, and, dancing his horse sideways, held a long wicked lance, its pennant snapping in the breeze.

They came to a stop several yards away and surveyed the tumble of horses and mixed bag of handlers: the Filipinos, Adrian, the girl, and her grandfather.

"Hey!" said Razin, breaking the spell. "Is this trotting out of hanks of hair my horses?"

"Who are you?" Billy asked, unimpressed by his flash.

"You!" Razin said, pointing to Adrian as the only white man. "Who commands this trash?"

"The lady." Adrian bowed toward Billy.

"I want to see money before I move these animals," Billy said.

"If that's what you call them, you've been fooled."

"Money."

Razin looked at her for the first time. "What is this? A talking woman?" He turned to his companion. "Can you believe that? Better than a parrot."

"All right!" Billy shouted, turning to the others. "Stop the unloading! Get them back in the cars!"

Razin laughed. "Your money will be handed over on the delivery at my camp—that was what was agreed."

Billy hesitated; she knew the verbal agreement by heart. "Are you General Razin?"

"Of course, you ugly girl! Now follow me!" He wheeled his horse, dug in his spurs, and galloped off.

"What do you know, hay face!" Billy shouted after him, "That great lunk of a body will surely collapse that poor horse!" Then she turned to the others. "All right! Get the horses moving!"

Adrian mounted his pony and, before turning away, said, "You should have gotten your money first." It was an unnecessary barb, but he had the satisfaction of seeing that it hurt.

"I will! Don't you worry, I will!"

It had cost Sergeant Masaki his last twenty-five mex to be allowed to travel in a windy boxcar and sleep with no covering on a filthy straw floor and eat some kind of food he could only describe as gluey. The shock had been finding the American, Adrian Reed, Jr., among these people. Most remarkable! He hadn't recognized him at first, and before Max could cover his amazement and think of a story to explain his own presence, Adrian had been very solicitous and concerned about Max's condition.

"You look terrible, man! Come on, let's see if we can fix up those cuts!" Max had been taken aback. It was the first time he had been treated with decency by an American or, for that matter, even noticed. He explained that he was a salesman and had fallen off the passenger train by accident.

If Adrian was satisfied with the explanation, Max was consumed with curiosity as to why a "rich" American was proceeding across country in the company of horse traders. They were both cautious, and over the next few days each probed carefully into the other's business. Their mutual interest in horses gave them a common ground, and although Max never revealed his military background, Adrian found out more about him than Max intended. A piece of the samurai family history emerged, and Adrian began to suspect that this man was more than just a traveling salesman. As for Max, he was able to deduce that Adrian had missed his train and was pursuing Yü for "financial" reasons. This wasn't explained, but he was relieved that it seemed to have nothing to do with political purpose. What he found difficult to understand was Adrian's sleeping with the hulking Mongolian girl. But he knew for a fact that Americans were less than fastidious.

He had slipped away in the confusion of the unloading and stayed by the far side of the station until the last of the horses were driven off. He waited until the dust settled, then walked up the road the engineer had pointed out as leading to Sian. A mile or so along it he passed a compound of low temple buildings, but kept on going.

Lieutenant Liao had been awakened just after dawn and had found a Captain Sato being held by the Peking Guards. He examined his credentials, the letter from General Hojo's office in Hsinking, and took him straight to the Little Marshal.

Chan Chow-ki had been in touch with the Japanese Kwantung HQ for some time. Each had been maneuvering to use the other against their mutual enemy, Chiang Kai-shek, and up to this point had avoided any real commitments. Now that was all changed; the flirting was finished; he had to bend over and present his backside. By agreeing to let Captain Sato help them he was being mounted by the tiger.

They sat at a table in the marble salon, and with the slant of the first morning sun cutting through the arcade arches, Captain Sato told them the astounding news of the horses' arrival in the nick of time.

"Then it's not too late!" Chan said, beaming.

Liao slapped him on the back. "Hooray for the Russians!"

Sato was not so enthusiastic. He had immediately sized these two up for what they were: overaged schoolboys, immature politicians. "You say the army will stay out of this?"

"Yes, they have been paid to remain neutral until Yü can have me shot."

His maps were produced, and he questioned them closely about Cossack strength versus the soldiers guarding Yü. "Bad," he said, digesting the odds.

Chan's face fell. "But why? There are more than two hundred Russians to put against Yü's one hundred and forty at the station. Surely that is enough?"

Sato shook his head. "Without close support, those horses will be shot to

240

pieces by the machine guns. Unless they can be put out of order before the attack, it will have a small chance."

"I have a plan," Lieutenant Liao said. Sato found that hard to believe, then was surprised to find the plan had possibilities. It would require bluff and a great deal of nerve, but if it came off, they might have a chance. It had a desperate quality about it he admired, and at this point there were no real alternatives. They went over timing and agreed that the last possible moment the attack could be launched was sundown. A guide would take Sato to General Razin's camp at once, and he would coordinate the battle plans.

It was nine o'clock in the morning, bright and sunny, when they rode out across the fields toward the foothills.

The Cossack camp turned out to be a dreary Chinese farm with crumbling buildings, augmented with tin and thatch to make rude barracks and stables. To Adrian, used to only the best accommodations on the polo circuit, it was shocking. The horses were ruins, ridden into the ground. Obviously, there was a desperate need of remounts.

The Cossacks ran to meet them, leaping bareback aboard the closest animals, and helped them herd the others. Despite their miserable appearance, there was no doubt about the Cossacks' ability to ride. They were aggressive and foolhardy and began to resemble the Cossacks of popular imagination. When the horses had been secured in enclosures bounded by tangles of briers, Adrian dismounted and went with Billy and the old man to look for General Razin.

They found him on the front porch of what must have been the original farm building, a bleak structure with a broken tile roof and shaky poles forming an overhead screen against the sun. The immediate area around them was treeless and harsh, and Adrian wondered where they found grazing and fodder for the horses. Several noisy ducks and a goose waddled around the side of the house in a flap of dust, and he could see a woman holding a baby in the dark of the doorway.

They had been followed by a group of Cossacks and their women—wives, he guessed—and lots of children. He remembered someone telling him that the Russians in China did not intermarry with Orientals. From the look of this bunch, it was true. Adrian looked around at the faces of the men and was struck by their simple, uncomplicated features: wide mouths, deep-set eyes, and small turned-over ears, with only the occasional flare of nostrils or refinement of a chin line. Peasants, their expressions in no way dashing or warlike, rather dull and perhaps curious. Theirs was the hardship of mass exile, locked into the center of a hostile or indifferent country, at the mercy of political patronage.

The general, the focal point, tilted against the house in his chair. He

241

wasn't drinking tea from a glass, or even vodka, but instead tipped up a bottle of Peking Five-Star Beer. They watched while he guzzled.

"I will be paid now," Billy demanded without preamble.

"Who is this?" Razin addressed Adrian. "What kind of woman would be a horse trader? Maybe a Red, ha? They like to put women up to men's jobs."

"She's an Odros Mongolian and comes by her trade naturally."

Razin knew this, of course, and went on talking to Adrian as if she weren't there. "What kind of funny accent is that? Are you a Jew?"

"American."

"You don't sound like one. I speak English better than you—I was up along the Amur in Sibera in 1918 when Americans shoved their big noses in—were you there?"

"No."

"How could you be American then? They were all there, I'm told—staying in their holes and not coming out—it was a disgrace! The only damn good of it was learning English—if you can call that good—"

"I want to be paid."

Razin shoved his huge head toward her suddenly and snarled, "Shut your damn face! What kind of woman talks over a man? A big, ugly, elephant-legged, slant-eyed one, I say! Do not speak in my direction again!"

In that instant Adrian recognized the brute. Close, he also saw bad teeth, dirty pores, and more blackheads in the noble nose than he could count. The uniform that he had been so taken with at a distance was stained, perspired in, and badly patched—not an elegant green-black at all but dirty gray.

"My pay," Billy persisted.

"Quiet, you loudmouthed bitch! Are you some kind of Hebrew, always talking of money? Shut up, I say!"

"What kind of man bullies a woman?" Adrian shouted back. "We came here in good faith after a long, mean trip to bring your lousy horses, and you insult us! Is this hospitality? Before this I believed Cossacks were famous as horsemen and great hosts! Not true!" Adrian didn't give a damn if this moldy giant and flea-bitten army all jumped on him! He was not going to stand for insults. He would not have Mavis Ming Billy's marvelous, overbearing, aggressive pride, her maddening independence, trod on by this moron whose brain power was about equal to his horse's. Adrian also realized he'd become fond of her, and it wounded his ego that the girl he was sleeping with was being demeaned.

Razin looked at him for a long moment, then said, "Well, you haven't given me a chance, have you? I like to have fun with the girls—a joke, you know—then we can talk and break bread. I'm famous as a host." He got up. "Come inside."

If Adrian expected Billy to be grateful for his defense of her honor, he was mistaken. As they went into the house, she snapped out at Adrian, "Why don't you mind your own business! Who asked you to shove into this? I can take care of myself!" She pushed past him and followed Razin into the dark interior, the old man bringing up the rear.

Inside, the smell of cabbage cooking was nearly unbearable, but at least it was Russian. They sat at a flyspecked table without a cloth, and the woman he'd seen in the doorway put down glasses in filigree holders, the first sign of any refinement. "We're going to have tea," Razin said. "That's a great Cossack way of greeting friends."

"I want to show you how much you owe us," Billy said, producing a worked-over piece of paper.

Razin slammed his fist on the table, bouncing the glasses. "My sweet Moses!" he said, clutching his head. "Is this woman possessed? Does she have manners? I don't think so!"

"She's anxious, General," Adrian added quickly. "Why don't we get business out of the way, then we can relax."

Billy glared at him and shoved the paper over. "This is the sum."

Riding into the Cossack encampment, Captain Sato accurately estimated their number and evaluated their readiness. He was not encouraged. As a cavalryman himself, he was aware of the Cossacks' awesome reputation as horsemen and ferocious fighters. But he was inclined to put it down to size and swagger. The value of the cavalry charge had ended with the invention of the modern machine gun, if it hadn't already been buried with the Light Brigade at Balaclava or Union losses at Cold Harbor. Its only remaining value lay in the subjection of primitive tribes, crowd control, and the frightening of green troops. He was counting on the reputation of the "Baby Rapers" to supply the last.

The tea drinkers looked up as he was shown in. "I am Captain Sato, Imperial Japanese Army, acting on direct orders from Marshal Chan Chow-ki, and . . ."

"Well, by Jesus, I hope you brought the shekels!" Razin said.

"Wh . . ."

"This damn Hebrew has been screaming down the roof to be paid for her skinny horses! Get it up, for God's sake!"

Sato maintained his detachment. He spoke to the Peking guide, and the rattan basket with Yü's gold was lugged in and thudded on the table. It was a small irony that the funds Yü had attempted to bribe Lieutenant Liao with would now provide the wherewithall to mount the Cossack attack against him.

As the business of counting out the coins went on, Adrian tried to appraise Captain Sato. With his shaved head and wired jaw Adrian did not for a minute connect him with the "handsome Japanese with longish hair" he had seen briefly in the bar of the roof garden the night of the farewell party. Sato appeared now to be a martinet, a stiff-backed career officer, who as a military adviser was meddling in China's internal affairs. Adrian took in the Borsolino hat, the well-cut jacket and riding breeches, and disliked him immediately. He kept quiet, realizing that it would not be wise to reveal he was American. Closer, Adrian noticed that Sato had a curious scar on his cheek. It looked almost like an eagle.

Sato scarcely gave Adrian a look. From his appearance he automatically assumed Adrian was one of the Russians. He looked it. As it had gotten colder, Adrian had been forced to use the last of his funds to buy a quilted Chinese coat and a ratty fur hat from Billy. He had not bathed since the romp in the water tank and had not shaved since she had painfully pinched his skin the day they wrestled. Adrian had a dense, black beard, and what wasn't covered by a week's heavy growth of whiskers was stippled by cinders and dirt. So it was understandable that Sato didn't recognize him as the "typical rich American" in the full-dress suit he'd seen at that same roof garden bar.

Satisfied with her payment, Billy bagged the coins, abruptly got up with the old man, and went out without a backward look at Adrian. He stayed where he was, interested to find out what the Japanese was up to. He thought of the two cases of important documents of "a certain military power" that hopefully were in Yü's luggage. Homer Lea had alerted him—the Japanese were the enemy—and looking at Sato, Adrian believed it. If Razin didn't object—and he didn't seem to—he was going to listen in. Assuming Adrian was Razin's lieutenant, Sato unfolded his maps and began to explain how they were going to take Yü's train.

Bodine and Gibb were having a terrible time. Bouncing off the track in front of the freight train, Colonel Gibb, by skillful handling, got the armored car down a steep embankment without turning over. There they bogged down, and no amount of reversing and running through the gears would extract the five-ton machine.

The sun was coming up as Bodine stood in the turret, giving advice and swearing, while the colonel, his head out the side-door hatch, tried to rock the car by quick changing of the gears. "Too heavy," he said over the engine's revving.

"Let's leave the damn lead-ass can here an' leg it!"

"You really want to do that, old son?" Gibb let up on the throttle.

Bodine hesitated. "No, that wouldn't be smart."

"We'll have t' lighten the old thing then. Look 'round the rear boot and see what we can chuck out."

244

Bodine ducked inside. Lining both sides of the hatch were stacks of the oblong metal boxes containing cartridge belts. He opened one; it was full. "This tub musta carried the ammo for the rest of the slopes—at two-fifty a box there's got to be three or four thousand rounds here."

"That's why she was down at the tail." Gibb got up from the driver's seat, and, together, they off-loaded the cases next to the embankment. Stacking them neatly, they cleared out towing chains, tools, and whatever else wasn't bolted down. Gibb climbed back behind the wheel. As he eased it forward, the car came unstuck.

"All right!" Bodine shouted. "Let's go!" Gibb pulled ahead and looked back at the boxes of stacked ammunition. Bodine followed his line of sight. "Shit!"

The years of military training had left their mark, and it bothered both of them to leave the ammunition sitting there. They sighed, got out, and loaded it back in, shifting the weight over the rear axle.

Traveling along the right-of-way, they reached the outskirts of Lantien by noon and saw the long line of boxcars pulled up next to the station. Stopping, they both got out and stood on the hood while Gibb trained his field glasses. "Must be the fellow who nearly buggered up our tail last night."

"Don't look like it's goin' anywhere."

"Nobody hoppin' about . . . boxcars empty . . . doesn't seem likely to zip off." He lowered the glasses. "Better loop around it and find another way into Sian, don't'cha think?"

"The roads must be blocked?"

"Wouldn't doubt it."

"How far are we from it, ya think?"

"Judgin' by our petrol sop, can't be far. There's another river first, isn't there? The Wei?"

"Oh, Jesus, not another trestle!"

"Don't know, but why not cut cross-country and find out." They hopped down, found some rough trails, and set off.

Passing Lingtung at a safe distance and avoiding the main road, they bumped across fields and detoured around farms until they found the right-of-way. After following the tracks for an hour, Bodine saw the shine of water and another railway bridge. This one was low to the water and buttressed with stone piers.

"Piss!"

"Shall we have a run at it, old son?"

"How do we know another train isn't gonna come along while we're on it?"

"I say—that couldn't happen twice, j' think?"

"Wanna bet?"

*   *   *

At Huachingkung Resort Marshal Chan Chow-ki called his Peking Guards into the marble room and lectured them. He was in full uniform and looked impressive, face shining, hand gestures reinforcing a mellifluous voice. He talked for a long time of the Great Red Cause, Lenin, Marx, even, and Sun Yat-sen—leading up to the mission they must perform today, one that perhaps they might not return from. The Peking Guard were thrilled. None was older than twenty-three, and the very thought of dying in a glorious battle for a luminous cause seemed too much to wish for.

Once the political rhetoric was over, guns were broken out, checked, and loaded with stripper-clips. Most were Mauser pistols, Chinese-made in the Hanyang or Shansei arsenals, *Shiki First* (Type 1). Their manufacture was patriotic but questionable. A few were Nickl conversions to full automatic with twenty-shot clips. These were even more erratic, and at rapid-fire even the strongest arm couldn't keep the pistol from rising like a salute. The Peking Guard loved them; they made a lot of noise and quickly dispensed a large number of bullets—unfortunately with little effect. Lieutenant Liao understood this and was counting on a more proven device.

Several heavy wooden boxes were brought up from secret cellars and placed on the floor. The Guards nudged each other, convinced this was plum wine to be toasted in celebration of their upcoming bravery. But no, Liao gently pried open one of the boxes and withdrew a roughly circular pot from others bedded in straw. He held it up like a prize fruit, a rich yellow, the color of the soil and roughly formed. At its apex a twisted wick protruded.

"A grenade!" a young man shouted, clapping his hands.

"No," Liao said, revolving it. "Something older."

"Fireworks!" another said, as if he were a student in class.

"Closer, but no. The Saracens claimed to have invented it in the eighteenth century and called it 'Greek fire,' but we know Chinese did. The old emperors used it against the Tartars, and the Boxers against the Imperialists at Peking." Marshal Chan knew it wasn't true, but it sounded good and they all applauded.

"What's it made of?" one said.

"Naphtha, bitumen, pitch, sulfur, gums, resins, turpentine, and oil." He paused. "In these also are added quick lime to make 'moist fire' because water greatly increases its volatility."

"Remarkable!" they shouted as a group, clapping and cheering. Then a sober voice asked, "How will we get close enough to throw these on the gunners?"

For an answer Liao directed them to pick up the boxes. Bowing to Chan to lead the way, they marched outside. It was an enthusiastic procession, as Chan and Liao had intended it to be; if you were going to ask people to go to

246

their death for an idea, it had better be preceded by a noisy and mindless celebration.

They trooped around the worn marble buildings and stopped in front of the recess to a dark archway. Planting his feet, Marshal Chan Chow-ki put his arms behind his back and nodded at the shadowy depression. "Bring it out!" he said, using his head in an unusually threatrical gesture. The others leaned forward in anticipation, and a car appeared.

It was a Rolls-Royce. Not just any Rolls, but a great boat of a car with a phaeton body by Barker of tulipwood secured with copper rivets. Fully twenty feet long with double cowl windshields, it had side mounts and enormous spotlights on running board stanchions. Imported into China by a ginseng king, it had been captured and recaptured by a succession of upstart warlords. Like a totem or soccer trophy, it had been passed around to the winning team, ending up with the grand champion, Marshal Yü. At this point its rich regal red wore a patina of scratches, bumps, and bullet holes that gave it a certain panache.

The Rolls had embarrassed the Little Marshal and had been hidden away at the resort during his tenure. The sight of its splendor brought back painfully the memories of his father.

Hating him hadn't been a natural thing; it had been a learning experience seen to by his mother. Ti-lin had been his first wife and had spent her young life within the rigid structure of the inner family. She was not allowed to speak to her husband when others were present or, indeed, to speak to any elder until she was spoken to. She would not become the head of her own house until her mother-in-law died, then her sister-in-law. She was expected to accept that, as an important man, her husband would need other wives, mistresses, and children. She bore this, patiently waiting, only to have the family destroyed by scandal and herself humiliated.

Yü had four known wives and a dozen concubines. Then, traveling to the cities of the coast and on yearly trips to London or Paris, he began to bring back white women. This was a shock and a disgrace, not only to Chan's mother but to the other Chinese wives and mistresses. Chan remembered as a boy that four "white demons" had lived in their yamen at the same time. His father called them "house guests," but everyone knew better. He visited a different one each night, and the servants joked and called them Monday, Tuesday, Wednesday, and Thursday—saying Friday, Saturday, and Sunday would arrive next Monday. They were white and ignorant, treating his mother as a servant. Worse, Yü allowed it.

It was too much for Ti-li. When Chan was ten, she tied her feet together with a silk scarf and jumped into the canal next to their house, drowning in the flow of thick sewage and greasy water. But her pain had a legacy, passed on to Chan, who nursed it, then educated it at his father's expense, finding in communism the perfect vehicle to deliver it up. Years of tireless work and intricate intrigue had led up to the moment when he was able to use it all and topple his father. Then at the last when he had deposed him and had the means within his grasp, he had allowed him to slip away. He had prevented Liao from sending a death squad after him at that very train station he was holed up in now.

He knew that in his reluctance to act was all the pull of the family, the honor of the father. Now his father was back, to punish him like a wayward child. But that wouldn't happen. Chan would strike first. There had been rumors that his father had brought yet another blond white woman with him and—incredibly—a monkey! One of the soldiers had actually seen it. They would all be dumped in that same canal, feet tied together.

General Razin made no speeches. He shouted for them to mount up and damn well get ready to kill some Chinese for their keep. In the resulting stampede several were knocked unconscious and others suffered broken bones. As Adrian watched from the porch of the house with Captain Sato, it was an amazing transformation. Once the slovenly, sullen troops were turned loose on the horses, it was an explosion of vitality and erratic madness. He watched, amazed, as they charged about, wheeling the horses past each other, rearing, falling off, fighting over a lively animal, raging about as though possessed. By three o'clock they were mounted and ready to kill any-body. It was frightening.

Even Captain Sato was astounded. He had expected it to take hours to sort them out. It was military anarchy with no officers or command that he could see, each man for himself fiercely competing with the other. It certainly weeded out the weaklings. Now, if it was possible to get them going in the same direction and he could introduce a line of march, they might be on the station road at the appointed hour.

Adrian cut out a horse and saddled up with the odd Mongolian saddle, wood covered, and without stirrups. Swinging aboard, he rode over to where General Razin stood passing out weapons from a pile on the ground. He looked up as Adrian reined in. "Are you coming with us, American?"

"With your permission."

"Where's your arms?"

"I'll go along as an observer."

"The devil you will! You ride with us, by God, and you kill with us!" and he threw a bandolier at Adrian's head. Adrian caught it with one hand and just had time to catch a carbine in the other. At this sudden movement his horse reared and swung around, galloping off out of control. It plunged him into the vortex of men and animals, and he fought to stay clear of spurs and whips as the others crashed around him, lunging and lurching, hooves lashing out, the dust churning up, broiling in choking clouds—it was treacherous, dangerous—and, by God, exciting!

Had it been like this hundreds of years ago when men rode into battle from tribal villages or primitive fortresses? Before modern armies and rigid commands reduced them to ciphers for politicians to spend—when taking up weapons meant defending or seizing land from others—face-to-face, hand-to-hand combat between warriors that decided who would take the spoils, ride off with the women, have the children to pass on the strong blood, rule, survive among men. It was the call to war, that heady, riveting challenge that offered any man the chance to change his life with his own strong arm, to win and take what he could with the sword or die violently and go down to defeat and slavery. . . .

Adrian was strongly affected by this acting out of an ancient scene; the departure of the soldier. Around him the women were handing up lances to their men, and above the noise and stomp and dust he heard a terrible high-pitched screaming, a sound in the throat, a kind of *zagarette* that came from all of them: the men, the women, and children who would stay behind. A battle cry that froze the blood and was more compelling than any bugle or tattoo of drums.

At the height of this he saw the girl and the old man, followed by the Filipinos, riding slowly away. Adrian turned his horse and galloped after them, catching up with Mavis Ming Billy.

"Where are you going?!"

She looked at him as if he were simple. "Back to the Ordos."

She would have gone on, but he grabbed the reins of her horse and the others passed around them. "Just like that? Weren't you going to say good-bye?"

"What for?" She seemed puzzled.

"Billy, we've been together every day—and night—for weeks now."

"So have the horses—should I say good-bye to them too? You don't make sense."

"Damn! You are a hard lady!" He slammed his hand down on the saddle, laughing. "Then I won't see you again?"

"Why should you?"

"Come to Shanghai! I'm going back there—let me show you the city. Stay with me at the Palace Hotel! It's marvelous. I'll teach you to two-step, we'll drink champagne, then we can go sailing on the Yangtze, make love watching the lights on the Bund. . . ."

"I don't like water."

"There are the films, the theater! Yes! And maybe you could even see a monkey do the tango . . . and a million things happening at night—cabarets! Bars! Restaurants! In the daytime we'll go to the races or sleep till noon in pillowy beds, served all the food ever invented! Come on! I'd love to show you off to those stuffed shirts—it would be worth the Sun Account just to escort you through the Grand Salon of the Palace Hotel. It would—"

"You are a big talker."

He laughed. "Sometimes. Come with me."

"What would it cost?"

"Nothing, my sweet girl. I'll pay for all of it."

"How could you do that? You have no money." She jerked the reins away and spurred her horse ahead.

"Billy!" Adrian shouted. "One day I'll show up in the Ordos! Wait and see!"

"No, I would be embarrassed to be seen there with you. You're the wrong color, and your eyes are funny."

He watched her for a long moment, hoping she would turn and at least wave, but she didn't.

At last he rode back toward the Cossacks. They had formed up with General Razin and Captain Sato at their head. As he urged his horse forward, they put up the thin foolish lances, and with the ragged pennants fluttering, began to move in the direction of Sian.

TWENTY-SEVEN

MARSHAL YÜ LISTENED to his pocket watch; it was running, and it was five o'clock. He parted the tasseled curtains in the bedroom section of the car and, removing his pince-nez, squinted across at the tracks to the far gate, bracketed by two machine guns. Heavy shadows stretched out behind their skinny legs, and the light was fading; unfortunately dusk came early now. He still hadn't heard from that toady of a Lieutenant Liao. *What had happened?* There was no telephone service, and he had sent one of his bodyguards at three o'clock to try to find out something. *Where was he?* The car to pick him up would be here at exactly six for the drive to Sian HQ and his momentous announcement. *Had his son and the Peking Guards been neutralized?* Sighing, he tugged at his stiff collar and opened the door to the parlor.

As a pleasant reminder of his college years, he still liked to observe the ritual of the cocktail hour, no matter what the location or pressure. And this one was special; for the first time in years he had put on his uniform. Like all his clothes, it had been designed with the accent on individuality. An unusual shade of blue, it was silver-buttoned, with multicolored campaign ribbons and the shine of exotic decorations: the Star of Kwang Hsu and the Order of the Elephant. He came into the room, cap in place, and carrying a rather awkward marshal's baton of carved ivory.

"Well!" Lola said. "What have we got here? Don't you look like something! I believe this is the first time I've seen a real general!"

Yü bent over her hand. "Marshal."

"Whatever—I always did go for a fella in uniform." She wore the bulk of a full-length Russian sable over her pajamas. Yü had presented it to her that morning, and she hadn't taken it off since. He sat at the rococo table, and champagne was produced. He proposed a toast.

"To a princess who will sleep in a palace tonight." They clinked glasses.

"You mean like the Palace Hotel, Charley?"

"Oh, no, a palace, palace. There were once five palaces within the walls of Sian. The Han, Sui, T'ang, and Ming emperors all ruled from here—and sadly after the Boxer Rebellion the empress dowager, T'zu-hsi, retired here with the boy emperor, Te Tsung."

"Is that right."

"All China is historic, but in the North the most ancient battlegrounds are known. Great and stirring events happened here two thousand years before Socrates. Kings had been long buried when English minstrels sang of Beowulf's legend. Really."

"Woof who?"

"Beowulf."

"Oh."

"In the West who knows the location of Arthur's tomb, eh? Or even who he was? But the tombs of Yao and Shun and Yü, the first rulers of China are still here to see after forty centuries of change. Oh, yes."

"Yeah?" Lola said sipping her champagne. "Well, I hope they have a theater or a movie house here. I haven't seen a good talky in a long month of Sundays. I don't suppose they have vaudeville?"

"No, unfortunately, Western influence has been retarded in reaching us."

"They must have some dance halls for the young kids. I'd hate to give up dancing. Hey! I could teach you the tango!"

"Alas, to date the only dancing is Chinese."

"Maybe I could open a dance studio where I could teach Western dancing?"

Marshal Yü was depressed to hear this. The last thing he needed was a blond dancing teacher in his entourage. Despite himself, he looked at his watch again.

"You expecting somebody?" she asked.

The Rolls Royce came straight down the highway leading into Sian, passed over the Pa Ch'iao bridge to the astonishment of the sentries, entered the city through the wall at East gate, and was aimed at the new train station. No one had seen it on the streets since the "Big Marshal" had been booted out, and it

252

was true that it not something you expected to run across in the fastness of Shansi.

Lieutenant Liao was driving, and the Little Marshal, Chan chow-ki, sat in the back, arms folded, staring ahead between the snap of CNC pennants on fender tips. Crouched out of sight in the back seat (and front) around them were as many of the Peking Guards as could be jammed in. At a respectful distance behind them, a covered truck followed with the others.

The lieutenant in charge of the machine gun company heard the car coming at some distance. The men had just begun their late afternoon meal, and he was making sure the food had been rationed out properly. He had been newly promoted and took every ritual in army life entirely seriously, considering it a great honor to have been chosen to command the company that was to guard the great Marshal Yü. Actually, this officer and company had been picked by those who knew about such things, because they were green recruits and less apt to be tempted by squeeze. Then, too, the local generals were reluctant to commit their own men to a contest that might go either way. In the end, fresh troops were brought in straight from field training.

The lieutenant heard an excited shout from one of the sentries on the gate and, walking toward him, passed the machine guns. As he did, he noticed that both squads had fallen in the food line at the same time. He cursed and had started to turn back when another, even more urgent shout from the sentry hurried him on.

The street in front of the station was deserted, and as he went though the wide gate in the wall, both sentries were hopping up and down and pointing, cavorting like schoolboys. He ordered them back to their posts, severely, then, looking down the street, he stopped short. It was the Big Marshal's car! Amazing! He went farther out to make sure he was seeing right. Yes, it was the big red Rolls-Royce! He had seen the car many times as a boy in Sian and recognized it. But . . . what was it doing here? His stomach gave a lurch; no one had told him to expect this.

His orders read that a car would pick up Marshal Yü at six—*was this it?* He found that hard to believe. CNC flags were flying on the fenders, and he now recognized the Little Marshal in the back seat. Most strange. Was he here to escort his father to HQ? Again, no one had told him that. Thoroughly confused and apprehensive, he didn't want to make any mistakes in protocol and approached cautiously.

There had been rumors that the Big Marshal would move into town permanently, perhaps tonight. A covered truck followed—was this to transport the luxuries he had brought? The car was now only a dozen yards away, and he had to make up his mind. His basic orders had been to prevent anyone or anything from reaching Marshal Yü without authorization. He ran forward, waving his arms. *"Please to stop!"*

The car continued on very slowly toward the gate, and, forced to run alongside to keep up, the lieutenant formally saluted the Little Marshal. "Forgive me, sir, but may I request you please to stop . . ." He was relieved when the car finally did, squarely in front of the gate. As the lieutenant leaned in to ask politely for a pass, he was astounded to see several figures crouched on the floor under tarps. When he opened his mouth to ask about this, somebody put a gun barrel in it and pulled the trigger.

A mile away the 10th Lancers proceeded at a leisurely pace along the main street. Although Captain Sato had been urging them forward for some time, it did no good. General Razin said there was only one good spurt of speed in the cheap horses and he was saving it. They were nearly an hour late coordinating the attack with Marshal Chan, and Sato could only hope Marshal Chan was as tardy as Razin. Dealing with the Chinese in matters of promptness was frustrating. Sato heard no sound of gunfire, so he had to assume they hadn't arrived yet. The next thing to worry about was whether they would arrive at all.

For Adrian, riding with the Cossacks brought into play two sets of emotions; on one hand, he was apprehensive, with no idea of what he was getting into, and bright enough to know it could be dangerous. On the other hand, it was an incredible adventure, a step back into the past: lances shining, pennants fluttering, a page out of a boyhood tale of knights. With the bandolier across his chest and the ratty fur hat over one eye, he felt part of them. He held the carbine with no intention of using it. He was not a combatant and would not shoot or kill anyone. He hoped that the "enemy" would take one look at this savage retinue and cave in. He was here because it was the only way he knew of to catch up with Yü. He was along for the parade.

For the Chinese along the route who had the nerve to peek out of their shuttered houses and shops, it was less colorful, and there was no doubt at all about their emotions. As the long line of men and horses trotted by, weapons at the ready, they could only ask themselves once again, why were they cursed with foreign armies?

Then they all heard it: a shot, very clear, followed by the rattle of automatic fire. Razin raised his arm, shouted a single word in Russian, and the horses began to canter, then gallop, hooves sending up sparks on the cobblestones.

Minutes earlier, as Marshal Yü and Lola were sitting down to cocktails in the *Empress of the East*, the square, riveted nose of the armored car poked out of the dark of the railway tunnel, and Bodine and Gibb were through the Third Ring wall and into the Sian freight yards.

"Let's get off the tracks, huh, Gibbsie?" Bodine said, looking over his shoulder.

Colonel Gibb swung the wheel; the front end lifted, resisted, then bumped off the track. He stopped and let the big car idle as they examined the rail yard through the slits in the steel windscreen. "Not exactly zippin' with business, is it?"

The Lunghai line had been extended to Tuan-kuan in 1928 and to Sian early in 1931. The yards covered 1.2 square miles but were yet to be fully developed, with only a rudimentary classification yard and tower. There was very little rolling stock on hand outside of a half dozen coaches, a line of boxcars, and a large tracklayer and crane. The private car, highly visible, sat parked off to one side, the baggage car behind it.

"See that Pullman?" Bodine said.

Gibb cranked up the front shield and got out the field glasses. "There's a name on the back . . . *Empress of the East* . . ."

"Lemme see," Bodine said, taking the glasses and refocusing. He tracked along the car's side, then suddenly stopped and backed up, tightening up on a figure standing by the side door. "By Jesus! It's one of Yü's pancake eaters!"

"Are you sure, old son?"

"Oh, hell, yes! That's one of the scissor-bills that grabbed me on the junk!"

"Then he's still here—the contest's not decided." Gibb gestured toward the far gate, just visible. "What's that over there?"

Bodine turned the glasses in that direction. "Emplacement." He fine-tuned the glasses. "Maybe a company, and it looks like a couple of Hotchkiss machine guns." As he watched, a young officer walked toward the gate.

"Yü's people?"

"Either keepin' him in or them out. We better try to settle up while we can."

"Why don't I pull the Austin 'round the far side of the *Empress,* so's t' be out of sight from that lot?"

"Sounds good."

Marshal Yü was just about to look at his watch again when he heard the noise of a heavy engine quite close. A minute later the outside bodyguard slammed through the door, shouting and pointing. The two inside men joined him, all talking at once, wildly excited.

Lola looked from one to the other, startled by the sudden break in their smooth routine. Yü held up his hand, and they broke off. Excusing himself, he got up slowly, went to the window, and pulled aside the curtains. The turret of a large-caliber gun was trained on him. He jerked back, and for a minute it was completely quiet. Then there was a polite knock on the door.

"What's going on, Charley?" Lola already felt a chill of apprehension.

"Please forgive me, princess," Yü said in a low voice. "It would be safer if you went into the sleeping room."

"Safer? Safer from what?" But she now saw that the bodyguards had drawn large handguns, aiming them toward the knocking. "Jesus! What is this!"

"Please!" Yü said firmly. "Now!"

Without a further word she went into the sleeping room, locking the door after her.

Crouching behind a chair, his own tiny automatic drawn, Yü nodded, and a bodyguard opened the door while the others pressed against the wall on both sides. The door stood open for a minute, then a voice said, "Mr. Min?"

Yü found no difficulty connecting the voice to the man, and if he was surprised, his own voice didn't show it. "Captain Bodine?"

"That's right."

"Most good to know you have arrived safely! I left full instruction with the bank to be passed along to you at my sudden departure. I hope you received them."

"No, I can't say that I did."

"What a shame! What rotten service! And I don't suppose you received the checks either?"

"Colonel Gibb is with me, Marshal . . ."

"Delightful!"

"He's behind that gun trained on your car. Why don't you come to the door where I can see you?"

Yü holstered his gun and stood up. He motioned the guards to stay in place, then he stepped into the open square of the door. The armored car was pulled up almost flush with the train, its side door opposite the private cars. The iron window flap was dropped down on the driver's side, and Bodine rested his arms on the sill, so close that it had been easy to stretch out and knock on the bottom of the car door. Above and behind him Yü could see the gun trained on him. As he looked, it bobbed.

"Why don't you gentlemen come in and join me for the cocktail hour?" Yü said, smiling.

"My cut of this operation was to be seventy-five hundred Mex. I estimate that with time-in, per diem, and travel expense, it should run to about an even ten by now."

"Very fair, I'm sure."

"I think so. The colonel will settle for fifty-five hundred on his contract."

"Entirely deserved. I am only sorry that you were put to this so much trouble, those pesky checks!"

"We want it now."

"Of course. I am due to take over the management of government here at eight tonight—it will be a most impressive ceremony if you care to attend. I can positively guarantee the Bank of Sian will have your money in the form of a draft the first thing in the morning. Then—"

"We want it now, and we want it in gold."

There was the first hesitation from Yü. "Oh—I am most sorry, but that would be impossible."

"Then you're a dead duck." Yü's eyes moved ever so slightly toward the left. "If you're thinkin' about those people down at the gate, just remember we're behind you, and to get to us, they'd have to come through you. At the first twitch of signal we'll chop this car in half. You're a soldier; I don't have to tell you what large-caliber bullets will do."

"You are a most hard man, Captain Bodine."

"I never said I wasn't. But look at it this way, I ain't takin' it all."

Yü sighed. "Ah, yes. Think of your purse not as half empty but half full."

"Confucius?"

"Calvin Coolidge."

"That doesn't sound like him."

"If you insist on the weight and inconvenience of gold, you will have to wait until I bring my chest."

"No, you send one of your troops—how many are there?"

"Three."

"Wasn't there four?"

"One is off on an errand."

"All right, you stay there where I can see you and send one of the other ginks after it."

Yü spoke quickly in Chinese, and there was a rustle behind him. "Where is Mr. Adrian Reed, Jr.? I miss his appearance."

"Nanking, I guess—we got separated by the Chiang's Nats."

"Oh, too bad, you should have mentioned my name."

"Yeah. Lemme ask you somethin'—is that dancer and the monkey with you?"

There was a hesitation. "Yes. It would be most distressful if she were to enter into this." It was the first hint of a threat.

"Easy! I'm not here to rescue any bimbos—Gibb and I are here strictly on company business. You pay up and we'll be gone. The kid will have to settle his own account."

There was a shuffle behind Yü, and a large chest was placed on the floor. It had been hidden in the ice locker in the car's pantry and slept on each night by a different bodyguard. Yü opened it and, tugging out the heavy sacks, began to stack the gold coins. "Double eagles!" Bodine said. "Twenty-dollar gold pieces—they used to pay the fleet in 'em in the early twenties."

"No doubt," Yü said, shifting the coins into a rattan basket the bodyguard held.

"You don't see 'em anymore—but then you don't see any real Mex either." Bodine laughed. "Only a damn Chinaman—excuse me—would import silver from Mexico, leave the eagle and cactus stamped on 'em, and circulate 'em. But I guess it does explain why they call 'em Mex. Hell, I remember . . ."

The sharp, clean sound of a shot cut across the rail yard. The Maxim instantly shifted, and Bodine held his hand up. "It's okay, Gibb—it came from the gate." Yü had frozen, and they all listened, motionless. "Maybe some bird just let off his piece. . . ." Then there was the sudden crash of automatic fire, a sustained stitching sound followed by the ignition of Greek fire. "What in hell is goin' on?! You expectin' somebody, Yü?"

The machine-gun crews and foot soldiers at the gate had been eating their supper by charcoal braziers when the Rolls-Royce appeared. They poked each other, exclaiming over its fantastic appearance. Many stood on ammunition boxes for a better look, and all were excited to see an exotic object they had only heard of. Most were young farm boys. (After Captain Sato had questioned Liao and Chan about the troops guarding the station, he had cross-checked with the evaluation sheets from Hsinking and was relieved to find they were part of the 2nd Company, 9th Brigade of the 17th Route Army, formed up at Fen-yang eighteen months ago, and green recruits. It was one of the reasons he had hopes of success.)

When the shot was heard and the lieutenant dropped, the soldiers were stunned and could not grasp its meaning. Then in the next minute men leaped from the car and truck and began firing.

The Mausers were no more accurate than predicted, but the sheer fire power and noise were awesome. Holding them on full automatic and feeding the 20-shot stripper-clips in at a furious pace, the Peking Guards literally sprayed the air with bullets. Everyone had his head down, and this gave Liao's grenadiers a chance to come forward and throw the pots of Greek fire.

Inside the gate, the machine gunners had recovered first, and, dropping their rice bowls, clambered behind their weapons, frantically feeding in belts, locking-in and cocking. The first lit-wick pot hit at the feet of the gun on the right, smashing open and pouring out its volatile contents at their feet, but it did not ignite. Then the second hit alongside it, and again it didn't go off. Lieutenant Liao saw this and was ready to reverse the Rolls when the third exploded in a fiery mass, engulfing the others.

A cheer went up from the Peking Guards, and now each pot that was thrown ignited the one before it. The gunners scrambled up and fell back, desperately trying to beat the flames out on their uniforms. The gunners on the left saw this and were up and running as the first pot hit. Both guns were now out of action and in flames.

Twenty yards to the rear, the 130 foot soldiers hugged the ground as the incoming rounds whined harmlessly above their heads. Walking among them, several tough sergeants, veterans, shouted and lashed about with sticks, trying to form them into a skirmish line. At last some began to respond, actually firing their rifles in return, and soon badly directed fire was being exchanged from both directions.

At this point the situation for the Peking Guards became critical. Instead of overrunning the machine guns, they had destroyed them and now were unable to turn them against their enemies. The Nickl Mausers, always erratic, were heating up and breaking down, and the expenditure of ammunition had nearly exhausted the supply. As their rate of fire began to fall off, the return rifle fire increased.

Incredibly, up to this point few on either side had been hit. Liao and Chan were both out of the car now, lying prone with the rest, stretched across the opening of the gate. Heads down, bullets zipping over, they began to have their first real doubts about success or even survival.

Then they heard a galvanizing shout go up from the rear, *"Kazaki! Kazaki!"* Others took it up, and across the line the soldiers heard it, lowering their guns and squinting through the haze of gunsmoke. Then they saw them.

Swinging up the street and wheeling toward the gate, Captain Sato knew this was the vital moment. There was no way into the station other than that gate. Although built less than a year before, the station and freight yard were surrounded by the old Third Ring of wall, thirty feet high and nearly that thick. Only the railway tunnel at the back offered another egress. If that gate was well defended or they got hung up in it, lost their momentum, and had to dismount to fight . . . Damn! He suddenly saw that the stupid fools had parked the car and truck right in front of the gate, blocking it!

Bodine had climbed to the roof of the armored car where he had a clear view of the gate over the top of Yü's private car. He adjusted the glasses and watched for a second. "Somebody's rushin' the gate . . . don't look like many . . . Mausers . . . blue jumpers . . ."

"Peking Guard—fanatics!" Yü said. He stood in the doorway of the car, looking up at Bodine.

"How many people you got down there?" Bodine said, his eyes still to the glasses.

"One company, with two heavy machine guns!"

"Well, there go the guns—they've just fire-bombed 'em. The gunners are runnin' like scalded-assed-apes. . . . Listen, hear that now? Rifle fire—maybe your boys can hold them, they've finally formed up a skirmish line . . . rag-

259

ged, but they've got the numbers. Hey, what's that?" He raised the glasses toward the road outside the gate. "Jee-zuss! Fuckin' cavalry! They've just come flyin' up the road on big-ass horses lookin' like wild men with spears!"

"Russians!" Yü said in a flat voice. "Cossacks—the 10th Mukden Lancers."

"The baby rapers! Oh, those are rough-hewed white men—they're gonna clean house on your poor bastards!" Bodine jumped down from the hood. "C'mon, Yü! Shove that gold over—we're clearin' out!"

"No."

"What? What did you say?"

Adrian was pulled along with the flow. Blood pounding, he heard the gunfire as an odd, abstract sound, unable to connect it with anything to do with him. Then a truck and car loomed up, and they automatically spit around them without losing stride. It was a brilliant bit of horsemanship, and in the next instant they had charged through the gate, leaping the burning guns, and plunged through the smoke toward the firing line.

Around him he heard the ferocious battle cry go up, vividly saw the lances being lowered over the arched necks of horses, and the furious joy in the faces of the Cossacks.

Viewed from the perspective of your belly, it was an awesome sight: huge horses moving forward in a thundering, galloping wedge; thousands of tons of unleashed, driving horseflesh, sharp hooves, flying rocks, ground shaking—and above, the men—faces distorted, bent over pommels, lances held straight out, bright pennants trailing the points, tips double-edged and razor sharp. Lances! An ancient, simple weapon, terrible because the thought of being stuck like a pig, run through, pinned down with a sharp steel point sent a shudder up everyone's spine. The line wavered, then began to break. The sergeants flailed and threatened but couldn't hold them, and when the first went, the others followed.

This was exactly what the Cossacks wanted. Riding down the running men, they speared them from behind, then, working back and forth, chased them over the tracks, thrusting and jabbing. Herding the survivors like animals, they cut them to pieces, some using the carbines or their handguns, others hacking away with heavy sabers. Over the noise and screams of the victims were the joyous shouts of the lancers, having the time of their lives.

Adrian was appalled. He pulled his horse up. They had won! The charge was over, the soldiers dispersed! Why in God's name were they killing them? When the enemy surrendered, you took them prisoner! He shouted at General Razin, who sat his horse watching a few yards away, but he could not be heard over the screaming.

At that moment one of the terrified soldiers—a boy—darted past Adrian. Behind him, a Cossack rode after him, saber swinging. Adrian wheeled his horse and turned into him, body checking as he'd done many times on the polo field. The horse staggered, then recovered, and the man furiously swung the saber on Adrian.

Adrian put his horse over, stepping him nimbly to one side, forced the other to turn in a tight circle, twisting awkwardly behind him, to strike at Adrian. This kind of riding was perfectly suited to his rough-and-tumble years in polo. At last, skills were brought to bear in areas where he was clearly superior. The playing of country club polo worked as well on the battlefield; the Cossack was good but outclassed. Adrian kept crowding him, "riding him off," until he lowered the saber to try to turn out of the trap. Adrian slammed him off the horse with the butt of his carbine.

In the next instant an explosion went off by his right ear, and the horse dropped like a stone. Adrian, pitched over his head, remembered to tuck and roll, and scrambled up, stung by loose gravel and cinders. General Razin's horse loomed over him, and the general leaned forward in the saddle, aiming an enormous handgun. "Hey! What are you doing, you damn Jew!"

Adrian faced up to him, shouting back and pointing. "You're murdering unarmed soldiers! Stop it! Those men should be taken prisoner!"

Razin laughed. "Prisoner? You are a damned fool! Do you think this is a storybook battle? We take no prisoners. What good would that do?"

Captain Sato reined up and, saluting, ignored Adrian. "General, I suggest we get on to Marshal Yü. We don't want to lose him."

"All right," Razin said. "Let's get the fat bastard."

Bodine stood confronting Yü at the door of the private car. Behind him, Gibb had the Maxim trained on the spot. "C'mon, Yü! Don't give me any con! Pass that gold over or we'll chop you and these ginks up and take it."

"Listen please to me." Yü said in a calm, reasonable voice. "If those beasts break through, they will slaughter all of us. The young lady . . . the ape, everyone. As a military man in China, you know their reputation. They pride themselves on ferocity. No person will be left alive."

"Wouldn't doubt it for a minute, pal. Your joss just went doggo, and I ain't about to push mine by hangin' around. In this game you take your chances. Well, you just lost. Now fork over those double eagles or we'll chop you before the baby rapers get a chance to!"

"You can stop them! That armored car is worth a brigade of men! Horses are no good against machine guns! Protect us by turning them back! You can do that! Yes!"

"Oh, no. We had a deal, remember? We were gonna go along and help you take Sian with a swell new army. The kid was putting up his half of the Mex, and we were all gonna get rich. But you got cute. Well, you don't do that t' me more than once. Fuck me once, shame on you—fuck me twice, shame on me!"

"What may I say? You are correct. It is to my everlasting regret that I did not take your advice and strong arm. But will you condemn me—and the others—to death because of sharp business practice?" Yü had begun to sweat. He was bringing a lifetime of experience as a gifted speaker, negotiator, pleader, and con man to bear on Bodine. He was pulling out all the stops. He tried a new tack. "Think of our great countries, yours and mine—if those Cossacks win this battle for my son, it is Communists who will inherit Sian, and it will be the beginning of the end."

Bodine laughed out loud. "We got another yap-dazzler here, Gibb! Listen! Those Russians will make monkey meat out of all of us! They are madmen! I wouldn't stay here for my weight in gold!"

Yü seized on this. "You will have it! Your weight in gold!"

"What?"

"What is it? Your weight? How much?!"

Bodine began to smile. "One hundred and fifty-eight pounds."

"It is yours!" Yü began to shovel the sacks of twenty-dollar gold pieces into the basket.

"What's that in U.S. dollars?"

"Fifty, perhaps fifty-five thousand! A fortune!"

Bodine leaned over and pounded on the turret with a sound like a bass drum. "Did you hear that, Gibbsie? Fifty-fifty?" The machine gun nodded up and down. He turned back. "Can any of your people load?"

"Load?"

"*The guns!* I'll have to have a loader! Jesus, what we need's a squad!"

"Yes! Yes! Hao was in the army. He knows guns!"

"Then get his ass over here! Let him carry the gold!"

Actually, it took both Bodine and the loader to get the heavy basket into the armored car. While the sacks were being piled out of the way, Gibb climbed into the rear driver's seat and reversed the Austin in a straight line. Then changing to the front, he steered around the baggage car, over the tracks, and stopped, facing the expanse of freight yard in front of the gate. Bodine began snapping the ammunition tins open and pulling out the top feeder strips. As he did so, he instructed the loader in rapid Chinese. Next he and Gibb eased into the turrets, adjusted the slings to lean back on, and looked out the aiming slots along the top of the gun barrels. "What would you say, a thousand yards to the gate?"

"More like eleven hundred meters."

Bodine pushed the marker up on the sight. "This will have to be by guess. We sure as hell don't have a rangefinder or even a compass. And I don't guess you want to crawl out there and knock in a stake."

"Not really."

"I've never tried to stop a cavalry charge. How fast will they move?"

"Hard to say, varies really. A good gallop usually on the drill ground, but there are all those bloody tracks and odd bits and ends stickin' up about here."

"That's our dumb luck. They'll have to come straight at us to get to Yü—those coaches block one side and the station the other. It's like a funnel and we're the neck. I'll set the range at seven hundred yards."

"A bit close, isn't it?"

"We better work in close. If they bunch up, we'll get better travel on the slug and maybe catch two or three on one round. These are old weapons, and the barrels may be warped or outta round, y'know—so we're sure not gonna worry about accuracy. What we need is somethin' to knock the fuckers down. Now, here's the way it's going to work; since we can't set up a cross fire, we'll fire separately on short bursts until we go through the belt. That way we can try to keep the heat down and reload while the other guy is firin'." He kicked one of the water cans feeding to the water jacket surrounding the barrel. "Sounds about half full—they hold seven and a half pints. If one gun jams, the other takes over. Better let me free the stoppage—I don't see any extra barrels so we'll just have to shoot these till they curl up." He shoved a side lever forward in its brass half circle. "I'm gonna set the cyclic rate at about three hundred r.p.m.s. That should be fast enough to nail them without gettin' the casin's hung up. If they start to get through and we have to work together, give me a slap on the shoulder."

There was a pause, and Gibb passed the Tiger Bone as they leaned back in the slings, watching the Cossacks charging about, chasing the foot soldiers, whose screams could be clearly heard. In the background was the sound of carbine fire and the occasional crackle of one of the Mausers that still operated. "Crazy bastards!" Bodine said.

"The Inja army had a kit full of lancers—Bengals, of course, Empress of Inja's, then the Queen's Royal on and on. These fellows are all horse. That's all they eat and sleep, j'know—racin', polo, dashin' about. Has very little to do with the military. They're all for the sport of the thing—however, they make little distinction between the pig-stick and the odd wog. Fancy themselves as gentlemen who just happen to be detained in the army. Silly buggers, I mean what bloody good is a stick with a knife on it in this age of zip, blast, and blewie! What? They do make a nice parade, though."

"Think we can stop them?"

"A char, m' dear. In the Matabele war fifty of our chaps, irregulars at that, with four Maxims stopped the massed attack of five thousand warriors—killed three thousand of 'em in an hour an' a half."

"Yeah, but those were sambos on foot with a bunch a sharp sticks—this bunch are fuckin' Cossacks ridin' great big horses!"

"Adds a bit of spice, don't it?"

"Maybe we'll turn 'em around with a few bursts—why would anybody wanta ride a horse into a machine gun?"

"Well," said Colonel Gibb, "we're goin' to get our chance to find out—here they come."

He was right. The 10th Mukden Lancers had finally formed up and, trotting their horses, moved forward in a wedge. They held their lances up, only this time the tips of the blades were too caked with dried blood to shine.

TWENTY-EIGHT

ADRIAN WATCHED THEM go, sick with the shock of what he had just witnessed. No film or book or telling had prepared him for the reality of it. Nothing could erase the sight of men on horses chasing down and spearing other men. The sounds of their screams were louder than all the stirring battle cries, drowning out the panoply of uniforms, charging horses, and fiction of manly combat. He had seen plenty of blood and even death on the polo field, but nothing like this. Men had killed other men with no reason that he could see but the pure joy of it. He considered himself lucky that Razin hadn't shot him. Looking around, he would have gone to the aid of the wounded, but there were none.

Captain Sato had stayed behind, too, but for other reasons. He did not want to be directly involved with Marshal Yü's slaughter. As a "military adviser," the first rule was to stay clear of fatalities among those at the top. He was here to push forward his government's policies, not as an assassin—and there was always the possibility he would be on the other side next time. He dismounted and walked over to the Rolls-Royce. It had been pulled up inside the gate, and the Little Marshal, Chan Chow-ki, sat in the back seat, all puffed up, taking the congratulations of the Peking Guard, who jumped about hurrahing like idiots. Only one had been slightly wounded during the brief engagement, and he wore that wound like an honor. Ass.

265

Sato spoke to Lieutenant Liao, who stood leaning on the car's windshield, smiling down at Chan.

"It would be a good idea if your men formed up to command the gate and road approach. It offers wide-open access."

"Let them enjoy their success," Liao said with a condescending smile. "They have earned it."

Sato was astonished at this unprofessional attitude. It only confirmed that these two were military dabblers, unreliable fanatics. He was a realist and knew their success so far had hinged on green troops and the luck of catching them at supper—just that. He pointed at the two guns knocked off their tripods and blackened by the Greek fire. "You might be able to salvage one of those guns if you combined the parts. It could then be set up to protect our rear."

"There is no more rear, Captain," Liao said in a slightly superior voice. "From now on, for comrades it is all forward."

Sato couldn't believe his ears! Spouting Red slogans to him! He turned away angrily.

In the back seat of the Rolls, Chan accepted the childish excess of the Peking Guards. Enveloped in their hysteria, he remained aloof, but his stomach was doubled up like a fist, and he could feel his heart contract. *He had personally given the orders to kill his own father.* He tried to picture his mother's face as it must have been when she choked to death on the slime of the canal—but he couldn't. Instead, he saw his father's eyes, amused, intelligent—the same eyes he saw every time he looked in the mirror.

The orders were simple, the kind the 10th Lancers perfectly understood: kill everybody they came across. They took their time walking the horses across the freight yard, picking their way over rails and around the switches and signals. The animals were almost done in, blowing hard. Barely recovered from the long trip in the boxcars, they had just been marched ten miles and charged into action. Riding along in their loose wedge formation, General Razin at the point, the Cossacks joked and called to each other across the ranks, bursting into laughter over colorful insults and outrageous bragging. They were in a marvelous mood, feeling like men who had done what they were made for.

At eight hundred yards no one noticed the armored car. This was not unusual; its dull gray color and boxy shape blended in completely with the sidetracked railway coaches and other rolling stock. Colonel Gibb had parked it head-on to give the smallest profile, and there was no reason they should have been watching for it.

It sat at the neck of the funnel, both turret guns pointed straight ahead toward the 10th flowing in.

Bodine watched them come, estimating the distance. He had sighted in on the upright bar of a switch lever at the 700-yard mark, and would hold until the first horse crossed this imaginary line. In the opposite turret Colonel Gibb rested his elbows on the gun and looked through the aiming slot with the field glasses. He still wore his tweeds: coat, tie, and vest, matching cap at the correct angle and pants tucked into canvas gaiters. He was to shoot second, and now softly described what he saw: "Scruffy-looking lot . . . damn big fellow in the center, though—must be the colonel. Horses are full sized but showin' their bones, terrible-lookin' plodders. . . . I'd fix your sights at about twelve hands—forty-eight of your inches, old son—to cut them across the heart line. Figure seventy-two to the trooper. If you stay under two meters—six feet or so—you're bound to rip somethin'."

Bodine depressed the elevation. "I'll try the first burst low to see if we can turn them."

"In that case, it might be better to catch the nags at the knees, try a half meter, say eighteen inches . . . wounded animals thrashin' about are bound to be more dangerous to the poor devils on the ground than dead ones. . . . Seven-hundred-yard marker comin' up . . . I'll count off, shall I? Ten . . . nine . . . eight . . . seven . . . six . . ."

"*Load!*" Bodine shouted, repeating it in Chinese. The loader slapped the ammunition belt across the feed block, Bodine pulled the right-hand crank back, set the lock, and loaded the first round. "Safety off!" Flicking the safety catch with his left finger, he pulled the trigger back with his right, freeing the firing pin.

". . . five . . . four . . . three . . . two . . . one!"

"*Firin'!*"

The first rounds were low, zinging off the metal tracks with a sustained ringing sound and deflecting up. For just a fraction of a second the riders paused, puzzled, and the jingle of bits and accouterments could be clearly heard. The horses picked their ears up and began to shy. Then General Razin looked toward the flashes flickering from the armored car and raised his arm, shouting in Russian. They dug their spurs in and charged the guns.

"*Jee-zuss!*" Bodine shouted. "Here they come anyway! The crazy ginks!"

He elevated the gun, and the next burst caught the front runners across the legs, shattering forearms and shanks, and sent them sprawling, riders over their heads. The others veered around them and kept coming, General Razin still at the head, looking straight ahead. As the gun passed down the line, tearing gaps in the charging lancers, they closed up, shouting their battle cry. Some choked off, plunging into the wreckage of men and horses. Cossacks were trained to charge straight at the guns, go hell for leather, come to grips with it, get there, destroy the tormentor. This rigid discipline often panicked the gunners, so they urged their terrified animals on, increasing the stride, digging in, forcing them forward no matter what.

"Loadin'!" Bodine shouted. "God damn dumb hunyocks! They're gonna get their asses shot off! Christ! For what? Why?"

"Theirs not to reason why, eh?" Gibb took over, cranking the gun up to the four-foot level. "FIRIN'!" This time the hits were solid thumping sounds that went end to end, dropping the horses in their tracks and literally tearing the men off their backs. Bullets were so thick that one man might be hit three or four times in a split second. Gibb worked the line from right to left where Bodine had stopped, the loader shifting over to feed his gun, the belt undulating out of its tin box, swaying back and forth as though self-motivated. He moved the weapon at a slow, even pace, fighting the temptation to pump back and forth rapidly or stop for misses. He seemed to have his best luck catching the horses at head level, so the round traveled through to the rider at chest level.

In the other turret Bodine felt the bronze water jacket and jerked his hand back. Sizzlin'! If it got too hot, a round could explode in the breech, and then good-bye gun, or even gunner. The noise inside the car was horrific, with the hammering of the gun amplified by the metal box, the empty cartridges clattering to the floor—and the talking. Neither man could understand the other while firing, but they both carried on a conversation: "Get over there! Stop—stop!" "That's it, go down!" "Christ! Missed that one!" "Look out! Look out! . . ."

Outside, the smoke blew across their view, and the dust and cinders kicked up by the riders obscured them by half. Bodine could see them closing at about a hundred yards and still coming on. "Jesus!"

"Loadin'!" Gibb shouted.

"Firin'!" And Bodine picked up the line of fire close enough now to begin making out features of the men. Damn! He really hated that! Didn't want to see any silly ass face! Didn't want to remember an odd little thing that might stick in his mind. He had shot men like this in France and Haiti—it was what he did—and he could still remember the look on some faces. Why did the bastards keep comin'? Killing themselves for what? Where were the officers? It was indecent! Stupid! He also knew if they didn't stop them on this next swing, they weren't stoppable.

Behind the lines at the gate, Captain Sato had unceremoniously climbed up on the hood of the Rolls and was watching the action with his small field glasses. "An armored car! At twelve hundred meters! Where did it come from?"

"It wasn't there yesterday!" Lieutenant Liao shouted back.

"The damn fools are charging the guns! Throwing away the brigade!"

"Maybe we can send someone to stop them!" Marshal Chan said, standing up in the back seat, clutching the center windscreen.

"Too late for that! What a stupid waste!" Sato turned to Chan. "The only way to knock that gun out is to flank it—send your people around the back while the gun is busy . . ."

"Wait a minute," Liao said, stepping forward. "I'll command my men—"

"*Shut up and listen*! Do you want to save what is left of this mess?! Do you know what is happening here? Do you? This action is being decided by *two* machine guns! I am a professional. Pay attention to me or you may all be killed today!" This was said with such ferocity that Liao actually stepped back a foot, and the Guard were chastened. They stood behind Liao, fiddling with their ruined Mausers, and begged to be sent in, like some high school sports team.

"You are in command," Chan said calmly, sitting down in the backseat. "Once through the station you will be in a good position to advance on the car. But—be sure Marshal Yü's train is covered—then get in close and throw those bombs. Armored cars are very vulnerable to fire, and it should drive the crew out." He jumped down from the hood. "I will work my way around the other side and wait until I see your attack before I open up." He turned away without waiting for an answer.

Picking up a carbine, he ran past Adrian, who was standing next to a ruined horse, watching the charge. Sato stopped and turned back, speaking to him in Chinese. When Adrian looked at him dumbly, shaking his head, Sato gestured with the weapon. "Come with me! There!" He pointed, but Adrian stood his ground, shaking his head. Then Sato leveled the carbine at him, and there was no doubt the man would shoot him. *"Come with me!"* Adrian went.

Bodine finished his sweep with the machine gun, and Gibb began with his. They had broken the line of Lancers, stopped the main thrust at eighty yards in a little under four minutes. The ground was churned up in a hideous mass of dead and dying horse and men, and those that still could, crawled toward the rear. Not one man had dug in and fired his carbine from behind cover; they had just kept coming. "Jesus!" Bodine said. "Dumb rubes! Bohunks! They must like gettin' killed!"

"*Loadin'!*" Gibb shouted. "Damn fine concentration, though—they didn't break pace, not a man jack—a real eighteenth-century exercise."

"Assholes!" Bodine was furious that they had allowed themselves to be thrown away like that. It was the bone-headed simps of officers who got them into it! "Firin'!" But now it seemed all that was left to shoot at were riderless horses, and he couldn't bring himself to kill any more of the dumb plugs.

Instead of bolting to the rear, cavalry mounts ran forward. They were trained to remain steady under fire and stay in line—and when they lost the weight and control of a body on their back, they went crazy and, galloping forward, tried to attach themselves to another leader. There was only one left and they bunched around him: General Razin. He had managed to pass through the curtain of fire, with men and animals dropping right and left. Without looking back, he still had no idea his entire force was decimated. But this would not have mattered to Razin anyway; the point of a charge was to overrun the enemy position, and that is what he intended to do.

Bodine had let up when not fifty feet away a single man rode out of the smoke. "Jee-zuss!" He swung the gun over at almost point-blank range, pulled the trigger, and for the first time it hung up. "Jam!" he shouted, and flipped up the top of the case.

"Still loadin'!" Gibb shouted back. But the loader had tangled the fabric cartridge belt and, fumbling, he dropped it.

General Razin closed. All he could see of his objective was an unpleasant-looking iron box on wheels with the dark opening of a few odd slits and slots. He had taken a lance from the hand of a man who dropped next to him, and lining it up with the half circle opening above the left machine gun, bore in. He intended to drive it through the gunner's aiming eye. Coming abreast of the car with the last of the horse's wind, he perfectly thrust the lance through the opening—just as he had done hundreds of times in practice on a much more difficult target, a swinging apple.

"Look out!" Bodine shouted, catching the flash as the blade came through the gun port. Colonel Gibb had been leaning over the belt, and he moved sideways at the warning, but too late. The tip of the lance was driven through his left chest nearly in a line with his foulard pocket handkerchief. He grunted and fell back, pulling its shaft in with him.

Working frantically, Bodine cleared the gun and pulled back the crank lever, fed in a round and traversed to the left. But he couldn't find the rider in the slot of the gun port. The thing about an armored car was, when the enemy got under your guns, you were in the soup.

Lieutenant Liao moved the Peking Guard through the deserted station to a window on the far side. From here they could see the nose of the armored car. To its left was Yü's private train. If they crawled between it and a flatcar on one of the spurs, they could be on top of the car before they were seen. He reasoned there wasn't time to split his force and cover Yü's train, gambling that anybody in the private car would surely have his head down with all the noise of the machine guns.

Then the firing stopped. In the hush that followed, they watched as a single Cossack rider rode out of the dust and thrust a lance at the armored car. Don Quixote tilting at the windmill. It was an odd, chilling sight. At that moment they broke out the fixed window, letting themselves down to the ground. Then, crawling along, towed the box of fire bombs.

In Yü's private car they heard the breaking of glass in that momentary letup. Crouching below the windows, Yü and the three bodyguards could see the Peking Guards crawling toward the armored car. They eased up several windows and, resting Bolo Mausers on the sill, lined up.

The Guard edged forward, without cover for the crucial stretch. When the bodyguards opened up, they were trapped between the armored car and the train, bullets kicking up dust a dozen yards away. The short-barreled Bolos were notoriously inaccurate, and they were in no real danger of being hit, but Bodine had been alerted by the firing, and swiveling the gun, saw the figures on the ground and began firing. Caught in a cross fire, they panicked and, jumping up, ran for it. They were cut down in one short burst, and only Liao survived, still in the window of the station.

Bodine immediately tracked the gun to the rear, but he still could find no sign of the horse. *Where was it?*

The general's great charger, lathered and blowing hard after the 800-yard gallop, had stumbled, sunk to its knees, rolled over and died. General Razin stepped off without any discomfort, and drawing the enormous old Russian Nagant revolver, walked toward the back of the armored car. Keeping out of line of the gun, he found a footing on the frame extension and climbed up onto the rear deck.

Inside, they heard his amplified scuffling. Gibb lay on his right side, gritting his teeth and sweating heavily, eye rolled up. Behind him, the gunner froze, still holding the belt. Bodine, in the sling, hands on the gun, knew that in one minute whoever was up there would push a weapon through one of the slits and commence firing. He reacted by suddenly shoving open the turret hatch above his head with a loud clanging sound.

On the rear deck Razin saw the hatch fly open and prepared to shoot whoever emerged. He waited, and when no one did, crossed over quickly, shoved the gun over the edge, and began firing down into the car's interior. Bodine jumped out of the rear hatch to the ground, turned, and leveled the trench-cleaner. The Russian swung around, aimed the revolver, and pulled the trigger. There was a loud click, and both men stood and looked at each other. Then Razin calmly lowered the gun, replaced it in its holster, and crossed his arms.

Bodine stood with the shotgun poised. Above him was a figure in the full Cossack uniform of a general, hat cocked over his eye, mouth pulling up his beard in a kill-me-if-you-dare sneer. Bodine got mad. "Are you the dumb son of a bitch that sent all those poor bastards into our guns? *Huh!?*" There was no answer. "You ought to be ashamed of yourself, you big tub of shit! Just what in hell did you think you were doin'? *Huh? Huh?*" There was still no reply as

271

General Razin maintained his aloof position, disdaining to acknowledge this wretched foot soldier. "Get down off of there!" Bodine shouted, gesturing with the shotgun. "C'mon! Move your lard butt!"

General Razin walked to the edge of the car roof and with dignity climbed down. Bodine shoved him roughly ahead. "I oughta shoot you right in the ass where your brains are! But no, by God, I'm not gonna do it! I wouldn't waste my time shootin' a moron! You don't deserve to be shot by a soldier, you clown!" He pushed him harder. "Go on! Take a walk, damn you! Walk back through all those men you slaughtered!" The general walked straight ahead, past the bloody mess of men and animals. Bodine fired the shotgun once, sending up gravel at his heels, but he kept going at the same pace. "If I ever see your miserable face again, I'm gonna kick your balls inta your tonsils!"

Then Bodine realized he was standing alone, out in the open, and extremely vulnerable.

Captain Sato lined up the sight on the carbine. He had watched with disgust as Lieutenant Liao sent his men into a trap of his own making. Had seen the general's horse collapse, the general's climb to the roof, then one of the crew shouting at him and driving him off. He didn't understand this, but for the first time he had a really clear shot. At about a dozen meters, even with the carbine, he should have no trouble hitting him. Then as he sighted in, the Russian behind him began shouting, "Bodine! *Bodine!!*"

Bodine? Sato found that impossible to believe, then as he looked closer, he knew it was Bodine! That same self-important, posture was visible even from here. The flash of red hair, yes! That damned dog of a Marine who had humiliated and insulted him and very nearly killed him with his bare hands! It suddenly seemed to Sato as though it were meant to be, that by some design this single man pursued him, was directed by a force of fate to test him at the crucial junctions of his life.

He now knew that the uneasy feeling he had carried with him was correct: Bodine had not been killed by Sergeant Masaki, and he also knew the sergeant's disappearance had something to do with this hated man. It was as though Bodine had been deliberately chosen to represent that part of the West Sato despised most; the crude, pushing, aggressive white man who, by his very gestures and tone of voice, indicated without a question of a doubt that he was superior to any Oriental, black, brown, or tan—anyone who did not look like him or come from a place that he approved of as civilized. It was a man like this who had shoved his way unannounced into Sato's own country in the last century and, backed by ships' guns, demanded that trade begin. It was the reason Japan had let go of the old ways and turned around to meet the challenge with a modern army and navy, because not to do so would mean to become as enfeebled as China, to be at the mercy of redheaded mongrels like this one. He was the mix of a dozen different rotten breeds and yet looked down on a homogeneous people who had remained pure. It was men like him who had enacted laws in their own country to exclude Chinese and Japanese while they poured into Asia grabbing everything in sight, ready to go to war if one tourist felt threatened.

A portent of things to come. He knew it was his fate, his destiny, to meet this man here and now—that between them they represented the best and worst of their two nations—who would survive now would forecast the victory of yellow or white in the coming struggle. It was meant to be.

"Captain Bodine!"

Bodine had heard the first shout, and without questioning who would know his name in the middle of a Sian battlefield, instantly dodged behind the car. Now he heard it again, this time in a different accent. He hesitated, then shouted back, "Who is that!"

"Captain Tetsuo Sato, Imperial Japanese Army!"

"Who? What do you want?" Bodine found it incomprehensible that a Jap was out here—were there others? Were they here in strength? And if so, what in hell business was it of theirs, anyway?

"A duel! I want to fight you!"

"What!" Bodine laughed out loud. Jee-zuss! Of all the crazy damn fools! Were they all like that? He remembered the other Nipponese who had challenged him to a duel at the party. What was this, a national disease? "The only duelin' I'm gonna do is with my dobber, Jappo! Why don't you go back to Tokyo and your fujiyama mama!"

"You are a dirty-dog of a cowardly fuck! A Marine pig afraid to come against a real soldier!"

"There ain't a day of this year I couldn't kick the shit out of a bagful of you little monkeys!"

"Prove it then! You broken wind from the ass of a snake! You handful of spent scum! I dare you to fight me, man to man! You have not got the stomach or heart to do such a thing! I say to you a Japanese soldier can beat you! I challenge you on the field of combat! If you refuse, then we both know you for a dirty dog of an American coward! The white race will lick our asses and we will fuck your sisters and pull down the White House! If you do not believe me, meet me! I dare you!!"

Despite himself, Bodine got mad, furious that this damn maniac of a Jap would single him out here for an idiotic dare. But it struck at a chord in his nature; with all the insults, Sato had instinctively picked the one thing that he could not let go by—a dare. Then, thinking about it, he smiled, knowing how to call the maniac's bluff and back him down. "All right, you slant-eyed mistake! You wanna duel? None of them puny little fuckin' swords or pistols! You're challengin' me, right? Then I get choice of weapons—agreed?"

"Agreed!"

"Okay! Let's see what kind of hair you got on your balls! I'll meet you out in the open—machine gun to machine gun at fifty yards!" Bodine chuckled to himself, waiting to hear him swallow that one and start weasling out.

"I accept," Sato said. "Tomorrow at dawn, here."

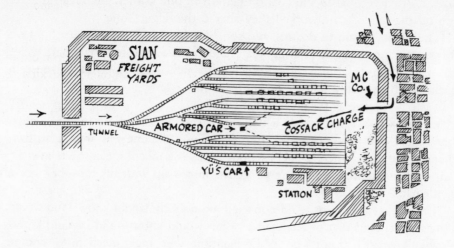

TWENTY-NINE

IN THE FADING light Bodine backed the armored car through the rail yard and managed to get it up on the rail tracks that would lead out of town. He parked it with one gun pointing toward the distant gate. If anyone was going to attack, they would have to come through the space between the station and sidetracked coaches to reach the car. But he didn't think that would happen tonight.

He left the loader they had borrowed from Yü on watch and helped Colonel Gibb out of the car. They had pulled out the lance with some trouble. Penetrating one side of the left nipple, through the pectoral muscle, it had entered the clavicular fibers and nicked the third rib. What had prevented it from going clear through was the tangle of pennant balled up just below the blade. Bodine cleaned it as best he could with Tiger Bone Whiskey and bandaged it with what was on hand. It was a nasty irregular wound, deep and with every chance of turning septic. As it was, Gibb was capable of walking, and with his left arm bound in tight, moved painfully, but nevertheless moved. He attributed his mobility to the efficacy of heavy drinking. Bodine helped him to an empty boxcar within sight of the armored car and settled him in with a gallon of Tiger Bone. Then, returning to the car, he dismounted one of the maxim guns from the turret. He took the bipod stored in the boot, along with tools and a lantern, and carried them all back to the

275

boxcar. After setting up the coal oil lantern in one corner, he began to strip and oil the gun. As he worked they shared the Tiger Bone.

"There's no reason to do this, old son," Gibb said. "Why not just light off the Austin, zip on back to Tung-kuan, and catch a train for Shanghai? We've got paid, j'know, fairly weighed down with nick. There's no damn sense in duelin' with that silly fellow, no profit in it."

"Yeah, well, I've gotta do it. That's all."

"I mean who's t' know if you don't show up? Here we are in the godforsaken middle of nowhere—and after all, it's not like one was among his own chaps at the club, where a duel's serious—this is a joke! I mean the fellow is a Jap—a damned wog! You can't go gettin' mixed up with his lot—he's not a gentleman."

"That makes two of us. And don't tell me nobody would know. You would know, right? And that peckerhead of a Jap would know—and I would know! Now let's forget it. I gotta do it." Dismantling the trigger mechanism, Bodine began a careful adjustment of the spring tension. "Besides, there's not a damn thing to worry about. This is what I do, for Christ's sake—I'm a gunner, remember? I know how to adjust this weapon so that a tickle will let it off."

"But I say, be serious! Heavy machine guns at fifty yards! Too bloody much! It's a suicide pact! Both of you are goin' t' blow each other to pieces with the first burst!"

"Don't you believe it! It only takes *one* bullet between the eyes t' stop a man squeezin' any trigger, right? Well, I plan to get that one bullet off first. I know a few tricks on these pieces, an' I'm gonna play 'em like a roller piano. That crazy Jap hasn't got a prayer."

"What d' you suppose was wrong with the fellow in the first place that he took such personal affront t' you? D'ja know him?"

"Hell, no, never laid eyes on the asshole before. But I'll tell you there is somethin' wrong with those people, all of 'em. I mean anybody who'd stick a knife in his own stomach and carve out his gizzard just because the cherry blossoms didn't bloom or some fuckin' thing has got to be half nuts, right? An' it's more than that—those people actually believe they're gonna run over the top of all of us! It's true, they've swallowed all that half-baked horseshit about the emperor bein' the son of heaven and the rest of 'em bein' the first people on earth. I mean it took Perry—old Bruin—t' go over there and pry the dummies out of their cocoons. Hell, if it hadn't been for us Americans, the silly slants would still be sittin' around in paper houses in their stockin' feet, drinkin' tea outta little bitty cups and actin' like there was somethin' special about a couple of rocks in the backyard."

Gibb passed over the jug, and Bodine took a long pull. "Never been t' Japan, have you, old son?"

"Not me! Wouldn't go near the place. Your average Chinaman is a good-natured gink, happy really, considerin' the shit they got t' put up with. They know a joke and will laugh along even if the joke's on them. Not your Jap, no, sir—they are all business, they're on their way to get somewhere, an' nothin' is gonna stop 'em." Bodine finished wiping the parts down and, satisfied he'd done his best, reassembled the gun. "This piece is sound. Believe it or not, the sears ain't too worn and the barrel lines up. Hell, they don't make 'em like this anymore—all brass, hand fitted." He leaned his back against the boxcar, suddenly very tired. "Jesus, Gibbsie, I'm beat. I mean, killin' a couple a hundred Russkies will take a lot out of you."

Gibb started to laugh, then choked it off as the pain clenched up.

"Startin' to pull on you?"

"No, no . . ."

"Lousy luck."

"Just odds catchin' up."

"Damn," Bodine said. "We're both gonna sleep t' night."

Adrian sat by a low charcoal fire and listened to the moans of the wounded. He had done his best to help, along with a Chinese doctor and several nurses sent out from town. The Cossacks who were able had loaded others who weren't on the backs of wagons, and using the few horses that survived, walked off into the darkness, he guessed, to their camp. The doctor told him those who were left behind would be taken to the hospital in town the next morning. The word was, troops would move in at nine tomorrow. Spies and observers had reported back the day's action to the generals who waited in their barracks for the results of Yü's coup.

There was a great deal of confusion over just what had happened. The machine gun company guarding Yü had been decimated; then in a turnabout the 10th Lancers had been broken by an armored car. It was uncertain whose. Underground American and Japanese interests seemed to be at work. The regular army would move in tomorrow and clarify the situation (the joke was that whoever met them at the gate to the station would be the next warlord). There had also been rumors about a duel that was to take place at dawn between opposite commanders, but this was hard to believe.

When Adrian thought about it, he realized he shouldn't have been surprised to have seen Bodine. He (and probably Colonel Gibb) were bound to be where Yü was. But why were they defending him? To hang onto the gold? Again he would have to wait until morning to find out. There was no way he was going to cross that no-man's-land of animal and human corpses in the dark and probably get shot in the bargain.

The business of the duel was crazy. Why was the Japanese officer so obsessed with killing Bodine? Had they met before? Were they old enemies? He would probably never know.

He sat now with the Chinese doctor, both men staring in the fire and unable to communicate. Not because of the language, but because each was embarrassed to look into the other's eyes after what they had seen tonight. It seemed indecent to be alive and whole. Adrian looked around; they appeared to be alone. The big wooden-bodied Rolls still sat in front of the gate, but where was the "Little Marshal?" He had vanished. For that matter, where was the Japanese? Adrian didn't like the idea of him skulking around in the dark. He shivered and looked at the sky. It was getting colder, and he could see clouds obscuring the moon. It looked like snow.

Captain Sato rummaged through the parts of both burned machine guns and put together one working model. He had carried them into an empty train shed and set up a light in its machine shop. The gun was a French Hotchkiss. Manufactured under Maxim patents, it was basically the same gun as Bodine's—a later model that had been refined by the French, using the same components. The only difference was that this gun had no water jacket, was fed by 30-round metallic strips, and more important, was faster with a cyclic rate of 600 r.p.m. Like Bodine, he believed the first to fire would survive.

It hadn't occurred to him that he was on a suicide mission or throwing his life away when he accepted Bodine's outrageous terms for a duel. He was calling his bluff and would have agreed to anything to come to grips with the man. The rules were simple; each would appear with a second, who would set up the machine gun exactly fifty yards apart from the other. The duelists would take their positions behind the guns, the seconds would walk to the exact middle ground (twenty-five yards), take one corner of the same silk scarf, hold it over their heads, let go, and run for their lives.

When the scarf touched ground, the firing would commence. . . .

What was that! Sato looked up quickly. He heard somebody come in the door and walk quietly but deliberately toward him. He jerked the Nambu pistol out of his belt, "Who is that!" But there was no answer.

"When I went to West Point . . . "

"You went to West Point?" Colonel Gibb said, interupting a long monologue. They had been passing the bottle for several hours now, and Bodine had segued into a biographical stretch.

"Oh, hell, no!" Bodine said. "I didn't *go* there, I *went* there."

"How's that?" Gibb said, puzzled.

"When I was a kid, we lived in the Red Hook section of Brooklyn—Jesus, talk about tough! But never mind that—I had an uncle with a farm in upstate New York in a burg called New Paltz. It was fulla rubes and had been settled by the French Huguenots. What a hard-assed Irishman was doin' among all them frogs I got no idea—anyway, when things got too hot in the city I was sent up to my uncle's farm and the mean old bastard would work my ass off for free all summer.

"This one time I got sick of it and thumbed a ride down to the river—the Hudson—and got let off at West Point. Well, I had never seen anythin' like that! It looked like it was right out of the picture books—a big damn fort hanging out over the river, with battlements, canons, and a tree they said George Washington had taken a leak under, or somethin'—the place was fulla history. And here were all these guys walkin' around with tight little asses in swell soldier suits, brass buttons, braid, and neat caps squared over their eyes. Well, that was it! I knew right then and there I wanted to join this army, whatever the fuck it was. So I marched into the first buildin' I saw, an' up to a desk with this guy sittin' behind it, and told him I wanted to enlist—you gotta remember I was sixteen at the time and what did I know about gettin' into West Point? This gink behind the desk had these big curved stripes on his arm, a haircut like a convict, and was maybe two or three years older than I was, a plebe or whatever they called the assholes. Anyway, he gives me this look like I'm somethin' he just scraped off the bottom of his shoe, and says—I can still remember— 'We're not taking midgets this year.' Then smiles like this was suppose to be funny and I should laugh.

"I knocked that bird off that chair an' up against the wall quicker than it takes a mink t' blink. I was standin' there with a piece of his tooth still stuck in my knuckles when a regular Army sergeant hustles me outside and points me up the road. 'Son,' he says, 'if I were you, I'd go right downtown today and enlist in the Marines—they deserve you.' And that's what I did." Gibb took another swig of the whiskey. Looking at his eyes, Bodine wondered if he was drinking this much because he knew it might be all he would ever get.

Sato was ready to pull the trigger when the figure of a man came into the light with his head down. *"Masaki!"*

Max was still wearing Sato's old suit, torn and filthy, but with the tie in place. He said nothing, offered no explanations, because, of course, none was valid. He had not told Captain Sato that Bodine was alive, knowing his life depended on finding him first, killing him, and then reporting it.

Leaving the train, he had walked into Sian and had been promptly arrested. They had questioned him most of the day, and after his papers were checked, he had been allowed to leave with no explanation other than that he would find Captain Sato at the train station. Riding there with the doctor, Max heard the story of the battle he had missed and the amazing gossip that a duel was to take place at dawn between a Japanese captain and an American who commanded the armored car. No one had to tell Max who the American was.

He walked toward Captain Sato, head bowed, stopped, dropped to his knees, and, putting his forehead on the floor, bared his neck. Sato understood what was needed, and, stepping forward, placed the barrel of his pistol on the last knob of his spine. As he did so, he thought of a famous farewell poem the great warrior Masatsura had scratched on the temple door at Yoshino with an arrowhead in 1348, and was there to this day:

> *I could not return, I presume.*
> *So I will keep my name*
> *Among those who are dead by the bow*

It began snowing after midnight, blowing in unexpectedly from the mountains in a fine powder that at first dusted, then covered the bleak hills. Snow was unusual in the Wei Valley this early and especially in Sian. Along with the snow a cold front brought the first real frost.

Marshal Yü saw the beginning streaks of dawn through the train windows. He had slept on the floor next to Lola to shield her body against any stray bullets. They both had tried to coax Ramon down from the luggage rack, with no luck. The sustained firing had frightened him badly.

Yü got up and, looking out through a gap in the curtains, was surprised to see snow. It covered the bodies of the Cossacks and the horses, suggesting a startling icing, a macabre confection. Yü couldn't decide if it was a good or a bad omen.

"What's happening, Charley?"

"It's snowing."

"Have they finished shooting?"

"Yes, yes, I think so—it's safe now."

Lola didn't believe that for a minute. Yesterday had been a nightmare, sounding like tommy-gun battles in gangster movies. She had recognized Bodine's voice outside the car yesterday, and Charley had said he was protecting them. He didn't say from what.

Yü heard from the bodyguards about Colonel Gibb's wounding and the impending duel. If Bodine *was* killed (and unless there was some tricky business, he was sure they both would be), who would guard the gold? Gibb? Hardly. There would be very little to stop him from getting his own back. It had been extortion that got it away from him—robbery, really. As things were now, with him and his son at a standoff, those extra funds might see him over the top.

He crawled back to Lola and put his small automatic into her hand. "Take this, princess, I have to go out for a while."

"Jesus, Charley! I don't want this—I couldn't shoot anybody!"

"No, no—please keep it for the emergency—then I will feel better." He

leaned over and kissed her. "I am desperately sorry you had to become involved in so bad a thing. It was not meant to be this way. I would not have
involved you if I thought it would happen."

She smiled. "Listen, we made a deal. Nobody promised me it was going to
be heaven."

"You are a most remarkable woman." Keeping low, he got up and went out
the door.

Some swell speech, she thought. Baloney, she would have traded all her
gold, the fur coat, her ass, to be back at Frisky's right now getting ready to
go on. She just couldn't win. If she wasn't falling for some collar ad, who was
only interested in getting into her knickers, it was a con man like Charley,
working some kind of Chinese shell game.

She looked at the gun. It was a pretty little thing, all shiny with a pearl
handle. For the first time it hit her—Charley wasn't telling her to use it on
anybody else—he meant she might have to use it on herself.

In the boxcar Bodine slept hard, exhausted and drunk from the whiskey.
Across from him, Colonel Gibb sat, legs splayed out, body awkwardly supported by the doorjamb, head against it at an odd angle. The Tiger Bone
Whiskey was finished and the telescoping cup had rolled away. As the feeble
sun came up, it lit first the bronze machine gun barrel, then the colonel's
face. Both eyes appeared to be staring, and it was hard to tell if he was dead
or alive. It was his job to wake Bodine.

Adrian was shaken awake and woke freezing. He didn't know how he had
managed to sleep under such horrible conditions. And to wake and find yourself covered with drifting snow was a real eyeopener. His fur hat was pulled
down over his ears, and his legs were tucked up under the long padded coat.
The snow had stopped falling, but a stiff wind blew its fine particles up and
sent them swirling through the air like a subtle, shifting curtain. He made out
Captain Sato, bundled up to the ears with scarfs, the damn arrogant Borsolino
hat at its cocky angle. Had he shaken him awake? He heard him shout something over the howl of the wind and then saw he was pointing a carbine at
him. He gestured, and Adrian followed him into a train shed where a machine gun was set up and waiting.

My God! He wanted him to help with it—be his second in the duel with
Bodine!

It seemed at the very least ironic, but at the moment there was no one to
share this with. Reluctantly, he grabbed one leg and they picked up the
heavy gun. As they went out, he caught the flash of a figure lying wrapped up
on top of one of the benches. He didn't ask who it was.

Together, they lugged the awkward weapon across the expanse of the freight yard. It was necessary to walk straight through the battleground. Picking their way around the stiff, white-powdered bodies of men and horses, Adrian felt this was about as abstract a scene as he was ever likely to see. The sun rising to the east cleared the foothills of the Lisham range and its rays instantly transformed the jutting legs, kinked elbows, and mounds of horseflesh into a vivid pink landscape of arrested motion and sudden death.

When they reached the straight stretch of track agreed on, they put down the gun. At a distance Adrian could make out two figures approaching from the opposite direction. It was impossible to get a clear view for more than a few minutes through the screen of blowing snow, but he recognized Bodine, head ducked into the storm, battered campaign hat tilted forward at the usual cocky angle. They put down their gun, and the other second walked toward them. Sato gave Adrian a rough shove, and he realized they were to meet in the middle. Head down, hands in his pockets, he started out, and as he walked the snowy ridges of track to what he guessed was the approximate middle, he wondered if he should call out to Bodine—wave, let him know he was a friend—but thinking it over, he decided the last thing to do was make any quick movements between dueling machine gunners. He kept still.

When they met, Adrian remembered the second as Yü's chauffeur. He held out a silk foulard scarf, and when Adrian looked puzzled, indicated by wagging it that he was to take one end. He did and had his arm tugged up until they held the scarf aloft together. Then it hit him! This was the signal! When they dropped the scarf, the machine guns would start firing! Jesus! He looked down the line and between gusts of snow could see that both men were in position, heads ducked into the wind, lining up.

It suddenly occurred to Adrian that once the signal was given and the guns opened up, they would be in the middle. Before he could digest this, the Chinese nodded, they dropped the scarf, turned, and ran for their lives in opposite directions.

Adrian's long legs stretched out, arms batting against the stiff padded coat, feet sending up puffs of fine snow as he dodged around ground obstructions, jumped unknown white lumps, running flat out into the snow-coated field of the dead. Desperate not to step on anyone's dead, yielding body, he ran like a deer, up on his toes, feet scarcely touching the ground. Finally, diving behind the mound of a dead horse, he rolled, and swinging around, was in time to see the scarf float down.

Long afterward, it seemed to Adrian he had seen the duel in slow motion. This curious thought persisted, and it may be he dreamed it so many times this way that he came to believe it; the scarf floating on the air, dipping this way, then that, pushed by the bluster of the wind, a bright wisp of silk suspended over the straight stretch of white-capped track— punctuated by the two gunners as though carved in flat relief—each hunched at his position, facing profiles, figures fixed with a dusting of snow, absolutely still, the descent of the scarf, languorous, lazy, then vanished as if swallowed—and instantly the voice of the guns speaking simultaneously.

The two bursts couldn't have lasted more than a split second, but to Adrian it seemed they went on for long minutes, a sharp double-hammering, the crossing spew of bullets, like converging fine lines that leaped from the muzzle of one to the other. As he watched, the two fanatics literally shot each other to pieces. Clothes, hats, belts, buttons, flesh disintegrated in colorful contrast against the snow. The bodies appeared to move in jerking, almost gay motions, bouncing with the rhythm of the bullets, hopping up and down as they flopped in their own unnatural dance. When at last they collapsed, fell in on themselves, Adrian saw that the hands of both were still locked on the handles of the guns, fingers crooked around triggers. Each man (unknown to the other) had tied his hand to the gun.

Then it was silent, and as the wind dropped off, Adrian found himself staring across the track into the face of the Chinese. Each was at the same distance from the line of the duel. They looked at each other for a long beat—with what Adrian liked to think, for the first time, was understanding. What they had witnessed was man acting out animal behavior; survival of the fittest at its most extreme, life canceling out life.

The minute Marshal Yü heard the firing stop and saw the predictable results, he swung into action. Bundled up in his elegant sealskin coat and hat, he and the two bodyguards let themselves down from the train and cautiously proceeded through the snow to where the armored car was last parked. By moving fast they would take over the car before the wounded Gibb could act—if he was still capable.

Rounding a string of coaches, they found the armored car straddling the tracks at several hundred yards. As they came in view, it coughed to life and with a noisy mesh of gears began to move in reverse. Yü shouted out his alarm and the bodyguard sprinted ahead, firing the Bolo Mausers. As Yü puffed after them, he cursed his timidity for not releasing one of his men to watch! Where was the man he had lent them to load? Out of breath, he stopped by a patch of blood in the snow and a tangle of foul bandages. Gibb obviously had been put in the car when Bodine went off to the stupid duel, then when Gibb saw the finish—and the bodyguards approach—he had decamped. Damn! The car had a long lead now, moving toward the tunnel in the wall. Yü had a thought—the Rolls was still out by the gate! They could loop around by the road and catch the slow armored car easily! He had opened his mouth to call back the bodyguard when there were two sharp sounds like abrupt claps, and his men crumpled.

Turning, Marshal Yü saw a dozen men with long rifles run toward him. He immediately stopped where he was and stretched his hands above his head.

They wore crude uniforms and padded coats with a large cutout of a red star hand-stitched to skimpy caps. He was seized, the seal coat stripped off, and his pockets searched. He allowed this with good humor and knew better than to ask who they were. He knew.

At that moment Lieutenant Liao came up. Apparently recovered from the loss of the Peking Guard, he now seemed to be in charge of this group. Yü smiled. "Is that not my sister's maid's son? Nephew of the 'great man'?"

"It is your executioner," Liao said dramatically and without preamble.

"That's odd, it is my memory that my funds sent the young man I speak of to Oxford College."

"It was not your money that sent me anywhere! It was money stolen from the people that completed my education that I might serve them by destroying a rotten, imperialistic capitalist like you!"

"Well, you certainly learned the rhetoric—it's a shame they weren't teaching manners along with it. It does not hurt one to be civilized as well as radical."

"You are the 'civilized' Chinese that has destroyed our country by taking on the ways of foreigners, giving them what they wanted for a snout at the trough!"

"Bad simile. And I would have thought those wretched red stars on your pitiful caps would have identified you as having friends other than Oriental."

"This is a world revolution! It will make brothers of all men!"

"Are you sure? Jesus Christ had something like that in mind, I believe, and so, of course, did Buddha—and before them who knows? Reform through fervent persistence is not new; what is new are high ideals pronounced as the gospel without a hint of the metaphysical or one decent God, other than that hairy bore Marx." Lieutenant Liao opened his mouth, but Yü overrode him. "I knew him in London, you know, his breath was as bad as his ideas. What makes you think that anything you spout has not been spewed out a thousand, a million times before by each irresponsible younger generation? There are no new ideas for social reform, you silly young man! There are only the same answers to the same questions—listen to history! The only hope is not to repeat yourself too often."

Livid, Lieutenant Liao gave a quick command, and one of the smooth-faced soldiers came forward, drawing a beheading sword from his backpack. Yü held up his hand, and such was his presence that the man stopped. "Let my son kill me if he means to take my place! Is that too much to ask? You soldiers here!" He looked around the group of young men, and they found it difficult to meet his eyes. "If a son wishes to kill his father, then he should have the courage to do it himself. When you are asked later to kill your own mothers or fathers, you should have a leader to tell you how it's done!"

The Little Marshal stepped around the corner of the boxcar where he had

284

been listening. "I curse you, Father! Do the rest of you hear him? Do you know what he is doing? Making you ashamed, twisting the words and facts. His cynicism and muddle of half-formed philosophy is to charm and confuse you. Like his face, it suggests the scholar instead of the sybarite! He is the honey-talker, confounding the simple with his 'logic.' If you're not careful, you'll forget he's taken the food out of your children's mouths for whores and gambling. Give him the chance and he'll use you all up in bloody conflict to pay for his pleasures. He is what we are here to destroy—the warlord!"

"Oh, my God! Enough of this elocution! Spare us your bleeding heart!" Yü said. "Take the sword and whack off my talking head. If you mean to be a doer rather than a proselytizer, then make an example of your father's whim to speak at long wind."

Chan Chow-ki very deliberately reached for the sword and took it out of the soldier's hand. His face was pale and his eyes liquid, but by the set of his mouth, Yü knew he had lost.

Adrian had heard the shots and ran toward the sound. His only chance now that Bodine was gone was to try to find Gibb, and then Yü. He knew it was dangerous, but after the last couple of days he didn't think twice. Coming around the string of boxcars, he was confronted by soldiers and threw his hands up. They herded him to where the Little Marshal stood with Lieutenant Liao. He recognized the portly figure of Yü on his knees in the snow, arms twisted behind his back by one of the soldiers. This was the man he had chased halfway across China, the man who had stolen his inheritance and Lola—still, seeing him in this undignified position, man-handled, he felt a stab of compassion. "Marshal Yü! What's happening here?"

Yü angled his head around awkwardly. "Ah, it is Mr. Adrian Reed, Jr.! Now our company is complete—but I'm afraid you arrived late for the settling of any financial agreement . . . as you see I am about to leave."

Adrian looked at his son, sword in hand. "Certainly you're not going to . . ."

"Get out of the way!" Liao said. "Your turn will come next!"

"Wait a minute, please!" Adrian said, as he was jerked back by the soldiers. "Marshal Yü, what about Lola and Ramon?"

He spoke very quietly. "They are in my private car, Mr. Reed, Jr. Try to protect them. Oh, and your father's 'books.' They are in the baggage car, I never meant to take them, it was a mis—" The Little Marshal suddenly stepped forward and swung the sword up. Yü smiled up at him sweetly. "Well, good-bye, my—"

The heavy blade came down with such force that it struck sparks from rocks beneath the snow. The marshal's head hit the ground with a soft thud, rolled a few inches, and came face up, the pince-nez still in place, the mouth forming the unsaid word. The Little Marshal stepped back, ashen, and Liao took the sword before he dropped it, handing it back to the soldier.

"Now this one!" Indicating Adrian.

"What in hell are you talking about? I'm on your side, remember? I was riding with the Russians!"

"You ride with whoever offers the most profit. You mercenaries are anathema to China! We will see to it you are all wiped out."

"I'm not a mercenary! I'm a—a businessman! I came here to try to get back funds Yü swindled me out of in Shanghai!"

"It doesn't matter whether you use money or weapons to exploit us! You are the enemy!"

"That's not true! My father supported Dr. Sun Yat-sen and Homer Lea during the revolution!" These names had worked magic for him once before, and he was praying they would again.

"Sun was the bought man of the concessionist. He sold off pieces of China to the highest bidders—and Lea was just one more rotten mercenary—a puny little dwarf, puffed up with his own self-importance, who used China as a platform to write dangerous nonsense!" Liao nodded his head, and Adrian was pushed to the ground, the neck of his coat jerked back.

"Marshal Chan! Don't do this! It's crazy—what have you got to gain?! There's a whole field of bodies out there! What good will one more do? If I go home to America, I can tell them what happened out here—what you stand for and what your father did to corrupt his trust. . . ." Adrian was on the right track. Chan looked at him for the first time. "I know important people in San Francisco and New York. I can—"

At that moment there was a burst of gunfire in the distance. It sounded as if it came from the road outside the gate and was followed by a rapid exchange of automatic weapons. Chan spoke quickly in Chinese, and Adrian was pulled up and towed along as they all ran toward the gate.

When they got there, Adrian could see that a large column of troops was being engaged by a Red brigade, ranged along the sides of the road with rifles and light machine guns. It was obvious even to him they were fighting a holding action. He guessed correctly; the generals and the regular army had decided to intervene before the nine o'clock deadline, and had unexpectedly run into a guerrilla group sent to take the Little Marshal out.

As Liao urged him forward, Chan turned to Adrian. "Go back and tell them the future of China is colored red." And then he was gone, running with the others toward the road.

"Anything you say!" Adrian shouted after him. There would be only minutes until the troops closed, and he looked around frantically. The Rolls! He sprinted to the big car and leaped over the side into the front seat. He adjusted the spark on the steering wheel quadrant, choked it, hit the starter, and drove away, tires spinning in a shower of gravel. He'd learned to drive on his father's Rolls town car, and he knew the drill by heart.

Putting the car in low gear, he accelerated as fast as he dared across the tracks of the yard, cutting a virgin path in the snow. He skirted the battlefield, then slid to a stop beside the *Empress of the East*. Leaving the car running, he jumped up the steps into the parlor compartment. "Lola! Lola! It's Adrian!"

There was a pause. He heard her voice behind the sleeping room door. "Who? Who?"

He rattled the handle. "It's Adrian! Come on—for God's sake, open the door! We've got to get out of here!"

Adrian? Lola found that hard to take in. Adrian was here? How? Why? It wasn't possible that he had followed her . . . but what other reason could there be? She opened the door a crack, still bewildered. "I don't understand . . ."

"There's no time to understand! Come on! We've only got minutes to get out! There's a car outside!" He reached for her hand, and when she jerked back, he saw she was holding a tiny handgun. "Lola, please . . ."

"No! I'm not going without Charley. Where is he?"

"He's dead, Lola. I'm sorry . . ."

She didn't believe him. "Oh, no! You're just saying that! He wouldn't leave me!"

"I was with him when he died, Lola." He said this quietly. "He asked me to protect you."

She began to cry, like a child, in great heaving sobs. "It's not fair. It's just . . . not fair . . ."

The door was open and he could see she wore an enormous fur coat. Where was Ramon? He reached for her again, and again she pulled away, this time furious. "What the hell are you doing here anyway!" Eyes squinted shut, tears flying. "Who asked you to follow me!" Then, as an afterthought, "I thought you said you were going on a trip!"

"This is it, Lola," Adrian said firmly. "This is the trip, and we're all on it." In the moment that followed, the acceleration of gunfire could be heard from the road. "You've only got one chance, and it's right now. I'm leaving. Come with me or be buried with Yü."

"All right . . . all right . . . Let me get Ramon."

Adrian was already running out the door. "I'll be back in a second! Be ready!"

He took a tire iron and hub mallet from the car boot and ran down the track to the attached baggage car. Forcing the hasp, he slid back the door and was confronted with crates of furniture and a grand piano. Where were they?

Lola wiped her tears back and looked up at Ramon, face peering through the bars of the luggage rack, fists clenched around it so tight his knuckles were white. His eyes were dialated with fear and his muzzle puffy. She reached her hand up. "Come on, baby, we've gotta go!" Ramon drew his lips back and showed his teeth. It was the first time he'd done that to her in all their years together.

Adrian kept looking until he found the two cases of books, still stenciled with his father's name on top. He dragged one to the door and shoved it off on the ground, then began laborously hauling it back to the Rolls.

Lola began crying again, tears streaming down her face, carrying the eye makeup in vivid lines across the white powder. "Oh, Ramon . . . is this the way it's going to end? Are we going to die here not touching? A million miles from nowhere . . ." *Are you just an animal after all? . . . Are you going to bite me too like you did all the others? . . . Are you going to turn away at the last?* She reached her hand closer. "Well then I'm going to stay too. I won't leave you alone . . . but please . . . hold my hand. . . ."

Very slowly the fist unclenched and reached down to her.

When Adrian had dragged the other case from the baggage car and hoisted it in the back of the car with great difficulty, he found Lola waiting on the step. Ramon clutched at the coat. "Get in!" he shouted. "Come on!"

"I'm not going without my dowry! It's under the bed!"

"Your *what*! Lola, for God's sake . . ."

"I'm not going without it!"

"Damn!" Adrian ran back to the parlor car and found the heavy chest. It weighed more than both cases of books, and he had a great deal of trouble bumping it down the steps to the door of the Rolls. "You're going to have to help me! I can't lift the damn thing!" With her help, they managed to work it up on the running board, then onto the backseat floor. Then he clambered over the front seat, Lola beside him, and swung the big car around in a circle of flying snow, heading for the gate.

As they tore by the station and entered the approach through the front gate to the street, fighting had just broken off, and the Reds deployed to the hills. It was that crucial time when one body of troops pull out and the other probe forward, before committing themselves. It was into this vacuum that Adrian charged. Changing down, he shot out of the gate, foot to the floorboard, Roll's engine peaking. The first of the Tungpei troops ran up to close the gap and raised their rifles, but when they saw the CNC flags flash on the fender tips, they hesitated. Then the big car turned in a squeal of tires, and in the front seat was a blond girl and a monkey wearing a Chinese cap.

They watched, mouths hanging open, as the Rolls-Royce disappeared up the road in a cloud of rich exhaust.

SHANGHAI,
WINTER
1932

THIRTY

ON FEBRUARY FOURTH, nearly seven months after he had arrived in Shanghai, Adrian Reed sat in the outer offices of the American Consulate on Whangpoo Road.

He had an appointment with the American High Commissioner, and as he waited, listening to the grumbling of befuddled tourists about passport and bowel troubles, he clutched one of the secret Japanese books. The other twenty-nine were locked in the vault of the Palace Hotel. His original intention had been to take the books straight to Washington, and through his father's contacts release a leak to the press that would suggest his father's role in obtaining a key to American defense. Eventually the old man would have recognition for his patriotic vision of the coming danger, and the stigma of Teapot Dome would be set aside.

Now, however, he was convinced the books should first be turned over to the Far East Command. After the horrors of war and death he'd witnessed, it was vital to alert others to what could happen. Now, certainly, here were clear Japanese military intentions, and the detailed orders and documents to carry them out.

Maybe in some way it would make up for all the poor devils who had been caught up in the ill fortune that the Sun Account caused.

"Mr. Reed, you may go in now." He got up, nodded to the male secretary, and went through double doors into a room that overlooked the docks and Whangpoo River. It was raining outside, as it had been since they arrived in Shanghai, and the cold came straight through his only Palm Beach suit. The beard had been trimmed, and he thought it suited him. It went with a firmness of purpose he had acquired in the last few months. Although he'd been trained to danger and pain playing polo, here he'd learned firsthand about war and politics. Like Bodine, he now believed the Japanese were the enemy, and it was his intention that everyone recognize that fact.

The American High Commissioner stood up from behind his desk and put his hand out. He was a handsome man, impressive in a dark, well-made suit and hair cut in the English style; eastern establishment by way of a Rhodes scholarship and old family money. There was also charm. "Nice to see you, Mr. Reed. I remember meeting your father years ago in Santa Barbara. A very colorful man." Just right.

"Thank you, sir. It's really because of him that I'm here."

"Oh, how's that?" Still smiling.

Adrian unwrapped the book and placed it on the highly polished desk. It was large, about the size of a ledger, bound in scarlet leather and embossed in Japanese characters. "I have in my possession thirty of these books containing highly secret Japanese mobilization plans. The complete documentation of regulations, orders, and details of all phases of their military structure to be directed toward the United States in the event of war." He stood back to let that sink in and produce the expected thunderclap.

"Where did you come by these?" the Commissioner asked in a voice that ended small talk. Adrian believed the authenticity of the documents was being questioned.

"They were deposited in a bank here in Shanghai in March 1910"—he paused—"and were given to my father personally by Dr. Sun Yat-sen." He laid the copy of the Sun letter to Homer Lea on top of the book.

The Commissioner glanced at it. "Not signed."

"No, but . . ."

"And where did Dr. Sun get them?"

"He doesn't say . . . perhaps when he was exiled in Japan. I'm positive they are authentic—it should be possible to check . . ."

"The point is, Mr. Reed, if these 'books' are authentic, then that means they were stolen from the Japanese government."

Adrian was taken aback. "Yes, I suppose so, but after all, it's in the best interest of Amer—"

"We do not buy stolen information in this office, and we most certainly do not traffic in the confidential property belonging to a friendly nation. Stealing is stealing."

"Wait a minute!" Adrian said, getting mad. "I'm not selling anything! And I didn't steal them! I brought them here because I thought it was my patriotic duty!"

"Well, in that case you have been misguided. I suggest you return the books at once. Surely you're bright enough to realize that the military in most countries make up war-games."

"Damn it all! It's not a game! You don't seem to understand! The Japanese are the enemy! Sun Yat-sen said so, Homer Lea did, and—"

"Please! Spare me! Dr. Sun can perhaps be excused his manipulation of Japan and America on China's behalf—however, as an exile in Japan he was extended hospitality, and it seems a poor way to repay it. As for Homer Lea, I am sick to death of hearing about him!" He said this with some conviction, his complexion darkening. "That man and his book have been no end of trouble for us out here! At best, he was a romantic dreamer, an armchair adventurer who fastened on China as he might on Timbuktu or any other exotic place if it had suited his purposes. He was also a paper general, like your Kentucky Colonels, but worse, a dangerous warmonger and a propagandist of wrong-headed ideals distorting Social Darwinism to his own aims." He paused, and his voice dropped. "Can you imagine anything more ludicrous than an eighty-eight-pound cripple preaching survival of the fittest?

"Lea has undone the goodwill of many men!" He came around the desk, speaking with such heat that Adrian stepped back. "Have you ever read Baron Kaneko? No, of course not! Because he wrote about peace, not war—he was a privy counselor to the emperor, and said in essence that war was impossible between our countries because each depends on the other for vital trade—and this is a quote, '. . . the Japanese cannot live a single hour without American supplies . . .' The Japanese are far too intelligent to go to war. It would be unthinkable!"

He stopped suddenly, realizing he was on the wrong side of the desk. Returning to his chair, he looked up at Adrian. His tone was a bit kinder as he said, "We are professionals here in the foreign service—people who have spent our lives observing the Orient. Lea was in China no more than a few months. His education on things Chinese came from disaffected laundrymen in San Francisco and Los Angeles. Please leave the real China to us." The interview was at an end.

"Excuse me, sir," Adrian said, trying again. "But wouldn't it be worthwhile to let the military have a look at—"

The High Commissioner held his finger up. "Young man, let me give you some advice an English friend of mine offered: 'gentlemen do not spy on gentlemen.'"

"Thanks," Adrian said, and picking his book up, headed for the door. As he got there, the Commissioner had one more gem. "And if I were you, I'd shave that beard off. It doesn't suit you."

Adrian got into the cab feeling thoroughly depressed. Rationalizing, he realized he *had* taken a great many things at face value: Sun Yat-sen's manipulation of both America and Japan, Homer Lea's pedantic "Things to Come" outline, and his own shallow, surface observations of the country, the Chinese—and Japanese. The Commissioner had made a strong case for leaving these things in the hands of experts. If he believed Japan was America's friend and there would be no war, then he should know. Adrian knew only one thing: it was time to go home.

When Adrian and Lola returned to Shanghai (driving the Rolls to Tung-kuan and taking the train), they checked into the Palace Hotel and separate rooms. She was thrilled to be at last in a first-class hotel. Having Adrian just down the hall made her feel easier after the trauma of the last weeks.

On the trip back, he had tried to explain the ins and outs of the Sian adventure, but Lola either chose not to understand or wasn't interested. He didn't begrudge her the gold from Yü. That it had come from his Sun Account he took with a shrug (he may have been a snob, but he was not a hypocrite). But there was something like sixty-eight thousand dollars' worth in her "dowry" chest which she insisted on keeping under her bed at the Palace. Adrian tried to talk her into depositing it in the bank, but no. In this Depression year of 1932 banks were not to be trusted.

Their time together since leaving Sian had been difficult; unspoken accusations, wounded pride, and recriminations hung between them like a curtain. Each was convinced the other was at fault, and neither would be the first to speak of it. When they arrived back in Shanghai, the sexual tension was electric, building like a coming storm. In the end it fizzled out.

To cure his own finances, and with a great deal of reluctance, Adrian cabled his mother. He promptly received a draft accompanied by a long verse from the Bible. He had settled his debts and would buy a ticket on the *Gripsholm* sailing for San Francisco the following week. That morning, with the Japanese code book under his arm, he showed up at Lola's suite. She sat working a jigsaw puzzle at an ornate French desk, head down, frowning in concentration. The light from sections of the quadrafoil window flooded the rooms and lit her in a yellow negligee. A giggly maid let him in, and Lola looked up, smiling. "Hi, cowboy."

"I'm going to the consulate, Lola, then over to the shipping office to get my ticket on the *Gripsholm*. It sails next week—the tenth."

"You're really leaving then?"

"Yes, it's time."

"Sure."

"What about you?"

294

"Yeah, well, I'm beginning to like it here. You can't beat the prices, and . . ."

"Ramon?"

"I know, it's crazy, but he's so old—I don't think he'd make the trip back—he hates boats."

Adrian looked around. "Where is he?"

"Sleeping."

"He does a lot of that."

"Yeah."

"Well . . ." He knew all he had to do was reach out, grab her, and say, "I love you, I don't give a damn for anything else." But he didn't. He could never tell her what really bothered him. Not that Yü was an old man, that he was Chinese, a crook—no, what rankled him, God help him, was the description of Yü as the great lover. He could not live with that; it stung his pride. If she had once said . . . anything to indicate this wasn't necessarily so . . . given him a reason to smooth it over . . . but she hadn't.

There was an uneasy silence. Their eyes held too long, and finally Adrian said, "Good-bye, Lola, and good luck—you deserve it." He turned quickly.

"You too, cowboy. Happy trails."

Lola waited until the door closed behind him before she began to cry. Oh damn! Why had she said that? Why was she always trying to be so fucking funny?

Lola went into the bedroom and looked at Ramon. He slept curled up on a cot in the corner of the room. Thank heavens he had gotten over his "trees" regression. She bent over and shook him, but he just pulled up tighter in a ball. The whole crazy Sian thing had set him back.

She crossed over to the Victrola (a new one) and selected one of the records she'd bought since coming back. It was nice to be able to buy what you wanted when you wanted it. She wondered if someone like Adrian would understand that. Poor to him was a whole other thing than poor was to her. He had his ace down in the hole; confidence that his education, friends, relatives would always be there to tap. Hadn't he got on to Mama for the wherewithall to pay off the hotel and buy a ticket home? And the galling thing was, he looked rich! You knew from talking to him that he was different from you. It hit her that there was no way that they would have ever really understood each other. Every girl's dream of marrying a rich, handsome lover was just that—perhaps it was the unlucky ones who got their wish. Anyway, she was doing okay, set for a long spell, thanks to Charley. God bless his chubby hide.

She even had a maid now—an honest-to-God maid! A giggly Chinese girl who was just her size and she could fix up in her old clothes. They laughed a lot together, and Lola was teaching her the tango. Talk about a scream!

This made her feel better, and she poured a small whiskey. She'd begun to drink a bit during the day, but what the hey . . . What was the old vaudeville joke? When told somebody doesn't drink, the comic says, "You mean when he gets up in the morning, that's as good as he's ever going to feel?"

She laughed and put on the record, a Brazilian version of "Jealousy." It began with a sustained note played full out by a large orchestra, Bandonreons wailing their hearts out. It was the kind of marvelous exuberance that she dimly remembered the big pit bands playing for Billy and Inez at the height of their fame.

One of her first memories was of watching Inez and Ramon dance. To her, a little girl, he had seemed enormous, an almost mythical figure, a fairy-tale beast who she was sure one day would be changed back into the handsome prince. Backstage he was her friend, a playmate. But once on that stage, with those lights, that music, he was another thing. Magic.

She had never really considered his getting old. He had looked the same to her for years—then in the last months the change was dramatic. When they had stopped dancing at Frisky's, she thought the rest would do him good. But it was the beginning of the end.

As the music approached their rehearsal cue, Ramon stirred and rolled over. He had heard this one tango thousands of times. Lola stood in the center of the room, holding her hands out. "Come on, baby, your cue's coming up!" He put his feet down and, standing, shuffled out to her. Taking his hand, she led him through the steps. He was sluggish and behind the beat. Then she detected a gradual change: he began to tighten up, hit his marks.

When it ended, she clapped her hands. "Thank you, sir!" Breaking off, she opened the closet. "Wait a minute! Let's do this right!" She got out his faded dress suit.

Lola helped him into it: wide suspenders over the shoulders, connected shirtfront, tie and collar, tied in back. Finally the coat. "There! Now you look like something!" She swore when he died she'd buy him a brand new suit to be buried in. She put the record on, and they spun off again. This time they got it right.

The sun streamed through the quadrafoil window, its beams infused with tiny particles of dust stirred up by the dancers. As they moved together, sharing the cadence of the music, its exaggeration, the long, significant pauses, the tango seemed sad. *Tears of Salt*, they called it in Buenos Aires; frustrated love, fatality; emotional hopelessness. But to Lola at this moment it seemed just the opposite; she was happy, delighted that Ramon was responding. He may have been an animal, but he was also a dancer.

Lola's Chinese maid Lin-Ti let herself in the servant's entrance and, hearing loud music, stuck her head around the pantry door. She had never seen Lola dance with Ramon and the sight convulsed her. Clamping a hand over her mouth, she fell down laughing.

Lola saw her and stopped. "What's the matter, silly? You've never seen anyone dance with an ape?" The maid had slid to the floor on her knees, both hands over her mouth trying to hold it in, but a high-pitched hyena-giggle blew through her fingers. Lola went on keeping a straight face. "Why, in Cafe Society all the swells dance with monkeys. Who else have they got? Tommy Manville?"

Lola left Ramon and pulled the girl up, dragging her across the waxed floor. "You think it's so funny, huh? Come on, you're going to dance with us. That's right." The maid shreiked with laughter and pulled back, but Lola got her in position and together they continued the dance with Ramon. He wasn't particularly happy with the arrangement, but he didn't bite her either. Lin-Ti was female. Around they went, Lola showing Lin-Ti steps, Ramon repeating familiar routine, and all making their own particular sound of enjoyment.

When the record ended, Lola rushed to change it, dropping the needle back at the beginning. At his cue, Ramon swept Lin-Ti away. She squealed but followed. "You're getting it!" Lola shouted, clapping her hands. "That's great! Go on! Go on!" She ran toward the bedroom. "Keep going! I'm going to get you one of my swell tango outfits!"

Lola shoved the rack of dresses back and found a pleated number cut in flamenco style. She was having a marvelous time. It brought back memories of days as a little girl when she dressed up in Inez' costumes. Carrying the dress over her arm, she hurried back to the living room. As she did, she passed a clock reminding her of a dentist's appointment. One of the dubious benefits of being rich was getting your teeth fixed. Hooey! It also meant you didn't have to go.

Adrian's cab continued on to the shipping offices on the Bund. He hadn't bothered to rewrap the big scarlet book, and looking at it his feelings went from depressed to foolish. How could he honestly have believed a skimpy little island like Japan would overrun the zillion-and-one Chinese, let along go on to attack America? He had been infected by militant bigots like Bodine and Sato who *wanted* war. A big sigh. The books would go back to the bank to be filed away and forgotten. There were better ways to honor his father's name. It occured to him exactly how to do it. He had been trying to influence his government from the outside. What he had to do was enter politics and get inside. Now that he was a "far-East expert" and had faced the "Yellow Peril" in person, he was qualified to instruct stay-at-homes on American's policies in Asia. Not an impossible proposition if given the backing of his rich friends from the polo circuit, oil world, and maybe even a wife with social clout . . .

That stopped him. He saw very clearly a picture of a tidy, self-assured finishing-school graduate. After knowing Lola, would he ever be happy marrying someone who never said, "Oh, fuck!" when she flubbed a putt, or grabbed your ass when you weren't looking? He felt depressed all over again.

At exactly five o'clock the door to Lola's suite flew open and a man filled the frame. He was dressed in a black kimono with a scarf tied around his head so that only the slits of his eyes showed. The dancers stopped and looked at him in horror. He was at once so sinister and theatrical that they were unable to utter a sound. Then as they watched, struck dumb with terror, he came forward in a strange walk and, passing a hand behind his back, produced the bright flash of a sword like magic. Very slowly, elbows held out, he raised it over his head with both hands. As he did, Ramon, infused with fear, drew his lips back and snarled. The swordsman hesitated one second, then went forward.

Adrian stopped by the shipping offices on the Bund and booked passage aboard the *Gripsholm*. As he walked back to the hotel, finally committed, the terrible depression deepened in him. He knew what it was: he could not bear to leave Lola behind. The thought that he would never see her again was unacceptable. Then it hit him. Why? There was no reason it had to be that way. It was within his power to change it instantly! All he had to do was tell her he loved her and couldn't live without her. It was as simple as that! To hell with everything else!

He bought flowers at a sidewalk stall and ran back to the Palace. At six o'clock he was at the door of Lola's suite and found it ajar. Opening it, he pushed the flowers in and called out, "Lola! I—" Then he saw the ooze of blood.

There was a wide smear on the rug, skidding across the shine of bare floor leading to the bedroom. His heart pounding, he followed it, then pulled back, breath coming hard. The pale room was painted with it, white satin sheets on the bed soaked with it, the lacquered dressing table, chairs, and loveseat splattered with it. A curve whipped up the wall, fanning out and even flecking the tall ceiling. On the floor to the right side of the bed, a body was twisted up in the sheet, the turns of cloth blood striped and stippled. A small hand protruded, reaching out and still gripping the pillow.

He couldn't see the head, but both feet had been chopped off at the ankles and were missing.

Adrian staggered back, drenched with a cold sweat, unable to swallow, mouth locked open. He still held the flowers; now he flung them away.

When he finally began to function, his first thought was robbery. The bed had been struck a dozen times, the headboard showed deep hack marks, one of the panels had completely spilt out by terrific force, and in several places the mattress and springs were cut clear through. Reluctantly, he bent down and looked under it. The gold was still there. He thought about it for a long moment, then, throwing a towel over it, dragged the chest down to his room and called the police.

When Adrian had made his trip to the American Consulate earlier in the day, he had been down the street from the Japanese Consulate (also on Whangpoo Road and overlooking the docks). Had he passed by at nine that morning, he might have even run into Captain Sato coming out, just finished with a debriefing on the Sian situation.

It hadn't turned out exactly as the captain predicted, but nevertheless, Marshal Yü had gone down. If his son went over to the Communists, that was just one more Chiang Kai-shek would have to deal with. The generals had been reshuffled and a young Marshal named Chung Hsuch-lien assumed control. It was thought he would be more tractable.

Sergeant Masaki's death had been unfortunate but heroic. He saw to it that he was buried with full military honors as befitted a true samurai. His family was brought over from Kyushu at Sato's expense to take the sergeant's ashes home. He personally told them the heroic story; he had been shot to death in a suicide duel with a mercenary officer. Captain Sato recommended him for the Order of the Golden Kite (2nd class).

He had been ready to pull the trigger as Masaki knelt before him—then Masaki said four words: Let me kill him. Sato realized he wasn't asking for Sepuku, but for another chance to kill Bodine. He pleaded that it had been his fault Bodine had escaped the first attempt, and as a samurai he asked to serve his lord and fulfill his revenge. As Sato thought it over, he was satisfied that his honor would be intact. In fact, as the lord, he was acting with best possible motives in allowing him to cleanse his own honor.

He helped Masaki dress in his clothes and personally tied the hachimaki *headband under his hat. At the end they bowed together and Masaki had gone off a happy man.*

When the regular Sian army took over the train station, Captain Sato presented his papers, and after some negotiation they were back to doing business again. Kwantung HQ at Hsinking was pleased with the outcome, and Sato received warm personal regards from his mentor, General Tojo.

There was one thing left that would cleanse his honor. He had to face the ape. The first thing he'd done upon arriving back in Shanghai was to locate Lola and Ramon at the Palace Hotel. Then, after watching their movements (or lack of movement), for several days he conceived a bizarre ritual, or joke, as he liked to think of it. With inside help he was able to use the hotel service elevator and secure a key to her room. Knowing when he was apt to find her there, he arrived punctually at the cocktail hour.

There was no intention to kill the woman. He had come for the ape and instantly struck it down with the flat edge of his sword, knocking the animal unconscious. But the woman began a terrible screaming and scrambled into the bedroom. This infuriated him, and when she would not stop, he began to strike out in a frenzy with the sword, over and over . . .

Later, under control, he hamstrung the ape and dragged it out of the hotel in a laundry bag. Driving to the docks in the Ford that night, he placed the maimed animal in the jinriksha. This was the point of his joke. It was meant as a symbol that the Chinese would understand—a portent of things to come. It was the year of the monkey and the monkey could not move.

Adrian sat in his room, stunned. If he had longed for Lola when it was still within his power to have her—his feelings now after her horrific murder were absolutely unacceptable. He had been so consumed by what *he* wanted that he had never once considered that events could be irreversibly altered by others. She was gone for good.

When Adrian called the police, he had not told them who was reporting the murder. He simply could not cope with that. They would soon enough discover his identity . . . then came a jolting thought: he would be a major suspect. Who else was close to her? The gold belonged to his father and he had taken it from her room. Why? Because he believed it would disappear down the sewer of police corruption. Could he tell them that? Ha! Now that he began to think clearly he had another disturbing thought: where was Ramon? There was no way he could be separated from Lola but he had been. How?

What to do? Who could help him? As he puzzled over this, he fingered the Masonic fob on his watch. There were those who owed him. He found the card tucked in his passport. The front advertised: WIDE AWAKE GOOD STOM-ACH NOODLE COMPANY. On the back was a telephone number written in pen.

An hour later he met with his Masonic brother and Stanford classman—the cosmopolitan young man who was a power in the Green Gang. The heavy Horst waited in front of the Palace Hotel and they sat stiffly in the Palm Court over tea. While the Viennese string quartet sawed away at "Time on My Hands," Adrian explained the tragedy.

"I am most disturbed at your hideous loss," the young man said, bowing his nose nearly to the tea cup.

"Thank you for your condolences," Adrian answered with his own stiff bow. "What also disturbs me is the missing pet. She thought of Ramon as family and I feel responsible for his safety. I've got to make an effort to find him. It's the last thing I can do for her."

"I understand. If you can give me until the morning, I am sure we will make a discovery." He was relieved to be able to repay his debt to Adrian.

Adrian sat back and rubbed his head, a thing he did constantly now. "The whole thing is so bizarre, it makes no sense—perhaps it was the act of a madman or maybe someone who hated foreigners—or even apes."

"Wherever there is effect, there is cause. We will find the person who accomplished this, be assured."

Adrian sighed. "She's dead now and nothing can be done about that. It doesn't really matter who did it."

"Oh, yes." His brother handed him a card. It contained a poem paraphasing Ssu-K'ung T'u:

> The soul dwells in regions ethereal
> An atom at random in space;
> What will keep it in that dreaming place?
> Behind, the phoenix doth clang and rise;
> It is time to lash leviathans,
> And enter the contest
> Where revenge is the prize.

Adrian had been unable to sleep and by noon the next day his nerves were pinging. He began to have second thoughts about using the Green Gang to find Ramon. As he paced the hotel room waiting for some word, he wondered if he should contact the authorities. When he had called down to the desk early that morning, there had been a message that he get in touch with M. Bonné of the French Concession police.

There was a tap at the door and he crossed over as a folded square of rice paper was shoved under it. He snatched it up and unfolded it. On it was the address of a small private hospital in the French Concession, and beneath this the single word *monkey*.

Adrian went at once and found Ramon in a private room at the back of a small hospital. The building was isolated from the main wing, and it was necessary to enter by a metal gate. Inside, he crossed a covered corridor with rain hammering on its tin roof and was shown into a vaulted room with peeling paint and heavy mesh on the windows.

Ramon lay in a chipped, enameled bed, bandaged and sedated. It was the first time Adrian had ever seen him without clothes, and he was shocked. The hairy body stretched out on the white sheets didn't fit and seemed shrunken in size.

Under the noisy tin roof, Adrian found the doctor. He appeared amused but busy. "You know of this animal?"

"Yes, his name is Ramon."

He smiled. "The police brought him in several hours ago—over my objections. They say he is a valuable performing animal. Is that true?"

"Yes . . . he dances."

"Not anymore he doesn't."

"Will he live?"

The doctor raised his eyebrows, surprised by this. "Yes, he could. We have closed the wounds and they will heal—but the animal is hamstrung, useless. Certainly you'll want him destroyed."

"If he were human, would he be destroyed?"

"Of course not!" the doctor was offended.

"All right, then listen—he is to have the best of medical care, no matter what the cost. When he's ready to be moved to his own quarters, I want him provided with a nurse."

The doctor looked at him. "Are you joking?"

"Tomorrow there will be an account established for him in the Hong Kong Shanghai-Bank, and a trust set up. As long as he lives, I want him treated decently."

"This is badly out of proportion. There is a great deal of suffering and sickness in Shanghai—would it not be better to apply this money to *human* misery?"

"No," Adrian said. "No, it wouldn't." And he turned and walked toward the exit.

As he went down the long covered corridor, the rain continued its assault against the roof. At the end, a man stepped in from outside, snapping the water from his hat against a battered trenchcoat. Adrian meant to step past him and out the door, but the man blocked it, smiling. "Hello there."

"Hello." Adrian reached for the door handle.

"I say, aren't you Adrian Reed Jr.?"

Adrian was taken back. "Why . . . yes. Do I know you?"

"No, but I recognized you from the polo circuit. I used to do sports as a *Times* stringer in Rio. I'm the correspondent for the *North China Daily News* now."

"Is that right? Well, good to see you." And he reached for the door handle once again.

"Are you here about the monkey?"

"What?"

"I was at the docks with Bonné. We found it."

"Who did you say?"

"Bonné, chief of police of the French Concession—didn't they get in touch with you?"

"I've been very . . .

"I mean that was quite a thing at the dancer's place—Miss Ryan's. I'm told she had a regular fit. Hysterics. I hope you'll tell her the animal is getting the best of care." He stepped aside to let Adrian pass.

"I don't understand . . ."

"You can thank Bonné for getting the ape in here. They didn't want to take it in with humans you know, but—"

Adrian suddenly grabbed him, jerking him forward by wet lapels. *"What in hell are you saying?"*

The man from the *North China Daily News* drew back, conducting himself cooly under fire. "My dear fellow, I'm talking about the chopping of Miss Ryan's maid . . ."

"Maid?" Stunned, Adrian released him.

"Poor thing, whacked up like a gorgonzola."

"Lola?"

"Miss Ryan went off in all directions at once looking for the ape. This was yesterday, before we found it."

Adrian could not arrange the facts. After accepting Lola's death, he refused to gracefully accept her being alive. "How . . . how could that be?"

"She went onto a dentist's appointment, I believe. By God, maybe there's something worse than having your teeth pranged on after all."

Adrian slumped against the wall and began to cry.

The correspondent was embarrassed. "I say . . . you didn't know that? I am sorry. I assumed you were in touch. I mean you're being here about the ape and all."

"No . . . no . . ."

"My dear fellow, you should really answer your messages. Bonné would have explained . . ."

Adrian pulled himself together. "Where is she now?"

"The management of the Palace moved her to another room, of course, but when I called to tell her we'd found the ape, she was out. No doubt searching for the poor thing on her own."

"God!" Adrian exploded, frustrated and exhilarated at the same time. "I've got to find her right now!"

"Well, I don't know about that," the correspondent said, "but I know where she'll be tonight." And taking a rumpled copy of the *North China Daily News* out of his trenchcoat, he turned to the entertainment section.

At nine o'clock that evening the Japanese consul received a call at his private residence on Szechuan Road. He was annoyed at this intrusion into his privacy, but the caller had a cultivated accent and urgently directed him to go to Captain Sato's assistance. He would be found on Chunghsing Road in the Chapei District. He gave precise directions and hung up.

The consul was inclined to believe him. He knew of Captain Sato's covert work and was also aware that he had the patronage of General Tojo. It would not do to pass this off without checking. Sato was being promoted to major and was clearly a man with a brilliant future. The consul sent for his driver and, arming themselves, then set off immediately.

It was about an hour's trip into the country, past the North Railway Station to where Chunghsing Road turned into the Puto District. There was no traffic at all here, and the few squares of lights seemed miles away. The consul couldn't help wondering what had brought Sato to such a remote spot, and his anxiety increased. He began to look for landmarks the caller had described, and soon saw the humps of burial mounds off to the right. The car slowed, and ahead in their lights they saw a man sitting by the side of the road with his hand raised. It was Captain Sato.

The car pulled up and they jumped out and ran to him, pistols drawn. He seemed all right, remaining perfectly still, perhaps dazed, his eyes wide open, staring straight ahead. The consul called out and, when he didn't answer, threw the beam of his pocket flash on the face. It was ashen, bled white, and he saw now that the eyelids had been sewn to his eyebrows with green silk thread. The body was propped up by a stake driven in the ground and his coat was buttoned around it, the arm held in position by a stick shoved up the sleeve. His shirt front was open and other stitching could be seen; the body had been cut apart in many pieces and then carefully sewn back together again.

As the consul leaned in, he noticed that with blood drained from the face, the scar on the man's right cheekbone appeared in the almost perfect shape of an eagle.

At ten o'clock that evening a well-dressed man stopped at one of the stalls on Canton Road and bought a red carnation from a little girl in a doorway. Bending down, he allowed her to tuck it in the buttonhole of his suit. Walking on, he passed the Gothic towers of Scott's English Cathedral. Its fenced park of very British trees and scrubs seemed at odds with coolies bobbing along under yo-yo poles.

Further along he came to the entertainment quarter where the sudden intensity of light increased in brilliant jumps of neon and electric bulbs, culminating in the clash and blink of a hundred invitations and advertisements, each canceling the other out in kilowatt confusion. He stopped in the middle of the block and looked up at a blaze against the night that outdid all the others. Forty feet long and eight feet high, it announced:

THE ALL NEW FRISCO DANCE HALL
Girls of All Nationalities—Girls

The door was swept open for him, and he went up the stairs, bowed to the top by employees on each step. Pausing before the doors to the main ballroom, he took out an Upmann double corona and, nipping the end, placed it at a tilt in his mouth. A light was instantly produced, and puffing it up, he nodded. The doors were swung back, revealing dance hostesses arranged in two long lines, forming a path to the bandstand. At his appearance the band struck up "For He's a Jolly Good Fellow," and the girls all began to sing in Chinese, clapping their hands.

It was Warren Bodine, living his dream, surviving as few did to see it come true, walking between lines of beautiful, exotic, desirable girls—each one a different race, shade, and shape—all leaning forward, smiling and turning on the charm for the big boss—the new owner. All doing their best to impress him; bosoms out, tummies in, tucked into little slinks of dresses, they preened, posed, squeezed, and shimmied their bodies for his eyes alone. He responded to them all, beaming, resplendent in his custom-made suit; boutonniere, dollar cigar, freckles shining, red hair slicked down—a strutting cock of the walk, acting out every man's fantasy—a rooster loose in the hen house.

When he reached the bandstand, he turned, held up his hands, and the noise fell off at once.

"Girls—just remember this. Every one of you is gonna get your chance!"

A cheer went up and the band segued into "Tiger Rag."

Awakened from heavy drunken sleep by the sound of machine guns, he stumbled out of the boxcar in time to see the two figures on the tracks shoot themselves to pieces. In the next minute men were running across the snow toward him. He got in the armored car and started it, backing away as they fired. He didn't understand yet what had happened and didn't want to think about it.

Hiding the car outside of Tung-kuan, he smuggled the gold into the train yards that night. A brakeman got him aboard an outbound freight for a double eagle, and he made connections for Shanghai at Cheng-chow.

As he rode along, he thought about what had happened and puzzled over why Gibb had taken his place and given up his life. It didn't make sense—why would he do it? Later he felt a lump tucked into his shirt pocket and withdrew a twisted piece of paper. When he unwrapped it, he found Gibb's "eye," the great pearl. Written on the paper were two words: "Tweet tweet."

Passing through the crowd, Bodine was startled to see a familiar figure. Her back was to him but the strawberry-blonde hair in tight ring curls and bouncy little ass could not be mistaken. Pushing his way through the crush, he stopped behind her and tapped her shoulder.

"Hey, sugarcakes, how about a dance?"

Lola swung around and threw her arms around his neck. "Oh, Red! Red!" And she began to cry.

"Hey, I know . . . comin' back from the dead takes a lot out of you." He gently disengaged her. "How did you find out I was runnin' this place?"

"A reporter showed me an ad in the paper that it was opening. He knows you."

"Oh yeah—a limey scissor-bill with a long nose to poke in other people's business."

"But why didn't you contact me?"

"The wife for one, the government for another—and every chisler I ever knew who wants a piece of me now that I made it. Better they think that dumb-ass Bodine died up there in the mountain shootin' it out with a maniac Jap. My name's Colonel Marian Gibb now."

"But you don't look like a Marian."

He smiled. "Listen, kid, it's gonna be a tough name to live up to—but what are you doin', where's the college boy?"

"Gone back home. Oh, Red, terrible things have happened—my maid was murdered and Ramon has run away or something—I can't find him." And she began to cry again.

He lifted her chin. "Come on now, we'll find him. Didn't I find that Mr. Min for the college boy? Don't cry, leave it to me. I can't have my girl losin' her monkey."

The heavy rhythm of a tango struck up and he turned her toward the dance floor. "Hey! They're playing our song. Come on, babe, let's dance."

"Red, I can't . . . I just feel so bad about everything that—"

But he wouldn't hear it. "What's this? Isn't there somethin' about the show goin' on in your racket?" And taking her in his arms, he swung them into the dance.

They were the first thing Adrian saw when he entered the ballroom. Standing and watching the two, he remembered the last time he'd seen them together at Marshal Yü's party. He'd been jealous then of their smooth precision, of Bodine's cocky style—well, by God—not anymore!

Bodine felt himself tapped on the shoulder and, turning, saw Adrian smiling. "Oh, no! It's the college boy."

Lola could only stammer. "But . . . you said . . . how . . ."

Adrian took her in his arms without preamble and they moved off connected by the electricity of sex and music. There was no need of questions, answers, or long-winded explanations. Both knew in that instant that they were made for each other and nothing—not money or monkeys—would keep them apart again.

Above, a great mirrored ball revolved, its prisms of refracted light multiplying, langorously circling the room. At the center of its orbit, dappled by revolving patterns, Adrian and Lola, cheek to cheek, arms extended ahead, fingers locked, glided across the room—suddenly reversing with perfect timing on the beat. As the sensual, compulsive rhythm accelerated, drums pounding, they pressed even closer, heads bent together, oblivious to everything but the two.

Not many blocks away, Ramon lay in a private room of the concession hospital. At one side a plump Chinese nurse dozed. If the windows had been open, it's even possible he might have heard the beat of the tango drifting across the rooftops from the Frisco Dance Hall.

As it was, he lay very quiet, his head turned toward the door, eyes fixed, waiting. He wanted to be the first one to see her when she came in.